STEALING THE BRIDE

NADIA LEE

To Dawn.

1

COURT

THE BRIDE IS OVER MY SHOULDER, WRIGGLING LIKE A TROUT caught between a bear's paws. And it's true: my paw is on her ass, so maybe she *feels* like a trout, even though we're on a beach and there are no bears in Maui. And she's screaming like a banshee.

I run like hell down the aisle, past the tropical flowers lining each side, feet churning the sand. Somewhere a Chihuahua is barking insanely. The bride's head bounces on my back, the white veil brushing my thighs and knees. The guests in semi-casual beachwear are too stunned to move. They just stare, their mouths open. It looks comical—like something from a third-rate chick flick.

"Stop, you son of a bitch!" comes from behind me. The groom's finally gotten his shit together.

Sissy. I didn't even push him out of the way that hard. I look over a shoulder to give him a superior smirk.

He's started after me, his feet pounding the sand. But the guy's not fast enough. Even with a struggling woman over one shoulder, I can outrun him. I didn't get my muscles from one of those jiggle dumbbells that simulates jerking off. I got them the old-fashioned way—sweating on Icarian fitness equipment in a gym.

Oh yeah. You aren't getting married. Not until pigs win the Super Bowl.

Besides, he's going to thank me. As soon as the fact that his intended and I slept together only two weeks ago sinks into his microscopic brain.

My getaway Maserati convertible is waiting. Hell yeah. Stealing this bride in *style*.

I dump her in the passenger seat. Cursing, she struggles against the tangled veil and a small sea of white fabric.

I start the car. The engine roars like a lion, while the bride screams like I'm Hannibal Lecter coming off a month-long fast. The Hawaiian breeze ruffles my hair. I smack the wheel in triumph and give the car some gas.

Someone in red runs right in front of the car. *Shit!* I slam on the brakes.

"You fucking crazy?" I shout, my heart knocking hard against my chest. The Maserati could've turned her into a bloody human pancake. "I almost ran you over!"

A tall, slim brunette places her hands on the hood of my car, almost like she's daring me to run her over. Then she lifts her chin.

What the fuck?

The familiar aquamarine eyes send a jolt through me. I blink. The bride is right next to me, still cursing. What the hell is she doing over there in that red dress? Am I seeing things? I've been thinking entirely too much about her over the last two weeks.

"Skittles?" I say.

"Yeah." The same husky voice.

Damn... It *is* her.

I glance at my kidnapped bride...who has finally gotten her veil out of the way and has the exact same face as Skittles. *What the fuck is going on?*

2

2

———

COURT

My phone goes off again, but I don't bother checking it. I know who it is, and it's better for my sanity that I don't look at the notification.

Besides, the car's coming soon.

Sure enough, within a minute, a blue Prius rounds the corner and starts slowing down. Finally! Time to forget parental drama for the night.

Nate stares at it the way a zoo tiger might stare at an offer of hay. "Oh, come on! Court, man. Seriously?"

I try not to laugh at his tragicomic face. "Do you see anything else?"

"That's a..." He squints. "What *is* it?"

"Pretty sure it's called a Prius." I slap his shoulder in mock sympathy. "Uber drivers don't usually tool around in Bugattis."

"But...a Prius?"

I shrug. "So? It's environmentally friendly, reliable and will take us where we need to go."

3

"You know I have a brand spankin' new Lamborghini right over there." He gestures at the valet parking.

"Uh-huh. And how many beers did you have with dinner?"

"Two. No more than three."

I don't know why he even tries. "Four. You need to go back to preschool."

He gapes at me. "You were counting?"

"I saw the receipt."

"Oh." Nate takes a moment to regroup. "Well, I can hold my liquor."

"The Pryces can hold their liquor," I correct him, referring to his older brother's in-laws. They drink scotch and whiskey like water. "The last time I checked, you were Nate *Sterling*. And it was your idea to go clubbing, which means more drinking. You don't want to wreck your car so soon, do you?"

He bristles. "I'm a great driver."

True enough. And he actually can hold his liquor. I've seen him execute perfect backflips and make complex, six-figure stock trades after more than ten whiskeys. Still...I have my own rules.

I give him a quick pat on the back. "Don't be a snob."

That's guaranteed to annoy the crap out of him. Even though he was born with a gold-plated silver spoon, he hates it when people treat him like he's snooty. According to him, liking the finer things in life doesn't make him stuck-up.

"I'm not a snob," he says stiffly.

"Of course not. Which is why you won't mind riding in a Prius."

He rolls his eyes and sighs, then climbs in with all the enthusiasm of someone forced to share an airlock with a bunch of Klingons who've eaten too many beans.

To be fair, Nate has been looking forward to taking his brand new car for a drive. And as far as I know, he's never ridden anything that costs less than six figures.

Me? I'm more...down to earth. It's a small price to pay for some semblance of a normal life.

The driver confirms our destination—Z, a club my brother Tony owns—and the car takes off. Well, "takes off" as much as it can in L.A. traffic. There are lies, damn lies and car commercials.

Open roads and just you and your car, my ass. The reality is crawling along over-congested streets full of people, cars and busses. Count your blessings if they aren't farting black smog that smells like the love child of an oil rig and a rotten egg.

My phone goes off again. The knot that's been sitting in my gut for I don't even know how long tightens some more.

"Got a vibrator in your pocket?" Nate says.

"I wish. At least that would come with some entertaining possibilities."

"Shouldn't you answer it? Whoever it is has been texting you all evening."

"Eh. It's nothing important."

"How do you know?"

Sigh. He won't let this go until I tell him everything. "Because it's the nine million, ten thousand, six hundred and fifth text from Mom." I should charge her a penny a text. It'd push me into a new tax bracket.

"Or maybe it's Tony. And didn't you say Edgar's in town?"

Edgar's the oldest of us three brothers. Tony's the middle one, and I'm the youngest. "Tony doesn't need me," I say. "He has Ivy." Whom he's married to now, and so in love with I feel like I'm inhaling cotton candy every time I'm around the two of them.

But I pull out my phone to check anyway. Just in case Tony or Edgar needs me for anything.

Buuuut it's from Mom. While I'm glancing at it, her nine million, ten thousand, six hundred and *sixth* text arrives. Why couldn't it be one from God telling me I won the superpower lottery? Like the power to disable pointless texting.

Fed up, I shove the phone back into the pocket. "My mother. Told you."

"Oh." He grows silent.

Like the rest of the world, he knows about the scandal that blew up like a Molotov cocktail last year. The law says Mom didn't do anything illegal, but it sure as hell doesn't feel that way. A pit in the bottom of my gut burns. I swear there's a lava pool inside me that wants to spew its rage.

She should've done something. And not just her. *Me too.*

Every time I think about it, part of me wonders if I was

complicit. After all, I indulged her and catered to her whims. If I'd pushed just a little more...

"You know you could just block her," Nate says finally.

"I've thought about it. But once in a while, she gets hospitalized and needs somebody to be there with her." I'm almost certain she does it to get attention, but I can't ignore a call from a hospital. So I go, like a well-trained puppy, because Dad certainly isn't going to, and Tony and Edgar... Well, they're too strong-willed and experienced to put up with her theatrics.

"Maybe it's something important," Nate says.

Yeah, important to her. "It's not. You know what's really messed up?"

He waits.

"Why do moms who hate texting in general stoop to doing exactly that to get their son's attention?" I pause—dramatically—but I'm not expecting an answer from Nate. He's too normal to know. "They text you things like... *Hey, when are you getting married? When are you going to give me a grandkid or two? I met just the girl for you. When are you free?* You know what I'm saying?"

"Uh, I guess?"

Why the hell is he turning that into a question? He's my best friend. He's supposed to just agree with me. "Yours does it."

He winces. "Yeah, but only because Justin gave her a baby. Now she wants one from me, too, so she can have a nice set of two to bounce on her knees." His face scrunches like an aluminum can under pressure. "She forgets I need to find a woman first."

Sometimes it slips my mind that Nate's mom is normal. "At least yours doesn't want you to fix her marriage. Mine does."

He pulls back in surprise. "Isn't the divorce already final?"

"She's trying to delay it." Like that's going to change what she's done.

"And *you're* supposed to fix it? What does she think you can fix? And why you? You're the King of Short Flings and One-Night Stands."

"Dunno."

Now that you're finished with your Master's, you can spend some time convincing your father, one of her texts said last month.

She's obviously forgotten that my degree is in Gender Studies, not Matrimonial Repair.

Nate gives me a look full of sympathy, and I glance away. I don't need his pity. He doesn't understand what it's like to be in the mess my family's in. The worst drama he's ever been through was his grand-uncle Barron throwing a temper tantrum once or twice because he didn't get his way. But unlike my mom, Barron isn't morally bankrupt.

A tiny bit of resentment squirms like a worm pulled from deep, dark soil. I hate myself for feeling jealous of Nate for having a normal family. I should just be happy for him.

And I *am* happy for him. I just wish I had some normalcy, too.

Mentally I stomp the worm into a petty little death, then look out the window, hoping something out there will make me laugh or forget. There are twelve million people in Los Angeles. Surely someone will do something to put a smile on my face.

But no. People rush like slithery eels on the streets, and cars move with impotent fury, as though there's some massive conspiracy to keep them going well below the speed limit.

It's too bad my sense of humor isn't warped enough to find any of that funny. Maybe it's time I develop one.

Harcourt Roderick Blackwood. Laugher at All Things.

But until then, I need to settle for more standard fare—drinking, clubbing, finding a hot girl to spend the night with... The usual.

The Prius makes the final right turn. I start to say something to Nate, then something catches my eye. I stop, then stare at a woman in the long-ass line to get inside Z.

I can't pinpoint exactly what about her that captured my attention. The lights show her face, and it isn't stunning. She's not ugly or anything. But every feature on her face is just a little too large. The aggregate should look slightly off...maybe even unattractive. But not in combination, not on that heart-shaped face. It's not classically beautiful, but it's arresting.

My gaze drops to her body. Long and slim, it's the exactly opposite of what I like. I prefer melons and a bountiful ass I can grab. But she does have T and A...just smaller. Like going from a watermelon to a peach.

But somehow the size doesn't matter. Heat curls inside me anyway as I watch her. How weird. Is my taste changing for some reason? Even steak can get old if you eat it all the time. Maybe it's that tube dress... It's bright red—the same shade of red as a Skittles wrapper. Her heels are hot too—high and strappy and sparkly silver.

Then it finally hits me—why she's so mesmerizing.

Everyone around her is feigning a bored "I'm too hot to wait" expression, like that will move the line faster. But she's moving to some kind of music only she can hear.

Her hips swivel, her waist sinuous. Her movements aren't big or wild—she's on a sidewalk, after all—and they aren't the slickest, but there's so much joyful exuberance in her. It's bubbling like hot, sugary syrup, and I want to lap—it—up.

When she gives a small smile, I swear a rainbow arcs over her head.

"You getting out?"

Nate's question is like an annoying gnat. "What?"

"We're here."

I blink and look around. Oh yeah. I didn't even realize the car had come to a stop. The driver's staring at me like I'm an intellectually challenged sloth. With a broken leg.

I climb out and glance back at the girl. That line is *long*. She's going to have to wait an eternity in those heels. And a woman bubbling with that much joie de vivre shouldn't have to.

I start toward her, but Nate stops me. "Where are you going?"

I raise my hand to point, but catch myself. I don't want him to see her. Not yet. Not until I put up an electric fence around her and hammer a huge sign on it that reads: *Harcourt Blackwood's Woman. Keep Out. Trespassers Will Be Beaten and Fed to Rabid Piranhas.* "Sorry. Thought I saw someone I knew."

A plan forms in my head. Step One: get Nate out of the way.

We go to the VIP entrance. Nate and I are both on the list. The bouncer there looks like the result of a lab experiment involving a silverback gorilla and a T-Rex. His black shirt is stretched so tightly across the pecs that I swear he's going to pop a few buttons if he breathes too hard, like a bride who's sucked in everything she can to fit into a vanity gown. His scowl seems permanent. Every time he smiles, his face looks like it's going to crack.

But he smiles anyway. Good customer service matters, especially for VIPs. "Hi, Harcourt."

"Hey, Zack." I smile at Nate. "Why don't you go ahead and grab a booth? I need to talk to this guy for a minute."

He gives me a "don't do anything stupid" look, but shrugs and goes inside.

I go to the guardian of the VIP lane, then point at Red... No. That's not right. Her hair's brown, and she can always get rid of the dress. Ideally with me. Tonight.

But back to the present—what does she remind me of that's delicious?

Skittles.

That's a perfect temporary name for her. "You see that girl over there?" I point her out carefully, since there are a lot of women. He knows my taste, and I don't want him to get confused and pick a blonde with extra-large melons who's too above it all to look happy.

"The dancer? In red?" He sounds a little surprised.

"Yeah." I hand him a few crisp bills. "Let her in."

"Why don't you?" He shoots me a sly grin, which makes him look positively sinister. But his voice is as soft as melted candy. "Play the VIP card. Girls dig that shit."

Clichéd, and definitely not. I pat his fifty-inch chest, the pec muscles oscillating under my hand. "Zack, my man. I don't want her knowing it's me. Just tell her it's her lucky day."

I want her to like me because she thinks I'm awesome to be around, not because I have pull at a swanky club like Z. Being liked for me matters. That's one of many reasons I left Tempérane, Louisiana. Everyone there knows my family's filthy rich...and treats me accordingly.

I go inside. The music pounds, the bass hard and fast—perfect for dancing. The place is already heaving, as the Brits say. A huge number of people around the bars. Z has your usual array of alcohol, but it also has fancy top-shelf liquor for those who can pay. It gets more than its share of celebrities, who like to feel important by drinking stuff so expensive that you could fund a war on their tab.

Should I send her something pricey?

Nah. Dumb move. She might not be into hard liquor. And even if she is, if she doesn't recognize it, it's going to look stupid to explain how much it costs, because what the hell kind of douche does that anyway?

I'm not thinking very clearly today.

You care way too much about how she'll react. Normally you'd just send it and be done.

I flick away the annoying voice in my head. Nate's in one of the second-level VIP lounges overlooking the dance floor. He waves, and I plop down in the circular leather seat.

"What was that about with the bouncer?" he asks.

"Nothing." I signal a waitress for a whiskey.

"Uh-huh."

I like Nate because he's astute. But right now I wish he were a bit less shrewd. Skittles is more his type than mine. He likes lithe, leggy brunettes. "Just wanted to know if Tony was coming."

"Why would he be coming? Isn't tomorrow his anniversary or something?"

"How the hell did you know?" Is Nate tracking my brother's life? I only know about it because he asked me to drop by and distract Ivy tomorrow morning while he gets the anniversary gift delivered.

"His crazy mansion made the news, and they said it was for his wife, blah blah blah, who he married tomorrow. Well, tomorrow last year."

Nate gets shunted back in my "normal" column. The mansion Tony commissioned is insane. He only got it because he decided his wife deserves one, plus he figured he could install better security. It basically has everything except a force field.

The waitress brings me my whiskey, and I take a huge swallow before turning to Nate. "I like the mansion, and you know what's really cool?"

"No, but I'm sure you'll tell me."

"He gave me his penthouse."

"For real?" Nate downs his whiskey. "Justin didn't give me shit when he got married."

That might be true, but Nate doesn't really care. He has more money than he can spend in a lifetime. And if he ever did somehow need more, his brother would write him a check, no questions asked.

"He needs somebody to keep the white baby grand safe."

"What white baby grand?"

"His wife's old practice piano. He's buying her a concert grand for their first anniversary."

He snorts in amusement. "So you scored a penthouse in exchange for piano-sitting?"

"Yup." I search the dance floor below. It's been long enough that Skittles should be down there by now. But it's impossible to tell. Too damn many people. "I'm going dancing."

Nate looks at me like I just told him I want to roll around in a pile of dogshit. "Dancing? Now?" He knows that when I'm in a crappy mood due to my family, I prefer to drink and brood.

"Yup." I stand and lean over the rail, scanning the crowd for red cheeriness. "I might get lucky and find the love of my life."

Nate laughs until he nearly chokes.

3

PASCAL

MAN, THIS LINE'S SOOO LONG. HOW MUCH LONGER ARE WE going to have to wait? Or should I come up with something else to do to celebrate?

Except if I do, Curie's going to roll her eyes at me...affectionately, of course, but, still, an eye-roll is an eye-roll.

According to her, Z has the best music, the best drinks and, most importantly, the best crowd. Super-famous people come here. I've seen pictures of models, actors and everyone in between at this club. Apparently this is the place to be if you want to be cool and have fun. And since my sister is exactly that—cool and fun—she's been here many times.

I, on the other hand, have never been here before, which is sad considering I'm an L.A. native. But I've been a busy girl. Majoring in math sucked up a lot of my free time. And I went to college in Chicago, so technically I haven't been here the whole time.

And that's the only reason I haven't come to this club, not because I'm a geek.

Keep lying to yourself, Pascal. You know what you really are.

Ha, whatever. I'm not going to let the annoying voice in my

head ruin my evening. Actually my whole week. It's been fantastic, and—

"Hey." A gentle tap on my shoulder.

I blink up at a guy who's built like the Mountain from *Game of Thrones*. And he looks just as scary, minus the armor. "Hi...?" I say, unsure what he wants.

"You can come in through the VIP entrance."

Wait, what? The VIP entrance? It doesn't compute. "Who are you?"

"The large hired help." He smiles, which only makes him more terrifying.

Right. Must be a bouncer. But... "Me?" I place a hand over my chest. "VIP?"

"Yup."

"Oh my God. You know I'm not anybody famous, right?" As soon as I say it, I almost smack my cheeks. Why am I measuring teeth on a gift horse?

His steely gaze sweeps over me. "Yeah, I know."

Oh. So it's just my lucky day, then. I shoot him my sweetest smile, hoping I can push for a little bit more. "My sister and her fiancé are with me. Can they come, too?"

He shrugs. "Yeah, why not?"

Yay! "Thank you so much! You're awesome."

He gives me a smirk, like he knows some secret of the universe that I'm not privy to. "My pleasure."

I gesture at Curie and Joe to come quick, before the bouncer changes his mind. They keep lagging because she can't decide if she wants to have their towels monogrammed and is going over options with him. Apparently, that's the thing according to some bridal magazines. And Joe is too in love to resist the onslaught.

"Wait, why are we going over there? What did I miss?" she says.

"I got lucky. The VIP entrance, baby!"

"Wow, how did you get that?" Joe asks.

"Dunno. But I'm not complaining. Let's go."

Mr. Bear Arms leads us to the front of the line and holds up a velvet barrier rope with a big smile, which makes him look like a shark before dinnertime. But I'm too excited to care. We're in!

We walk through the door and touch down on another planet. The music is like a living thing, pulsing in my veins. I immediately feel drunk on the dynamic energy of the crowd. It tugs like a whirlpool of manic electricity, more alluring than a siren's song. No wonder Curie loves this place.

She steers us toward a bar. "I'm going to start a tab," she says. "My treat. You deserve this. We are *celebrating*."

She gets three shots of tequila, and we all clink glasses and knock them back.

A fireball seems to ignite in my chest as the liquor goes down. It's been a while since I drank like this. "Hell yeah." I pump my fist. "I'm totally vindicated. That bastard. Trapping him with a baby, my ass."

"No kidding. Who does he think he is? Can't believe he tried that crap with you."

"Totally. You should've seen the deadbeat's face when I dumped him on the spot."

Tom's a freelance journalist with spotty paychecks. I'd never met a guy more eager to move in with me before. Or more shocked when I told him to pack his trash and get the hell out. I'd already told him my period isn't really regular. He was either going to believe me or not, and I'm not keeping a guy who thinks I'm a liar.

"You know, he never apologized for going through my phone behind my back." That's how he discovered my period was late; I have an app that tracks it.

"Next time I see him, I'm running him over with a car," Curie says.

I frown. "I thought you're getting a Harley."

"Cars hurt more. Don't they? I'm pretty sure that's science."

"Yeah, they do." You don't need Newton to explain that. I wish *I'd* thought of running him over, though. It would've been soooo satisfying.

"Well, whatever. I'm flattening him."

I grin. My twin is the best sister ever.

Joe gets a text, and he shows it to Curie. It's probably about their wedding. They start giggling and talking, their heads pulled close together. They look so cute. They've been together since high school—one of those meant-to-be couples. And even though my love life is about as attractive as the bottom of a sewer, I'm thrilled that hers is soaring above the clouds. She deserves it.

So I let them do what engaged couples do when they're not debating china patterns and monogrammed towels. I go to the dance floor so I can move to the music.

All day long the Hallelujah chorus has been going off in my head. Today's just that kind of a day. I even danced to that outside the club while I was waiting.

Hallelujah, my life is awesome.

My period just ended. And I'm free!

And by free, I mean single. I would've celebrated sooner, but wasn't in the mood while Aunt Flo was visiting.

It kills me I didn't see that Tom was a rat earlier. And not just any old rat, but a dirty, mangy wharf rat. Not diseased at the moment, but he will be soon, with a case of incurable hemorrhoids. He's an asshole, and I believe in karma. It's insulting that he lost it over a late period, like I'm some kind of breeding goat.

And I'll be damned if I ever beg a man to keep me, especially someone like Tom. He's not God's gift. If he were, he would've been hung like a horny elephant, ripped like a fitness model and able to fuck like a lion, which I've read can do it up to forty times a day.

Thankfully, Tom and I had only dated for three months before I kicked his ass to the curb, so I wasn't overly attached to him yet. It's nice to be over and done without any emotional baggage.

Sweat mists my skin despite the cool air blasting through the vents, but I'm having a fabulous time. There's nothing like dancing to decompress. A couple of guys start to move in, but I'm not interested tonight. I put out the "men not needed or wanted" vibe. And they slink away, like frat boys realizing there's no free booze.

Except for this one guy.

He moves toward me as though he's impervious to my keep-out vibes. No asking for permission verbally or otherwise. He just joins me. Maybe I should tell him no, but I can't, even while thinking it's too bad his stay-away radar is broken.

Because—call me shallow—he is hot. Like, "I might need to wipe the drool off my chin" *hot.*

He's tall with broad shoulders—my catnip. The planes of his face keep drawing my eye. Everything about him is perfectly proportioned, and the mathematician in me is utterly fascinated and thrilled. It's like he's a living embodiment of the Golden Ratio.

The totality of his appearance is like getting punched in the face with a whole new understanding of the wonders of the universe. So screw the no-man rule. I'm going to enjoy him moving with me tonight.

He starts dancing up close. Every time our bodies brush, an electric sizzle prickles over my skin. My heart thumps harder and faster, but it has nothing to do with the exertion of dancing. It's purely him.

This close, I can smell his subtle scent—some kind of liquor and something piney. It makes my stomach flutter, like it's full of newly hatched butterflies ready to take their first flight. It has to be the kind of excitement Columbus experienced when he finally saw land after his endless voyage.

The thing is, we aren't even moving against each other overtly. It's beautifully subtle, his fingertips stroking my shoulders, the contact feather-soft. Coaxing me to see where it goes.

I didn't come out tonight to hook up, but now I'm thinking, *What the hell.* One-night stands were invented for this—a chemical moment you have to seize and enjoy. Otherwise I might never experience it again. And it's the sort of thing that makes a woman wonder and regret for years to come. All the best discoveries in math and science happen by chance. Who says it can't happen in someone's personal life?

After five or six songs—I'm not counting—I realize that I'm thirsty. But I'm reluctant to leave and break the spell.

Leave it to fate. Tell him and see if he comes along with you.

I lean close. "I need something to drink."

The sizzling look in his eyes makes me shiver deliciously. "Perfect. I'm starting to get thirsty, too."

He puts his hand on the small of my back. The touch is firm and sure, and I love it. It's like a brand, the heat radiating and spreading over my body. Even though I'm already warm from dancing, I don't mind it at all. Actually, I move slightly closer, so my shoulders brush against his chest. Just a little.

We go to the bar. Luckily, I don't see Curie or Joe. They're probably dancing or making out in some dark corner. Since I don't plan to make this more than a one-night deal, I don't want to bother with introducing this guy. It's better—easier—to keep things anonymous.

The hottie catches a bartender's eye quickly. He's very tall, after all. Probably six four or five. He flexes his hand on my back. "What you want?"

You. "Gin and tonic." *Drizzled all over you so I can lap it up.* My cheeks warm at the idea. I bite my lip.

The bartender nods, then turns to my dance partner. "How about you?"

"Whiskey."

I give the hottie a quick glance, to see if I'm still feeling the same sizzle. Yup. I text Curie.

Found a guy. Might be the one for the night.

She responds. *Woohoo. Take a pic.*

I hide a smile. *And scare him away? Just take my word for it.*

Fine, fine. Go for it. Bone voyage!

I shoot her a few laughing emojis. She and I have tracking apps on each other's phones for safety, and I also know she won't bother me for the rest of the night. Just in case.

The bartender gives us our drinks. The hottie reaches for his wallet, and I put a hand on his wrist.

"I have a tab," I say.

I lean in until I'm practically on the other side of the counter and give the bartender my sister's name, so the hottie can't quite catch what I'm saying.

"That's cool, but I don't let ladies pay for my drinks." He hands the money over.

"Fine by me." To be honest, I prefer that we don't pay for each other's anything. That way, there won't be any weird expectations or disappointments.

I drain half my gin and tonic, much thirstier than I thought.

"What's your name?" he asks.

Name. I hesitate. Although my body's going yes-yes-yes, something pulls me back. Probably the same cautious nature that makes me double-check my work, even when it's something as simple as one plus one.

"How about we don't exchange names?" I say. "An anonymous fun night."

"Anonymous?" He arches an eyebrow and lets his gaze skim my forehead, eyes and mouth. "I've seen your face, and you've seen mine."

Touché. "That doesn't mean we need to exchange names, does it? It can still be incognito. More thrilling that way."

He smiles that easy smile that sends heat shimmering through me. "Okay, but I still need some kind of name. I don't want to be going 'hey you' all night."

That's a point. Besides, I want to do a final test to see if he's worth the bother. "How about a nickname? I'll let you come up with one for me."

He considers.

I wait, anticipation building as seconds tick by. *Come on, don't disappoint me.* I want to know what he'll come up with. Is it going to be something silly or something amazing or something surprising? His answer will determine how the rest of the evening's going to go. No matter how pretty he is, I can't deal with a guy who's empty in the head.

"Skittles," he says.

"Skittles? Like the candy?" I'm not sure exactly how I feel about being named after something chewy and diabetes-inducing. I thought he'd choose something like Gorgeous...or if he's clever, pick something from literature or pop culture.

"They're sweet and colorful. And cheery. Just like you."

Oh wow. Something warm and delicious unfurls. I really like him. It's not even his face. Or his body. Sometimes the hottest guys can make themselves utterly repulsive by opening their mouths. Like that guy who tried to pick me up a few months ago by comparing me to Marilyn Monroe, as though I would be stupid enough to buy that I look anything like that.

But the hottie? Everything coming out of that gorgeous mouth is multiplying his charm. It's pulling me to him like gravity and Newton's apple.

"And how about me?" he says, leaning closer.

My gaze flicks to his lips, and I know exactly what I'm going to call him. "Whiskey."

"Really?"

"Yeah, because you've been drinking it. I bet you taste like it, too."

"Probably true." Something bright and wicked glimmers in his eyes. He puts a hand between my shoulder blades, and my heart starts to thud.

"Let's see if you taste like Skittles." His mouth swoops down.

4

PASCAL

HE BRUSHES HIS LIPS OVER MINE. HIS TOUCH IS SOFT, inviting rather than taking.

Hot sparks of excitement crackle over me. Even my fingertips are tingling.

I open my mouth and flick my tongue over his lips. I want to know if I'm right about him tasting like whiskey. But he's so much headier. More addictive.

He feels like the hottest dream and sweetest endearment. There's a breathtaking confidence in the way he meets my tongue, slips his into my mouth.

My heart is racing like I'm still dancing hard, sweat filming over my heated skin. His breath fans over me, and I fit our bodies closer, wanting more...needing more.

His erection pushes against my belly, hot and hard. And I freakin' love it.

A vague voice from deep inside says this isn't like me. I'm much more careful about who I tangle tongues with, more judicious about my relationships. But I've never felt this way before. Why not embrace this new feeling, the kind you always hear about in movies and books?

This is going to be incredible. Carefree. And, most importantly, *simple*, without any attachment or complications.

The word that comes to mind is *thrilling*. I wrap my arms around his neck and deepen the kiss, wanting to go all the way. Gotta find someplace private.

After what seems like an hour or so, he breaks off. The lust in his eyes stokes the heat burning inside me. "You're delicious." He licks the corners of my mouth. "Let's get out of here."

"You have a place in mind?" The things I want to do with him will get us tossed in jail if we do it in front of an audience.

"Actually, yeah. Come on."

My response is immediate. "Okay."

He reaches out. Our fingers link, and I grin as our palms touch and the hot tingles intensify and radiate throughout my body. My heart is pounding, like the first time I bungee-jumped. I can't remember ever feeling like this. It isn't just that I'm excited. He makes it all seem new, as though I've never experienced sexual attraction or chemistry before.

We make our way outside. He doesn't get his car or hail a taxi. Instead, he leads me down the sidewalk.

"Where are we going?" I ask, wondering if he lives close by.

"The Aylster," he says as though the exclusive hotel is his backyard pool. "It's only a couple blocks."

Another place I've never been to, even though I've lived in the city all my life. A uniformed doorman greets us, and the revolving door dumps us into a lobby glinting with marble and crystal. There's some kind of abstract bronze sculpture thing in the center.

Whiskey goes to the front desk. Since we agreed to keep it anonymous, I stay far enough away that I don't overhear his name.

I look up at the murals on the ceiling. Wow. This must be how a medieval peasant felt when she saw Notre Dame for the first time. It's awe-inspiring...but not off-putting. Down on the floor, there's a hint of elegant hospitality in the careful arrangement of the seats and tables.

My gaze slides toward Whiskey. After all, he's the most fascinating thing in this hotel. He's obviously got money, but seems too down to earth to show off. My experience says if he's the type who can afford a room at a hotel like this, he should've done something like show off his Porsche or whatever to attract me. But nope. Nothing of that sort.

And the fact that he's confident enough to not bother with such inane attempts stokes my desire for him.

I shift my weight, trying to relieve the hot sensation between my legs. As soon as the smartly dressed clerk hands over the key card, Whiskey takes my hand again. He leads me unerringly into a waiting elevator, as though he knows the layout of the hotel.

Before the doors can close, a couple of people join us. I bite my lip, my shoulders sagging a bit. If they weren't here, I'd totally be jumping him right now. I haven't felt this reckless in...well, ever. And it feels damn good.

Freeing.

Since there are other people with us, I prop my hands on the horizontal bar behind me and lean the back of my head against the wall. I run my tongue over my lips, then my teeth, trying to grab what little flavor of him lingers there.

Mmm. I close my eyes so I can savor it better. Something chocolatey and laced with liquor—the best combination. But what makes it unique is the special taste of him that's all male and confidence.

Whiskey slides a discreet hand between me and the wall, cups my ass and squeezes. My eyes pop open. Oh God. It's illicit and so damn hot. My gaze moves to the people in front of us. They're checking their phones. With an uncharacteristic impulsiveness, I brush my hand across his crotch. Delicious lust shoots along my veins at the knowledge that the others have no clue I'm soaking between my legs and Whiskey is hard and ready.

What I'm feeling isn't like me at all. But I don't care. Tonight, I'm going to be irresponsible and carefree. It's my reward: stocking up on fun before I spend the next several months focusing on my career.

The people exit the elevator five floors below ours. As soon as they're gone, Whiskey nuzzles my neck.

"You smell *so* good."

His breath tickles, and I place a hand on his cheek. "So do

you." And in the small confines of elevator, his scent seems to intensify until my senses are saturated with the pine and male. Why isn't the car moving any faster?

The elevator doors finally open with a ding. We rush out, laughing breathlessly like a couple of horny teenagers. He stops in front of a door and sticks his key card in. The light blinks red. I drum my fingers against the wall. The hotel needs to upgrade its card reader. Doesn't their management know their guests' time is money?

He tries again. But the door remains locked.

"Shit. Why isn't this working?" he mutters.

"Maybe they made a mistake." Which is possible. But very irritating in a hotel of the Aylster's caliber.

"They better not have." He checks the envelope that key card came in, then swears under his breath. "Damn it. Wrong room."

I laugh at his chagrined look.

He pulls me down the hallway. Finally, we stop at the door at the end of the long corridor.

He sticks his card in, then dramatically intones, "Open sesame."

The lock clicks. *Finally!*

He turns the handle, and we spill into a semi-dark suite together. He puts the plastic in its slot next to the door, and all the lights in the suite come on. Very convenient, because I want to see him.

He pushes me against the wall, his mouth ravenous over mine. I kiss him back, my need no less intense than before. It's like all the logistics of leaving the club and coming to the hotel and checking in and finding this room have whipped my lust to an Everest-like height—as though they were necessary steps before the most sumptuous meal ever.

And that sumptuous meal is definitely worth the wait and effort. I've never felt a hunger this deep. His dick, thick and hard, is pressing against my belly. I'm embarrassingly wet.

Our mouths still fused, he pulls the zipper on the back of my dress, his movements as urgent as the need inside me. He tugs the garment down, letting it pool around my feet. A soft sigh of admiration slips between his lips as he takes me in, his face stark with carnal delight. I'm glad I put on my best underwear today. I don't have the biggest breasts or the roundest ass.

But the sheer male appreciation that glimmers in his gorgeous blue eyes heats me up. I feel like I have the best body in the entire universe.

"You're perfect," he says, soft awe in his voice.

My toes curl in my shoes. "Take off your clothes," I demand, feeling bold and powerful. I've never been wanted like this—unabashedly and so openly. It's liberating, untying the knots of inhibition around myself and my lusty instincts. Wanted and wanton.

With a wicked grin, he gets rid of all of them in a few quick motions. Fully naked, he's stunning. Most guys actually look better in clothes, but he's an exception. It's a crime against women that he has to put something on for propriety's sake. Positively sexist.

His body is lean and beautifully muscled, not an ounce of excess fat anywhere. And his cock. It's long, thick, veiny and pulsing, curving up like a very, *very* large finger beckoning. The sight makes me lick my lips.

"Gorgeous." I flush, because I didn't mean to say it out loud.

He laughs softly. "Glad you think so." And then his mouth claims mine and he tunnels his fingers into my hair, pulling me closer. He's no longer coaxing or gentle. It's all intense heat and lust, white-hot and searing. He nimbly undoes the clasp on my bra and lets it fall. Then he's pushing down my panties, and when they reach mid-thigh, I wriggle my hips and legs until they join my dress on the floor.

"Keep the shoes."

The way he says it makes it sound positively filthy. I smile saucily. "You like?"

"Fucking love 'em."

He carries me to the bed, kissing me, and lays me on the cool sheets then covers my body with his. His weight is anchoring, secure and solid. I rest my hands on his shoulders, feeling the power in the muscles, then his ass. This doesn't seem like a dream that vanishes when you blink, but one that you can hold on to.

Our mouths seem endlessly fused. I've heard of drugging,

addictive kisses, but I never realized what they were until now. My head is spinning, desire pulsing with every beat of my heart. Then finally, he's moving down my body, nipping, licking, tasting. Unquenchable fire seems to burn in my gut, so hot I feel like I'm about to combust.

He pulls my nipple into his mouth and sucks hard. I arch off the bed, a strangled scream caught in my throat.

It's insane how much I want him. It's like my body is no longer mine to control. It can only feel and obey what he's doing to me—and the crazy attraction between us.

"You taste amazing, Skittles, I love every inch of you." He slips one of his long, agile fingers between my thighs. "You're so wet. So slick."

My muscles clench around him, but it isn't enough to soothe aching emptiness. I spread my legs, needing more.

"I love it that you're so hot for me." He takes the glistening finger and licks the juices off. "Tasty."

My cheeks heat. But the need crackling between us burns away any mild embarrassment. "I bet you are too." I stroke my index finger across the tip of his cock and pull the fingertip into my mouth.

His blue eyes grow so dark that they're almost black. Deep red colors his cheeks. "Skittles, I don't think I can wait."

"I'm not asking you to. We can do the slow stuff later. I want to take the edge off now."

He laughs, the sound light, happy and just a little bit wicked. A small part of me does an ecstatic dance that I can make him like this. He puts on a condom and glides into me, big and hot and thick and *Oh My God* good. My vision blurs, and I clutch him hard. He braces his weight on one hand and uses the other to caress my ass and leg, all the way down to the ankle and back up. "Sexy and sweet. All mine."

I smile up at him. He's all mine too—for the night.

He puts my calves over his shoulders and drives into me. With every thrust, pleasure builds exponentially. He seems to know exactly how hard to push and what angle to hit. The bliss swells until I think I'm going to explode, and it finally rips through me, burning me inside out.

I scream. Then I crest again, harder and faster than I've ever done before. He shudders over me, his cock jerking inside my still-spasming pussy.

I manage open my eyes and see his beautiful face, ecstasy twisting his sublime features.

A vague regret surfaces. I wish I knew his name, so I could scream it...or call him by it softly in afterglow.

But as our breathing settles and he wraps himself around me, I tell myself that it's better this way. All I can commit to at the moment is this single glorious night.

5

COURT

I STIR, FEELING THE SOFT, LUXURIOUS COTTON SHEET UNDER my nude body. I stretch an arm to my left, then frown when I feel only the other side of the sheet.

Which is chilly.

I crack open an eye and glance over. *No one.*

Maybe she went to the bathroom. I close the eye and shift until I'm more comfortable. I can feel a huge grin spread across my face.

Last night was amazing. We had this *connection.* And I came five times, which is a record.

As for Skittles? I lost count after ten. My grin grows wider. I seriously love how responsive she is, and I can't wait to start the morning off right.

Another half-dozen orgasms between the two of us should do. Then a leisurely champagne brunch—I know the Aylster has it on the room service menu. Exchange phone numbers. See each other again. I can't remember the last time I felt something like this with anyone.

We should definitely explore what we have between us. Have

a very normal and nice relationship. No drama, no crazy people. Just me, Skittles and our awesome chemistry.

Thinking about that makes me heat up. The bitter and slightly sour knot in my chest is now gone, and my heart is at peace, beating normally. The small pit in my stomach that felt like a burning acid pool? That's gone, too.

And it's not just the sex. There's something more.

Hmm. Wait a minute. It's too silent. No sound from the bathroom. No TV.

Women are never quiet for this long.

I open the eye again and look at the bedside clock. *Damn. Already ten o'clock.* I open the other one and sit up. Did she have to leave? I don't have any plans, but some people have to do stuff, even on Saturdays. For all I know, she has to work today. We didn't talk about anything like that last night. Something to rectify soon.

I get up and look around. Sure enough, her belongings are gone. Guess she really did have to go. A little seed of disappointment wedges deep, just under my solar plexus. She could've at least said goodbye. I wouldn't have minded being woken up.

Maybe she left a note. I look around. The suite is too damn big, but I'll find it.

A good five minutes later, I glare at her side of the bed. She didn't leave a note! There's nothing on the coffee table in the living room or the counter attached to the built-in bar. Sad to say, but Skittles has skedaddled.

Then I see a stiff green rectangle, almost hidden under the sheets. *Oh, no way.* I snatch it up. It's a fifty-dollar bill.

I examine every square millimeter on both sides, in case she wrote a phone number. But no, there's nothing. And I'm quite certain this isn't a tip for housekeeping. Nobody tips fifty bucks. We didn't mess the room up that bad.

What the hell?.

I stare at it, and could swear Ulysses S. Grant is smirking at me.

Suddenly the peace and happiness I've been feeling dissipate. My stomach is rumbling with something that feels like a volcano ready to erupt.

What that fuck is this? I deserve better than this bullshit.

I'm going to find her and kick her ass—well, not actually kick her ass, because she's a girl. But I'm going to yell at her. Set her straight.

But first things first.

I hop into the shower. Might as well be fresh and clean before I track her down. Then I'll shake her until her bones rattle and whatever gear that came loose in her brain goes back into place.

But as the soap sluices down my body, my outrage starts to build. She didn't drop that money by mistake. She meant to leave it.

Is this some kind of a cheap shot? Some sort of *payment*? Even if I were only charging ten dollars an orgasm, she'd owe me more than fifty bucks!

This is what happens when you sleep with a woman who can't do math. But then, not a lot of people can after a fabulous night full of hot sex and very little sleep.

It doesn't soothe the hot, jagged edge of my temper much. I yank on my clothes and go to the front desk to check out. A clerk in a crisp black uniform smiles at me.

"Good morning, Mr. Blackwood. Did you enjoy your stay?"

I'm this close to telling her that it was anything but enjoyable. But it isn't her fault that Skittles insulted me and skipped out. I force a smile of my own. "The room was great. Thank you."

I give her my credit card, and she swipes it. While she deals with the payment system, I glance around, impatience nipping at me. A smiling concierge hands an envelope to a guest.

Oooh. Why didn't I think of that before? We don't have to leave a note in the room now, do we?

"Are there any messages for me?" I ask.

"I don't see anything on the screen here, sir."

"No, I mean like a real note. On paper. Like in one of those old movies, where two people are staying in the same hotel, but one of them—"

"Let me check, sir." She disappears into the back then returns within a few moments. "I'm sorry, there doesn't seem to be anything."

"Okay." What miniscule hope I've been nurturing is dashed. Just like that. "Thank you."

Now the volcano isn't just rumbling. It's shaking. And fiery steam is hissing out of the top. I'm not taking this gross indignity. Skittles will pay.

My whole body tense, I start toward the sitting area in the lobby, ready to call for a car.

My phone buzzes. A text from Tony.

Hey, you coming over?

Oh shit. I totally forgot. I told him I'd be at his place. He's getting Ivy's gift delivered today. I'm supposed to get her out of the house and distract her. Ugh. Guilt and annoyance tug at me.

I'm coming, I text back. While I'm there, maybe I can get Tony to let me borrow TJ to help me track down my girl.

6

PASCAL

SHOULD I HAVE WAITED UNTIL HE WOKE UP? BUT I WAS already running late. If I woke him up, he might've wanted to talk. What if he wanted to exchange numbers or something?

Maybe I should've left him a note? But I wasn't looking for anything except the one night. What if he took things the wrong way?

"Pascal?"

Or what if—

"Pascal."

I start, turn around and see Curie staring at me. "What?"

"I asked you about the veils." She's holding two in her hands like pompoms. Which fits, since she was head cheerleader in high school. "What do you think?"

My cheeks grow warm. I'm here at the bridal boutique to help Curie finalize everything for the wedding in two weeks. But instead I'm obsessing about Whiskey, who I'll probably never see again.

I clear my throat. "Well... Your gown is pretty simple, so I think the veil can be little fancy."

She lifts the one with sequins and lace trimming. "So, this one?"

"Yeah, uh-huh. And it'll reflect the sun, so you'll look extra radiant."

"Great." She turns to the hovering salesclerk. "This one."

The clerk jots down Curie's choice and then takes both veils to put them back.

Curie loops an arm around mine. "Are you okay? You've been really distracted all morning."

"I'm okay," I say, weirdly reluctant to talk about it until I'm more certain what I think about Whiskey. I'm still mulling the whole evening over, and all the dirty things we did. Until last night, I honestly didn't know you could come from just—

"Is it that guy from the club?"

I look at her earnest face. The same as my own, but different. Softer. Lit up with love.

Whiskey is nobody now. Well, he's somebody I slept with, but I'm never going to see him again. On the other hand, it isn't like Curie is oblivious to the fact that I'm in the same red dress as last night.

"Yeah."

"How was he?" She grins.

"Pretty, uh... You know."

Even though I'm a fully grown woman, somehow telling my sister about the hot stranger makes me blush like a teenager with her first crush. It's crazy, too, because I've never giggled or blushed over a crush before, first or otherwise.

"Oh-ho!" Curie's aquamarine eyes sparkle like stars. "You've got the look. He was good, wasn't he?" She nudges me.

The butterflies are back in my stomach. This time, they're fluttering so hard and fast that I feel the heat in my belly. I lower my voice. "Amazing. Like, he knew *exactly* what I needed."

"Good for you." She leans closer. "So where does he fall?"

"Definitely top three." I tap my chin. "No, that's unfair to him."

"So...top two?"

I shake my head, then point my index finger upward.

Curie's perfectly shaped eyebrows rise. "Better than *Brian?* Wow."

"Oh my God. A whole 'nother order of magnitude."

Curie laughs. "So what's his name?"

"We, um, decided not to use our real names." My tone is super casual. It seemed like such a great idea to keep our identities secret last night. But now, in broad daylight and with no alcohol flowing through my veins, it feels...a tad silly.

"You don't know the name of *the guy you slept with?*"

"Shh!"

My sister leans in and hisses, "The guy you just said was the best you've ever had? And you didn't get his name, not even *after?*" She stares at me like I've lost my mind. "What if you want to see him again? Or maybe he might want to see you again. The experience could've been mutually mind-blowing."

Hot jitters shoot through me as the memories from last night flash in my head. *Oh, he had a great time, too.* The man was insatiable. "I know, I know, but I need to focus on my career. If I don't get promoted this year, I might as well get LOSER tattooed across my forehead. In all caps."

"You won't have to. There's no way you're not getting promoted this year. You're one of the smartest and hardest-working people there is. Dad has to know that. Everybody else at the firm does."

I smile because there isn't any better response. Curie's being supportive, but she doesn't really understand the depth of my anxiety.

I pray she's right about this year, but there are no guarantees. Dad refuses to tell me why he won't move me up, except to say that he doesn't want any appearance of nepotism, which is understandable but also totally unfair. My work is just as good as—if not better than—all the men who started with me and who already managed to score promotions.

I pack away my resentment with some effort. It won't do me any good to dwell on stuff I can't control.

"I studied the qualifications of everyone who either started with me or after and got promoted," I say. "You know what I found?"

I wait a beat, but I'm not really expecting a response. There's no way Curie can possibly know the results of my analysis.

"What?" she says.

"I found out none of them had a serious relationship."

"You looked that deep?"

"Of course." I'm just that thorough. Or desperate.

"So they were celibate for...how many years is it?"

"No, no, no. I'm sure they hooked up here and there to blow off steam, but there was nothing serious, you know? So it's pretty obvious. The evaluation committee wants somebody who's married to the firm. Good thing I discovered it in time."

"That's crazy," she says. "Almost everyone at the top is married."

"Yeah, but that's later. I can't be a VP until I get promoted out of being a junior analyst first."

Her jaw slackens, her eyes growing wide. "So your Mr. Amazing Lay never had a chance? Even if he could be The One?"

"Well, maybe not *never*." I clear my throat, shifting because Curie's making my findings seem a little ridiculous. "Just, you know...later."

"Except you were so determined to keep it casual that you didn't even get his name. How are you going to find him later, after you become a VP?"

Good point. I wasn't thinking very clearly last night. Hormones aren't the best for clarity. But if we were meant to be, I'm sure we'll bump into each other again.

Besides, there are over three billion men in the world. Surely I can find someone suitable later, even if it's not Whiskey.

But my stomach twists hard at the idea of never seeing him again.

"Maybe I'll hang out at Z again," I say, trying to sound nonchalant.

"Is he even from around here?"

"Um." I never asked, but she might be right. He could just be visiting.

Curie checks texts on her phone. "I'm having brunch with Joe. Do you want to come?"

I start to say yes, then catch myself. Instead of going with her and Joe, I should go back to the hotel. If nothing else, I owe Whiskey more than fifty dollars for the room. I only left him that little because it's all I had in my purse this morning, and I was running too late to grab more from an ATM.

But that doesn't mean fifty dollars is enough to wipe the slate clean. I prefer to keep financial transactions tidy, without one person owing another. I'm a modern, independent woman with my own money. No reason he should pay for the whole thing when I used the room too.

"It's all right," I say. "Nobody likes having a third wheel on a romantic lunch date. Besides, I need to go home and get some sleep."

"Ha ha, I'll bet. It's a shame, though. If he was that good, he's definitely worth exploring more with. He could be the one for you."

It'd be nice, wouldn't it, to see if we're compatible out of bed, too? "Maybe I'll run into him after the promotion."

"The next few weeks aren't going to make or break anything." She squeezes my hand. "Don't stress over it. You'll only end up second-guessing yourself and making silly mistakes."

Curie is one of the smartest people I know, and she gets me better than anybody. "Yeah, you're right."

We say goodbye in front of the boutique. I get in my car and drive to the Aylster Hotel. I give my key to the uniformed valet, but tell him, "I'm visiting someone. I'll be out soon."

Probably. Or maybe not so soon, if I'm lucky.

And the little belly flips are screaming, *Get lucky! Get lucky, get lucky, lucky, luckyluckylucky.*

I step inside the lobby. In the corner opposite of the front desk, I spot an ATM. I withdraw five hundred dollars. Even for a suite, that should be enough. I mean, are they really going to charge more than a thousand dollars a night?

As I make my way down the hall to the suite, my heart thumps. Each step makes my insides throb, the flesh between my legs becoming slicker and hotter.

God, I'm acting like one of Pavlov's dogs. What am I, a nympho?

I'm only here to give Whiskey the money to cover the half the room. There's not going to be any second screwing because I have plans—Pascal's Promotion Plan.

My subconscious doesn't buy it. It whispers what I want is more than one night with him. So *I'm* not the nympho here, it's my *subconscious*. But it's been deprived. The orgasms I had before Whiskey were nice little bangs. He gave me nuclear explosions.

When I arrive at the room, I see the door propped open.

Did he think I'd come back? If so, that's awfully confident of him. Not that I could blame him after the number of times I came in his arms.

My cheeks warm, I push it in and call out, "Whiskey?"

A few rapid, thick-soled steps hit the floor. I flip my hair over my shoulder and paste on a bright smile, ready to face him. He might've been slightly irritated I left without a goodbye, but I'm back. Sooner than I expected, too.

A middle-aged woman in a white uniform comes out.

I blink, deflating like a punctured soccer ball. *Housekeeping.*

"Yes, ma'am. Can I help you?"

"Sorry to bother you." I clear my throat. "I'm looking for the guest in this room...?"

"He checked out."

Already? Don't suites come with late checkouts? "Did he leave a message?"

"I didn't see anything here. But you should check with the front desk."

Right. A great suggestion. I shouldn't bother this woman while she's trying to do her job. "Thanks for your help."

I get inside an elevator, going down toward the lobby. I tap the shiny floor gently with one foot. Damn it. I didn't think he'd check out so quickly. If I had a room like that, I'd linger. Take a nice hot soak in the huge sunken tub I saw in the bathroom.

But it's really for the best, I tell myself. The more you linger, the more you talk, the more trouble you get into. Every legal drama has the attorney hero telling everyone to shut up. Hell, you can't even talk to your spouse if you're going through a divorce. This is the universe trying to protect me.

Now, if I can just convince my heart...

I should go home, but I tell myself he deserves to be paid for the half the room. So that's the only reason I trot toward the spotless marble toward the front desk when the elevator opens.

A uniformed clerk smiles at me, her golden name tag embossed with *MEL*. "Good afternoon. Welcome to the Aylster Hotel. How may I help you?"

"Hi. I'm looking for a message that one of your guests might have left for me." I give her the room number.

She taps a few things into her computer. "What's your name?"

"Pascal Snyder. But he wouldn't have left a message under that name. He calls me, um, Skittles."

She looks up, then her gaze drops for a fraction of a second to my less-than-fresh, slightly wrinkled dress.

I squirm. Her expression doesn't change, but she isn't an idiot. She knows exactly what Whiskey and I were doing in the suite. This is a hotel. We didn't get a room to pray together.

I straighten my shoulders and stiffen my spine. "Like the candy," I add.

"Of course. Just one moment, please."

She slips into the back office. I wait, drumming my fingers on the cool, smooth countertop. Even though I didn't give him anything except for the fifty dollars this morning, he probably left me something. Curie's usually right about men, and like she said, he probably wants to see me again. He would also predict—just as he predicted what I needed in bed—that I'd regret sneaking out.

Mel returns. "I'm sorry, but there's nothing for you. Not under either name."

My shoulders sag, and something between regret and chagrin dulls the fluttering butterflies in my belly. "I see." I think rapidly. I don't want to wave a white flag. Not yet. "Do you mind letting me know his name?"

Her composure finally cracks. "Excuse me?"

"His full name. I...didn't catch it." I flush, knowing how this sounds. "I want to get in touch with him."

The professional mask returns, but her eyes flicker. I don't need to be a psychic to read her thoughts: *Wow, what a stalker fail.*

"I'm afraid that's not possible, Miss Snyder."

I grasp for the most persuasive argument I can think of. "You know I was up there with him."

"Yes, I gathered that." Her smile says, *Congratulations, ho.* "But if he didn't tell you who he is, I'm afraid there's really nothing we can do. For security reasons, we cannot give out a guest's personal data without a warrant."

Oh for Pete's sake. She's just doing her job, but I hate it that she's doing it so irritatingly well. The firm expression on her face says she's not changing her mind until a new ring forms around Uranus.

I try a different tack. "I just want to give him some money for the room. I owe him half the amount."

"If he wants to be reimbursed"—she doesn't say *further*, but she's thinking it—"I'm sure he'll contact you." Underneath her smooth voice is a mix of amusement and a tinge of derision. Must be the training. How to Smile Hospitably But Still Be Bitchy 101.

I spot two security guards who... *Did they just put their hands on their weapons?* The last thing I need is getting beaten up then tossed in jail for stealing the information off her workstation, so I nod with a graciousness I don't feel. "Thanks for your help."

"My pleasure."

I turn around and leave, my shoulders threatening to slouch. No, no. I stand tall, doing my best to pretend I'm not feeling a bit of disappointment. It's better that I don't know who he is or have a way to contact him. Definitely. For the best.

If I tell myself that a hundred times, I'll start to believe it for real, even as a small part of me wishes I could get in touch with him so we could explore...that thing we were going to have *after* my promotion.

7

COURT

Tony's new place is huge. Not that the penthouse he had before was small, but the new mansion could be converted into a boutique hotel.

Unlike some of the overpriced places in the area, his doesn't have a pool. Instead, it has a shallow water garden. Ivy isn't the best swimmer, and has a problematic history with water.

I tip the Uber driver, who seems a little awed, and get out. Hope he doesn't get distracted and hit something on his way back. That little cherub statue over there probably costs more than what he makes in a year.

When I ring, a housekeeper answers the door. She's dressed in a pristine shirt and tidy slacks. Her comfortably rounded face creases with a big, welcoming grin. "You must be Court. Tony told me you'd be coming by. I'm Shelly."

"Hi, Shelly." I smile.

"Come on in."

She leads me into the foyer. Lots of shiny marble, chandeliers dripping crystal tears and bright natural light. The interior is classy and modern at the same time, nothing like the sterile place Tony used to live in. Ivy clearly had a hand in the design.

Shelly brings me to a living room large enough to host a football game. My eyes zero in on its best feature—a fully stocked bar in the far corner.

Shelly leaves, closing the door behind her. I spot Edgar and Tony in armchairs set near huge bay windows. A couple of thick rugs sit in front of a huge unlit fireplace.

Edgar is sturdy and physically imposing, like our dad. Unlike Tony and me, he took after our sire in more ways than one. That includes his drive to see Blackwood Energy succeed and grow even more. And not even an azure polo shirt and shorts can diminish the stark intensity of his presence.

Tony, on the other hand, is more like me, at least in appearance. We both got our looks from our mom. He's totally relaxed in a simple V-neck green shirt that matches his eyes and loose, lightweight khakis. His pose is lazy and content—Ivy's doing. She's done a lot to turn him from a tormented soul into this epitome of satisfaction and bliss.

"Where's Ivy?" I say, ready to whisk her away so my whipped bro can prep for their first anniversary.

"Julie came by this morning to take her shopping," Tony says.

"Oh. Well, okay. Cool." That's probably more fun for Ivy than hanging out with me. Julie's not only hilarious, but Ivy's best friend. "Was she my backup?" He never said anything about having one.

"Nope. She just showed."

"Why did you ask me to come, then?"

"Because Julie wasn't here when I texted you."

"So I came here for nothing," I say in token protest, then move to the bar and pour myself a drink, which is clearly the least I deserve. Not for showing up, but for putting up with how the day began.

Tony quirks an eyebrow. "Not nothing, apparently."

"Why don't you get me a drink too?" Edgar says.

"What are you in the mood for?" I ask. He usually prefers brandy or whiskey, but sometimes he drinks wine.

"Whiskey's fine."

I bring both the drinks.

"So. The gift. Is it here yet?" I say, settling into my seat.

"The guys should get here any time now to set it up."

Just then, the intercom buzzes. Tony checks his phone. "Aaand speak of the devil."

While he goes to take the delivery, I drink the whiskey. I should be relaxed and happy with my brothers around. I like them, and they're cool and supportive. But relaxed and happy is the last thing I'm feeling right now. I keep thinking about Skittles —and what she did.

I tap my knee slowly. *Did I do something to upset her last night? Maybe I said something I shouldn't have?* But no matter how hard I try, I can't come up with anything. Unless Skittles doesn't like being told how hot she is.

And let's say I did say something stupid I don't remember. Why did she run like that? If she was upset, she could've just said something.

Did she think I'd go through her stuff and try to find out who she is? It's true I want to see her again, but I wouldn't violate her privacy that way.

Maybe she *went through* my *stuff...* Hmm. No, I doubt that. She didn't seem like the type. Besides, it isn't like my name is Harcourt Bluebeard.

Maybe she had a bad experience with some motherfucker. Damn it. This is why there needs to be an anti-asshole society that beats up assholes who scar women.

"Everything okay?" Edgar says.

"Huh? Why?"

"You look really pissed. Is it Mom?"

I tense up. She hasn't texted me since last night. She probably got tired—or maybe her battery died. Permanently, one can hope. "No, it actually isn't. For once."

"So what's the problem? Your fancy school just realized that you didn't take enough gender classes and is taking your diploma back?"

Ha. That would be hilarious. "My degree's safe enough."

"Then what? Dad still giving you a hard time about taking a position at the company?"

I shrug, feigning nonchalance. Dad knows there's no way to

have Tony be part of the company. So he wants me instead. His sons will continue the family legacy, whether they like it or not.

Except... Working for Dad would mean living in Tempérane. And living in Tempérane means fawners. I have this thing about people who like me because of my family connections and name. I try to stay under the radar as much as possible, be the irresponsible kid who people with ulterior motives overlook. "Not really. He knows he can't really force me. I'm taking control of my trust in three weeks."

"That's true." Edgar finishes his drink. "He is really unhappy about that."

Thank God it was Grandpa who set up the trust. If Dad had it his way, I'd never take control over the money or the stake in Blackwood Energy. The second part is silly because he knows I'll always do what's best for the company—in other words, I'll always vote with Edgar. The company is too important to the local economy to mismanage. "Even if I had zero money in my bank account, I wouldn't work for him. There are other jobs."

Edgar stares at me like I just told him I could do matrix algebra in my sleep. "You have one lined up?"

I shrug. He takes this kind of stuff too seriously. "I can work for Tony. I can be his club auditor."

"Club auditor? You don't have any accountant training."

"No, not like that. I go to his clubs and see if I like them or not. And get paid for it." To be honest, I don't know if that's a real job. But if not, it should be. Clubbing is serious business.

"So you want to be paid to party?"

"It's not partying if it's a job." I smile, liking that idea.

Tony walks in. "Who's paying Court to club for a living?"

"You," Edgar says.

Tony turns to me. "Did Wei promise you that job?"

"No, although he should." Tony's assistant is a sensible man. Surely he can see the wisdom of having such a position filled by someone like me. "We were just talking."

"Why do you need a job, anyway?" Tony asks. "You're going to be worth about a billion dollars in three weeks."

"Yeah, for a guy who's going to be a billionaire, he looks pretty glum, doesn't he?" Edgar gestures at me with his empty glass.

Since both of them are here and have more experience than me, I tell them what happened with Skittles. They listen, leaning close and nodding from time to time.

When I'm finished, they pull back. Tony rubs his chin thoughtfully. Edgar's brow furrows, and he taps the rim of his glass. Then they look at each other and both burst out laughing.

"Oh man, I can't believe that happened to you," Edgar says finally, wiping imaginary tears from his eyes. "Fifty dollars? She probably faked it. Just how bad were you that she didn't even leave a C-note?" He looks at Tony. "You think the fifty included a tip?"

For fuck's sake. "She definitely did not fake it! I would've known."

"Then why the pittance?" Tony asks.

My jaw tightens. "That's why I'm asking you. Which I see was a mistake, because both my brothers are idiotic, red-faced baboons."

"The red faces are 'cause we're laughing too hard," Edgar says.

Tony taps his chin. "I can't think of any other reason, unless you took her to some hundred-dollar roach motel and the money was supposed to cover half the room."

"Come on, I'd never take a girl to a place like that. It was the Aylster."

Edgar purses his mouth. "Had to be the performance."

Asshole. "I'm telling you, it was not. We had a great time. Both of us."

"Then track her down and ask," he says. "Or better yet, throw the money in her face."

"Yes." Tony snaps his fingers. "Oh, and at a public event...like her high school graduation. Except that'll only show everyone what she thought of the night."

I bare my teeth. "You guys are dicks."

Tony grins. "Dicks worth more than fifty bucks." Edgar laughs, slapping the arm of his chair.

Damn it. I should've known nothing useful would come from my brothers. Why did I think otherwise? Hope springs eternal only for idiots. "You know what? I am going to find her, and have my revenge."

"There you go. Revenge is the best..." Snapping his fingers, Tony looks at Edgar.

"Revenge," he finishes.

My brothers are dumber than goats dropped off a cliff. "At least I'm not whipped enough to spend half a million bucks on a first anniversary gift."

"Well." Tony shoots me a bland smile. "First you have to *have* a first anniversary..."

"He's going to build her a copy of Versailles for their second," Edgar says.

"Like I said. Whipped." I make the whip-snapping sound.

Ivy walks in, carrying a shopping bag. She's a pretty strawberry blonde with soft gray eyes. She's even more beautiful now. Must be the love she's feeling for my brother. I'm not the mushy type, but when I look at those two, I feel like fate does exist.

"What's up with the whip?" She sweeps her gaze across the room, over all three of us, then raises her palm. "No, no. Never mind. I don't want to know. Just don't do anything I wouldn't do."

Edgar and I laugh. I don't know why he's laughing, but oh man. Ivy should know by now that I basically exist to do what she wouldn't do.

"Did you buy something pretty?" Tony asks.

"Shoes. I needed something comfy to wear."

I exchange a glance with Edgar. Since Ivy's home, it's our cue to get out. Bet Tony's dying to show her the gift.

We get up and bid them goodbye.

When I reach the foyer, I see TJ.

I overheard Ivy refer to him as a Visigoth once, and that's a damn good description of the guy. He's a giant—a mountain, really, with lots of hair and a nasty expression that says he's going to kick your ass, your dad's ass, your brother's ass and your Doberman's ass. All at the same time. The suit he's wearing doesn't lessen the aura one bit.

His biggest responsibility is ensuring Ivy's safety. But he also works for Tony, and everyone at my brother's company knows TJ and does what he asks them to do. Which means...

"Something happen to you?" TJ says.

I blink at him. "Huh?"

"You look unhappy."

It must be pretty obvious for him to comment. His communication usually consists of grunts.

I shouldn't tell him because he'll just mock me like my asshole brothers. On the other hand, he doesn't have to know all the details. And he can find stuff. Everyone at Z tells him what he wants to know.

Stick to the bare facts. Give him just enough to help without prompting any unnecessary commentary.

"I met this woman at Z," I begin. "I'm trying to figure out how to track her down."

He shrugs, like I've asked him to pick up a napkin or something. "What's her name?"

Damn it. I should've insisted on exchanging names, rather than going along with her silly "anonymous" routine. "I, uh, don't actually know. I called her Skittles."

His eyebrows twitch. "Was your blood sugar low?"

"Come on, man. I don't need this crap."

"It's not crap. I can help."

"Really?" I feign surprise. "What will I owe you?" In TJ's world, there's no such thing as a free lunch. Only free beatings.

"Nothing. You've always been loyal to Tony." He turns his head and spits. "Your parents treated him like the plague." TJ's loyalty to Tony could put a samurai to shame. "Did she do anything at the club? Buy a drink, use a credit card?" he asks, although he doesn't look optimistic. He knows I always pay.

"She was running a tab. But I don't think she settled it before we left." Thinking about how hot we were to get private makes me hard...and the memory of the post-sex morning pisses me off. Now I finally understand how people can have hate-fucks.

"Doesn't matter. We always take their credit card first, just in case. Who was the bartender?

"Diego," I say. "Benny was working, too."

"Lemme check." He taps his phone screen.

After a couple of beats, I ask, "So...?"

45

He shoots me a mildly irritated expression. "This might take more than four seconds. But don't worry. I'll let you know."

"Okay, thanks." Nothing to be done about the wait. But while TJ is working on getting me Skittles' name, I can fantasize about my revenge.

8

COURT

ALMOST TWO WEEKS PASS, AND NOTHING FROM TJ. THE fiery need for revenge is no longer burning as brightly as before. More like I'm annoyed with TJ for being so friggin' slow.

I bet he forgot. Typical.

Now I wish I'd insisted on exchanging names. Then I wouldn't be having to rely on him.

Of course, if I'd insisted on real names, I might not have gotten laid.

I think about that for a while. It's like the tree in the forest. Kind of philosophical.

I could've used Skittles' bright cheeriness since our night together. It's seriously annoying dealing with my parents, both of whom call me at all hours for very different—but equally annoying—reasons.

Dad wants me to work for him because...Family Legacy. Mom wants me to take his offer...on the condition that he reconciles with her. But they need to have their lawyers figure all that stuff out, not me.

Actually, even if I could bill them a thousand bucks an hour, I wouldn't want to be involved. I'm neutral. An island. A son called Switzerland.

Even Nate senses my piss-poor mood, because he drags me out to a comedy club, saying tonight's acts are especially funny. I'm not big on comedy clubs, but I humor him, trying to be a good friend.

People around me laugh, but I tune them out, the way I tune out the laugh track on a TV show. So irritating.

I gesture at a waitress for another drink as the crowd hoots. Nate, who should have better taste and maturity, is clapping like a baby who's seeing somebody blow a raspberry for the first time.

"What are you scowling about?" he says.

"Nothing," I say.

"You haven't laughed at a single joke."

I gesture at the stage. "That dude isn't funny."

"Why the shitty mood?" Now he's the one scowling. "I thought the comedy club would cheer you up."

"I'm fucking cheery, all right? Look." I point at the new drink that just landed in front of me.

He leans closer. "You still hung up on that girl? Snickers?"

"Skittles," I say dryly, opting not to mention the Parental Unit drama because he's probably just as sick of it as I am.

I already told Nate what happened with Skittles...minus the fifty-dollar part. I don't need my best friend giving me shit for the rest of my life. He'd probably put it on my gravestone.

"Snickers is better," he says. "It's got peanuts."

"Unlike you, I don't date nuts."

"You should. They're crazy in bed."

"So is Skittles. She screamed like Chewbacca getting his legs waxed."

Nate laughs. "You sure they weren't screams of disappointment?"

"She was sleeping with me, not you." But my heart isn't in the banter. I down my drink. The liquor heats my insides...and the irritation simmering in my gut. TJ said he'd find the girl for me. I'm entitled to a follow-up.

I stand up and pull out my phone to text him. But before I

can send anything, someone with arms like a squid wraps herself around me.

"Court!"

Ah, crap. You can't mistake that voice—it's perkier than a chipmunk on helium. Freakin' Tiffany. My ex, whom I parted with amicably, not because I like her, but because I didn't want to deal with the neediness and drama that would've ensued otherwise.

I turn and see the bottle-red hair, the stylish handbag. "I got a second interview with Blackwood Energy!" she squeals. "I'm going out there next week for it!"

"Great!" I say with a fake smile. Maybe she'll fetch coffee for Dad and leave me alone.

"I told your dad I was a *really* close friend of yours, and he was *so nice* to me."

Ugh. I need another drink.

"He asked me about you! I swear, he said he'd love to hire me to be your assistant. Wouldn't that be cool?" Her eyes are entirely too shiny. She even flutters her eyelashes.

"It would, but I won't be there, so maybe you should look for another position."

"But why, Court? It'll be great. You can work for your daddy, and I can work for you. You know how hard it is to get a job?"

"I can guess." She's proof that God is fair. He gave her the body of Jezebel after a stupendous boob job and the intellect of a lobotomized amoeba. I can see why Dad thought she could tempt me, but it's not going to work. The girl can't even sneeze without someone's help, and she treats me like a black AmEx card.

"I gotta go," I say, and walk away, not caring that I'm being rude. I no longer have any patience for people who only want to use me.

Outside, I text TJ, demanding to know Skittles' real name.

A few minutes later, he replies. *Forget her.*

Excuse you, TJ, but I didn't ask you to advise me on my personal life. *Why?* I pause for a second, then add, *You couldn't figure out who she is?*

Of course I did. His text is practically pulsing with wounded ego. *She's not worth it.*

49

He thinks that because he's never slept with her. Or felt the buoyant happiness she inspired. *Her name, man. Come on. You promised. I've been a great, loyal bro to Tony, remember?*

Curry Snyder.

Curry Snyder? It almost makes me laugh. No wonder she didn't want to tell me her name.

Another text arrives. *Ducking autocorrect. Curri.* Then another. *CURIE. Curie Snyder. But seriously, forget her.*

Why?

She's getting married tomorrow.

Everything inside me slams to a stop, like a locomotive crashing into a mountainside. *Where?* I manage to text, despite shaking fingers.

Maui.

To an ugly guy who propositioned her parents? The movie *Indecent Proposal* had something similar. Well, it was an old dude offering a million bucks to sleep with a young married woman in that flick, but still. Some old fart could've done the same to her parents. Stuff like that probably still happens.

Is she being forced? I text.

Forced? She's marrying her high school sweetheart.

Is this some kind of cosmic joke? Her high school sweetheart? My lurid *Indecent Proposal* fantasy shatters. No way this can be right.

Screw texting. I call TJ. "Hey. You sure about all this?"

"Of course I'm sure. She paid for the drinks with her credit card. Her groom's name is Joe Washington. Good, all-American boy."

What the fuck? "Then why the hell did she sleep with me?"

"You asking me? Didn't your fancy professors teach you anything in your gender studies class?"

"Who remembers any of that shit after they graduate?" I clench my hair, then cut the connection, my mind churning.

TJ's right. I should let her go. But...

I feel like I was holding a rainbow in my grasp, only to have somebody snatch it away.

Okay, forget the sex. What I want most from her is that sense of peace and happiness. There's no way this Joe guy is going to take that—take *her*—from me. If he were her true love, she wouldn't have danced with me that way or slept with me.

"Hey, you all right?" Nate has appeared, and places a hand on my shoulder.

I unclench my hair and run my fingers through it. "Not really. But I need to borrow your plane." I might be set to inherit a billion dollars in another week, but that doesn't mean I have a private jet lying around, ready to just take off whenever.

He stares. "The Learjet?"

"Yeah."

"You want to borrow the Learjet?"

"I gotta get to Maui."

"To do what?"

Oh geez. Hundreds of thousands of possibilities spin in my head. But there's only one logical option. "Confront Skittles."

9

PASCAL

Whoever came up with the phrase "tossing one's cookies" is a moron. They obviously never throw up because if they did, they'd know there's nothing cookie-esque about throwing up.

I clutch the toilet rim, feeling like my stomach lining's being ripped raw. My throat is aching like a million microscopic bees have stung the delicate tissue there.

Curie crouches next to me, her gentle hand on my back. "Are you all right?" she asks.

I nod, panting, even as cold sweat beads on my face. "Give me a second."

That's such a lie, though. I need at least a week, flat on my back. Damn it. I clench my teeth as my stomach churns dangerously, sloshing its contents like a raft in a storm.

I look down and see the lace trimming on Curie's white gown. Crap. Today's the day, and I'm here, trying to empty everything from my stomach...and then some. I feel like I'm going to empty my liver and gallbladder as well.

"You don't have to come, especially if you feel this bad," she says softly, blotting the sweat off my hairline with a Kleenex.

"It's your wedding. Once-in-a-lifetime deal."

The whole thing comes out in a whispery whine, and if I had the strength, I'd smack myself silly for that. I, Pascal Snyder, do not whine. Not so pitiably, anyway.

Besides, I'm being unreasonable. There's no way I can stand next to her as her maid of honor when my stomach is roiling to a "Ride of the Valkyries" that only it can hear. The worst thing is, whatever vile substance is making me puke should be out by now, but my belly is refusing to settle. It's like a rowdy hamster on crack.

It's so unjust. I *really* wanted to be part of her wedding. I've been looking forward to it all year long.

"Sorry. Letting you down," I say, finally turning to face her.

She hands me a small towel to wipe my mouth. "It doesn't matter. What I care about is you getting better soon. I'm going to miss you at the ceremony."

"I should've just fasted. I'd look better in my dress." The joke is flatter than a road-kill possum.

Still, Curie's awesome and manages a smile. "Yeah, but there's gonna be photographer...and of course the video. You can watch it later." She squeezes my hand.

"Okay." The response comes out listless and pathetic. Even though she and I are trying to be positive, we both know it's not the same thing. But what can I do? If I could will myself to be healthy, I would.

Even squatting next to me on the bathroom floor, Curie's gorgeous. And I'm not just saying that because she's my identical twin.

Her dark brown hair is twisted into a simple, elegant updo. Subtle makeup brings out the blue in her eyes and adds fullness to her lips. The dress is perfect too. It's not too heavy or complicated, since the wedding's going to be on the beach. The bodice fits her tightly, pushing her breasts up. The long skirt is made of a light material that should move freely to the breeze from the Pacific on the beach.

"You're the most radiant bride ever," I say. "I'm so happy for you."

"I couldn't have planned all this without your help, Pascal. I love you so much." She hugs me tightly.

Mom sticks her head into the bathroom. She's in her new hot-pink dress and full makeup. "It's time." She turns to me, looking sympathetic. Curie and I took after her. "How you feeling, hon?"

"Could be better." I turn to Curie. "You should go."

She starts to bite her lip, then catches herself. Her carefully penciled eyebrows pinch together. "I hate leaving you alone when you don't feel good."

"I'll be fine. Just gonna go lie down."

I'm not letting my hateful stomach of evil ruin Curie's special day. I even force a smile for her behalf, although the worry stays on her face. Still, she leaves with Mom.

My legs shake a little as I stand up, but they hold. I rinse my mouth and look at myself in the mirror. My makeup is useless. It can't hide the greenish pallor underneath. The blush makes me look actively ridiculous. Like a color-blind clown who's trying too hard.

The mascara and eyeliner are smudged from sweat. I scowl at the dark rings around my eyes. Waterproof, my ass. But if I try to sue them for false advertising, I bet their lawyers would say, "We never claimed it was *sweat*proof."

It doesn't matter. I'm not going to be at the wedding anyway. Who cares how I look?

Slouching, I prop my hip against the edge of the sink and sigh. Damn it. I really wanted to be there. Curie's only getting married once. It's unfair that I'm going to miss it...

But do I really have to? I could go stand in the back and watch the ceremony from a distance, even if I can't take part. Hell, given the amount of time and effort I put into helping her, I deserve to see it live, not on some TV screen later.

I take a sip of water and wait a couple of minutes. My stomach stays relatively okay. I take another small swallow and give myself five minutes. The bathroom remains stable; my stomach does not rebel although it still feels queasy.

I sigh softly. Even though I'm not a hundred percent, this is a sign. If I lie in bed, I'm going to regret missing Curie's wedding for the rest of my life.

My mind made up, I grab a plastic bag—just in case—and leave the room.

10

COURT

I OBJECT.

The phrase hack scriptwriters insert into a wedding scene for drama when they're out of fresh material. Who would've thought I'd be using it?

But this ceremony definitely calls for it.

And the décor isn't even that nice. I mean, it's not bad if you like pastel and white and girly-girl shades. But I expected a more...vivid liveliness.

Even the flowers are pastel pink and lavender.

It's so pervasive that I feel the colors ought to leach from my clothes and shoes to fit in.

What the hell happened to your taste, Skittles?

She isn't the woman you thought she was. Nate's words haunt me. They circle like a vulture waiting for my heart to die. *I don't think she's worth it. You can do better.*

Still, he lent me his jet because that's how our friendship goes.

I arranged for the Maserati. I'm not stealing her away in a cheap rental.

Set off against the picture-perfect beach in Maui, the bride and the groom face each other and hold hands. Their vows are as lovely as a jackhammer starting up at seven a.m. on a Sunday.

"So amazing." A busty blonde next to me tears up.

I look at her, wondering if she's talking to me. Nobody else is sitting on the other side of her, so maybe she is.

I don't have any Kleenex to offer, so I let her sniffle away. She's probably mourning the inevitable outcome.

Fifty percent of marriages end in divorce. Pretty shitty batting average if you ask me.

Now, if the bride slept around as late as two weeks before the ceremony... Well. I'd wager all my voting shares in Blackwood Energy that *that* particular marriage is definitely going to fail. Probably within the first year, if not the first week.

I squint at the altar. The bride's gown is blindingly white under the dazzling Hawaiian sun. Her dark chocolate hair is perfectly coiled over her crown, the pearly bodice fitted over her slim body. Although I can't quite make out her eyes from this distance, I know they're the pretty aquamarine of the Caribbean.

And they deepen into the color of the Pacific when she comes.

I shove my hand into my pocket. Feel the crisp texture of the fifty-dollar bill, folded neatly in half. I've carried it around the last two weeks, wondering about its meaning, why Curie left it on the dresser after our night together, and why the hell I needed to track her down so badly...even after TJ told me she was marrying somebody else.

Just walk away. She isn't worth it.

Logically, yeah, she isn't. But logic doesn't matter when my mind keeps recalling her brilliant smile, how she made me feel that night—carefree, hot and happy.

Sharp nails scrape against my belly lining at the idea of some other guy making her his, receiving that stunning smile. Yeah, I'm looking at you, Groom Dude. You must be an epic failure in the sack if she went out looking for bedroom action with someone else.

Probably impotent. He looks a little young for that, but erectile dysfunction is an equal-opportunity medical condition.

"They're going to be so happy together." The blonde next to me weeps openly into her hands.

No, they're not. I'm going to stop this farce before it hits its climax.

Almost time. I wait for the officiant for my cue, all the words ready. I rehearsed them during the long, long flight from LAX.

The man grins like a mule on ecstasy. "Now I pronounce you husband and wife."

What the hell? Why is he skipping the only question that really matters at a wedding? What if someone has a serious problem with this union?

I didn't sit through this dull joke of a ceremony for nothing. *Screw it.* I don't need the officiant to ask.

Outrage sizzles through my whole body like electricity. I jump to my feet, leap to the center of the row and take a step toward the altar, then point my finger at the bride, so she knows she's the reason. My heart pumps with hot—and slightly petty— anticipation as I shout the words I'm here to say. "*I object!*"

The guests' gasps are loud over the sound of waves. Satisfaction surges inside me over this ceremonious interruptus. Everyone's heads swivels in my direction. The couple turns as well.

Hundreds of gazes bear down on me, making my scalp tingle, but I don't care. I'm finally going to say my piece.

The groom frowns in confusion, which I understand. But the bride is staring like she has no clue who I am.

Which only pisses me off more. Not just because my pride is hurt. Something else more volatile is churning.

I whip out the fifty-dollar bill like a triumphant prosecutor whipping out a murder weapon with the perp's bloody fingerprints all over it. "Remember this, Skittles?"

The bride's looking at me like I'm off my meds. She glances at her almost-husband.

Outrage knots into a ball so big that it sticks in my throat. *Oh no, you don't.* "You dropped it on the bed after we had sex. Two weeks ago."

She turns pale, then red, and says something to her intended, gesturing with her bouquet. The groom turns bright crimson, murder in his eyes as he glares at me. Everyone else is looking at me like I should be committed.

After the groom beats me up, that is.

It annoys me that people can't see I'm right and she's not. Do they have any idea how much a decent divorce costs these days? It's like five hundred dollars per billable hour.

My hands clenched into fists, I walk up to the altar. The groom—Joe the All-American High School Sweetheart—steps in front of Skittles.

Yeah, like that's going to stop me now. If I were going to let this small an obstacle get in the way, I wouldn't have bothered to fly all the way to Maui.

I shove him to one side. Before Skittles can slip away, I grab her and toss her over a shoulder. She doesn't weigh much, but she's wriggling like an eel.

I smack her ass once. She gasps, then hits me with the bouquet. It kind of tickles. I run down the row like a receiver rushing toward the end zone. Somebody cue up the *Rocky* theme song.

The guests stare, their mouths open.

Hell yeah. Bet this isn't the show they thought they'd see when they flew to Hawaii. At least the weather's gorgeous. They can enjoy the champagne and banquet food under the pristine blue sky.

I have a list of questions I made in my head on the flight here.

Why did you go to the Aylster with me?

Why did you sneak out?

Why did you leave the money?

Why are you marrying that guy?

And a hundred other *why*s...

As soon as I get Skittles away, we're going to have a talk.

11

PASCAL

I HAVE TO BE SEEING THINGS. THROWING UP ALL NIGHT LONG has probably messed up my vision. Or maybe this is just a fever dream.

I squint at the ceremony. Some tall guy is dashing off with Curie over his shoulder, her veil billowing out behind in the Maui breeze. Thankfully she's sensible enough to not smack him too hard with her bouquet, because she'll need it for later.

I slap my cheeks lightly and blink a few times. But nope. Not seeing things.

If he weren't ruining the wedding, I'd be admiring the stamina and strength required to do what the man is doing. He's moving faster than even Joe, who is in hot pursuit.

It's hard to see the bastard with the sun behind him, although something about him seems familiar. Probably a member of the Curie Admiration Association. I can't remember the last time she didn't have a stalker or two.

My sluggish mind finally kicking into gear, I look at the distance between me, the creep and Joe. I'm closer to the kidnapper. It's up to me to stop the scum.

Don't worry, sister. I'll save you!

Adrenaline pumping through me, I kick off my heels and run toward him. My belly protests—a lot—but I clench my teeth and keep going. I can heave after I rescue my sister.

The kidnapper dumps Curie in the passenger seat of a fancy convertible. I have to keep him from leaving, so I jump in front of the car. He slams on the brakes.

"You fucking crazy?" he screams. "I almost ran you over!"

Yeah, he did. My legs are shaking, and it's not all from the sickness earlier. I breathe hard and place unsteady hands on the scorching hood of the car for balance. I'm afraid my knees are going to fold otherwise.

Come on, Pascal. Keep it together. Just long enough until Joe gets here.

Then, after two gulps of air, I lift my chin to face Curie's kidnapper.

What the... *Whiskey?*

Shock punches me in the chest. My mouth parts, but then I close it again quickly to forestall more puking.

What is he doing here? Why is he trying to steal Curie from Joe?

"Skittles?" he says slowly.

"Yeah," I croak, my throat still raw.

He takes a quick look at Curie, then turns back to me. He flicks a thumb at my sister. "Who the hell is this?"

What? He doesn't know? "You're asking *me*?" I try to straighten, but it doesn't work. Now that the adrenaline is waning, I feel entirely too weak.

So I settle for a harsh rebuke instead. "You're the one who kidnapped her!" Except...it doesn't come out very strongly. Damn you, stomach bug!

"Hey, you! Shithead!" Joe finally arrives, puffing and red-faced. He immediately softens his voice. "Are you all right, darling?" he says to Curie.

"I guess...?" She finally pushes the veil out of her face. "I don't think I'm hurt."

"Are you guys...sisters?" Whiskey asks.

Given that his gaze is jumping from me, to Curie, to Joe then back to me, I have no idea who he's talking to. But I should probably step in and fix this. After all, Whiskey is my mess, and I'm supposed to be the maid of honor. Comes with the job.

"Yeah." I clear my throat. "Twins."

He looks at the sky, then places a hand over his eyes. "Oh for... Fucking TJ."

"Fucking...?" A light dawns in Curie's eyes. "Oh my God. Is this your anonymous one-night stand from Z?"

And, of course, at that *precise* moment, Dad finally runs up. Why couldn't he have waited five more seconds? Maybe I'll get lucky and get swept away by a person-sized tsunami.

Usually, Dad's calm, with an even temper. He's not physically imposing, despite his height. But right now, his face is red as though he's been burned, which is impossible, because Mom's fanatical about sunblock. He's clamping his teeth so tightly that I'm afraid steam's going to start coming out of his ears, and his brown eyes are bulging. The last time he was this mad was when I was ten. I climbed a tree he explicitly told me not to and fell down and broke my arm.

"One-night stand? Do you know this man, Pascal?" he demands in a booming voice.

Why don't you speak louder, Dad, so everyone on the island can hear it?

Embarrassment crawls over me. If I could, I'd bury myself under the sand. "Yes." So much for anonymous fun. Next time, I'm not doing it unless I'm in Tibet...or at least some place twelve time zones away from anywhere in America.

"Can we continue? Kiss my bride? Have our reception?" Joe asks.

"Yes," Whiskey answers, the hand still over his eyes. "And sorry for the, uh, you know. Interruption."

Joe helps Curie out of the car, and they leave together. The guests who were inching closer for better view follow them back to the altar.

Dad gives Whiskey a look.

Whiskey drops his hand and looks at him. "Hi."

Dad's eyes narrow. "I know you. You're—"

"A lot of people do," Whiskey says with a tight smile.

They do? How come I didn't recognize him, then? "Are you famous?"

"Not really," Whiskey says.

Dad shakes his head at me, and I brace myself for some scathing words. Well deserved, since I screwed up, but that doesn't mean they won't hurt.

"We're going to talk about this later. Without the audience," he says.

"Yes, Dad." I look down at my toes. Can this be a puke-induced nightmare? Maybe I fell asleep on the bed after Curie left. But given how raw I feel in my worthless stomach, all this is probably really happening.

He follows the couple. Palpable disapproval radiates from his retreating back.

My gut twists. He's probably going to disown me now. After he fires me. And you know what? I can't even fault him for it. I'd do the same if I were him.

And that's not all. My instinct says something else is very wrong with the situation, except I can't quite grasp what that is. By the time I figure it out, it's probably going to be too late.

Suddenly, my stomach roils violently. I try to turn away, but it's too late. I projectile-vomit all over the shiny hood.

"Oh *shit*!" Whiskey jumps out of the car.

Since there's no food in my belly, it's mostly clear liquid. But that doesn't mean it isn't gross. I yank my hands off the metal and take a couple of steps back, too sick to calculate what it's going to take to clean this thing.

If only my day would end now. This craptastic incident is going to culminate in Whiskey yelling at me over this damned fancy puke-mobile, even though this is one hundred percent his fault for trying to kidnap my sister. I gird myself for a fight, but all he does is put a gentle hand on my back. "Are you okay?"

"If you hadn't tried to kid—" *Wait.* Did he just ask if *I'm* okay? I frown at him. "What did you say?"

He gives me the slightly exasperated look of a man annoyed with a dimwitted toddler. "I asked if you were okay."

"Uh." I glance at the car and finally notice it's a Maserati, the kind of vehicle men fantasize about. The kind they worship. "You aren't upset about the car?" Everyone I know would be pissed off. Hell, *I'd* be pissed off.

"Huh?" He notes the condition of the hood, then shrugs. "Nothing that can't be washed." His eyes skim over my face. "You don't look so good."

He grabs a wad of Kleenex from his car and blots the sweat on my forehead and temples. His touch is incredibly tender. My brain is trying to reconcile this with the man I met two weeks ago —the fun, carefree type who fucked like a god.

Most guys I know don't do *caring* very well. And I can't quite figure out what to make of his reaction.

At the same time, I can't forget he's crazy enough to kidnap a woman from her own wedding, even if he did think it was me.

I cross my arms. "How did you find me?"

"Well...technically I found your sister."

"Yeah, whatever. How'd you do it?"

"The tab."

The unfairness of the universe is unbelievable. "The *club* told you?" The hotel clerk was so freakin' rude to me when I asked for his name, but the club just *handed over* my sister's name? "They just *told* you?"

"They wouldn't normally. I know the owner."

Of course he knows the owner. Ugh. Just my luck. This is why I go to clubs that aren't as cool and hip as Z.

"qo' 'oHbe' 'IH," I mutter. It's Klingon for "The world is unjust."

"What?"

"Nothing." I'm too tired and sick to explain it. "How did you know I was here?"

"The wedding announcement."

Of course. The damned wedding announcement. I swear they exist only to let anonymous one-night stands track you down.

He peers at me. "Do you want to sit down?"

What I want is to see what's left of the ceremony. But I'm too embarrassed to go over there, especially with Dad having over-heard the thing about me and the one-night stand. What will Mom say? What do I say to her? And how on earth am I going to face Joe's parents?

Forget watching the rest of the ceremony. I want to go bang my head against a palm tree and just erase the last fifteen minutes.

But since it isn't possible to selectively delete memory, I say, "Yeah."

Whiskey takes me to the passenger seat, and I sit down gingerly. It's a convertible, so I can just hang my head over the side if my gut decides to empty itself out again.

He settles behind the wheel. "So. Your name is Pascal. And the last name is Snyder."

"Yeah." So much for anonymous fun. Sighing, I try to look at the bright side. Like...how I was hoping to run into him later anyway. But really, couldn't he have waited until my promotion first? "And you?"

A second of hesitation. "Court."

I nod. It's a good name. Solid. Strong. I like it entirely too much.

I rub my forehead. What's wrong with me, thinking about how much I like the guy's name in a situation like this? He's proven himself seriously unstable. Who kidnaps a bride from her wedding just because you *think* you slept with her once?

I should be repelled by his...weirdness. But instead, my hormones are lighting up like a conifer on Christmas. They also note he's painfully gorgeous with the Hawaiian breeze stirring his dark hair and the sun giving a golden glow to his skin. His eyes are the most perfect shade of blue, and I feel like I could stare at them forever.

Temporary fling, Pascal. You have bigger goals than hooking up with a guy.

And no matter how wrung out and lightheaded I am at the moment, I must not forget that he's insane. And criminally inclined. He tried to kidnap Curie. He's probably a mafia boss or something. Although...do mafia bosses come this young and good-looking?

To hide my discomfiture, I clear my throat and shift a bit. "So. Why are you here?"

He pulls out a folded bill from his pocket. "Remember this?"

I stare at it for a second, then pull back upon recognition. The fifty dollars that I left him. It waves like a flag of shame between his fingers. "Yeah. What about it?"

"What's the meaning of this? I thought you could do math better."

The shield that never fails to go up every time somebody questions my competence snaps into position. "Of course. I studied math in college."

He looks at me up and down. "Where? Five-dollar-diploma-dot-com?"

"The University of Chicago," I say between clenched teeth. Then, very deliberately, I relax my jaw. He probably jumped to the wrong conclusion. The amount is inexplicable and weird. "I didn't mean to leave you only fifty bucks, okay? That's all I had at that time. I went back to the room to add to it."

Propping his elbow on the headrest, he leans closer. "How much?"

I purse my lips with annoyance. Does he think I'm that ignorant? I know how much a suite like where we stayed costs. "About five hundred."

He considers. "That's not bad, although I think an orgasm from me is worth at least a hundred bucks."

"What? You charge by the orgasm?" Is he, like, a hooker? "Did you get into trouble with your pimp?"

I thought hookers were mostly women, but that's probably sexist. There's nothing that says men can't do it, although it would be such a waste if Court was a gigolo. He's too handsome and nice... Actually, being good-looking and great in bed probably makes him very good at his job. A high earner for sure.

And why does that bother me so damn much?

"My *pimp*? Did you think I was trolling for"—he has trouble finding the right word—"a *client* at the club?"

"Well. Not at the time."

"Then why did you leave me the money?"

He's upset about that? "I was trying to pay for my portion of the room."

"But I already took care of it. Didn't you see me give them my credit card?"

"So? I pay my own way. We both used the room, so why should you pay for everything?"

He stares at me like I just spoke some more Klingon. Maybe I should have, since he doesn't seem to comprehend anything anyway.

"Are you rich?" he asks.

Maybe he fell out of the bed and cracked his skull after our one-night stand. "I don't understand what that has to do with anything, but no, I'm not rich. I do, however, have a job, and I do make my own money."

He runs a hand over his face, then stares at me like an English major facing a multivariable calculus problem. "It's just that...I never met a woman who insisted on splitting the bill when there was no, you know, obligation."

My head is hurting, and I don't have the energy to explain, but I plow on. Somehow it's very important that he understand. "I think it's smart to pay your own way. That way, there aren't any weird expectations."

"You mean like wanting to have brunch the next morning and possibly exchanging phone numbers?"

"Look, I didn't mean to make you feel bad. I had to leave because I was scheduled to meet Curie to help her with the wedding stuff."

"Okay."

"And I don't know why you came all the way to track me down. Most people would just try email or something," I say, my exasperation growing. "What would you have done if I were really getting married?"

Court runs his long fingers through his hair. "I don't know. Ask what the hell you were doing with me?"

He isn't quite meeting my eyes. The reddish tint on his face is from more than the sun. I start to speak, but his attention shifts. I look over my shoulder and see Dad standing there, staring at the two of us.

The sun glints off the silver streaking his otherwise brown hair, and his eyes are narrowed. Anxiety knots in my throat.

"Hi," I say, but it comes out a nervous squeak. "I thought you were going to go back to the wedding."

"The ceremony's finished." The lines between Dad's eyebrows deepen.

Oh crap. This can't be good. What's he going to do? If he plans to yell at me, surely he can wait until Court's gone.

"You." Dad points at Court, some kind of calculation taking place behind his unreadable expression. "Since you're here, you might as well join the reception."

"What?" I squeak. "But why?"

Court glances at me. *Say no,* I will him. If ever there was a time for telepathy...!

His mind deflects me like a coat of Teflon. "Sure," he says with a smile that belongs in a bank commercial—inspiring trust and confidence.

"Pascal, you should've said something about him earlier so we could avoid the...spectacle."

Dread descends like a cluster of heavy clouds. Dad actually swung a bat at one of my exes when I snuck out with him in high school. (Thankfully, he missed.) There's no way this is a friendly gesture. "Yes, Dad. Sorry."

"If you were just more like Curie—"

"I think Skit—Pascal is great," Court says.

"Do you, now?" Something light and glowing breaks through the dark thunderclouds in my dad's expression.

That's either an "I forgive you" or an "I'm going to stab you in the back in the first opportunity" look. Since I don't know which, I say, "I feel sick again. I really need to lie down." To add verisimilitude, I put a hand over my belly and moan with as much pathos as I can muster.

"Pascal, you should've seen a doctor," Dad says, crouching closer. His voice is full of sympathy, which means he's buying my act.

A hand pats my back—Court's hand. "I'll take her to her room and make sure she rests."

"You?" Dad squints.

"I studied nursing for a while." Court flashes him another of his trusty bank-commercial smiles.

"Well then." Dad leans closer and whispers, "Don't do anything your sister wouldn't do."

"Okay," I say, although I have no clue what he means. Curie's been with Joe since high school, and there's very little she wouldn't do with him.

"The reception's starting. Your mom's holding her own, but…"

"Yeah, you should be there for her and for everyone, really," I say.

Dad gives Court and me an inscrutable look, then leaves.

I slump in my seat until Dad's out of sight. Then I reach for the door.

"What are you doing?" Court asks.

"Going back to my room."

"Didn't you hear me tell your dad I'd keep an eye on you?"

I stare at him, unsure why he's asking me this. I can't think of a guy who'd voluntarily play nurse to a sick woman. It isn't like Court and I are anything. We just slept together once. "You can't be serious."

"More serious than prostate cancer."

I pinch the bridge of my nose, doing my best not to snort at his choice of disease. "You didn't study nursing." If he did, I majored in quantum physics.

"I read a biography on Florence Nightingale. Picked up some stuff." He makes a circle around his face. "And this mug of mine is known to cure many female ailments."

"And the source of your boundless ego," I mutter in Klingon.

"What's that?"

"Nothing." This is one good thing about speaking a language not that many can understand. I can say what I want.

"Where are you staying?" he asks, starting the car.

He's not going to give up. A guy who flew all the way here to screw up a wedding isn't going to just roll over.

I have no idea what his idea of nursing is, but I gotta marshal all my strength to deal with his persistence.

69

12

PASCAL

"YOU REALLY DON'T HAVE TO. I THINK I THREW UP ENOUGH, and really, I'm just going to lie down. It's going to be super boring," I say for the tenth time in the elevator.

"Cool. I like boring," Court says.

I want to punch him. But I won't because I'm a civilized person. Also because my punch is going to make him laugh rather than give up and go home. I can't even fart to horrify him because speaking Klingon doesn't make me one.

"Besides, I promised your dad."

"You shouldn't have."

"Least I could do after ruining his daughter's wedding."

Crap. That makes me feel worse, because it was really my fault. "Fine," I say between my teeth.

We enter my room. Housekeeping's come by, so it's tidy now. I grab a shirt and shorts from the dresser. "I'm going to change. Stay here and do nothing."

"Gotcha. Nothing. Take your time."

I go to the bathroom and lock it with a loud click. The mirror shows an extra-pale, extra-tired woman. Probably all my pigment got used up doing the Technicolor yawn.

First things first. I brush my teeth with extra toothpaste to get the taste of the stomach acid off my tongue. Once I'm satisfied, I change out of my dress and put on the comfy shirt and shorts. Then, without thinking about it, I reapply my lipstick. The second I'm done, I groan silently. It looks like I'm trying to impress him. *Ugh, Pascal!*

I pluck a Kleenex, start to wipe it off, then stop with a loud groan this time. Now he's going to know I wiped it off.

Annoyed with myself, I toss the crumpled tissue in a bin and walk out. The only thing that matters here is making myself extra clear to Court. I wasn't kidding when I told Curie no dating until promotion.

When I'm out, Court herds me to the bed. "Sit," he says.

"Aren't you supposed to say lie down?" I blurt, then bite my tongue. That sounds like I'm flirting or something, doesn't it?

"Not yet. Can I borrow your phone for a sec?" he says. "I want to check something."

"What happened to your phone?"

"It's got a problem. I can't use it."

"Okay." I put in my passcode and hand it over.

He taps a few keys. His phone buzzes, then goes quiet. He hands my phone back to me.

"What's that about?" she asks.

"I put my number in for you. Just in case you need to get in touch."

Does he honestly think we'll be texting and calling each other? "You're the one who followed me here. And didn't you get my number too?"

"Yeah. So next time we can do that email thing you mentioned, like civilized people." He pops a can of icy-cold Coke and hands it to me. "Here."

I take it automatically, then stare at it like it's a coiled snake. "Where did you get this?"

"The minibar." He gives me a slightly indulgent look that says he's not going to rag on me because I'm obviously sick. "Want me to call for ice?"

I cringe. "You know this Coke isn't worth the twenty bucks the hotel will charge, right?"

"It is now." He places a few bills on the dresser, then takes a chair by the bed. "There. I'm paying."

"But—"

"Coke is a cure-all for stomach issues."

I give him a dubious look. "Right, Mr. I Read Florence Nightingale's Biography."

"Don't knock it. It's got a lot of useful information."

"Yeah? Like what?"

"Like how patients should just do as their nurses say without any back talk." He points at the can. "Now drink, before it gets warm."

I take a sip. It's surprisingly refreshing. Without intending to, I down more than half fairly quickly. "Anyway, you don't have to pay for it," I say.

"I insist. It's up to the nurse to provide what the patient needs."

"So you can bill me a hundred bucks for it?"

"I would *never* try to wrangle compensation." A wicked gleam sparks in his eyes. "Not money, anyway."

His brilliant smile tells me everything I need to know about what he wants. And the problem is that it's too damn tempting, like a Garden of Eden apple. But I remind myself of the big picture I have for my life. I can't give that up for some momentary fun. "Look, Court, I'm flattered by your..." I search for an adequate word. *Stalking, obsession* and *insanity* are probably not what I should go for here. "Your, uh, interest...and determina-tion...but really, it isn't going to work. I'm not dating anybody anyway."

"Really?" He arches his eyebrows. "Explain, because I'm lost."

I don't think I said anything too esoteric. "What I mean is, I'm not interested in a relationship."

"Ever?" He leans closer, his gaze turning quite intense. "Were you secretly hoping to land that Joe guy yourself?"

The damned Coke goes down the wrong way. I cough and sputter. "No! What are you... You're crazy." I snatch the Kleenex from Court's hand and wipe the tears in the corners of my eyes. "I've never felt a thing for him."

"So why the relationship embargo?"

"Look, I'm up for a big promotion this year," I say.

"Congratulations."

"Thanks. Anyway, I can't jeopardize it by dating. I've been a junior analyst for four years at my company. I have to get promoted this year or my career is finished. Nobody stays a junior analyst unless they're dumber than a fruit fly."

His blank expression says he doesn't really get it. But he nods anyway. "In that case, I hope you get it. But I don't understand what that has to do with..." He moves his index fingers between us like a swing.

"Nobody at the firm who moved up from my level was in a relationship at the time of promotion."

He scoffs, which raises my hackles. It reminds me of the way Curie looked at me like I'd lost it when I told her.

"It's true."

"You researched this? Looked into everybody?"

"Yes. All the people who started my year or after." I don't add that I bribed my friend at HR with a box of Godiva and gossiped —casually, of course—to dig up the information.

He shrugs. "Still, that's not enough to prove causation. Besides, who cares? There are plenty of other jobs."

"But none at SFG. It wouldn't be the same."

"SFG?"

"The Snyder Financial Group. My dad founded it, and grew it into an amazing private wealth management firm." Pride swells in my chest like it always does when I think about what the company means to him.

Court looks scandalized. "You want to work for your daddy?"

"Why not? It's family. And I want to be part of that legacy. I've worked hard to be a part of it."

He shudders at the word "legacy." "That sounds hellish."

"You wouldn't understand because your family doesn't have a company for you to help run," I mutter. Well, I'm not sure if his does or not, but my money's on not. Why else is he being so dismissive?

An ironic look crosses his chiseled face. "Of course not."

"Definitely not. You—" A sudden burst of gas pushes up.

Panicked, I put a hand over my chest, but it's too late. A small belch slips from my lips.

He blinks. "Wow."

Oh hell. Kill me now.

I bend over and bury my heated face in my knees, wishing I could teleport to some other planet, preferably in a different galaxy. Why hasn't NASA invented beam-me-up technology?

"Are you okay?" Court asks, his voice full of amusement.

"No."

"You know, it really wasn't that bad. It was a...uh...a ladylike belch."

I keep my head down because I'm still too embarrassed to face him. "Ladylike...? I don't think you know what the word means." I'll buy him a dictionary. It's only fair—he bought me the overpriced Coke.

"I have two brothers. What you did barely even qualifies as a burp."

"Oh, well, that makes it better. I'm so thrilled to hear I don't erupt as loudly as your brothers."

"Hey, it's an improvement. You've gone from chunky liquids to gas."

"Just stop."

He continues as though he hasn't heard. "What, you think I don't know women pee, poo, fart and belch?"

I flop onto my back and put my hands over my ears. I can't listen to him anymore whether he means to make me less embarrassed or not, because it's only making me feel extra humiliated. "Stop! Shut up! Aaah!"

My eyes squeezed shut, I roll around on the mattress, hoping the motion will make me unable to process whatever's coming out of his mouth. I'm already pretty lightheaded from the stomach bug. The rolling motion will take care of the rest.

Except I feel sudden vertigo as my body goes over the edge of the bed. "Ah, shi—!"

But I hit a solid male body instead of the floor. Court has caught me. I blink and look at him.

"Thank you." I clear my throat. "Those're some reflexes."

"Yeah." His arms tighten around me.

The feel of his bare arms and hands sends hot shivers. *Warning! Warning!* my mind blares.

Too late. He's already breached my force field. I know because my heart is beating erratically and I don't want to move from where I am. His thumb brushes my cheek gently, and I sense my resolve to keep him at arm's length until I make senior analyst weaken. Until now, I thought people were being ridiculous when they talked about pheromones. But holy crap, they're real.

Brisk knocks at the door make me freeze. "Pascal?"

Shit. *Dad.* I scramble off Court. He stands and smooths his shirt, his expression bland. "Sit. I'll get the door," he says, and opens it before I can reply.

Dad comes in. His sharp eyes sweep over me and Court. "Your color's better," he says to me.

"Yeah. Thanks. Court's been a great...nurse." I add a pat smile.

"Good to hear." Dad nods. "Thanks, Court."

Court flashes a wholesome, all-American boy-next-door smile at my dad. It's so damn convincing that I almost see a halo around him. "No need to worry, sir."

Dad clasps Court's shoulder. "You know, we have a family dinner next Saturday when we return home. Consider yourself invited, if you'd like to come."

Whaaaat? Why isn't he swinging a bat at Court? Not that I want him to, of course, but that's what he would normally be doing. "No," I say.

At the same time, Court says, "Thank you. I'd love to."

If either of them heard me say "no," they don't show it. *Oh my God.* Doesn't anyone care about my opinion on this? "Dad, I'm sure Court is very busy."

"And I'm sure he can speak for himself, Pascal," Dad says, with a let's-not-pursue-this smile. He turns to Court. "Can we impose on you to bring a bottle of wine?"

"Of course. Red or white?"

"Rosé. Dry, if possible."

"Shouldn't be a problem. I know where I can get a good Tavel."

"Excellent choice." Dad turns to me. "Anyway, I need to go back to the reception. Just wanted to check up on you."

"Is it bad out there?" I ask, doing my best to suppress a cringe but not doing such a great job.

"No. Curie turned the, ah, attempted abduction into a big joke, and everyone thinks it was amusing. Joe is also putting a good spin on it. You know how they are—lemons into lemonade and all that." He leaves.

I cover my face with my hands, feeling very much like I've fallen into a rabbit hole. I don't understand why Dad wants to see more of Court. It isn't like we're dating or anything. Besides, even if Curie and Joe are laughing about what happened, Dad isn't the type to let it go.

"You should find an excuse not to come," I say.

"Why?" Court says. "I think it's nice of him to invite me."

"You tried to ruin his daughter's wedding. Do you know how much it costs to have a wedding in Hawaii?"

He considers for a moment. "No. Should I?"

"He's going to try to kill you. The dinner will probably be poisoned."

He laughs. "All right. I'll only eat bread from the basket and drink the wine I brought."

Ugh. Typical male, not taking what a woman says seriously. "I'm not being silly here. Dad really *can* hold a grudge. You don't understand."

A shadow passes over Court's handsome face. "I have some experience with something similar myself. And your dad doesn't seem like the type to be that petty or vindictive."

I want to argue, tell him he's totally mistaken. But somehow I can't, not when there's pain flickering in his eyes.

Suddenly uncomfortable, I lie down on the bed and put an arm over my eyes. "All right, fine. But you can't sue me if you get poisoned. I did warn you."

He laughs. "Want me to sign a waiver?"

"Yes. Do that, and then please leave."

I hear a pen moving over paper.

"Here." He places a sheet on my palm.

I glance at it.

I hereby hold Pascal Snyder innocent for anything that happens at her family dinner this coming Saturday. If I'm poisoned, maimed, abducted, buried in cement at a construction site, so be it. She did warn me. All my money should go to Make-A-Wish.

It ends with his signature. And he has really nice handwriting. Like, "he could make money as a calligrapher" nice.

I sigh. "Great. Thanks. You can go home now."

"I know. I need to return the jet by tomorrow." He sounds vaguely annoyed.

That should cheer me up. But instead, I'm feeling slightly disappointed and irritated. Disappointed because he's going to leave like I want him to, and irritated because I want him to linger.

What is wrong *with me?* I don't get conflicted about guys. But with Court, everything's different...which makes him entirely too dangerous.

13

_____

PASCAL

ON MONDAY, I WALK ACROSS THE GLITTERING VESTIBULE OF the Snyder Financial Group. To make sure I don't look too ill, I put on a bright pink and pearly-white dress. It puts some color to my otherwise sallow cheeks. I'm not back to one hundred percent yet, but I can't afford to take time off. Not until I'm promoted.

The announcement is coming in four weeks. I can do this. Every one of my quarterly performance evaluations is excellent. My boss told me I was doing well. I just have to make sure I don't give them any reason to pass me over again.

Dad's admin, Megumi, smiles at me in the hall, carrying two mugs of fresh coffee. She's tiny, with neon-magenta hair and long hot-pink nails. I admire her bold sense of style...and the fact that she can keep up with my dad while maintaining a serenity I can only aspire to. The whole building could be crumbling, and she would be utterly calm and telling people not to run as they evacuated.

"Morning, Pascal. How was Hawaii?"

I wonder for a moment if she's heard about the...incident. But if she has, she doesn't show it. She's always diplomatic and sweet. So I opt for an innocent smile. "It was nice. Sunny, breezy."

"Doesn't look like you saw much sun."

No kidding. I put a hand over my belly. "Stomach bug."

She winces. "Ouch."

"Next time, though."

"By the way, your dad got here ten minutes ago."

I grimace—inwardly, so Megumi doesn't see me make a face. I always try to arrive earlier than Dad, but somehow can't seem to manage it. No matter how early I show up, he's here before me. If I didn't know better, I would think he's having me watched.

And somehow Megumi always pops in at the same time he does. Mind melding—apparently some non-Vulcans can do it as well.

"He asked to see you the minute you arrived."

That's...unusual. Dad's way too high up the food chain for me to interact much with him professionally. "Got it."

I stop by my desk to lock my purse in the bottom drawer and boot my laptop. Then I make my way to where Dad's working.

As the founder, he could've had the most opulent office, but he chose the one with the best view of the city. Says he likes to see the city where he's trying to make a name for himself.

I want to be part of that so bad—creating a legacy. After all, I'm a Snyder too. Curie never cared about math or financial modeling, but I've loved both since I was a kid. I learned to read using the front pages of the *Wall Street Journal* Dad left on the breakfast table every morning.

Even though Dad never said it to my face, I overheard him and Mom talk about how he wished he had a son. But that's okay. I can be the son he never had and carry on the legacy. I'm just as smart as any guy, and I can do the work. I just need to prove it, even though he isn't too keen on me working here. He probably assumed I chose to work here because he'd be easy on me. It's up to me to prove that I'm serious. I want to help him. I want to make a name for myself, just like he has.

The door to Dad's office is open. I knock on the frame and stick my head in. "Hey. You wanted to see me?"

"Come on in." He gestures with his free hand. He's holding a cup of coffee in the other.

I take a seat and a calming breath.

"You look better," he says.

"Thanks. I feel better." Not a lie, even though I'm not fully recovered yet. Although he's my dad, I'm aware that while we're inside Snyder Financial Group, he's my boss. I need to be careful about being overly frank.

"So. The man."

I clear my throat, but the tiny, uncomfortable knot refuses to budge. "Uh. Yeah."

Here it comes. We never got a chance to really talk about it in Hawaii because Dad had to leave early when the Asian stock markets and currencies had a meltdown, with some of the indexes dropping over five percent. But that doesn't mean he's forgotten about the scene. Who could? Or the fact that Court and I slept together. Mom told me that I'm always going to be a little girl to Dad, even when I'm sixty. Just like I don't ever want to think about my parents doing it, I'm sure the feeling's mutual on my dad's part.

On the other hand, he invited Court to dinner. I'm still not sure what to make of that.

Dad leans back in his seat and gazes at me over steepled fingers with the same thoughtfulness he gets when he regards exasperating market movements. "Did you know who he was when you slept with him?"

Thank God I'm not drinking. Otherwise I might've spat. Time to keep it brief. Dad is the last person I want to discuss my sex life with. "I had no clue. It was just a one-time thing."

Dad's eyebrows dip lower, like thunderclouds ready to unleash their fury.

Shit. Wrong thing to say. No father wants to hear his daughter's sleeping around. But I don't want him to think I'm not serious about my career. "I mean," I say, "he and I decided to keep things casual, and...uh..."

Dad's expression darkens. It's no longer just thunderclouds. A hurricane is forming. At least a category three.

Crap. I shut my mouth and smile, since I'm not going to come up with anything clever enough to come back from the blunders I've made already.

"It doesn't look casual. He flew out to Hawaii to stop *you* from marrying. And dress pretty for Saturday."

"But why?" I blurt out. If I had the power, I'd make this Saturday vanish from the calendar.

Dad looks at me like I'm an imbecile. "Because I invited him to dinner."

"I'm going to be busy."

"No, you aren't. You never miss the Saturday family dinner, and you will not miss this one."

But Court hasn't ever been there. I don't want to give the wrong impression to Dad. I don't normally talk about my professional aspirations at SFG with him because I don't want him to think I'm trying to influence him to act on my behalf. But it physically hurts me to shut up about how I'm trying to avoid dating right now.

Dad scowls at my silence. "Say yes."

"You should've asked me before inviting him. I'm really busy, and all my nice stuff is in dry cleaning."

"Your mother is going to be upset."

That's a cheap shot, but effective. I love Mom, and there's no way I can let her down. She loves cooking for us and fussing over us, even though Curie and I are in our late twenties. "Okay, but I just want you to know I'm trying to advance in life. Like, I'm really giving it my full attention." There. I said it, albeit obliquely.

"You will advance if you quit wasting your time on the likes of Tom."

Dad's derisive tone hurts, but it also reconfirms the data I gathered about the promotion. Still, I can't stop myself from saying, "You didn't think so when I was dating him. As a matter of fact, you told me it'd be good to have a date for Curie's wedding."

Ignoring that detail, he glances at the Nikkei chart. "Your new man is Harcourt Blackwood."

Dad speaks like I should know that name. Except...nothing pops into my head. Court is definitely not a key client at the firm, either, because I make it my business to know all the top ones.

Dad sighs. The sound says I'm beyond help.

My mouth dries. I clench and unclench my hands and shift in

my seat, trying to regain the calm I need to navigate this minefield.

"Is he somebody you know?" I ask tentatively.

"You should look him up. Google has plenty of data. Even your mother recognized him."

Yeah, but so what? Mom recognizes a hell of a lot more people than me all the time. She's extroverted, loves to host parties and social gatherings and reads society gossips and tabloids with the zeal of a devout Christian studying the Bible.

I refrain from pointing this out to Dad. Then I realize he said Google, not Facebook or other social media sites. Is Court famous enough to have stuff written about him? "Got it. Do you need anything else?"

"No."

Pasting on a smile, I return to my desk. It's so weird that Dad's showing this much interest in some guy I picked up at a bar. Actually, his interest isn't the strange part. There's this faint undertone of *approval* that's bugging me. It's like...he *likes* Court or something. But why?

I immediately Google Harcourt Blackwood. The next time Dad quizzes me, I'm going to be ready.

Google returns hundreds of hits. Harcourt Roderick Blackwood, a.k.a. Court, is the youngest of the Blackwood brothers. His family is royalty in Tempérane, Louisiana, where Blackwood Energy is headquartered. And within the week, he's set to control a billion-plus-dollar trust and a huge block of voting shares in Blackwood Energy.

Wow. I stare in shock. I had no idea he was a...*somebody*. He even has a Wikipedia page with sections. I'm not famous enough to warrant a Google hit. When you look up my name, the search engine returns results on Blaise Pascal, the French mathematician.

It explains so much—the VIP treatment at the club, the easy way he got the suite and the free time to look me up and follow me to Maui. And the jet. I bet he never flies commercial.

I return to Google and skim the search results. There are some articles about him and his family. They're mostly of the scandal-rag variety, about how his mother covered up some crime against his brother's wife. Somehow what his mom did wasn't technically illegal, but his dad is divorcing her anyway. Sympathy stirs. That must be awful. I can't imagine being in the center of something like that, knowing someone close to you did something reprehensible.

I scroll down some. There's a snapshot of his mom, taken earlier last year. Margot Blackwood is a beautiful blonde, her chin angled in a proud tilt. Her skin is smoother than some of my college friends', and she's slim and fashionable. There's nothing about her that says she's a mother to three fully grown adult men. But something about the shot is...slightly off-putting.

I bite the tip of my left thumb, wondering why. I've never even met the woman, and you don't know how much of what the "news" is saying is real. And her mouth is curved in a small smile. Then I finally lock in on the steady coldness in her gaze. That's what it is.

An article with a particularly lurid headline about the family pops up next. Coincidentally enough, it has Tom's byline on it. My lip curls in distaste. Just like him to sniff around someone else's misfortune. I click on it out of morbid curiosity, then roll my eyes at the ridiculously sensational lead. *Killer matriarch*—really?

I close the browser and get ready for the morning meeting. I have this new financial product I want to propose to expand our private wealth management client base. Even if we don't implement it immediately, I want to be recognized for thinking big about our future and growth. It's my attempt at getting some bonus points before the promotion decision is made.

Excitement lightens my steps as I go toward the conference room.

Rodney, a fellow analyst, falls into step with me. "Hey," he says with a bright smile.

"Hey." I smile back at him.

He started a year after me and got promoted last year. But it's impossible to be upset about that. He's one of the nicest and most genuine guys at the firm. His large, square glasses sit on a sharp Roman nose. Dork potential is high with those specs, but actually they balance out his narrow face. His brown eyes are always so earnest, and I swear clients love that about him.

A lot of women at the firm love that about him, too. Unfortunately, he's taken. After his promotion, he found the man of his destiny. From what I understand, they're head over heels about each other.

"I heard that Curie almost got kidnapped at her wedding. Is she okay?" he asks.

I cringe, wishing I could teleport to a place where people don't gossip. Like Mars. Hard to talk without air. "You heard that already?"

"Everyone probably has. She's the big boss's daughter." He scratches the tip of his nose. "I mean, you are too, but you know what I mean."

Yeah, I do. I was hoping the crappy market movements would be the main topic around the water cooler, but an almost-kidnapped bride is so much more interesting, especially when she's the founder and managing director's daughter. Maybe I should've just called in sick today. Or became an astronaut. "It was just a case of mistaken identity."

"So, the guy wasn't a psycho or anything?"

"Nope." Just a super-rich guy with no sense of proportion , who my dad seems to like for some bizarre reason.

Rodney and I enter the meeting. Every market team has one on Monday, and all the members covering Asia are already seated around a long table. I take an empty seat, and Rodney sits next to me. The meeting follows the agenda, like always.

Dad doesn't say much, but he almost never does. One of the VPs explains that although many markets dropped, we still made a significant profit off our short positions, which doesn't surprise me. This is why clients pay us the big bucks.

I jot down some notes from the projections. They seem solid, albeit a bit conservative. But some of our clients loathe losing money more than they love making it. Totally risk-adverse.

Toward the end, we have the time to bring up any ideas or suggestions. So I do.

"Right now, people are jittery and nervous about the unpre-dictable ups and downs, even though they're very interested in growing their money," I say. If I pass this stage, I'll have to make a formal presentation. "I think it'll be great if we can start a new product catered specifically to the upper middle class, which we haven't been serving. We can brand it as 'wealth building for the middle class.'"

"We only deal with people with real money," one of the VPs says, sounding bored and slumberous. Dad nods almost imperceptibly.

I expected this. If Dad didn't feel this way, he would've already started something similar. Undeterred, I continue, "Middle class doesn't mean people with no money. They're people with some savings. These days, even households that routinely make high six figures or more feel like they're middle class."

Many of the VPs start to close their leather folios, their movements crushing the fluttery excitement inside me. I glance at Dad, praying he sees the merit in my idea. But he taps his fingers twice on the legal pad in front of him, then shuts his.

I bite my lip. I didn't presume he'd be all over it immediately, but I thought he'd give it more consideration than a couple of finger taps.

"Anybody else have anything to say?" he asks, his palms on the table.

"I think Pascal's idea has merit," Rodney says.

Thank you.

"Even under her proposed financial products, the type of people who feel comfortable walking in here and opening an account are going to have some significant assets. It's a great way to increase our clients. And I like the branding she proposed. 'Wealth building for the middle class' is very welcoming and enticing."

"That's a good point, Rodney." It's the same VP who shut me down only seconds ago. "Catchy, too. Good job."

What the hell? A bitter knot clogs my throat, making it impossible to speak.

"It's really Pascal's idea," Rodney says.

"Great thinking, Rodney," Dad says, as though he didn't hear Rodney attribute it to me. "Outside the box."

The words are like hard slaps. They're what I wanted to hear from him for *my* idea. My hands start shaking, and I clench them so people can't see my reaction and pity me. You can't work at SFG if people start pitying you.

"Appreciate your bringing it up. Now if that's all..." Dad stands.

And just like that, the meeting ends. Everyone follows my dad out, little specks of iron trailing the giant magnet.

Except me. I stay in my seat. I don't think I can walk.

Rodney is leaving, but he turns back and sits next to me in the otherwise empty room.

"Sorry," he says.

I shake my head, suddenly drained. "Wasn't your fault. You tried to help." I attempt to give him a smile, but my cheeks are like rubber. "I appreciate it."

"But I feel terrible...like I took credit for your idea. I don't understand why they didn't take you seriously."

Even though he says he doesn't understand, his eyes show a glimmer of understanding.

I'm a woman. Somehow the fact that I have a vagina makes everything out of my mouth not worth paying attention to, according to some jerks. When the same words come out of someone else's—a man's—they're worthy of notice.

I expect that from some of our subtly sexist VPs...maybe. But my own father?

That's an unexpected blow.

Rodney pats my shoulder. "You know, one day they're going to realize what an amazing analyst you are."

"Thanks," I say, although I'm not sure if that day will ever come. I hate feeling this negative, but right now, I don't have a whole lot of positivity left.

"That model you created made everything more efficient, too. They should recognize that."

"Hopefully."

I worked my ass off on the model because I knew it'd make a difference. Nobody from management has said anything. I've been hiding my disappointment because I don't want people to think I'm starved for praise. I'm just hoping they see the contribution I made despite their silence.

But given how the meeting went today...

"Or maybe not..." I tap my mouth with the end of my pen.

The tone Dad used earlier in his office comes back to me. The way he pointedly mentioned my advancing in life and Court. Does Dad think the work I do needs a bigger impact? Greater than the model or a possible new product line?

"Do you think my dad wants me to bring in an account?"

"What do you mean?" Shock twists Rodney's face. "Bringing in a new account is a VP job. A junior analyst would never be expected to do that."

But Dad brought up Court. In *that* tone. "There's this guy..." I start.

"Yeah?"

"I met him, and we became sort of...um...friendly." Rodney doesn't need to know the details of just how friendly we became. I tell him about Dad's reaction—how I should get to know Court.

When I'm done, Rodney looks at me like I've turned into a Vulcan, minus the logic. "So you think your dad brought it up because he wants you to bring this guy in as a client?"

"Maybe...? He's taking control of a trust worth more than a billion dollars. He's going to need someone to manage his money, right?" I say, even though part of me wonders if I'm insane to even think it. Court probably already has people taking care of his money. And isn't it awkward and ridiculous to ask him to move his account here just because we slept together once, especially after I made a big deal about not associating with him anymore?

"Well... If you can swing it, that'll definitely get you noticed. You might end up working for the VP managing his account, too."

Right. And the devil on my shoulder says I should go for it. If I get passed over again this year, I'm done at SFG.

Rodney continues, "But if that's what it takes to earn you the recognition you deserve, I think it's really unfair. You've already proven yourself. I don't understand why you keep getting overlooked."

"Thank you." The annoyance behind his words soothes the anger inside me.

It doesn't do any good to stay irritated at the circumstances I'm in...or the fact that I'm not taken seriously because of my gender. I need to figure out what I'm going to do to get noticed by the people who determine my fate at the firm. And I need to consider what Dad might've meant when he brought Court up the way he did.

14

COURT

THE NEXT MORNING, NATE AND I ARE AT ÉTERNITÉ, A FANCY French fusion restaurant, for brunch. I've mooched off him from time to time, and joked that I'd treat him if I ever became rich, which is about to happen in a couple of days.

Besides, he lent me his jet. I owe him this mimosa brunch, even if it does have a price tag that would make most financially sensible people clutch their pearls in horror. The restaurant is worth the cost, though. The décor is elegant and light, the food is prepared perfectly and the service is impeccable.

And while we're waiting for our food and drink, Nate gets the gist of the story about how I made a mistake because Curie and Skittles are twins, and how I played nurse to Skittles.

Nate nods. "Smart. Nursing chicks always earns you points."

"Obviously." Except she said no dating because of some promotion, of all things. Was she playing hard to get because she regretted the one-night stand? Some women are weird about that sort of thing. They don't want to look easy. Personally, I like easy women, especially when they're easy only with me.

Our brunch arrives. Nate shuts up and starts attacking his

bacon like he hasn't eaten in a decade. He has a strict motto: life is uncertain—eat bacon first.

"Your phone's quiet," Nate says after polishing off his bacon. "Your mom give up?"

I wasn't thinking about her, but I'm not about to tell Nate I've been obsessing about Skittles and her promotion. "Maybe."

But that isn't like Mom. She'll hold a grudge for decades, even against her own flesh and blood. Her silence makes me worried, but I shove the unease aside. It's possible she finally understands the futility of trying to get me to fix her marriage.

Right. And Klingons are really Vulcans on Halloween.

"Your dad leaving you alone too?"

"Nope." I down a mimosa. "He called me twice over the weekend, but..." I shrug.

As I do so, I feel the solid weight of my phone in my pocket. Should I text Skittles? Maybe I should ask her out to Éternité. She'd probably enjoy the mimosas too.

But she said no dating, remember?

Brunch isn't really *dating*. It's eating. Everyone has to eat.

"What are you stewing about?" Nate says.

"What?"

"You're staring off into space. I know it's not the food, and definitely not the company. So what gives? I thought things went well with Starburst."

"Starburst?"

"You know, the Maui wedding twin."

"Oh. She doesn't want to see me because she's hung up on some silly promotion."

Nate shifts around. "No promotion is silly. It means more money and authority. And sometimes a better office."

"Okay, you're right. The promotion isn't silly. Her beliefs around what it takes to get one are." Then I finally unload what she said.

He listens. Confusion, disbelief and incredulity get into a mud-wrestling match on his face.

"Really?" he says when I'm done. "Has she considered the possibility that she just sucks at her job?" He raises a hand before

I can respond. "Scratch that. People who suck never think they suck."

"I think she's probably okay," I say, more out of wanting to defend her than any concrete basis. Nate could be right, but I don't want to hear any talk about Skittles being incompetent.

"Performance in bed and performance on the job are two very different matters. I know because I made a mistake of hiring an ex once. She was impossible. We had to let her go after a month."

I give him a look. I'm trying to date the woman, not hire her. "I can theoretically wait until she's promoted this year."

"And if she doesn't get promoted this year?"

"Why do you have to be so negative?"

"Just saying." He cuts into his French toast, which is swimming in syrup. "Look, if she doesn't want you enough to disregard some fucked-up no-dating rule, screw her."

That's the problem. I want to screw her. Over and over again.

Nate reads my face. "Dude. There are billions of women out there."

"But none of them is like Skittles." Well, one is almost like Skittles. But she's married now—and not quite right, if you know what I mean. And none of the others has lightened my heart the way Skittles has.

"When the lights are off, they all feel about the same in bed."

Spoken like a true player. "Might as well date an inflatable doll, then."

"They *should* invent datable inflatable dolls. Cheap, low maintenance, easy." Nate guzzles down his mimosa. "It isn't like you to spend this much time and energy on a girl. You're hung up on her because she made you chase her all the way to freakin' Hawaii. Otherwise, you wouldn't have spared her another thought. Trust me."

"But she did," I say, irritated at Nate's attitude, even though I understand where he's coming from. Normally, I never bother because I hate exerting too much effort on women. However, with Skittles, things are different.

But only a little, I swear.

"Fine. Then stop thinking like the old Harry."

I flinch at the nickname Mom gave me to show my brothers how much she favored me. Too many bad memories there.

Nate continues, "Think like the new Court. Like a billionaire."

"I won't be one until after Friday."

He waves a hand. "What would Tony do?"

I give Nate a strange look. "Lie?"

"Okay, yeah, but that's not—"

"Make everyone else lie to cover up the lie?"

"No, I mea—"

"Shoot a guy?"

"No! Look, shut up for a minute. What I mean is, he wouldn't have waited for the promotion. And there are ways to get her to see you *now*. What does she do?"

"An analyst at a private wealth management firm."

He sits up. "Perfect! Open an account there and insist that she manage it for you. A hundred million will get you whatever you want."

Huh. "That isn't even that much money."

"I know, right? But it'll be enough. And getting a new account should get her noticed. So when she gets promoted, she'll have *you* to thank and won't stick to her silly rule. And if she doesn't get promoted this year... Well, you can just drop by every so often to discuss the portfolio."

"Right. Like every day."

He spreads his hands. "Why not?"

"A hundred million is a *fortune*," I say, making my face look oh-so-serious.

"A huge one. Very concerning amount. Enough to make you want to check in as often as possible."

"You're a genius."

Nate leans back, cocks an eyebrow and swirls his wine. "Tell me something I don't know."

15

COURT

On Saturday, I wake up a new man.

Well, not a new man, but a billionaire.

Dad's lawyer changed everything solely into my name yesterday. And I swear, the heavens opened up this morning, bathing me in radiant light. Somewhere cherubs are playing harps and singing to celebrate this occasion. Probably drinking mead, too, and getting ready to have a little cherub orgy.

Even the shower water feels softer and sweeter. It's like the world is happy for me—except Dad, of course. Hard to try to control me now that I'm one hundred percent independent.

Billionaire or not, I take my Maserati to Tony's house to raid his wine cellar. Although I'm pretty decent with wine, a man's got to recognize his limitations. My brother is much better with vintages and so on, and his collection is phenomenal.

Since I made the kind of scene that got the tongues working overtime in Maui, I need to redeem myself. And the first step is bringing the right wine.

Skittles' dad said rosé. So I'm going to pick up the best rosé from Tony's and a bouquet of flowers for her mom. Every woman loves flowers.

It's time for maximum charm. I've taken care to dress well—a blue silk shirt and light slacks. This is L.A., so you don't want to go too formal. The key is tastefully luxurious without being overly stiff or ostentatious.

When I arrive at Tony's mansion, Ivy greets me. She's in a simple T-shirt and shorts, her face free of makeup except for some lipstick, her feet bare. I like it. It's almost like we're back in time—before Mom ruined it for everyone. Ivy used to dress like this when she was home from Curtis.

Since I'm not a total idiot, I brought donuts for her. A grad student who got pregnant was stuffing her mouth with them constantly last year, saying all pregnant women crave sugar. Between the calories and the baby, she blew up like dough in an oven, but she insisted she "pregnancy-glowed." Anybody who disagreed got shit-listed. I can't ever be careful enough.

"Here you go, fresh donuts for you and my nephews or nieces. Love your pregnancy glow." I kiss Ivy on the cheek.

She laughs. "I don't think the glow happens until later. I just found out, like, three weeks ago."

"Yeah, but the babies look magnificent."

Her perfectly drawn eyebrows go up. "How do you know?"

"Tony texted me the ultrasound picture." I still have no idea what the thing was supposed to show, but it's probably best to just go with the flow.

She pats her belly. "There're just dots right now."

"*Magnificent* dots."

She laughs again, and I grin. It's good to see her happy and relaxed.

"And you're going to be a magnificent uncle," she says.

"Of course," I say. "I'm going to be so awesome that they will openly prefer me to Edgar."

She arches an eyebrow. "Oh? And how are you going to pull that off?"

"I'm naturally charming, so it won't be that hard. And gifts. Lots and lots of gifts."

She laughs, takes my arm and, carrying the box of donuts, leads me down the wide corridor toward her new practice room.

Inside, the brand-new concerto piano sits in the center. A couple of couches take up space nearby.

Damn. That thing is huge. Like a baby orca. It looks expensive as hell, too. But then it was handmade in Austria...and even supposedly has extra keys compared to your standard pianos. Tony went on and on about how amazing the Bösendorfer is when I made the mistake of saying no piano is worth half a million bucks...and how it's only fitting Ivy got an Imperial. The side even has a tiger lily embossed on the wood, which I'm sure isn't a standard feature. It's Ivy's favorite flower.

She sits down on one of the couches and picks out a donut with extra chocolate glaze and sprinkles. "So. What do you need?"

I shoot her a wounded look. "What, I have to need something to visit?"

"No, but you brought donuts."

She's got me there. "Just some wine."

"You know you're welcome to take any bottle you like."

"Tony grumbles if I take too much, but if I say you let me have it, he shuts up about it because he's crazy about you and you're the best."

"I know I am. By the way, did everything work out with your fifty-dollar girl?"

Ah, great. Should've known Tony would tell her. "Tony has a big mouth."

"We have no secrets. But I won't tell anybody." She leans forward. "Tony said he gave you a hard time, but don't mind him. I think the situation is very intriguing."

"You do?"

She nods. "It doesn't matter what the explanation is or what Tony said. Leaving the money is asking you to contact her. Fifty dollars is an intriguing amount, you know? Otherwise she would've just walked out of the room."

"Precisely," I say, since she's basically telling me what I want to hear. It's always best to get a woman's perspective on stuff like this. Hopeful and excited, I tell her what happened in Maui and the dinner invitation, while she devours two more donuts.

"Flowers always go over well," she says. "You have anything in mind?"

"Not really. I was thinking maybe taking something cheery, but..." I shrug to hide a mild discomfiture at not having figured out what yet.

"How about something pink? Carnations or roses. They're both classic and elegant."

Not pink roses. They used to be my mom's favorite. "Carnations sound perfect. You're a genius."

She laughs and pulls out another donut.

"So what have you been practicing on this super-fancy piano of yours?" I ask because I know it'll please her to tell me. It seems like the right topic to steer her to, since she's been so helpful.

"I was working on a piece by Schubert, transcribed by Liszt when you came. Wanna hear it?"

"Of course."

Listening to Ivy isn't like enduring some amateur's painful attempt. She's a concert-level pianist, and the sound she can pull out of a piano is pure magic.

She wipes her fingers off, opens the Bösendorfer up and lays her hands on the keys. The notes she teases out of the piano are soft, delicate and haunting. Her long fingers move gently and seemingly effortlessly. Her eyes start to close, and it seems like the music is coming straight from her soul.

I'm not particularly gifted in music, but something I can't quite pinpoint stirs inside me as I listen. When she's finished, she opens her eyes and looks at me. "What do you think?"

"Riveting."

"It's not bad. Just getting there. I need to smooth the phrasing in some places and give it a little more...depth and emotion. The sense of...you know...unrequited love and the deep longing and melancholy that won't go away."

I just nod, not because I agree with her, but because that's the only response I can muster. I don't understand how she could think that there's anything wrong with what she just played. But that's why she's a concert pianist and I'm not. I used to play the piano, and made everyone within hearing range throw the back of their hand against their forehead and despair. It didn't help that I hated practicing.

"Thank you for the lovely mini-concert, but I've got to get going if I don't want to be late."

"Have fun." She stands, then suddenly snaps her fingers. "Oh, I forgot to tell you, Yuna's flying in tomorrow."

"She is?" She's Ivy's soul sister and one of the funniest people I know. Like Ivy, she's a gifted pianist. I don't get to see her as often as I'd like because she lives in Seoul.

"Uh-huh. She's dying to meet her honorary nephews or nieces. Actually, she's convinced that they're one of each."

"She could be right. That girl is right about a lot of things."

"Yeah. It'll be fun if we have one of each." She grins. "If you can, drop by tomorrow and we'll have a nice dinner to welcome her."

"I'd love that." The evening will be hilarious with Yuna around.

Ivy gives me a look. "Bring a date."

"Ha." What a thinly veiled attempt to meet Skittles. "We'll see after I wow her with my wine."

But I do plan to invite Skittles to dinner. It's only right after today's dinner with her parents, but I have no intention of letting her meet mine. They'd scare her away like snakes scare away... well, most normal creatures.

Besides, since I have no intention of going back to Louisiana, Tony and Ivy are the only nearby family that counts. Most importantly, they're sane. Since I acted a little bit crazy in Maui, I want to show Skittles I'm a well-adjusted human being with a well-adjusted family.

Ivy walks with me to the cellar. I take Tony's best rosé. He won't miss it. Not when Ivy says she gave it to me. "How about I take this?"

"Go for it." Ivy gestures carelessly. "Good luck with your girl."

I smile, liking the way she calls Skittles my girl. "Thanks."

I don't think I'm going to need much of it with Skittles, especially with my action plan. But I will definitely need some luck to smooth things out with her dad. I get the feeling that he doesn't dislike me, exactly, but in my experience, what people say and do don't always reflect how they really think. Just look at my mom. Besides, dads can be weird about their baby girls. Gotta count my blessings this isn't Texas, where every father owns a shotgun.

Then there's Skittles' mom, whom I never got to meet in Hawaii. She was probably busy trying to salvage the ceremony and reception after I crashed it. I sigh softly. Let's hope she doesn't sprinkle my food with broken glass.

Skittles' parents' home is surprisingly modest. It's in a nice neighborhood, of course. But it isn't a mansion or anything ostentatious. I expected a bit of crassness after doing my homework and looking her family up.

Her dad is the founder of SFG, a mid-sized financial services and wealth management firm. It does well enough, and from my experience, a lot of finance guys like to splurge on big houses and swanky cars. And trade their old wives in for newer models.

Steve hasn't done that, though. He's still with his first wife, whom he married three decades ago. Wonder if she's unusually well preserved...

Like your own mom? I scowl. She's the last person I want to think about right now, especially since she stopped calling and texting over the last few days.

Taking in a breath, I look around the small fenced yard. The house may be humble, but the lawn is immaculate. Carrying a huge bouquet of carnations and the wine, I walk up the smooth concrete path and knock.

High-pitched barking greets me first. Then a small, tidy woman opens the door with a big smile. A bright yellow apron is wrapped around her slim body. Her face is slightly lined with wrinkles and laughter. But they don't make her look old or haggard. They make her face lived in, and show that she's had a full, good life. The eyes that twinkle with humor are the same aquamarine as Skittles'. Even if the eyes didn't give her away, I would've known she's no hired help. She's entirely too comfortable and assured.

"Welcome." Her voice is full of genuine warmth. "You must be Harcourt. I'm Esther, Pascal's mom."

I smile. "Call me Court, ma'am." I extend my hand and give her the pink blossoms.

"How lovely! And how thoughtful of you. Do come on in."

She doesn't look like she's going to stab me with a kitchen knife for almost ruining her daughter's wedding. I take a step in and get a whiff of meat and potatoes cooking that makes my mouth water.

A tiny white Chihuahua rushes at me and barks, its tail raised high and quivering with every yelp.

"Hey now. I'm a guest. I'm invited."

Esther shakes her head. "Nijinsky thinks she's a Rottweiler."

"Nijinsky, huh?" Interesting name, since Nijinsky was probably the greatest ballet dancer of his generation, maybe in history. I watched a video of him with my ballet-crazed ex in college, and even I had to admit the man was divinely touched.

"She chose it. We couldn't decide on a name—Steve and I—so we put down top three names we wanted and let her sit on one."

"What were the other two choices?"

"Einstein and Spock. I thought they sounded perfect for her." She looks down at the dog. "Don't you?"

"Yes." And this explains why Skittles and her twin sister have the names they do.

Esther leads me to the living room. "Pascal isn't here yet, and Steve's on a call. He's always working. Saturday, doesn't matter. The market's open somewhere in the world. He's always worried about these things, but people shouldn't work on weekends."

I find myself sympathizing. The man is responsible for not just his clients' money, but the livelihood of everyone at the company. Dad and Edgar are always working too. "Your husband sounds like a very successful and ambitious man," I say instead.

She laughs. "He's done well enough in his career. Thank God. When we first married, it wasn't like this. It wasn't until the girls turned fourteen that we could afford this home. I fell in love with it the moment I saw it."

I nod, unsure how to react. Mom always acts like the family's huge mansion is just...normal. But people in Tempérane always seem to look at the Blackwood family mansion with undisguised envy.

In many ways, it's a huge relief that Esther is nothing like my image of a rich man's wife.

She continues, "My friends think that I should trade up, but the girls are gone. It's just me and Steve now in this home, and if we get a bigger place, who's going to clean it and take care of it?"

A butler and a small army of housekeepers and gardeners. But I'm pretty sure that's not the answer she wants, so I keep my mouth shut.

"I can't imagine having a stranger home all the time," she adds. "Not that there's anything wrong with meeting new people, but it would be awkward, I think. Besides, I enjoy taking care of the house."

I wonder for a moment if she's pretending. It's a little bizarre to hear that from a wife of a financially successful man, because why wouldn't she want to have somebody take care of chores to maintain her home? Mom certainly never lifted a finger to clean or cook. That's what our housekeepers and cooks are for.

I look around the homey living room. No portraits of important-looking men gazing down at everyone from the walls. The TV and the sound system are all top-of-the-line, but the leather couch has a nice worn sheen to it that says this is a place where the family gathers regularly.

"I can see that. Your home is very charming." An afghan is folded neatly over the back of the couch. I run my hand over the soft material. "It feels nice."

"Thank you. I made that myself."

I run my hand over it again, just to get more of the texture. "I hear it's very time-consuming." Maybe Esther really does enjoy doing homey things.

She laughs. "It's an old hobby. I went through a phase."

I look at Esther more closely. There's a comfortable, confident glow to her that shines from within. It reminds me of the happiness radiating from Skittles at the club.

For a fraction of a second, an odd longing pings in my heart, creating a small ripple. Before I can process the emotion, loud thuds come from above and then Steve appears on the stairs. "Ah, you're here now. Sorry about that. Business call," he says.

Unlike my dad, Steve is thin, with a long nose and a serious mouth. But his voice booms, like a professional announcer at a wrestling match.

"Harcourt." He shakes my hand.

"Just Court, sir."

"Court." He reaches down to pet Nijinsky. The dog closes her eyes and wags her tail in undisguised joy.

"Look what he brought." Esther shows her husband the flowers.

"Nice." Steve's eyes warm, but I think it's more in reaction to his wife's pleasure than my gesture.

I lift a glossy bag I filched from Tony's place along with the rosé. "Wine, too."

At that moment, Skittles walks through the front door. An eye-searing purple maxi dress hangs from her long frame. Her presence is like a burst of sunshine, something that puts an intense bliss in your heart just by existing. And the odd pang that put an ache in my chest is gone, replaced by beautiful warmth.

She lifts the plastic container she's carrying. "Cherry pie. Your favorite, Dad."

Steve's stoic face splits into a smile, and he leans over and gives her a kiss. "Thank you, dear. You bake the best pies."

I eye the round container and look at Skittles. Culinary talent. Who would've thought? Every business major I ever met lives on cup ramen and pizza.

The flush on her cheeks looks delightful. And eminently kissable.

I want to pick her off the floor, hug her tightly and twirl around, absorbing her body heat and scent.

Control, control. Her parents are watching.

"Hi, Court," Skittles says, staying by her dad.

Smart. "Hi, Ski—Pascal," I say with my most charming smile. "You're looking well."

"I've recovered. It's been a week."

"I heard you took care of Pascal during the reception," Esther says. "How sweet of you. Steve said you studied nursing. Very unusual for a man, but so useful, isn't it? There's a huge shortage."

Skittles purses her mouth. I can imagine all the acerbic words she's holding back.

I bite my tongue so I don't start laughing. "I only studied for a semester. No hospital's going to hire me."

"What a shame," Esther says.

"He has other options," Steve says. "Like his family company."

I smile blandly, since I don't want to tell him I'd rather be a bum. That isn't the kind of thing that impresses fathers.

Something beeps in the kitchen. Esther wipes her hands on the apron. "Oh good, the food's done. You all must be hungry. Let's go eat."

She guides us toward the dining room, which isn't exactly grand, but big enough. The open floor design lets diners see the kitchen island. The hardwood on the dining room floor is lightly scarred from use over the years. But a careful layer of wax shows that it is lovingly cared for. The cherry-colored table has six chairs around it. It's already set with a bowl of salad, some rolls and mashed potatoes with gravy.

Skittles takes the carnations and puts them in a vase. Esther walks into the kitchen and brings out a large covered dish. "Hope you like pot roast," she says.

I inhale deeply. It smells like hearth and heaven. My mouth waters, and I grin at Esther. "I love food, especially when it's home-cooked. I almost never have it."

She looks at me like I'm some beggar out of a Dickens novel. "Is that so? If you want, I can pack some for you to take home. It's better the next day."

No way am I going to turn that down. If it's half as good as it smells, I might just polish it off later tonight. "That sounds fabulous. Thank you."

We all sit down. Steve takes the head of the table, Esther to his right and Skittles to the left. I sit next to her and enjoy the nearness and the subtle scent of her shampoo. It makes me hungrier, but for an entirely different reason that's wholly inappropriate with her parents around.

Patience.

I can't tell her what I'm planning to do with her parents listening. I want to make sure she isn't already overloaded. The point is to monopolize her time, not make her work until she drops dead. I've considered telling her dad I want Skittles' undivided attention on my hundred million, but that isn't nearly enough money to make a man jump through a hoop.

Besides, this dinner is anything but social. It's an inquisition to see if I'm a sociopathic loon. Poor Skittles—no wonder she's so tense. I wish I could tell her I got this.

Everyone digs in. The food is amazing, everything perfectly seasoned and prepared. I wasn't buttering Esther up earlier; I can't remember the last time I had a homey meal like this.

Mom's idea of cooking is whatever our housekeepers put together. When she wants to get fancy, she hires a professional chef to prepare a six-course meal.

I'd much rather eat Esther's food than whatever lavish junk Mom's chef can concoct.

Something taps my foot. I look down and see Nijinsky. I glance around surreptitiously then slip her a small piece of meat. She licks my fingers.

"This is a great choice." Steve's sudden remark makes me straighten and pay attention. "Didn't know you were a connoisseur."

"I'm not," I say quickly before he decides to quiz me. I know a little about wine—like a few famous labels and vintages—but not like Tony. "I had a recommendation from a friend." Or, more precisely, Ivy telling me to take whatever I wanted. But Steve doesn't need to know that.

Steve nods, then concentrates on the bottle, slowly pulling out the corkscrew. "So tell me. What are you doing with my daughter?"

Damn, that's blunt. Esther rolls her eyes and grabs a roll.

Skittles shoots me a look. Unless I'm mistaken, she's even shaking her head a little. She obviously wants me to claim that there's nothing serious between us. Except I don't want to do that because I'd be lying. After all, we slept together. Had sex at least five times that I can remember. And I gave her at least twelve orgasms. That sounds pretty serious to me. Not that I'd say any of that in front of her mom and dad.

"I like Pascal," I say. "And I'd like to continue to see her. I wouldn't have gone to Maui if I didn't feel that way."

Beaming, Steve hands me a glass of rosé. I wait until everyone has a glass and a chance to clink, then take a sip. Damn. This is seriously excellent shit. Thank you, Tony. A point for moi.

"Good, good," Steve says. "I did wonder about you last weekend. But it's about time Pascal takes her personal life more seriously. Her sister's already married, but she's still single."

Guess her dad's getting antsy. Well, well. Maybe Skittles is wrong about the dating equals no promotion thing.

"*Daaaaad.*"

Esther seems to take pity on her daughter. But not so much on me. "Court, when you came to Hawaii, you thought Pascal was marrying Joe. That had no effect on you at all?"

Her tone is polite, but the glitter in her eyes says she wanted to ask the second I showed up with the flowers and wine. And she isn't the only one looking at me like I'm Moses holding the stone tablets. Steve is staring too.

I look at both of them, meeting their gazes. I'm so ready for this question. "I figured she had a reason. A woman happy with her fiancé wouldn't have been with me. So I decided I owed it to us to at least look into what was going on. For all I knew, she could've been being forced into something."

Pain explodes on the side of my calf, and I almost drop my fork. Skittles' kick carries more viciousness than a horny goat forced into celibacy.

But if she thinks she can punt me into silence, she has another think coming. And regardless of what she said in Maui, there definitely is an "us."

"And then what? What would you have done if she were being forced?" Steve asked, leaning forward. It's almost like he's living the hypothetical scenario I've concocted.

"Rescued her, obviously. And if everything worked out between us, maybe we'd go back to Maui for our own ceremony." I leave it at that, drink the wine and smile. Let the parents put their own rosy ending to it.

Skittles' knuckles turn white. Her glare stabs my face like an ice pick. Guess she's mad because I'm not disavowing everything and acting like there's nothing between us. But what the hell did she think I'd say? *Hey, I screwed your daughter for fun, but don't expect anything else. The best part of her is what's between her legs. The rest I can take or leave.*

I have no desire to be skinned alive. Besides, doesn't she want to keep her parents out of jail? Murder is a serious matter. "That motherfucker screwed my daughter" is not a valid legal defense.

And based on the happy, glowing smile on her dad's face, he is definitely not upset about the Hollywood ending I described.

Steve notes my half-empty glass. "Have some more wine."

"No, thank you. I'm driving."

Esther nods with approval. Steve looks at me like there's a halo around my head.

"Responsible and sensible. You're a surprising young man," he says.

"Well," I say, trying for some false modesty. This trick never gets old. Tony taught it to me when I first entered school. He said if I behaved like an angel for a week, I could get away with murder for the rest of the year. Apparently teachers always create their long-lasting impressions of each student based on how they behave during the first week.

Skittles' parents are a bit trickier because of the whole twin thing, but now they think I'm a perfect man for their precious daughter. I can see it in their eyes.

And if Steve thinks that, surely he won't get in the way of Skittles' promotion.

Her mouth tight, Skittles looks like she wants to cut more than the meat on her plate with her knife. The she mutters in Klingon, "Men. I should've been a nun."

Laughter bubbles in my chest. She's peeved because she's been proven wrong. Smart people can't stand it when they're wrong. I'm almost tempted to respond with something clever, but I get distracted when Esther pushes the bowl of mashed potatoes in my direction.

"I baked a pie for dessert." She beams at me. "If that isn't enough, we have seven different flavors of ice cream."

16

PASCAL

COURT IS EITHER INCAPABLE OF READING PEOPLE'S expressions or being deliberately obtuse for the sole purpose of driving me crazy. Did I not make myself clear in Maui? Should I have sprinkled his food with rat poison—not enough to kill him, of course, but enough to make him spend all his time in the bathroom?

No, probably not a good idea. With Dad being so weird lately, he might ask me to nurse Court back to health. As payment for what he ostensibly did for me in Hawaii.

This relationship of ours... Actually, it can't even be called a relationship. We spent a night together. But he's acting like it was some kind of grand romance that got interrupted.

Damn those fifty dollars. I should've ignored my principles. If I had, maybe he wouldn't have shown up in Maui to ask me what the money meant. Better yet, I should've never gone clubbing. This is what happens when you deviate from your usual routine and have too much fun.

But you like *fun!*

Yes. But the aftermath sucks, I tell the voice in my head.

After the dessert, I paste on a fake smile. "Mom, Dad? Do you mind if I take Court out for a short walk? Kind of need some help digesting the food."

Mom glances at Court. "He might want to have some coffee, or tea—"

"It's all right," he says, patting his belly. "A walk sounds perfect. I'm actually pretty full."

So he's not *totally* oblivious.

Mom looks at him like he just handed her a winning lottery ticket. It's positively nauseating. No guy I ever dated sucked up this hard. Or this *well*. Other than trying to kidnap Curie in Maui, he's been killing it with my parents.

"Let's go," I say. I try to lead him out without holding his hand, but he's too quick. He links his fingers with mine, and I can't pull away without making a scene.

Shooting me a smug smile, he squeezes. Our palms press tighter, and I swear I can feel his pulse. And mine throbs and matches his rhythm.

This kind of connection is ridiculous. I've never felt anything remotely like it before. And why now?

Focus. This is not the reason I took Court out of the house.

Because I know about Mom's propensity to eavesdrop, I walk in silence for a couple of blocks, then look around. We're clear.

"Now we can talk," I say.

I expect Court to look concerned or slightly upset, but he just gives me that easygoing smile. "Sure. About what?"

"Did you hear *anything* I said in Maui? My 'no dating until the promotion' thing?"

"Sure, how could I forget? I've never heard anything so crazy."

I shake my head. "You don't understand." And he never will because he's a man. "The firm's very male-dominant. It's hard to stand out or be heard as a woman. A man and I can say the exact same thing, and everyone's going to praise him for his great idea, while acting like I said nothing."

I brace myself for an argument. *Things like that don't happen anymore.*

Companies are much more egalitarian now.

Maybe it's just you, not your gender.

"That sucks. And what a waste. Fifty percent of the population is women. Ignoring them is stupid."

My anger and resentment recede like a tide at his sincere tone.

"I'm surprised your dad lets people do that to you." He stops for a second. "They *do* know who your dad is, right?"

"Yeah, but he doesn't want any appearance of nepotism." Actually, it's worse because he acts just like the VPs. But I don't want to admit that to Court. It seems...somehow disloyal to speak that way about Dad to him.

Court frowns. "He still should say something. If they're doing it to you, they're probably doing it to other women, too."

Maybe. There are two other female junior analysts, but we don't socialize much, since they're both covering Europe. And "Hey, is your boss ignoring you, too?" isn't something you can just bring up at the annual Christmas party.

"It's better he doesn't. I don't want any special treatment." My tone is prickly as the scene from the meeting flashes through my head. Frustration and anger entwine around me. I shouldn't have to feel the need to defend how I'm treated by other VPs or my own dad at work.

But I don't think my defense makes a difference. Court is still looking at me like Dad should say something.

He shakes his head. "Never mind nepotism and your dad. If the promotion is that important, wouldn't you get it if you had a huge account that you could manage?"

It's sweet of him to try to help, but it's obvious Court knows nothing about how SFG works. "I could bring in an account, but that's about where it would end. Nobody lets a junior analyst manage a big account."

"That's just a small detail. I can put some money in with the company. Let's say...a hundred million?"

I stare, unable to believe what he's suggesting. *A hundred million?*

He continues, "That should be enough to get you noticed... Don't you think?"

No kidding. My thoughts and emotions spin out in all directions. It's like what Rodney and I discussed after the meeting telepathically transported itself into Court's head. Rodney thought I'd have to do some convincing to do. But it doesn't look that way. Court is actually volunteering.

A hundred million.

The amount takes my breath away, but he's talking about it like it's nothing.

But why is he doing this for me? He doesn't know me well enough to do that. My promotion means nothing to him. What's his deal? In most normal cases, I'd say he's hoping for some nights out and getting laid, but a hundred million is a way too much for that.

He isn't finished. "And I can say that the condition of me keeping my money with SFG is you managing my portfolio. What do you think?"

Holy cow. "You know if you do that, I really will end up managing your money, don't you?" I say weakly. I do grunt work. Even if I get promoted, I'll be building models, not managing a full portfolio for a client on my own.

"Yeah, so? Aren't you good?" He smiles.

His grin pierces my heart like Cupid's arrow. It explodes into glitters and lights. Hot, intense emotions I've never felt before and can't quite identify surge through me.

But the strangest thing is that the scheme no longer sounds tempting. It sounds sleazy and manipulative.

"I am, and thank you. But I can't let you do that," I say.

He stops abruptly and gives me a look normally reserved for an asylum escapee. "Why not? It's really not that much money."

The question feels sincere, but I don't understand how he can be so blasé about that kind of sum. "It's not about that. It's about the fact that I want to earn my promotion. I need to make my place within the firm on my own. If you do this, I'm buying it, and it won't be right."

He considers me for a moment. There's none of the easy humor in his blue eyes now. "Is it your ego?"

I shake my head. "It's more than that. It's a matter of pride. I don't know all the reasons you're offering to do this, but I know it isn't because you think I'm the best choice to manage your money for you."

"I can respect that."

"Thanks."

And I realize something. I like Court in a way that goes beyond just physical attraction or chemistry. I can't remember the last time a guy I was dating showed consideration for my career ambitions. My exes usually presumed that since I'm working for my dad, I should just wheedle my way up the ladder. Even when I tried to set them straight, they thought I was just protesting as a formality or something.

"My brother's having a small dinner party tomorrow," he says. "Be my plus one."

My immediate instinct is to say yes, but I pull back. After telling him that we can't date so I can get my promotion, it sounds silly and hypocritical to jump on the invitation, even though I really, really like him.

He adds, "It's just a dinner. And not at all intimate."

"Well..."

"I know you did your survey and all, but I don't think what's going on at your dad's firm is about dating. I just can't imagine anybody caring that much about somebody's personal life."

I cross my arms, slightly irritated because my data is solid. The feeling is intensified by the fact that Court has a motive to see me incorrect—he wants to date me. "Then what do you think it's about?"

"Something at work you aren't considering?" He shrugs. "What you need to do is figure out the real reason you're getting passed over."

That feels like a slap. A hard one. My cheeks heat, and the muscles along my spine tighten. "Are you telling me I'm not good at my job?"

"No. If you sucked at it, you would've definitely taken my offer, because you wouldn't care how you hang in there as long as you do. But you have pride, which tells me you strive to be good at what you do. And you're smart, which means you probably excel at whatever you set your mind on."

I can tell he isn't saying it just to flatter me. My shoulders relax, and I let my arms drop.

Then he adds, looking off into the darkness, "So if you're good at your job, but you're still struggling to get recognition and promotion, somebody's probably sabotaging you. Think about that."

17

COURT

SKITTLES TURNED DOWN MY INVITE, AND STILL HASN'T called or texted. What I said probably came as a shock. I'm sure she hasn't experienced the kind of scandal my family has. But sometimes the people who hurt us the deepest are those who are closest to us. They know all our hopes, dreams and weaknesses because we're too unguarded around them.

Well. If she wants me to not open an account at SFG, so it doesn't look like she's sleeping her way up the ladder or something, that's fine with me. There are other ways I can scale the wall around her.

When I arrive at Tony's mansion, the huge place is in an uproar. It's to be expected, though. Yuna doesn't travel light.

With most people, that means traveling with a million suitcases. But in her case, it means traveling with an entourage.

When she first visited, she came with her father's secretary. The second time, it was with two of her mom's assistants. She's probably here with at least two people. Her parents are paranoid about her safety, and I can't blame them. They're worth tens of billions, and their daughter would be a juicy target for a fortune hunter—or worse.

But the biggest reason the place is bustling is Yuna herself. The woman just doesn't believe in restraint.

When I walk into the living room, Ivy and Tony wave from the love seat they're sharing. They're sitting with their arms and legs touching, like there are ropes tying them together.

"You made it." Ivy smiles warmly.

"And with flowers," Tony says. "Although that rosé you filched is worth more than tiger lilies and orchids."

"Oh, shut it," I say. "You have more wine than you can drink in your lifetime. Sharing is caring."

Yuna stands, looking like she's just come from a relaxing day at a spa instead of a trans-Pacific flight. Her hair is dyed dark auburn and is longer now, hanging almost to her lower back. There's a slight gold tint to her skin, which is always pale. But from what Ivy's said, milky is how she prefers her complexion. She's exceptionally slim, too. I swear, her family needs to spend some money on food, not fancy designer dresses and shoes.

"Court, so great to see you." She gives me a tight hug.

I hug her back. "Good to see you too. How long it's been?"

"Two months. An eternity."

I laugh. She's always so dramatic.

She tugs me toward another sofa. We sit together.

She cranes her neck, looking behind me. "So... You came alone?"

"Were you expecting someone?" I shoot her a teasing smile. "I have a good friend if you're looking for a husband. Ticks off *all* the boxes. Rich. Pretty enough. Educated. Decent personality, too."

Nate would skin me if he were here. He's enjoying his bachelorhood too much to settle down. But I know Yuna won't take my offer seriously.

Sure enough, her cute little face scrunches. "Don't even start." She leans closer and lowers her voice. "You see those two women over there?" She gestures surreptitiously.

I follow the line of her hand. Two impeccably dressed Asian women with their black hair pulled back give me polite smiles so identical that it's almost creepy. Must be Yuna's entourage.

I turn back to Yuna. "Are they going to report everything I say to your mom?"

"Undoubtedly. Mom says they're for my 'safety and comfort,' but they're really spies. And they're perfectly bilingual, with exceptional hearing."

I bite back a laugh. "I'll keep that in mind. No state secrets."

"And no talk of husbands. Mom's been trying to set me up with a bunch of *suitable* men." She rolls her eyes. "Do you know how hard it is to deflect her?"

I can imagine. Yuna's mom is just like her—a force of nature. It'd be easier to deflect a hurricane.

Yuna straightens. "Besides, I was wondering about the fifty-dollar girl. Ivy said you might bring her."

My mood darkens a bit. Should've expected Ivy to tell Yuna. Those two tell each other everything. "She's not coming."

"Why not?"

"She's busy." Not technically a lie, because Skittles might really be busy right now.

On Sunday evening. Yeah, right.

"Don't judge, but the headline was so trashy that I had to click on it," Yuna says.

Oh, shit. *The fucking tabloids.*

"I read all about how you went to Maui, and um..."

"And kidnapped the wrong girl," Tony says dryly.

"Hey, they're identical twins. And it's really TJ's fault. He gave me the wrong twin's name."

"Maybe you weren't specific enough. He's never made a mistake like that with me," Tony says.

"Whatever. If I'd gotten any more specific, he'd be walking around with her description etched onto his ass."

Yuna raises a hand. "I have a feeling about this girl. This is destiny."

Ah, jeez. I should've known Yuna would go into this direction. She's big on fate, soul mates and all that female stuff.

Tony snorts. "If it's destiny, he should've known which one was the right one."

"Well, I sort of did." When I first saw Curie, I didn't feel the same scalp-prickling sensation I had with Skittles.

"See? Your inevitable fate!" Yuna's dark eyes are bright with delight.

I roll my eyes. "Destiny" is what brain-dead poets and novelists blabber about. That's why I couldn't major in English literature. I could tolerate only so much idiocy. "If it is destiny, she should fall in my lap." And not after some far-off promotion. Destiny should jump me, legs spread and screaming, "Take me, make me yours!"

Yuna looks at me like I'm an unenlightened cave dweller. "I said destiny, not a free lunch. Heaven has no free lunch."

What kind of heaven has no freebies? "Then what's the difference between heaven and hell?"

"In heaven, you get to eat your cake after you earn it. In hell, you get nothing."

"Riiiiight."

"Work for this girl!" Yuna says. "Then you can marry and give me another nephew and niece to spoil."

Holy mother of God. I almost choke over her enthusiasm. Babies? Yuna's already counting *babies*? "Do you have names picked out for them, too?"

"Do you want some help? But your wife might feel strange about that."

I cover my face with my hands. But my head—that fucking traitor—is imagining Skittles in a gorgeous white wedding gown... and holding a baby. Well, not at the same time, obviously. And the baby has her eyes and my hair. Instead of making me shudder and want to throw up, the idea is weirdly warming.

Must be a mild fever. Or maybe I'm a little dehydrated.

"I'm just kidding," Yuna says. "But oooh, guess what I brought?" She turns to Ivy and Tony. "I went baby shopping and found the most adorable onesies..."

18

Pascal

All Saturday evening and Sunday, I felt like a jerk for not calling or texting back. It was a weird sensation, and it kept me restless. How do guys manage it?

On Monday morning, I tell myself I've been busy thinking about what Court said—about somebody sabotaging me. But for four years? I just can't think of anybody who could've done it for that long without me noticing.

After the morning meeting, I notice a text from Curie. What's she doing with her phone rather than enjoying her honeymoon? She still has almost a week left.

You've been holding out on me!

I cock an eyebrow. *How so?*

I saw Mom's post. Your man sent her flowers.

He brought them on Saturday when he came for dinner.

Ha! Nope. See?

She sends me a screenshot of Mom's Facebook post. A picture of daisies and a dog biscuit. Mom captioned it, "Sweet surprise this morning. My daughter's date sent them to me, thanking me for the delightful dinner. I love it when people appreciate my cooking!" It's followed by a bunch of hearts.

Totally like her to get excited about stuff like that, I think fondly. She loves her little herb garden in the back, but she also adores flowers of all types.

It's a nice, unexpected gesture. I mean, some of my exes tried giving flowers to Mom to suck up to my parents. But the treat for Nijinsky? That's a first. And it makes the gesture even more genuine and lovely.

I start to type a response to Curie, but the arrival of calla lilies at my desk interrupts me. The blossoms are large and gorgeous, the fragrance strong and delightful.

Pleasure unfurls. There's part of me that says I should be annoyed that Court is ignoring my no-dating-until-promotion rule, but somehow I can't muster the energy. The flowers are just too pretty, and I've never gotten anything like them at work.

"Hot damn." Megumi pushes her nose into one of the blossoms. "What did Tom do?"

"Ha." Tom bought me flowers *once*, from the closest grocery store to my apartment because he forgot my birthday. "Tom and I are history. Been that way for a while now."

"Then who?"

I pluck the card before she can. It merely reads: *Court.*

Most men would add something to focus on the fact that they sent the flowers. But not him. Confidence much?

The self-assurance makes me a little hot.

"Who *is* it?" Megumi demands.

"Somebody I met." I shrug with a nonchalance I don't feel and stick the card in my purse, and then my purse into the bottom drawer, which I lock again. I don't trust someone as nosy as Megumi not to read it otherwise. Megumi is a surprising mix of discretion and gossip. The problem is that I never know which way she's going to go.

My phone buzzes. It's Curie again.

What stories are you coming up with to cover it up? You know you can't keep a secret from me for long, don't you?

Of course not. I wouldn't even think to try. Besides, Curie definitely deserves some explanation, because she is not only my twin, but an unintended victim of my one-night stand with Court. I still feel terrible about that, even though she told me it was no big deal before leaving for the honeymoon. But first, time to set her straight about this "your man" stuff.

Dad invited him over. Mom cooked pot roast. He loved it, and she packed him some to take home. He's just thanking her for that. It's nothing serious.

The calla lilies on my desk chant, "Liar, liar, pants on fire," in what I imagine to be an angelic choir of tiny flower voices.

It's totally serious. Joe didn't send flowers to Mom until he knew he wanted her to be his mother-in-law.

Shock twists in my throat until I can't breathe. *Court is NOT trying to propose to me, if that's what you're saying. Marriage has made you crazy.*

Mark my words. Whatever the history between the two of you, Dad's going to approve of him because he's making all the right moves. You know Dad wants you to settle down, too.

He just wants grandkids, I text back quickly. It's so like Curie to think everyone wants love and family and all that because she wants those too. Besides, it's Curie Dad wanted to see settled down, not me. He knows about my career ambitions—to make a name for myself and more.

Bet he does, but if he approves of Court, it won't matter about the no-relationship rule. He owns SFG. He can override it, if such a thing really exists.

The skepticism is so palpable that even I'm starting to doubt my own conclusion. That's Curie's superpower—making people see things her way. She probably wins all her fights with Joe, too.

We'll see, I text. Trying to argue with a supervillain is useless.

I put away my phone, then stare at the flowers. There's no place to hide them, and no way I can throw them away.

Pretend they aren't here. Then take them home. If anybody asks, I'll say they're from a friend I did a favor for. And later today, I'll text Court and ask him not to send anything else to work.

My mind made up, I set the vase just so on my desk and spend the next few hours wrapping up calculations for the projection I've been working on.

Dad stops by my desk.

"Got any plans?" he asks. "If not, why don't we have lunch?"

I look up him and blink a few times. In all my years working at the firm, he's never asked me to lunch. Is this about the promotion? Or the idea I proposed last week? Maybe he mulled it over and decided it has some merit.

"Sure." I hit the save button on the Excel spreadsheet I've been updating.

He tilts his chin at the calla lilies. "Nice flowers."

Stick to the plan, Pascal. I paste on a smile. "Thanks."

"From Court?"

I wish I could demur the way I did with Megumi, but it's my dad. He knows me too well to be fooled. "Yeah. To thank me for the dinner on Saturday." I take the purse out of the bottom drawer. As long as I act super casually, he won't see anything. People give flowers to each other all the time, don't they?

"Huh. Your mom's the one who cooked."

He has to be so literal. "I brought the pie. He sent something to Mom and Nijinsky separately."

"What did Nijinsky do?"

"Be cute?" A thought strikes me. "Did he send you something, too?"

"Men don't send men flowers." There's a calculation taking place in his dark eyes. And it isn't reassuring. At all.

I stand up.

Just then, Court walks in, a laminated VISITOR tag around his neck. I pause and stare, suddenly hyperaware. All eyes—female and male—swing toward him. He's impossible to ignore. His gait is unhurried, like a man used to having the world wait for him. There's a sense of deep and calm satisfaction and confidence in his eyes and smile that say he's assured of his place and position and wealth. He's dressed in a simple blue shirt, slacks and polished loafers, but commands more attention than the asshole VP behind him in a thousand-dollar suit.

The butterflies from Z are back in my belly, fluttering like mad. And I can't seem to stop the happiness from bubbling within. *Oh God.* I have it bad.

"Hi, Steve." Although Court greets my dad, he stands next to me, making clear the real reason he's here.

Crap. If I will him to compliment my pie, is he going to notice and do exactly that? Or is that going to deflect off his Teflon brain?

Dad smiles warmly. "Hello, Court."

"Hi, I'm just about to go out for lunch with my dad," I say quickly, so grateful Dad wants to eat with me.

"Oh. I was hoping to steal you away for lunch," Court says with a small frown.

"Maybe next time—"

"We can always do it tomorrow," Dad says, then turns to Court. "She usually gets a little over an hour off."

My jaw slackens. *A little over an hour? Since when?*

"But you can take some extra time if you want." Dad's voice couldn't be warmer or more paternal. He has *never* been this this proud or happy, even when I graduated summa cum laude from the University of Chicago. "You've earned some comp time."

Comp time? We have *that* at SFG?

"Great, but I can't let her spend her comp time on me." Court smiles. "I'll bring her back in an hour."

Dad beams the delighted dad smile he usually reserves for Curie and Joe. He doesn't think Court and I are anything, does he? Court didn't even kiss me goodnight on Saturday.

"Have fun, you two." He waves us off with an indulgent look.

Court puts a hand at the small of my back and leads me out. And I go along, since that's better than being on the receiving end of Dad's weird...expectant look. Court's touch is firm but gentle. His palm tingles against my skin through the bright green dress I'm wearing, just like that night at the club and the Aylster Hotel afterward. My coworkers stare, and I see admiration and envy in some of the women's eyes. I feel like the hottest thing in the world...but a small sense of hypocritical shame wriggles inside me. After all, I've been telling him we shouldn't be seen together for the sake of my career. And I wasn't kidding about the promotion being important. If I'm passed over again...

Suddenly, everything inside me starts to deflate.

When we're inside the elevator, I try to take a step sideways to break the contact, even though my hormones want exactly the opposite.

But he moves with me, so that I'm trapped between him and

the wall, like taco filling in a hard shell. I should try to push him away. But instead, I'm inhaling his scent.

He smells good. Indecently so. It's the kind of scent that can make a woman lose all sense and logic. And I, Pascal Snyder, can't afford that.

"What did you do to my dad?" I ask him to buy myself some time to reorient. "Jedi mind trick? Vulcan mind meld?"

He laughs. "No."

"Did you send him something?" Dad said Court didn't send flowers, but said nothing about anything else—like a bottle of premium liquor.

"Of course not. He's a *guy*. Did you like the flowers? They reminded me of you."

It's hard to stay focused when he says things like that. His blue gaze is so deep that I feel like I could plunge right in and never come out.

"They were all right," I lie, hoping it'll discourage him. Those are some incredible flowers. If I act untouched by them, he has no hope of impressing me with any others.

"Next time I'll send you tulips."

"Why tulips?" I've never received anything other than roses. Bright red roses. Well...until today.

"They're cheery and colorful. Like you."

The smile he sends me is entirely too sincere and disarming. I can feel my shields drop despite my best intentions.

"By the way, you don't really have over an hour for lunch, do you?" he asks.

This must be a new routine. Mr. Astute.

Oh, this isn't new, my traitorous mind whispers. *He was damn astute in bed.*

The memory of what happened in the Aylster Hotel breaks through the dam I put up. Sweat mists over my suddenly hot skin, and liquid heat pools between my legs as though he has his mouth on mine, his hands on my breasts and his hard cock rocking against me. Sizzling shivers run down my spine. Closing my eyes, I bite my lower lip so I don't make an inappropriate noise.

"Skittles?"

He really shouldn't be saying my name in such a low, intimate voice. We're in an elevator, after all. "Hmm?" And maybe I shouldn't be responding in such a breathless tone. Or does it matter? We're the only ones in the elevator.

"The lunch break?"

What's that again? What about lunch break?

My brain finally pulls itself out of the crazy hormonal haze. Oh crap. The lunch hour.

"No." The word comes out husky and slightly raspy. Even though he can't possibly know exactly what was going through my head, my face is burning anyway. I clear my throat, unable to meet his gaze. "I normally take about half an hour or so. And usually at my desk." So I can stare at charts while nibbling on a sandwich.

"That's what I thought. And you don't get comp time."

"No. There's no such thing at the firm." It seriously annoys me that Dad said that. Nobody working in finance gets comp time. Except maybe if you're working in retail banking.

I steal a glance in Court's direction. He's smirking. What's so amusing?

"So. A fancy lunch is out. How about something simple and quick? Sandwich or a burger good?"

"Yes. Either one."

He takes me to a burger joint. It's not fast food, but not anything fancy, either. We have a table waiting for us. Must've been reserved.

"Aren't you presumptuous?" I ask.

"What?"

"How did you know I'd come with you?"

"I didn't. But if you were busy and couldn't come, I would've come alone." He shrugs. "Even faced with the harsh reality of a life-ending rejection, I still gotta eat."

I snort a laugh at his dramatic tone. And to be honest, it's a good thing he has a reservation. The place is packed.

"What's the deal? Are the burgers here that good?" I ask after we're seated.

"Their non-meat burgers are supposed to be good. Want to try one?"

"Non-meat? Like veggie burgers?" I try to hide my wince. Maybe this place has great fries and milkshakes.

"You don't like the sound of it?"

"I had one once in the college cafeteria. Let's just say I'm not interested in experiencing that culinary horror ever again."

He laughs. "Oh, come on. I'd never treat you to college food. Not even I could stomach most of it. The vegetarian burgers here are supposed to look and taste like real beef."

"Really?" I remember hearing something about some magical fake meat, but I didn't pay much attention. Let's just say I like my meat...well, meat.

"I have a friend who wants me to invest in distribution and maybe opening more restaurants. I told him I'd think about it after trying the food myself. Then I thought, why not get a second opinion?"

"Oh." I've never been asked to advise on a new restaurant venture, especially in a non-number capacity. It's sort of cool and exciting.

"So you see," he says slowly, as a winsome smile spreads across his face, "this isn't really a date."

I laugh at his ridiculously self-serving loophole, torn between being flattered and exasperated. "Oh, really?"

"Absolutely. It's *market research.*"

A server interrupts us, and we order the not-meat burgers and fries. The menu proudly declares if we don't like them, we can send 'em back and get something else. I also get spicy curly fries and sparkling water. Court gets the steak fries and a large Coke with extra ice in another cup. It reminds me of the way he declared it a cure-all for stomach issues in Hawaii and tried to take care of me in his own way.

He really is great boyfriend material, my mind whispers.

Yes, I know.

You should just forget the promotion junk. Good men are rarer than a Vulcan with a sense of humor.

I know that too, but... I just can't let go of the promotion or my wish to become somebody, to be recognized at work.

When the server's gone, I prop my chin in my hand. "So if this is research, then what are the flowers for?"

"Because you're beautiful. And for that cherry pie. I *really* liked it. I was hoping you could bake me another."

The look he shoots me is entirely too full of hope. And too adorable for me to reject. "Aren't you a billionaire?"

He shrugs, like it isn't that important. "Yeah."

"So don't you have an army of people baking you whatever you want?"

The light in his gaze dims a few watts. "Yeah. Back home. But it's not the same."

"The food in Louisiana isn't good? Really?" I heard from Curie, who's been to New Orleans twice, that the food there is enough to make you consider giving up a kidney...and a bikini body forever.

"Of course it's *good*. Just not the same."

I remember his enthusiasm over the home-cooked meal Mom made. She's an amazing cook, but it sounded like he hadn't had anything like that in...forever.

The coldness in his mom's gaze pops into my head. If that is how she is normally, I can't see her puttering around in the kitchen.

Sympathy stirs within me. And something else. Not pity. It's more profound and complicated, like abstract algebra. A man from such a wealthy family with a mother that cold should be a self-centered jerk. I've seen my share of them, from rich frat boys in college to many of the clients at the firm. It's always worst when they haven't made their mark yet and need to feel more important than everyone else.

But Court is different. He doesn't make any grand gestures to impress me or throw money around in an ostentatious fashion, but he shows he cares in small ways. He's considerate and kind to my mom and Nijinsky. He doesn't try to monopolize the conversation, and he's scrupulously polite to my dad. And he hasn't brought up even once that I didn't text him back over the weekend or that I didn't go to the dinner party with him. It's like he just accepts that I might have my own life with things that don't involve him.

It only makes me like him more. Makes me think there could

be more than just hot chemistry from before...that we can be friends, too.

This is the first time I ever felt like that about a guy I had sex with. And my fluttering heart says it might not end with mere friendship.

19

COURT

SKITTLES RELAXES MORE AS THE LUNCH GOES ON. SHE seemed happy to see me at first in the office, but I sensed her tensing up pretty quickly. It's as though she thought I was there to start an inquisition about yesterday or to embarrass her somehow.

Well... Okay, so I *did* embarrass her in Maui, but I thought I redeemed myself on Saturday. And the calla lilies were inspired, too. Yuna told me they're elegant flowers that represent good fortune and magnificent beauty. And Skittles certainly deserves that designation, and also a warning sign around her that says, "Stay away because she's taken!"

Besides, I like her. Before I see her, I think the effect she has on me is going to lessen. Hell, I can't even watch a movie more than once without being bored out of my mind, no matter how good it is. But instead, I crave more of her. More sex, definitely. But also just more time with her.

I resent the hell out of her dad for not having promoted her already. Then she wouldn't be on this ridiculous no-dating-until-promotion kick. Why couldn't he have half the zeal my dad does to have his own kids continuing the Family Legacy?

"So. What are you planning to do now that you have all your money?" she asks between bites.

That feels like an interview question. Too bad I don't have anything clever to say in response. I could make up something that sounds really grandiose. Like the junk people put on their PowerPoint slides to impress investors.

I'm going to conquer the world. Build an empire that's going to last a millennium. And start a dynasty to put all dynasties to shame.

But Skittles deserves better. "I don't know yet."

"Are you going to join your family business?"

My whole body tenses for a moment, but I force myself to relax. She doesn't know she's poking a sore point. "Probably not. My brother's doing a great job with it, and I don't see why I should get in his way. So, what do you think about the burger? Just as good as real meat?"

"Actually, yeah. I wouldn't have guessed." She wipes her fingers on the paper napkin. "Definitely worth considering investing in. I'd bring my friends."

I just smile. To be honest, I'm not interested in restaurant businesses. They're competitive and have horrible margins. But Skittles wants the veneer of us "not being in a relationship". And she doesn't want me dropping a hundred million bucks into her company. So this is my compromise. If anybody asks, she came out to lunch to help me make an investment decision. And the calla lilies are for being a mean baker.

A little sneaky, but all's fair in love and war. And that Chinese dude Sun Tzu said it's okay to use subterfuge to win. Besides, this is really win-win. She gets what she needs—lunch— and I get what I want—time with her.

When the bill arrives, Skittles reaches into her purse.

I raise a hand. "I got it."

"No, it's okay. I always pay for my own things."

Must be the same independent streak that made her leave that fifty bucks. So it wasn't just a one-time thing. I can respect that, but this is a date, even if she doesn't know it. "Yeah, but I asked you here for your professional opinion. So technically, it's a business lunch, and I plan to expense it." On the altar of dating funds.

She hesitates.

"Unless you plan to bill me...?"

Shock crosses her gorgeous face. "What? No. Of course not." I take the opportunity to slide a few bills to the server. "Shouldn't you put that on a business credit card?" she says, recovering quickly.

"Cash is easier."

And it's a habit. Since forever, banks sent all the bills to the trustee controlling my money, which happened to be Dad until a few days ago. Because I didn't need him knowing when, where or how much I spent, I always used cash unless it was something like an airline or hotel reservation. Trust me, that chafed like hell.

Her response is a skeptical look.

I merely smile wider, then take her back to her office, while making small talk about her family and the dog. I steer the conversation away from mine because I don't want her asking about my parents.

All the while, my brain's whirring. What should be my next excuse to see her? Another investment opportunity?

Maybe I can ask her to help me pick out some good wines to go with the burgers we had. There's a fantastic wine bar I've been wanting to check out. I climb out of the car as she does, ready to throw the question at her.

Before I can say anything, some scrawny guy in a slightly yellowed shirt and worn jeans runs up. "Hey, Pascal!"

He has eyes the color of burned coal and his tone is entirely too friendly. He puts an arm around her shoulders like it has every right to be there. Who the hell is this fucker and where did he come from?

I narrow my eyes. All cars should come with an ax. So I can hack away the offending limb, especially when it's attached to a guy who's still young enough to get it up.

She pushes him away. But she could have pushed harder.

"What are you doing here, Tom?" Her voice is appropriately cold, without any of its usual happy sweetness.

Freeze that idiot. Make him feel it.

"I'm back in the city," he says, spreading his arms.

"And...how does that give you the right to put your hand on me? We're through, remember?"

A clingy ex. Ugh. They're the worst. She could've slapped him to make her point clearer, but oh well. I'll settle for the verbal rebuke for now.

"Oh, come on." He scowls. "I know you're a girl, but you should be over that by now."

"E*xcuse* me?" She puts her hands on her hips, her feet shoulder-width apart.

Go, Skittles. Kick his ass. I'll be your backup if you need help. Better yet, let me hold that idiot down for you.

"It wasn't a big deal. Why you gotta be so emo about it?" he whines.

"I'm being 'emo'? Really?" Her voice goes low and dangerously cold. "You snooped around my phone and decided because my period was a little late, I got pregnant to entrap you. Well, guess what? I'm not. Never was. So we can be cleanly, totally *done*."

What an idiot. Why would Skittles want to entrap a guy like him?

"You gotta air our dirty laundry like that?" Tom says in a voice so loud he's drawing attention.

"I wouldn't have if you'd stayed away. And it isn't *our* dirty laundry. Just yours."

Damn, she's hot when she's mad, especially at somebody else.

"Is it because of him?" He points an accusing finger in my direction.

I preen inwardly. Obviously, if it's between you or me, she's going to choose me. She isn't blind or stupid.

"You're hanging out with a college kid?"

Huh? Where the hell did he get that from?

Skittles flushes at his tone, which makes her sound like some kind of cradle robber.

I make a subtle move so I'm shielding her from this jerk. Time to set the fool straight.

"First, I just finished grad school." I smile. You should always smile, especially if you plan to deck the guy, figuratively speaking.

He glares at me. "Nobody asked you, college boy."

"And nobody invited you," I say.

He smirks, but it's more forced than superior. "And why would you, when I know all about your family's dirty little secrets?"

My entire body goes rigid. It's been a year, but I can't help but react badly to any mention of the scandal involving my mom. How she looked the other way from a potential homicide.

No, scratch that. A homicide, because a girl did die. And the culprit went unpunished for nearly a decade because of Mom's spiteful silence.

"Do you think you're something special? You're nothing. I dug up everything about you and your family. I even wrote about it. You might have heard of me." He smacks his chest with his palm. "Tom Brockman."

The name makes me scrunch my face with bad taste in my mouth. Tom Brockman is a bottom-feeding tabloid hack who went after my family last year when the sordid details of what Mom did came out. Out of all the so-called journalists, his articles were the most lurid, trying to paint everyone, including Ivy, as people who deserved what happened.

"You didn't 'dig up' anything. You just repackaged what other, actual journalists researched to try to make a quick buck or two at someone else's expense. You write about other people's pain for profit. The Josef Mengele of journalism. Except you're not as creative."

His face turns bright red. His knuckles whiten as he clenches his fists.

Come on, motherfucker. Throw the first punch so I can break your nose.

I'm not stupid enough to punch him first and give him the pleasure of suing me for millions in pain and suffering.

"Tom, you need to go," Skittles says, placing a hand on my arm.

The gentle touch soothes my temper, but only a little.

"I'm telling you, you're making a mistake." But there's a frustrated understanding in his pale eyes. He knows he isn't going to get anywhere. The shitbag slinks away.

Then it finally hits me. He dated Skittles. Touched her and thought she was pregnant with his baby.

Pure outrage pours through me. What's wrong with karma? Is she on vacay? A man like that should be a virgin. *For life.* "Tom Brockman was your ex?"

Her lips grow tight. "Yes. I was dating him before I met you."

"Is he one of the reasons you decided to adopt your no-dating rule?"

"No."

I'm skeptical. The data she gathered probably helped her reach the decision, but surely dating a loser like that didn't help. I'd bet a kidney he wasn't supportive of anything she wants to do.

She checks the time. "I really have to go. I have a meeting." She starts toward the office. "Thanks for lunch."

Suddenly, I can't let her go like this. "Skittles."

"Yes?"

"What he said isn't all true." I look away, uncomfortable with this intense desire to explain the scandal. Obviously, she already knows about it. Everyone with access to the Internet does. "About my family and what happened, I mean. The tabloids, they really blew everything—"

"I know. And even if it were true, it doesn't matter." She gives me a warm smile. "You're you. Family is family."

A weight I didn't know was on my shoulders lifts. I stare, stunned that she knew exactly what I needed to hear. My phone buzzes, but I ignore it. I watch her wave, turn and disappear into the building. The effect of the smile lingers like a kiss, and I find myself smiling back.

Until I check my phone and see a missed call from a hospital in Tempérane.

20

I WALK TOWARD MY CUBICLE. MY BELLY'S FULL OF GREAT food, but my heart is churning. How dare Tom show his face at my work? It's like he's forgotten all about the horrible things he said when he thought I "entrapped him with pregnancy."

Or the fact that I told him we were through. Utterly. One hundred percent.

But that isn't all. He dragged Court and his family into our fight. Bastard. It must've escaped his notice that if he hadn't been such a dick, I would never have hooked up with Court.

If Tom shows up again, I'm going to forget everything my mom taught me about being a nice girl. I'll tell him how I feel in every language I know, including Klingon.

Rodney comes out of a conference room opposite my desk with a tall man in a charcoal suit. Not one of our lawyers. I know everyone on the SFG legal counsel team. And he doesn't look like an accountant, either. They always have this exacting air about them, an anal retentiveness that demands they calculate everything down to the last penny. The man's black hair's too long, and there's an arrogance and indolence to his dark gaze.

Rodney smiles broadly. "Cristiano, this is Pascal Snyder, the brain behind that new model you liked." As Cristiano turns toward me, Rodney mouths, *Your latest Nikkei prediction modeling.*

I try not to beam too hard. That one's my pride and joy.

The man's expression is cordial without being overly friendly. "A pleasure. When Rodney said 'Pascal,' I assumed it was a man."

"All woman," I say, hoping my gender isn't going to be a problem.

"Clearly. And beautiful as well." His tone is flattering but also scrupulously professional. He extends his hand. "Cristiano Cortez. Nice to meet you."

I shake hands with him. His grip is firm but not overly strong. This is a man very aware of his strength. I wonder if he is *the* Cristiano Cortez, one of the most important clients at the firm. I've never met the man, but I've heard about him. But there might be more than one. It isn't as though the name's trademarked.

"I did like that model. If I had a firm that managed money, I'd poach you," he says. His cool but penetrating gaze communicates that he always says what he means, and I can feel myself glowing.

He turns to Rodney. "Thank you for your time. You'll hear from my assistant by COB today."

"Excellent. I look forward to it."

Cristiano leaves.

"Tell me if that's who I think it is," I say to Rodney.

"The one and only. He likes your work. A lot. And he isn't shy about saying so."

I put a hand over my mouth. "Oh my God."

Excitement bubbles like a freshly popped bottle of champagne. He didn't just think I was good, but he *told others at the firm.* This has got to be my year.

Dad walks by with a fresh coffee in his hand. Before I can tell him what Cristiano said, he leans over the partition of my cubicle with a warm smile. "Back so soon? I thought I said you could take your time with Court."

Something feels wrong, but I'm too excited about the exchange with Cristiano to dwell on it. "It was just a business lunch to discuss an investment he wanted to make." And it's a good thing it didn't drag on, because I would've missed Cristiano.

Dad's expression tightens for a moment until his gaze falls on the calla lilies. "Then why did he send you flowers?"

"I told you it's about the pies." Then I add, "He wants me to bake him some more." I don't really believe he meant it—my pies are good, but not *that* good—but that's what he said, so...

Dad presses his lips together. "At his place?"

"Huh?" What kind of question is that?

"Does he want you to bake him pies at his place?"

"I don't know. He didn't say," I respond distractedly. I want to tell Dad about Cristiano. So I do, feeling like that first time I created pro-forma statements on my own in high school. "He loved my Nikkei model."

"Mmm." Dad's eyebrows pinch together and lower over his narrowed eyes. If he were a weather system, a tornado would have started by now. "I don't know why Rodney would make Cristiano think that your model is all that critical to our work. We've always grown his money for him."

It couldn't hurt more if he'd backhanded me. My eyes sting, and I blink furiously. The weight of people's gazes presses down on me. Their pity is too much to bear. Humiliation prickles like ants crawling.

"Then why don't you call him and tell him that?" I say coldly. Or at least I try to say it coldly. But my voice is shaking. And I hated it that I'm letting Dad know how hurt I am. A big girl doesn't let someone see her cry or be hurt at work, even if it's her dad.

"I haven't had the chance, but I will." He starts to walk away, then stops. "Pascal, everyone has something that they're really good at. Working here just isn't for you. Your talent is better off used elsewhere, in other fields."

The words punch me in the heart, and I almost double over. I gasp, and somehow air is stuck in my throat. My cheeks are hot, like he's slapped them. Tremors run through me, but I can't stop them, not even by clenching my hands. He's never, ever said anything like this to me before. If he honestly felt I wasn't any good, why didn't he tell me earlier? "Like what?" I say, my voice barely above whisper.

"Well, look at what Curie's doing. Be original. Make your own way."

He walks off.

21

FOR THE NEXT HOUR, I TRY TO FOCUS ON WORK. BUT IT'S impossible. Dad's words keep circling in my head over and over and over again. Each time, a new layer of anger, doubt, disbelief and resentment settles over me like mud at the bottom of a river.

Just look at what Curie's doing.

She graduated with a degree in art and photography. She used that, plus her extroverted personality, to become an influencer on Instagram. Does he really think I should be like Curie?

But I don't take that many pictures, and the only reason I'm on Instagram at all is to follow Curie.

And that's not all that's distracting me. Every time somebody walks by my cubicle, I feel like they're giving me a pitying look. Every time I hear a whisper, I feel like it's about how pathetic I am.

Intellectually, I know it's crazily egotistical. A junior analyst like me isn't that important at the firm. But I swear, it seems everyone has heard what Dad said. Combined that with how my idea was dismissed during the meeting last week, I might as well be sitting in the center of the bullseye of loserdom.

Annoyance at myself surges at the negative emotions. My

stomach is hurting too, mainly from stress, and I place a hand over, hoping the warmth will soothe it. My belly always acts up when I'm upset.

I go to the bathroom and sit in a stall. *Finally, no more pitying glances.* I pull out my phone and start to text Curie, then stop. Is this so important that I need to unload it on her during her honeymoon? Her wedding ceremony already got ruined because of me.

I put the phone away and stare at the floor. *Is Dad right? Am I deluding myself into thinking I'm good at what I do?* I just don't know what else I need to do to contribute and stand out. To make a difference at the firm.

If Dad doesn't think I'm any good, it makes sense the VPs will share the same opinion. And that explains how they're treating me in meetings these days.

Maybe it's time you update your résumé and look for something else.

The notion is killing me. But I haven't been promoted in four years. Dad could've been gently hinting that I should give up.

Well, until today. Today he just came out and said it.

I start to stand, but the door to the bathroom opens. I hear several shoes tapping on the tile floor, voices animated and excited in a hushed way that indicates they're having an extra-juicy conversation.

Oh geez. I hesitate, feeling like I'm back in seventh grade, when hiding in bathroom stalls was how you got the best gossip. I cross my arms and wait, not wanting to go out and see anybody. I don't have the energy to be social and pretend I'm fine.

"That poor girl. It's so sad that she doesn't know that she's going to get passed over again," one of them says. I hear water run.

My stomach knots tightly. Now I wish I hadn't had the burger with Court.

They could be talking about somebody else, a small voice in my head says, although without much conviction.

"I know, right? She's trying so hard to impress her dad, too."

Bitterness fills my mouth. How many female employees have a dad to impress in the firm?

"And failing. He's been objecting to her promotion every year."

The revelation slams into me like a freight truck. For a second, I can't process anything. Finally, what Court told me flashes through my head. He said somebody had to be sabotaging me. I dismissed it because the idea that one of my coworkers was stealing my work or trying to take the credit was crazy. But *my own dad?*

Why would he do that when he knows how much it means to me?

Maybe because you just aren't very good at your job...? He said as much earlier, a mean voice whispers in my head.

"Wonder why. Her evaluations look great."

"Who knows? Maybe he has ridiculously high expectations."

"At least she won't be fired. That's something."

"Yeah, but who wants to be a fifth-year junior analyst? It's already bad enough—"

I shove the stall door. It crashes open with a loud bang. A redhead whips around, while her friend—a blonde—drops her compact in the sink. I recognize them. Both are from HR.

"Is it true?" I demand, my voice shaking.

"What?" the redhead says, her smile unsteady, while the blonde grabs her compact and shoves it into her purse.

"My dad's the one who's been blocking me from getting promoted?"

They look everywhere but at me. "Um. I have a memo I need to wrap up."

"Yeah, I got to draft a hiring procedure for this year's interns."

Blood pounds in my ears, my muscles going tight around my neck and shoulders. No fucking way they're leaving after saying all that crap. They're going to tell me exactly what's been—*being*—done to my career.

I leap ahead and block the door. "What's going on? I have a right to know."

The blonde flushes, still unable to meet my eyes. "You can't tell anybody I said anything. I could get fired."

Oh for God's sake. "I won't. I promise."

She clears her throat. "Well... Your dad keeps vetoing your promotion. The managers have been wanting to move you up since your first year."

First-year promotions are as rare as unicorns. My knees shake at the realization that I did that well...and was robbed of the recognition I deserve. "Why?"

"He just kept saying you weren't ready."

That's bullshit. Not ready? "Is he the only one who didn't want me promoted all this time?"

"As far as I can tell from the files. But..." She bites her lower lip, smearing her teeth with the pink gloss. "You didn't hear it from me, okay? I'm going to get into *so* much trouble if you say anything." Her friend nods vigorously.

I breathe hard, my heart racing with uncontrollable rage. A scream strangles in my throat, and I swear my vision dims for a moment. I dig my nails into my palms. The pain anchors me. "I won't say who told me, but I'm not going to stay quiet about this," I say, then march out and toward my dad's office.

Betrayal swirls inside me, as violent as a summer storm. Dad knows why I joined the firm. He knows how important it is for me to make my mark, to be recognized, to be somebody. And when I shared my dreams with him when I first applied for a position here, I didn't mean I wanted to be a popular social media influencer. I want to make my path, using my own unique talents and skills.

And he, someone who should've been on my side all this time, made sure I could never have it. Never once did he hint he'd do this to me. Oh, no. And this explains the attitude of VPs. There's no point in giving opportunities to someone who'll never advance.

Megumi starts to smile, then stops when she sees my expression. "Are you all right?"

No, but it isn't something I can unload on Dad's assistant. "I need to talk to my dad right now."

"He doesn't have a meeting, but he has a client coming in ten minutes."

That is enough for what I have in mind. I walk into his office and shut the door behind me.

He looks up from his computer. "Pascal." He frowns. "Do we have a meeting?"

"No. I just need to know two things."

"Yes?"

Every cell in my body starts shaking with nerves. Now that I'm here, I want him to tell me those women in the bathroom were mistaken. I want my dad to be on my side. Suddenly, I don't even want to know for sure. But the question slips from my lips anyway, a lot steadier than I expected. "Is it true that you've been blocking me from getting promoted?"

His eyelashes flutter so minutely that if I weren't staring at him so intently, I would've missed it. "Yes."

I stumble, taking half a step back as though he's punched me. A million wasps buzz in my belly and ears until I think I'm going to throw up. "*Why?*"

He meets my gaze. "Honey, this is not where you belong."

That hurts again, but I cling to what I heard—that the managers thought I was good enough to be promoted my first year. I try to calm my racing heart, the furious roaring in my head. "I don't belong here?" I ask shakily.

"No. You belong with a man who's going to spoil rotten and treat you like a queen."

Wow. Sexist much? I've dealt with enough sexism in my life, but coming from my dad, it's extra hard. He adores Mom, and he's always been a great dad. "Do you think I went to the University of Chicago and studied mathematics so I can be somebody's trophy wife?"

"I'm not saying you should be someone's trophy wife. You're good enough to be your man's equal. And your education isn't wasted. You meet a lot of eligible men while in college. Besides, men of certain social standing and ambition do not want some barely literate high school graduate."

I don't even recognize my dad right now. Who is this person from half a century ago? He was so proud of me when I got accepted to college, but it...it wasn't about me? It was about my *marriage prospects*? Everything inside me is shaking so hard that it takes a while to gather myself. "Have you ever considered the fact that maybe I want to stand on my own, without a man's name or money behind me?"

"Of course. That's why I gave you a job, so you could get a taste of it. You did, too. The stress is awful for you, and you and I both learned you don't handle it well. It's been giving you indigestion for the last few years."

My molars grind together so hard that the muscles in my jaw start aching. "Yeah, because I was stressed out that no matter what I do, I'm simply not good enough!" My voice is nearly shrill despite my desperate attempt to keep it quiet and as unemotional as possible. Being emotional is bad in finance, especially if you're a woman.

"It'll be your man's duty to work and take care of you," he says as though I haven't said anything. "You should only enjoy the fruits of his labor, so to speak. Look how much happier your mother is now. She was miserable when she was working."

I put a fist over my pounding heart. I feel like it's going to break through my ribcage otherwise. "So? What does that have to do with me? She said she hated her job because she was working for an asshole boss at a small insurance company whose number one goal in life was to deny people's claims. I'm not her, and I'm not working for her old boss!"

Dad's expression remains the same indifferent, cold mask. Then I finally realize the truth—he doesn't care how I feel.

"Is this why you didn't beat the crap out of Court in Maui?"

He shrugs. "Court is perfect. He's rich and young. Seems like a nice guy, and he must care about you to have gone all the way to Hawaii like he did. Your mother and I are both very pleased."

I refuse to accept that Mom's in this too. She's always told me I should do what I want. Encouraged me to study math if that was what made me happy. "Does she know you've been ensuring I can't do what I want with my life?"

"Don't be ridiculous. She and I agree on many things, especially when they concern you and your sister."

All the air squeezes out of my lungs. Mom and Dad have always been very close, and I've never, ever seen them argue.

Suddenly, I can't take it anymore. The fact that I wasted four years of my life here pounds into my head until I feel like my skull's about to explode. "I'll give you what you want. I quit."

He smiles. And that makes me want to scream. But what did I expect? For him to tell me he's sorry? Or that he'd give me the promotion I so richly deserve?

"Great decision!" he says. "Now go spend some time with Court."

I'm tempted to tell him *over my dead body,* except that would be petty and childish. So I lift my chin and walk out with as much dignity as possible given the circumstances.

Megumi jumps up from her seat. "Pascal, are you feeling okay? You're so pale."

If the only thing she's noticing is that I'm unusually pale, I'm doing a decent job of pulling myself together. There's no way I'm falling apart right now. That'd be too humiliating. "I'm fine. Do you have a box I can borrow?"

"A box?"

"Yeah. Something about yay big. I just quit." I realize my hands are shaking. I clench them and force a smile.

Her eyes grow owlish. "Oh my God, but why? You like working here."

"Things have changed."

"Pascal, I'm going to miss you."

I stare at her. Her expression is positively dripping sympathy. But those two women from HR knew and never told me. How likely is it that Megumi didn't know how Dad felt about me being here?

Part of me wants to rail at her. I thought she was a friend. But I don't need to make a scene. Besides, what can Megumi do? Risk her job? "I'll miss you too." I force the words out between stiff lips.

Mechanically and quietly, I put my folios and the flowers from Court into the box. Next goes the framed photo of me and Curie. My hand stills over the one with me and Dad. A spiteful part of me says I really should leave it behind. But I snatch it off the desk anyway. It isn't the janitor's job to toss my trash.

Carrying the box, I go to the elevators. Rage, humiliation and frustration pulse through me, but I try not to show anything. I don't want to be the latest and hottest gossip around the water cooler. But maybe my effort here doesn't matter anyway. My coworkers stare. Their silence is louder than a scream. I hit the down button. Rodney rushes out from his desk.

"What's going on, Pascal?" His dark eyes fall on my things. "What are you doing?"

"Leaving."

"What? Why?" He runs a hand over his hair. "Did something happen?"

"I just realized..." I can't bring myself to say it. How do you tell someone your dad's stuck in the Dark Ages? "It's just better this way."

An elevator opens with a ding. Thankfully, it's empty.

Small mercies. I step into it, then turn to face him. "Don't be a stranger."

Confusion clouds his expression. But he'll never understand. He is... Well, he doesn't have a father who wants him to quit his job and get himself a sugar daddy.

I hit the garage level, then chide myself for the uncharacteristically unkind feelings toward Rodney. It isn't his fault Dad's the way he is. Rodney's always been one of the nicest people I worked with.

Doesn't matter now, though. I'm done here.

I spot my silver Acura right where I left it, next to a Saab and an empty space. Anger and resentment tug at me. It was Dad's gift when I got accepted to the University of Chicago. I adored that thing. I thought he was proud of me because I'd accomplished something amazing, not because he thought I'd land myself a husband with good earning potential and a portfolio brimming with blue chips.

I dump the box in the back, then sit in the driver's seat, my spine stiff. I'm afraid if I bend even a little, let myself feel anything other than anger, I'm going to be a mess. On autopilot, I put my hands around the steering wheel. I should go home. The Snyder Financial Group is not where I belong.

An unspeakable pain spreads from my heart to the tips of my fingers and toes. I put my palm over my chest, hoping it'll hurt less, but it doesn't help. I clench my jaw so I don't start bawling, even though I'm alone in the car. It's a matter of pride. I am *not* going to cry over something that I can't do anything about. It's just a waste of time.

A coppery tang registers. I realize I've been biting my lip hard enough to bleed.

Angry with myself, I blow out a breath. This isn't helpful. I should...

Out of habit, I pull out my phone and start texting Curie. Then I stop. *What am I doing?* I keep forgetting she's on her honeymoon. But then, she isn't just my sister. She's my best friend.

I start thumbing through my contact list, looking for someone to talk to?

Not Mom. And not anybody from work. *A lot of my friends are also my coworkers.* Shit. Ex-boyfriends are out...

My finger stops over Court. It's ridiculous to call him now, after telling him no dating, blah blah blah. Dad thinks I should spend more time with him on top of that, so calling would be like doing what Dad wants.

On the other hand, I wanted to see Court before the whole... fiasco blew up in my face with Dad. *Not* calling Court would be cutting off my nose to spite my face.

I sit, staring out into the gray expanse of the parking structure. Right now, I want a friendly ear and shoulder, plus no judgment. And nobody fits that better than Court.

22

COURT

"YOUR MOTHER... SHE'S HERE FOR CHEST PAIN," THE NURSE says, her voice slightly hesitant over the phone. Maybe she's wondering what the hell kind of sons Mom has that none of them are rushing over to see her.

I stare at the high ceiling of the penthouse, prone on the couch and wishing I hadn't called back. If this were a year ago, I'd be on my way to Tempérane. But now...

I have zero desire to go. What does that say about me as a son and a human being?

But I remember the first time she did this. And I went over there like a worried and dutiful son...

When I check in with a nurse, she takes me to a room. The condition of it shows how Mom's status has fallen. And it makes me more deflated than a punctured soufflé.

Before, she'd have been in a huge private suite that fit a five-star hotel more than a hospital. Silken royal blue and ivory wallpaper. Her gown would be elegant white with an expensive, pearly sheen. There would be enough fresh flowers to overpower the antiseptic. Soft music of her choice.

The room's still private, but nothing special. White industrial paint on the walls. Her gown is a shade between blue and dirty laundry water with the hospital name and logo. No flowers, and the odor of antiseptic stings my nose.

Seeing this hurts. It's a reminder that not only have things been terribly wrong with my family for almost two decades, but that they've hit the point of no return.

We'll never be whole again, never be right.

Mom's in bed, her gaze focused on something beyond the wall in front of her. She's a beautiful woman. The smooth porcelain skin, soft golden hair and the unusual green and blue eyes. Her mouth is soft and painted a light pink. She's always been slim, but she's lost more weight recently. The IV needle buried in her arm makes her appear even more vulnerable.

Bitterness ripples over me. What a waste. She could've had everything. She did have everything. Until...

"Harry, you've come," she says, her voice soft. She extends her hand.

"Court," I correct her, even as I go over to wrap her hand in mine. I hate that name, hate how long I let people use it.

Harry is the nickname she gave me when she decided I would replace my older brother in her affections. I let her, because I was ten back then, too young and stupid enough to believe I could help fix our broken family if I just went along.

Going along was precisely the problem.

"Harcourt," she says. Typical. She has to be the one in charge. The air of frailty she wears is a weapon she wields like a knife.

"The hospital staff who called said you were sick." I squeeze her hand. It's warm and soft, perfectly manicured. I'm close enough I can smell her classy, expensive perfume, and note the slightly rosy tint to her cheeks underneath her foundation.

"I am." She gives me a smile. "But I'm feeling better now that you're here."

I realize what she's up to, and I'm tired of the manipulation and annoyed with myself for not having seen sooner. "If you're feeling better, I should get going. I have things to do."

"You're going to start working for your father." A satisfied glimmer lights her eyes.

"No, I'm not."

She frowns, anger showing through the cracks in her composure. She's probably upset I'm not just going to go along anymore. Then she catches herself and tempers the irritation with disappointment. She knows disappointment is a more versatile tool. "But you should, Harcourt. You must."

"Why do you care?" She never did. As a matter of fact, she's the one who encouraged me get my master's in gender studies, despite the palpable disapproval from Dad over the years.

"If you please your father, he'll listen to you. I know you can fix this mess."

Suddenly exhausted, I run a hand down my face and swallow a sigh. Mom's refrain is always the same.

Fix it, fix it, fix it.

She cannot—will not—accept that her marriage is over. Dad's not going to forgive her. Hell, I'm not sure if I can. "I don't have that kind of influence over Dad."

"Yes, you do! All you have to do is convince him to give us another chance."

"Whatever mercy you showed Tony is what you're getting from Dad."

She stares at me as though I've spat in her face. Then finally she says, her tone defiant and proud, "Lane's love for me isn't dead. Not over what happened to those two. I did nothing wrong. Nothing illegal."

It kills me to see her in denial over how she almost ruined the lives of Tony and Ivy. They lost nine years because of Mom.

"What you did was morally wrong!" I say through a tangle of disgust, guilt and the need to get the hell away from her crazy obsession to regain her former glory as Mrs. Tulane Blackwood. It's lodged so tightly in my chest that it's hard to breathe.

Just what the hell am I doing here, anyway? I'm indulging her, which encourages her. She only turns to me because I'm the one stupid enough to run to her, talk to her, text her back.

"You will not talk to me that way, Harcourt Roderick Blackwood!"

That would've cowed me when I was a child. But she lost her moral authority when all the petty and selfish evil she's done came out. "I'm going back to L.A. Don't expect me to fix it, and don't *think Dad's going to forgive you just because you pulled this...this hospitalization stunt."*

I turn and walk out.

"Harry. Harcourt. Court!"

The second I get out of the hospital, I gulp in the hot, thick Louisiana summer air. It's infinitely more refreshing than the cool hospital air, the perfume on my mother.

"It'll be best if you can come. Soothe her, you know." The nurse's words pull me out of my bitter memory.

"You think so?" I don't mean to, but my voice is slightly mocking. Mom's had an easy, comfortable life. Why the hell is she developing chest pain?

My phone beeps, interrupting the call. I glance at the screen and see a text from Skittles. I put the phone back on my ear. "Look, I gotta go. I'll ask my older brother Edgar to stop by."

"She specifically asked for you."

"He's in Tempérane. I'm in Los Angeles." I hang up and check the message from Skittles. What does she want? A date, maybe? The plan could be working already, I think with a self-satisfied smile.

You there?

Why yes, I type, wishing I could hear her voice, its bright cadence. *Did you forget something?* That sounds cool enough. Not "I want to see where what we have between us is going to lead" eager.

Nothing for a while. I scowl at the phone. Did she get called into a meeting? If so, why did she ping me like she wanted to talk?

Then she calls. Heh. Maybe she needed to find a private place for a chat. Cubicles are terrible for personal conversations.

"Hey, Skittles," I say, not bothering to hide the happiness swelling in my chest. I'm all ready to hear her cheery voice.

"Court?"

I sit up, suddenly on full alert. She sounds muffled, and unhappiness permeates the one word, like an oil spill on a pristine lake. "What's wrong?"

She sniffles.

"Are you hurt?" I ask. Maybe that asshole Tom came back. If so, I'm going to throw him off a balcony.

"No. Yes. I don't know."

I jump to my feet and grab my keys. *She's too upset.* I need to see her in person and fix this. "Where are you?"

"In the underground garage. At SFG."

So much misery is flowing out of her, like blood from a deep cut. "I'll be there soon. I promise. Don't do anything I wouldn't do." Actually, that's terrible advice. "Just stay there!"

I get in my car and rush into the L.A. traffic. Just hearing the sadness and hurt in her tone twists my insides. What the hell could've happened to upset her this bad? Her shithead ex didn't come back, did he? Or did something terrible happen at work? Somebody lost a billion bucks on a bad trade and blamed it on her, maybe? I bet crap like that happens.

When I reach the underground garage, I realize there's no way I can locate her car. I don't even know what color it is. *God damn it.* Frustration and worry tighten their fists around me. I call her. "I'm in the garage now," I say. "Where are you? Honk so I can find you."

I hear a horn behind me, and the headlights come on and off on a silver Acura in the rearview mirror. I relax a little. That was easier than I thought. There's an empty spot right next to it, so I slide right in.

Time to calm down. I'm no good to Skittles otherwise.

I get out of my car and approach hers. A box in the back seat catches my eye. It has the flowers I sent her, plus a few frames sticking out on top like jagged mountains.

Oh, shit. I never held a job the way she did, but I know what it means. Fucking Steve. What kind of asshole dad fires his own kid?

I rap my knuckles against the window gently. The door unlocks, and I climb in. Skittles looks exhausted. Her shoulders are rounded and slouched, and her entire body has the collapsed look of an old and tired balloon. Even in the crappy garage light, I can see how pale and wan she looks. And suddenly I feel like somebody's robbed me of the sun in the sky.

She sniffles.

"Hey, what's going on?" No response. "Look at me, Skittles."

"I shouldn't have called you," she says finally. "I'm not sure what I was thinking."

"What the hell, woman. I gave you my number so you could call me." I'm pissed she thought to keep me in the dark or not lean on me when she needs someone. When I was in a shitty mood the night we first met, she was there to brighten me up. Whether that was intentional or not is irrelevant. "Look at me."

She sighs and slowly turns her head. The skin around her eyes is red, and unshed tears shimmer. They burn me like acid, maybe because Skittles is trying so hard to be strong. Or maybe it's just because it's her.

"I have something in my eyes," she says. "It's been irritating them."

I nod, determined to spare her pride. "I can see that. Have any eye drops?"

"No. It's okay. They'll get better soon."

"Okay." I hold her hand. It's cool and limp. I squeeze, trying to warm it.

"I quit my job," she says suddenly.

I stare at her, holding my breath, while my brain works furiously to process what she just said. Is this the same woman who told me she couldn't date because she needed to be promoted? It sounded like she was really close. If I didn't know her twin was on her honeymoon, I might've thought I was talking with Curie, not Skittles.

"I thought you enjoyed your job," I say, choosing my words with care.

"I do." Pain twists her beautiful face as though somebody sliced her gut. "Well, did. But it's different now."

Then, between sniffles, she tells me what her dad told her. I can't believe Steve crushed her spirit and ambition with such cruelty. Not only that, he's basically trying to put her on a path to end up like my mother. And I'll be damned if Skittles ends up as brittle and selfish as Mom. She deserves to shine, bubbling with delight.

"I know he's your father, and don't take this the wrong way, but he's full of shit," I say.

"I feel stupid." She sighs, deflating further. "Everything I did was for nothing. I was never going to advance—was never going to amount to anything."

If Steve were here, I'd punch him in the mouth. I thought he was better than this. Aren't all parents—I mean, except mine—better than this? "Don't say that. That's just one man's opinion. And he's dead wrong."

She dabs at her eyes. "You were right. Somebody was sabotaging me. I just never thought it would be my dad."

Damn it. I wish I knew how to fix this for her. But I can't even fix my own family; what do I know about other people's? The only thing I can think of to make it better is... "Do you want to grab a drink?"

She checks the time. "It's barely three."

"So? You, uh, seem to have the rest of the day off."

She gives me a look and then snorts a small laugh. "Yeah. You could say that."

"I can be your designated driver. And it'll be my treat." A few drinks, maybe a cheesy movie and dinner should cheer her up. And chocolate. Can't forget the chocolate. First rule of cheering—

"It's okay." She looks at our linked hands. "I should probably go home."

She doesn't move, though. Just looks infinitely sad and alone.

"Want to come over to my place?" I say. "It's close to here and has a few nice bottles of wine and whiskey." The stuff Tony left behind...and I "forgot" to take over to his new place. His wine cellar looks full anyway. "And a pool and tons of movies we can stream. I think I might even have some ice cream." Or at least I hope I do. I tend to go through it pretty quickly.

"You don't mind?"

"Of course not." It'll be my pleasure to put cheeriness back into her.

23

PASCAL

I FOLLOW COURT TO HIS PLACE, ALL THE WHILE WONDERING if I'm doing the right thing. But when he looked at me so earnestly, I couldn't say no. It's like he's a wizard with this magical ability to coax me into doing things I might not do otherwise.

Or maybe it's because I know that his desire to help is sincere. He isn't doing this hoping that I'll help him get a job with my dad or that I'll sleep with him out of gratitude or anything like that. If he just wanted sex, there are hundreds of uncomplicated, non-sniffling women out there whose makeup isn't ruined. So how can I not accept what he's offering in the same spirit it's being offered?

As promised, his penthouse isn't too far from SFG. The place is huge, with an open floor plan that makes it feel bigger than an opera house. The deck has a pool, and when I look at the spectacular view of the city from here, I swear I can breathe easier.

"Wow. This place is amazing."

I look up at the ceiling, where fans spin slowly. The floor is shiny marble, with a few rugs thrown around for comfort. The kitchen has all the appliances you can hope for, although from the looks of it, either Court has a dedicated housekeeper or he doesn't cook much.

"How long you've had this?" I ask, curious since I swear I read he didn't take full control of his money until very recently.

"Not that long. It was actually my brother's." Court goes to the kitchen and looks through the stuff in the wine cooler. "When he moved, he gave it to me because I didn't want to live too close to the campus anymore."

Wow. I know there are families that give each other houses, but it's surreal for me to actually know one in real life. "Is he the one who owns the club?" I ask, remembering how he got Curie's name.

"Yeah. He's married and wanted more of a family home, if you can call his mansion that."

I run my hand over a white baby grand. "This is a beautiful piano. Do you play?"

"When people overstay their welcome."

I look at him. He looks utterly serious. A small laugh bubbles, then bursts out. The heaviness in my heart seems to vanish, and I sigh, feeling like I could float.

"I'm just babysitting this thing because my sister-in-law got a new one."

Ah. I rifle through what I remember from the Google search, and recall that his older brother married a concert pianist. A prodigy, which gives this piano some added significance. I've never touched anything used by a prodigy before. Unlike Curie, I can't play at all, even though Dad did his best to get me to learn a few pieces. I wonder if he did that to have me impress some guy, then shake my head. I don't want to think about that right now.

Court brings a couple of glasses of white wine. "Here."

"Thanks." I take one, grateful for the distraction.

"One day to be angry."

"Agreed. One day. Then I gotta shake it off," I say, even though I'm not sure if I can limit myself to one day. But I need to try. I can't afford to waste my life and energy on this...injustice.

I clink my glass against his and take a leisurely sip. This is an excellent wine—not overly dry, but not sweet either. Just the right balance of acidity and a lovely hazelnut finish.

I sit down on a couch, and he sits next to me. We don't say anything...just enjoy each other's company. Our thighs brush, and attraction sizzles at the touch. I savor it, loving the way my blood courses through my body, heavy with hormones. Court smells amazing. Curie once told me that pheromones were real, and I said she had to be mistaken—they're stuff people make up to explain the stupid things they do in the throes of lust.

But now I understand what she meant. My body's completely attuned to his nearness, his heat, his scent. Still, I don't know if it's all just chemicals. I don't feel stupid with lust. Instead, it feels like comfort and connection. The kind that says this is a safe man—someone I can trust with more than just my body.

It all seems too fast and too sudden. How can I know Court so well? But my heart asks if there's some set time I need to spend with him before I can be sure. Two months? Three?

We had sex within hours of meeting. And we shared two meals together. He came for me when I wanted him to—despite the fact that he could probably hear tears in my voice—and really...how much more do I need?

I finish the wine and place the glass on the low table in front of me. I don't think I've ever been with a guy who I could share a comfortable silence with—being happy just by being close to him. And the way Court rushed to the garage when I called... The way he looked—concerned and anxious. All for me. We haven't known each other a long time, but he's done something each time we've seen each other to make me feel special and lovely. Is that why it feels like I've known him longer than a few weeks?

Slowly, I lean toward him, then wrap my arms around his neck and lick his lips. He tastes like wine we just shared.

No. Better. Warm and delicious with an undertone of hard male and a sweet, generous heart.

He pulls back slightly. "Skittles..."

I bury my nose in his neck and inhale the warm scent on his skin. "Don't. Let me take advantage of you."

"But—"

"No more talking."

I claim his mouth. It stays firm and unmoving, hesitation making his body tense. The fact that he doesn't want to take advantage of my vulnerable state makes me want him more. But I probe with my tongue...and finally he kisses me back.

I push my tongue in, then coax his into my mouth. I want to feel all the wonderfulness of him, all the heat. No indecision, no second guesses, and no thinking.

I pull his shirt over his head, then throw it on the other side of the couch. My hands greedily skim the hard planes of his lean, powerful body. His naked skin is taut and hot. I place my palm over his heart, feel it hammering underneath. I smile with satisfaction, my pulse racing to match the rhythm.

He runs his hands along my spine and unbuttons my top, his fingers shaking slightly with impatience. When he's finished, I shrug, letting the garment drop. He unclasps my bra, and I push it out of the way, the lacy thing sliding along my arms.

I cup the undersides of my breasts and push them upward. His eyes grow dark, a flush coloring his sharp cheeks. He dips his head and takes a nipple into his mouth, sucking hard.

I arch into him, needing more, wanting more. Heat flares between us, burning away my earlier misery, until only bright, beautiful light remains.

I've never felt this way before. And I know it's not the sex, but Court.

"I want you inside me right now," I demand.

"Not yet. You need to take very thorough advantage of me."

He pulls the other nipple into his mouth. I cry out, my toes curling as white-hot pleasure shoots all the way to my clit.

His large, warm hand rubs the back of my thigh. I shiver at the delightful contact. He cups my ass, then pushes my underwear out of the way until he can touch me skin to skin.

Yes, yes, yes.

He slips his fingers between my legs, grazing the most sensitive skin gently. I whimper, my hands clenched in his hair. He spreads my liquid heat all over me.

"Do you think I've taken enough advantage of you?" I ask, the question coming out in a needy whisper.

"Almost."

He starts to shift and gather me up, his muscles bunching, and begins to lift me. I can sense that he's going to carry me to a bedroom. But I don't want that. I don't want anything to break the moment between us. I want him right *here*, right *now*.

I grab the back of the couch and pull, forcing us back down onto it. I unbuckle his belt, undo the fastener on his pants and unzip him, then push his boxers out of the way and wrap my hand around his huge, hard cock. It pulses in my fist, and I smile when a low groan tears from his throat. I run my thumb across the tip and feel the slipperiness covering it.

My eyes on his for as long as possible, I lower my head and suck. His breathing grows rough.

"You *sure* I haven't taken enough advantage of you?" I give his cock a few slow pumps.

Cursing under his breath, he reaches into his pants pocket and pulls out a condom.

I arch an eyebrow. "You had that all this time?"

He grins. "I started carrying it after Maui, hoping I'd get lucky."

"Hmm. I think your numbers just hit."

He covers himself with the rubber. As soon as he's finished, I sink onto him, inch by inch. He's so big that he stretches me until I gasp. We move up and down together, his hands on my hips, then on my breasts, his fingertips brushing my nipples.

Our gazes connect and fuse. His is so blue, so brilliant. Desire and something soft and sweet shimmer in its depths. And a small ache starts in my chest, warm and beautiful.

My pussy isn't the only thing that he's filling. He's filling my heart with pure brightness. Searing bliss swells inside me, and I let out small whimpers and moans.

"You make the sexiest sounds," he says.

He rubs his thumb over my clit, and the pleasure crests so hard, so fast, that the room spins for a moment. I cry out, clinging to him.

"Again," he demands. He puts his feet on the floor and levers himself, pushing into me harder and faster.

I hold on to him, an anchor in a maelstrom of sensation. When I shudder with another incandescent climax, he screams my name and joins me.

24

COURT

I RUN MY FINGERS ALONG THE BEAUTIFUL CURVE OF Skittles' spine as we lie on the couch. Her chest rises and falls gently.

"It's really tiring, all this taking advantage of people," she mumbles against my chest.

My lips twitch. I flatten them into a sober line. "It is."

She taps her index finger right over my heart. "Just so we're clear, I took advantage of you."

"Yup," I say agreeably. "All I did was lie here."

To be honest, I don't know who took advantage of whom. We were chasing our pleasure, pushing each other to it, while I did my damnedest to erase every bit of pain in her heart.

But none of that matters. After the career she worked so hard to build imploded in her face, she probably needs to feel in control again. And I don't mind at all that she's using me.

The notion makes me pause. I never thought I would let anybody exploit me again after what happened with Mom. God knows, she used me for almost two decades to soothe her pain without really dealing with it like a responsible adult. It didn't matter how I felt...how anybody in the family felt.

But the funny thing is, even though Skittles is using me, I don't resent it. She's independent and strong—hell, she didn't even want me to pay for the hotel or lunch. I know this is just her leaning on me for a moment until she centers herself again. And I like it that she can be strong on her own. I don't want her to want me because she's helpless without me. I want her to want me because she likes me as a person, not as a crutch.

My phone, sandwiched between us in my pocket, buzzes.

Skittles shifts, her eyebrows arching. "That is some strong vibration. You've been holding out on me."

"Haha, not a toy. It's a call."

She starts to sit up. "You need some privacy?"

"No." I pull the vibrating gadget out of my pocket and see that it's Edgar.

Every three months, he calls to ask me to come home to talk with Dad. He's doing it because that's what Dad's been asking him to, and our father can be pretty persistent. If he could, he'd get all my exes, not just Tiffany, to guilt me into going back to Tempérane and taking a position at the company.

But sometimes he calls because of something truly urgent, and it hasn't been quite three months since last time he asked me to come to Tempérane. So I feel like I should answer...just in case.

"What's up, Edgar?" I say, keeping my voice brisk so he knows I'm busy.

"Where are you?"

I frown. It isn't like him to skip all the social niceties. "Home. Why?"

"Oh, okay. I thought you might be on your way here."

"Why would you think that?" He knows I'm not taking the job offer from Dad.

"The hospital call you about Mom?"

Oh, crap. I totally forgot. I squeeze my eyes shut and place a hand over them. "Yeah."

"It turned out to be nothing. Just the usual drama. I went over, and she's been discharged, no problem."

"Thanks." Guilt ripples through me anyway. I feel the weight of Skittles' curious gaze.

"Also, if you don't have a job or know what you want to do, consider taking a position at Blackwood Energy," Edgar says in a flat, lifeless tone, as though he's been given a line he's embarrassed to read in a play rehearsal.

"Oh yeah. Think about it every day. Hey, I have a guest. Gotta go."

"Okay, take care. Bye."

I toss the phone, and it clatters onto the coffee table. I sigh heavily.

"You all right?" Skittles asks, shrugging into her shirt.

I'm never going to be all right, not when it comes to my mom. "Yeah." I run my fingers through my hair. The tugs on the scalp seem to help clear my head a bit, but don't do a thing to relieve the tension creeping into my shoulders and neck. I pull my pants on. "I'm fine. It's just my brother."

"The one who owns the club?" she asks.

"No, Edgar. The one back home."

"Oh."

I can feel the questions in her gaze. All the junk that happened in my family... And of course she read all about it. Or heard from that intestinal parasite, Tom.

Normally I don't care that much what people think. I didn't give a fuck when I was at UCLA—and ignored all the whispers that followed me around. But I don't want Skittles to speculate or believe a bunch of Internet crap written by people out to make money off my family's misery.

She's going to have to know anyway, and it'll be easier if she knows now rather than later. That way, if she decides she doesn't want to touch my family with a hundred-mile pole, we wouldn't have been too emotionally involved for it to hurt.

Except the idea of never seeing her again makes my spine go cold.

I take a deep breath. "After our lunch, I got a call from a hospital. My mom was there, apparently with chest pain."

"Oh my God." She places a gentle hand on my arm.

The touch makes me feel better, rather than like some weird circus freak show.

"Is she all right?" she asks.

"Yeah, she's fine," I say quickly, not wanting Skittles to waste any sympathy on my mother. "She's done this before. When texting and calling don't work, she does this. I fell for it a few times and went to her, only to have her tell me that I have to go to work for my father and fix her marriage."

Her jaw slackens. "Working for your father will fix her marriage? What?"

"Dad really wants me at the company. She thinks that if I do that, he'll be so grateful that he'll do whatever I want in return. So then I'm supposed to ask him to make up with her, et cetera et cetera."

Her hand slides down my arm and curls around my fingers. "I'm sorry."

Her sympathy soothes, but at the same time the lid that I've been keeping on my bitterness comes undone. I can't stop myself from saying things I swore I wouldn't tell anybody. "It's always been that way. I'm the son that nobody really wanted." If my parents could, they'd have traded me for Katherine's life in a heartbeat. And the fact that I'm angry about that makes me feel like a shitty person for not being noble enough to want to sacrifice myself for my sister.

Skittles flinches as though slapped. "How can you say that? Of course you're wanted."

That's sweet of her to say. Maybe in her world-view, parents not wanting and loving their children is unthinkable. "What my mom really wanted was a daughter. She already had two sons when she had me. You know that my sister died, right?" Katherine's death always gets mentioned in articles about the scandal.

"Some sort of hunting accident, wasn't it?" she says, choosing her words with care. Everyone dances delicately around it when they want to talk about *that*. Unless they're asshole reporters or something.

"Yeah." I don't elaborate because if she knows enough to bring it up, she's already read all the details already. They're in so many damned "articles." "Until then, Tony, the one who owns the club, was her favorite. But afterward, I became her favorite

because Tony's the one who took our sister to the forest and..."
Old sorrow ripples through me, and I can't finish. Tony never
meant for any of it to happen. When it came out, it only brought
pain...to him and to everyone in the family.

"Her *darling Harry*." The nickname still grates, leaving a raw
wound. "That was me."

"Being chosen as her favorite wasn't your fault."

"No. But it was my fault for indulging her. Instead of asking
her to let it go or forgive Tony, I pretended like nothing was
wrong and tried to cater to her whims. If I hadn't done that,
maybe she would've forgiven Tony before...everything. And she
wouldn't have done what she did." I run my hand through my
hair, although I'm not sure if I really believe I have that kind of
influence over her. My mother is a very stubborn woman.

"What people said in the articles about your mom is
nonsense, Court. If she'd done something so wrong, she would've
gone to jail. You shouldn't let it bother you."

I shake my head, feeling the familiar nausea. "Not all of it is
nonsense. She knew there was an attempt to murder Ivy—who's
Tony's wife now, by the way—but she didn't do anything. She
claims she acted within the law, and she had nothing to do with
the attempt. And she's right. It's not illegal to look the other way.
But honestly, she did it to punish him. She did it because she
wanted him to suffer. And that, I cannot forgive. And I can't
believe the role I played in it, being her favorite."

Skittles brings my hand to her lips and kisses my knuckles
gently. "You must've been a kid when it happened. Whatever she
did, she was an adult and a mother. You were probably just trying
to maintain peace in the house."

Her aquamarine eyes shimmer with caring. The old, twisted
piece of ice in the center of my heart starts to thaw, and my chest
aches.

I lay my forehead on hers and look her deeply into her
eyes. "Stay."

I see the tiniest flicker of hesitation. This is probably too serious, too fast.

"And this time, don't try to leave fifty bucks behind and

vanish. This penthouse costs, like, at least a million bucks an hour."

As intended, it makes her giggle. Her lips curve into a small smile. "Okay."

25

PASCAL

I STRETCH LUXURIOUSLY ON THE SHEET. MY MUSCLES FEEL like warm goo after a good night's sleep and morning sex. Who knew that orgasms could be such a great way to start a day?

My body still buzzing, I wrap my arm around Court's pillow, since he isn't in bed with me, and bring it closer. Mmm. It smells like him, too. I bury my nose there and sigh.

"Morning."

"Morning." My greeting is muffled.

"Come on, Skittles. You gotta eat."

"I don't want to get out of bed," I say. "I want to relax." It's weird to say that because it's Tuesday, and I never miss work. But hell. I'm not going to feel bad about it. I promised myself I'd mope for one day, and that day's over now. I have plans—to indulge myself and sleep in a little. Then go get a job. Show Dad that he's totally wrong about my place in the world.

"Who said anything about getting out of bed?"

"Huh?" I tilt my head and see Court standing by his side of the bed with nothing but a pair of black shorts...and a tray and a huge Thermos pot. "Oh. Wow."

"I know. I look good." He winks.

I laugh. "That you do." He's facially stunning—all those chiseled angles and lines. But what I truly admire is his body. The broad shoulders, wide chest and well-muscled back that flow into a tight waist, narrow hips and long, strong legs. Anybody can win a pretty face in the genetic lottery. But you don't get a body like that without working for it. "And breakfast in bed, huh?"

He settles next to me. "Fried eggs, Pop-Tarts, and toasted bagels and cream cheese. I figured you'd like at least one of 'em."

I study the plates. The idea of Court cooking for me is incredibly sweet. "Sunny-side up only?"

"That's the only kind of eggs I can make with confidence. It takes mad skills to not break the yolks."

"Rocket science." I smile, arranging the pillows so I can sit more comfortably. "Thank you. I've never had breakfast in bed."

"You're welcome."

Touched by his effort and feeling pampered, I reach for an egg and half a slice of toasted bagel and cream cheese.

"Coffee?" he asks.

"Yes, please."

He serves both of us, and I enjoy the morning brew. *God. I could get used to this.*

"So, what are you doing today?" he asks.

"Making a résumé and sending it out." Something I never thought I'd have to do until yesterday. Anger and sadness clench around my heart, and I sigh. "There are other jobs."

Just because Dad never wanted me at SFG doesn't mean I have to give up on my career aspirations. I'll show him! Rapid promotions, a swanky corner office, an assistant of my own and everything else that comes with being at the top! I'm aiming for the stars—to be a managing director in the next fifteen years or sooner. Some of the people I worked for at SFG thought I was good enough to be promoted after only twelve months, so I know I can succeed.

Court pushes the cream cheese closer to me. "Yup. I'm sure you're going to get a lot of amazing offers. You might even get hired at a higher level going in."

Excitement sparks, and I smile at his faith in my ability. I hadn't considered the possibility, since I've been thinking more along the line of going in as an experienced junior analyst, but why not? I'm good enough to deserve better. "I hope so." After finishing my egg and bagel, I take the final sip of the coffee. "I need to shower and go home. My personal laptop is at my place."

"You don't have to. You could work on your résumé on my laptop. The weather's beautiful. You can do it by the pool. I'll even let you borrow one of my shirts."

I should probably turn him down, but it's so tempting. The sun is shining and it'd be nice to work by a pool—another thing I've never done before. I was always too serious when it came to my education and work. And I don't want to be that old stodgy Pascal anymore. "Well...maybe just today."

"Awesome." He picks up the tray.

"Let me help you clean up," I say.

"No, no. Today is Court Makes Skittles Smile Day. So, go take a nice, leisurely shower and then come down when you're ready." He kisses my forehead.

I feel the soft caress all the way to my heart. I hug him and give him a wide smile. "You're perfect."

"Tell me about it." He walks out, making me laugh.

Court acts like I make him happy, but in reality, I think it's him who knows exactly how to make me ecstatic. If I were strawberries, he's the whipped cream. If I were the cake, he's the frosting... Or maybe it's the other way around. Whatever it is, we're compatible and seem to be on the same wavelength all the time.

After the shower, I come out and see my clothes from yesterday, freshly laundered and laid out on the bed. *A housekeeper?* I go still and listen, but I doubt it. Besides, didn't he say that he made breakfast?

He must've done it. It's so thoughtful...and surprising. I assumed a guy like him wouldn't know how to use a washing machine or dryer even if the fate of the galaxy depended on it. If I hadn't seen it in those articles, I would never guess he's one of three heirs to a vast fortune and likely grew up as a one percenter.

I can't wear my work outfit to the pool, so I step into the huge closet for something I can put on. His clothes are laid out neatly, everything pressed and hung or correctly folded. There isn't as much as I thought there would be. Aren't billionaires supposed to be clothes whores?

On the other hand, what he does have is very high quality. A few bold, masculine rings sparkle under the light, and the belts are supple leather, the buckles shiny. I spot a midnight-black tux in one corner, and stick my hand underneath the clear dry cleaner's cover. The fabric feels soft and silky under my fingertips. I bet Court looks mouth-wateringly hot in it. It's too bad that tuxedos aren't something a man wears often.

I step back, pulling my hand away. Everything in the closet is also organized by occasion and color. This has to be the work of a housekeeper. I can imagine Court being neat and ironing...kind of. But to be this organized? Nope. That's definitely not a guy thing.

I change into a white button-down shirt long enough to pass as a micro-mini dress on me. The label says it's cotton and doesn't need to be dry-cleaned, so even if it gets a little wet, it won't matter.

The downstairs level feels different in the morning. The natural light pouring in makes the place appear even bigger and airier, every surface shining. The baby grand positively sparkles like a hunk of polished ivory. I go to the pool, where a huge parasol is set up. Court's already in a pair of navy bathing trunks. His smooth, bronzed body moves beautifully. This is going to be a great view to work to.

He hands me a bottle of sunblock.

"Want me to put some on your back?" I ask.

"Nah. You see how tan I am? I brought it out for you. You're probably going to burn."

I give him a mock glare, but note how pasty I am compared to him. Hawaii was going to fix that, until my stomach decided not to play ball. "Are you calling me ghostly pale?"

"Of course not, Casper." He gives me puppy eyes and a smile. "Don't be so hard on yourself, Skittles. You're perfect just the way you are."

I flush, pleasure and a warm glow mixing together. How can he say things like that without sounding corny and insincere?

Or maybe you're just that into him.

He takes the bottle and squirts the coconut-scented lotion on his hand, then rubs it between his palms. Slowly, he glides them over my jaw line, neck and below, dipping under the shirt to touch the valley between my breasts.

"You know the sunlight can't reach there, right?" I say, trying hard to breathe evenly.

"I understand sunlight can penetrate shirts."

I raise an eyebrow.

"But it's probably best to focus on the exposed parts first," he says, way too seriously, even though the corners of his mouth are twitching.

He dumps out more lotion then moves his hands to my legs, starting from my toes. He smoothes his palms over my ankles and calves and up...up...up... He moves between my legs, ostensibly to make it easier to apply the sunblock. My throat dries as hot shivers run through me. We had sex, like, how many times last night and this morning? But somehow it doesn't seem nearly enough.

"You smell delicious," he says, and kisses me.

"Mmm. So do you." And I could melt into his firm, skilled mouth and forget everything except the stirring of pleasure inside me. Part of me even encourages it, tugging at me to let Court set the pace. But the more logical part—the one that made me study when everyone else in my class was out partying late at night—says sex isn't on the agenda at the moment. "But I really do have to work on my résumé," I say, albeit half-heartedly.

"I know." He gives me a final peck, then pulls out a laptop from a bag set under a small drink table and places it on one of the loungers under the parasol.

I settle down under the shade and take the laptop. "What's the password? Or if you want, you can just type it in," I say.

"No password."

"Seriously? Why not?" Doesn't he have important stuff on here? Or things he doesn't want people to see?

He snorts. "What's there to steal? My thesis?"

He watches me open a Word doc. For a second, I wonder if he's going to hover, but he pats my shoulder. "If you want, I can reward you for your hard work with sex."

My lips tingle at the offer, and I swear I can taste him again on my tongue. "Isn't that more like a reward for you?" I say primly.

Laughing, he turns and dives into the pool in one smooth move. I admire it—and the way his lean body effortlessly cuts through the clear water. I'm not a bad swimmer, but he's something else.

He makes quick work of one lap, then grins at me. "When you need a break, you can always join me."

"I don't have a bathing suit."

"Yeah, I know." He gives me a grin. "Don't let that stop you. If you're just feeling a little shy, I can always take off my trunks, too."

"Haha," I say to cover up the naughty excitement that sparks through me. I've never been skinny-dipping. Never even considered it. But now it sounds like it'd be fun as hell. And illicit, too. "We'll see."

After shooting him an exaggeratedly stern look, I start working on my résumé. It's a lot harder than I thought. To start, I type out all my accomplishments in bullet points, but no matter how I try to word things, I can't hide the fact that I was at my dad's firm for four years without a single promotion or official recognition.

Damn it, Dad. If you'd just let people give me the credit I deserve, I wouldn't be in this situation.

The laptop pings. A small alert box pops up about a new email from Tulane Blackwood. That's Court's dad, if I remember correctly. The subject line reads: URGENT.

"Court, you have an email," I call out when he breaks the surface and runs a hand over his face. "It's your dad. Says it's urgent."

Court's expression freezes for a moment, then goes back to normal. But his shrug is stiff and unnatural. "Ignore it."

"You sure?"

"Yeah. It's really not that important."

I frown at the tight tone of his voice, but what he told me yesterday clearly showed that his parents are a complicated topic for him. Court's in such a good mood today that I don't ruin it by probing. If he says it's not urgent, it probably isn't.

So I focus on making my SFG years sound as impressive as possible, then finish the résumé and draft a simple cover letter template. By the time I'm done, it's lunchtime.

Court comes out of the pool and starts drying himself off with a sun-warmed towel. "I'm starving," he says.

"Me too." I email both documents to myself and hand the laptop to Court. "Wanna grab something?"

He tosses it carelessly on a lounger. "Sure. There's a cool little Japanese place we can try, if you like sushi."

"I love it. Can I grab a quick shower first?"

"Excellent idea," he says with bright eyes. "I'll join you."

My body starts tingling in places I didn't know could tingle. "No, because then we'll never eat."

He gives a mock sigh, but lets me use the master bathroom alone. I change into my clothes from yesterday and put on some powder and lipstick from my purse. For once, I wish I'd taken Curie's advice and carried a small makeup pouch with me. She's big on that, saying *you never know*. But my complexion's decent, and the lipstick does the trick, I think.

Court—because he's a guy and lucky—just throws on a T-shirt and shorts after a quick shower of his own. He drives to a pretty place with bright wood interior. A couple of Asian chefs are laying slices of fish over bullet-shaped rice balls at an open counter set opposite the door as the hostess leads us to a table. The seating area of the restaurant is rectangular, with an elegant square stone garden in the center and a bamboo water fountain.

I get my favorite—maguro sashimi with a small side of seaweed salad, miso soup and steamed white rice. Court gets a basket of edamame and a huge deluxe nigiri sushi set—aptly named "Sumo"—that has thirty-six pieces of sushi.

The service is brisk and efficient. A woven basket full of freshly boiled and chilled soybeans in green pods comes out first. Court wasn't kidding about being hungry, because he starts inhaling them like he's in an eating competition. I barely touch a couple of pods before the basket's half gone.

"If you want, I can pass your résumé around to some friends," he says, finally coming up for air. "I know some people."

For a fraction of a second, I'm tempted. If he puts in a good word with his buddies, the fact that I haven't been promoted in four years might not be much of a factor. But I'll be damned if I take a pity job. Stuff like that never stays quiet, and I'd rather die. "Thanks, but I really want to make this work on my own. I want to prove to Dad I don't have to be a guy to do what needs be done."

He smiles warmly. "Can't argue with that. But if you change your mind, I'm always available."

"I know." I start to reach for his hand.

"*Cooourt!*"

The high-pitched squeal stills my hand. I turn and see a well-groomed redhead in a bright lemon tube dress rushing toward us —actually to Court. Her face is so well made up, it actually looks airbrushed, and her nails have glue-on stones that glitter.

"*There* you are!" The woman comes clopping up, somehow sounding like she's running on cobblestones. "I thought you left town and *totally* panicked!" She laughs like she's on helium.

Even though his mouth is still curved in a smile, a combination of annoyance and disgust fleets through Court's eyes, as though he's looking at a lump of dog poop some irresponsible owner left behind.

"Tiffany," he says. "I thought you were busy job hunting. What are you doing here?"

"I am, but Daddy bought me lunch because he knows I love sushi." She laughs and rolls her eyes. "I just can't afford it here."

"Right." He nods.

My estimation of her is slowly going down, not that it started out that high anyway. I don't like the way she puts her hand on his shoulder or leans so he has a better view of her overgrown frontal melons. *Bitch.* Doesn't she realize he's with me?

"So," she says, "have you heard anything?"

Court, being a total gentleman, keeps his eyes on her face. "About...?"

"The *job.* Your dad never called me back." She twists her body this way and that, the fabric over her Himalayan boobs stretching tighter. And she's getting so close that they're almost rubbing against him.

Oh geez. Is this how she plans to score a job at the company Court's family runs? That's...sad.

Tiffany continues, "I mean, he hinted it'd be great for me to work for you because you're going to need an assistant—"

"I actually have zero desire to work," Court says. "I plan to be as lazy as possible. As a matter of fact, I'm going to be a professional bum."

The idea is so absurd that I almost burst out laughing. I can't believe Court can deliver the line so seriously.

Tiffany actually does laugh. "I'm not talking about vacations, silly."

"No. As permanent employment." Court uses his hands to frame an imaginary floating billboard. "Can you see it? 'Beach Bum Billionaire!' Has a nice, alliterative ring, doesn't it? Sadly, it isn't the kind of position that requires an assistant."

"But—"

"Tiff, you're interrupting our date." He glances at me meaningfully.

She finally turns toward me. Her eyes catalog me from head to toe—my hair, my face, my breasts and clothes. Then she dismisses me as though I'm no competition to her bottle-red hair, overly made-up face, huge tits and extra-tight dress.

I raise an eyebrow. *At least my tits are real.* And I don't need to cajole a man for a job.

"Sorry." She doesn't look sorry. "But like I was saying—"

"If you don't leave, I'm going to be really unhappy, Tiffany." Court is speaking entirely too mildly, like he's vaguely annoyed with a puppy that hasn't been housebroken yet.

"But..." She pouts. Then her eyes widen. "Wait! Are you going to hire *her*?" She points like I'm something that ought to be scraped off hot asphalt.

"I have zero interest in working for him," I say blandly. "I don't date my bosses."

"Tiff, meet Pascal. See how gorgeous she is? Scary smart, too. A strong, independent go-getter. Just my type."

He's probably saying all this to piss Tiffany off. But pleasure warms my cheeks anyway because those are attributes I'm working hard to achieve.

He continues, "Now listen. Good luck with your job hunting. I'm sure it'll be fruitful for you." His voice has turned coolly formal, his words hard. It surprises me, because he always seems so jovial and fun. "Don't ever interrupt my personal time again. If you want to talk to me about professional matters, you can make an appointment and pay my hourly rate of five thousand dollars, wired in advance."

Her mouth drops open like a maguro I can see on the cutting board. "How can you be so cold?"

"Quite easily. Goodbye." He gives a little wave.

Her massive chest heaves. I brace myself for a scene, but she inhales—very impressively—a few times and stomps out of the restaurant, making more noise than a rhino trying to kill a roach.

Court turns to me with an embarrassed smile. "Sorry about that."

"No, it's fine. Does, um, this happen a lot?" I've never had an encounter with an ex's previous girlfriend like this. I can't pin down how I feel about it. Annoyed, obviously. Awkward. And pitying...because it's just pathetic for any woman to do what Tiffany just did. But that doesn't mean I feel much empathy for her.

His left eyebrow twitches. "Define 'a lot.'"

"Like...a few times a month?"

"It happens. They know who I am, what I have, who I know."

"That must be irritating."

He shrugs. "It is what it is."

Our server finally brings our entrées. I start to pick through the beautifully laid out maguro with my bamboo chopsticks, my appetite no longer quite so hearty. Our mood is quiet and somewhat somber.

I place an elbow on the table and prop my chin on my fist. Court is eating like there's nothing wrong with *his* appetite. Maybe he isn't at all bothered by the fact that people try to use him because of his money and family. But I am. I've never dated somebody like him before, and I wonder...

"Do you ever wonder if I'm going to use you?" I blurt out.

He nods, his mouth set in a flat line. "You already have."

I have? When? How?

"Last night. It was great." He lets out a soft sigh, his eyes shimmering with something stormy that should scare me but doesn't. "You need to do it again."

My face flames, half with embarrassment and half with inexplicable pleasure. "You aren't taking me seriously."

"Of course I am. I can't believe you're worried about it. You aren't like them. *You* left *me* fifty bucks that first time, remember?" He taps his chin. "I think it maybe covered the service charge or something."

"You're never going to let me live that down, are you?"

"Nope. Gonna milk it for life. When I'm old and lying in a nursing home bed, I'm going to be like, 'Skittles paid me after great sex. One thousand dollars.'"

My eyebrows are probably disappearing under my hairline. "A thousand dollars, huh?"

"Adjusted for inflation."

I laugh. "Okay, buster. No more money for you after sex, regardless of performance."

"Not even a little?"

"Nope."

"Even after you take advantage of me?"

"Most definitely not," I say with mock severity.

He grins. "Deal."

26

FOR THE REST OF THE WEEK, I DEBATE LONG AND HARD about skipping this Saturday's dinner. Court invites me to spend the day with his brother and friends at his place, and it's really, *really* tempting. I still have no idea what I'm going to say to Dad. We haven't spoken since Monday, and my disappointment and anger haven't fully dissipated.

But Curie and Joe are back from their honeymoon, and they're going to come. No matter how upset I am with my dad, I can't let what happened at the firm taint my relationship with the rest of the family. And I also need to figure out how I'm going to deal with Dad. Avoiding him won't solve anything.

On Friday, when Court realizes my plan while we're having pizza and watching an old episode of *Buffy*, he asks, "Do you want me to come with you?"

Part of me wants him to. I've brought my exes to dinner before many times, but Dad's attitude on Monday makes me hesitate. "No, it's okay."

Court opens his mouth, then closes it with a frown.

I feel bad about turning him down, because he's just trying to help. So I promise to come by after dinner.

As I park my car and walk into my family's home, I can't decide if I made the right decision. Yes, Dad was weird about me and Court on Monday, but why should Court have to pay a price for that? If Dad hadn't said what he said, I would've definitely brought him. Not just for support, but why shouldn't he come with me when my exes did? He's worth a hundred Toms.

Argh.

Curie and Joe are already in the living room, showing their tablet screen to Mom. Curie jumps up when she sees me. "Pascal!"

"Curie! You look amazing!" And she does. The light tan highlights her aquamarine eyes more, and she's positively glowing.

We hug. Joe and I exchange a hug also. He's sunbaked as well, and I swear he's smiling even more now than before. Marriage must be good for both of them.

I sit on Mom's left, and Curie takes the right, Joe parking himself beside her. It's a little tight, but we all fit on the couch. I put an arm around Mom's shoulders and squeeze.

"How you've been?" Mom says.

What exactly is she asking? About my job hunting or just my general well-being? I can't tell, so I just tilt my flat palm to left and right with a small shrug. "So what are you looking at?" I ask, turning the topic away from me.

Mom smiles. "Curie and Joe were just showing me some photos from their honeymoon. Look. They're incredible." And then she adds in a stage whisper, "They're so in love."

Joe beams.

Mom shifts the screen closer and shows me the pictures. Curie and Joe are both very photogenic. One in particular catches my attention. Curie and Joe are sitting side by side on a low wooden platform over the pristine sea of the Maldives, their legs dangling off the edge. The tips of Joe's toes brush the water, and a gray-brown bungalow squats behind them on pylons. It looks like heaven—and just the most perfect place for a couple in love.

"Is this where you stayed?" I ask, tilting the screen so they can see it.

"Yeah. You should go," Curie says. "It's amazing. The floor

has a huge glass panel in it, and you can see the fish and coral and everything. It's pricey, but worth every penny."

"Yup," Joe says. "But don't freak out like her if you see a shark swimming below."

Given how strong an impression *Jaws* left on my sister, I can just imagine her reaction to a destination rife with man-eating marine creatures.

"It was *huge!*" Curie spreads her arms as far as she can. "Haven't you seen the movies? Sharks can break through glass."

"Only in Ocean Hollywood." He kisses her on the forehead. "Don't worry. If one breaks through, I'll save you from its humongous, ravenous maw." Then he mouths over her head, *Baby shark*, while holding his hands about a foot apart.

I grin at their obvious affection and bond. I wonder if they knew this was where they were headed when they first met in high school, and if this could be me and Court somewhere down the road. The thought is startling; I never daydreamed about anything like that with any of my exes. It was always just me and my career. Making a name for myself...making Dad proud.

Just then, Dad comes out from his office. There's no mistaking his heavy step.

Tension sneaks up my spine, all the way up to the base of my skull. I keep smiling so as not to wreck the evening. I hope he understands why—and goes along with it—rather than trying to ruin the family time by bringing up our unpleasant conversation in front of everyone. If he wants to talk about it, we can do that privately.

He looks around. "Fantastic, everyone's here." He looks exceptionally jovial, even when his eyes skim over me. It's as though Monday never happened. Then he stops. "Where's Court?"

Really? No "I'm so glad you decide to come"? No "How's everything?" "He had something to do today."

Faint disappointment crosses Dad's face, and it's all I can do not to shake my head. It's petty and small of me, but now I'm *glad* I didn't bring Court. If Dad isn't happy to see me without a man... then that's his problem, not mine, and I'm not going to cater to his medieval needs.

"Oh, that's a shame. I made extra because I thought he was coming," Mom says. "I hope he can join us for your promotion celebration, though. I'm planning to bake your favorite double chocolate chip cookies and cake, unless you want something different?"

My vision blurs for a second. "My what?"

Shifting his weight ever so subtly, Dad looks away. And then I realize he hasn't told Mom. Curie and Joe are looking at me like this is awesome.

Fury and resentment surge inside me. Dad lives with Mom. He should've said something by now. I breathe in, taking a moment to calm myself. "Well, I guess it's up to me to make the announcement," I say, slowly and evenly. "There's not going to be any promotion. I quit."

Mom, Curie and Joe stare at me for a moment. They're wearing identical expressions—slightly open mouths, wide eyes, their necks slightly forward. Joe shakes his head. "This isn't some kind of April Fools' joke, is it?"

Curie looks utterly bewildered. "But why? You love that place."

My gaze slides toward Dad, who is standing apart from the scene like he isn't the cause of the whole mess. Bitterness like I've never known coats my tongue. "I did. Still do." The relationship I had with SFG was long, almost as long as my life. Realizing that I'm not gonna be part of it anymore is like cutting off a piece of myself.

"Did you get a better offer somewhere?" Joe asks.

Dad scowls at his shoes. He almost looks uncomfortable. But does he feel terrible about ruining my dream?

Normally, I'd say something to smooth things over. But not today. I shake my head at Joe.

"What happened?" Mom demands, looking at me, then Dad.

"Yes, Dad. What happened?" I say, feeling slightly petty and irritated that he hasn't said anything to anyone, not even Mom.

He clears his throat. But he doesn't speak, as though his silence is going to satisfy Mom.

Since he isn't going to talk about it, I step up. I can't decide if I should be happy or mad that he seems ashamed of what he did on

Monday. "Dad blocked my promotion this year—again. Basically, if I stay at SFG, I'm never going to get promoted. I recently learned that some of the managers thought I should've been promoted after my first year." I swallow, the hurt rippling again. Dad should've been the one on my side. Member number one on Team Pascal.

Mom turns to Dad. "Darling?"

He doesn't meet her gaze. "She needs more experience." He rubs the back of his neck.

Bull-fucking-*shit*. Outrage bubbles. That's no reason to keep me unpromoted and unrecognized for years. He knows that, and everyone else under this roof does too. "No," I say coldly, my voice shaking with bitter disappointment and anger. "You thought I should just give up. You think I should just get a man who can take care of me."

He draws himself tall and straight. His eyebrows pinch together, two deep lines appearing between them. "What father wants his daughter to work like a dog? Financial services is very stressful."

"I love that job," I say harshly. "I love investing people's money, helping them plan for the future and save for retirement."

"*Steve.*" Mom's hands flutter around, as though she isn't quite sure what she should do with them. "You know why we named the girls the way we did."

"We?" He pats his chest with an open hand. "I wanted nice, normal names. Not some scientist or mathematician. My top choices were Molly and Emma."

"But you agreed mine were better when I told you why."

He sets his mouth in a mulish line. So like him to get stubborn when he's backed into a corner. I don't know why I never noticed that about him until now.

Mom continues, "I don't want them to live up to some social expectation that the girls should just be pretty and get married and have babies. I want them to do what they want."

Thank you, Mom.

"It isn't like Pascal never wants to get married," he says.

He's so set in his ways that he can't see how illogical he's being. "How is that mutually exclusive with my wanting a career or make my own way in the world?" I ask. "I can have more than one thing in life, Dad."

"So what are you going to do now? Business school, maybe?" he demands.

After taking a few breaths to control my temper, I say, "I'm sending out résumés and reached out to people I know. I'm waiting to hear back."

"And...?"

I cross my arms. I haven't forgotten him telling me to spend time with Court. I've been doing that, and it isn't because of Dad's wish, but because I want to. But I'll be damned if I let him know. That'll only make him smug, and I don't think I can control my temper if he starts acting superior on top of everything else. "And that's it."

"It's not easy to get a job. Matter of fact, it's damned hard," Dad says.

Would it kill him to say something supportive, like "good luck"?

"I'm sure you'll find exactly what you're looking for," Mom says.

"I agree," Curie adds.

Joe starts to nod, then notices the dark scowl on Dad's face and bends down to scratch Nijinsky's belly. Smart man. I don't want Joe put in an uncomfortable situation because of me. Dad can be petty, and upsetting him right after the wedding wouldn't be a smart move.

"That's what you think." Dad looks disgusted for a moment, then snorts. "You don't know what it's like. She has a huge hole in her résumé, too." I inhale sharply, incredulous he's making it sound like it's somehow *my* shortcoming that put the wasted four years at SFG there.

"What *hole*?" Mom says.

Shit. Her eyes are flashing, and she's showing her teeth in that threatening way of hers. I didn't come here to have my parents fight over me. "Mom, don't worry about it."

But even as I tell her to calm down, Dad's smugness really bothers me. It's almost like he's convinced that I'm going to fail no matter what I do. But how can he know that for sure? He has no clue where I applied or who I contacted. Even if he did, calling around and asking people not to hire me would make him look weird. That just seems so beneath him.

On the other hand, I didn't expect him to actively sabotage me at SFG. I'm obviously not the best judge of character—at least not where my father's concerned.

27

COURT

PROPPING MY FEET ON THE COFFEE TABLE IN MY penthouse, I wonder how things are going with Skittles and her family. I offered to go with her, but she turned me down, probably because her dad said that the only thing she's good for is getting married and having babies.

Even though I understand her wanting to deal with her caveman dad on her own, it doesn't mean I'm cool with it. Part of me resents Steve for putting such a weird wedge between us, making it impossible for me to shield her.

At least she isn't going to be alone...although, for all I know, her family could be ganging up on her now. I got good vibes from Esther, but it was only for a couple of hours, when we were trying to get to know each other. She married Steve, didn't she? She might share the same opinion he does, might even give Skittles a hard time for wanting more. And what about Curie? She might side with her dad. She's already fulfilled half of Steve's "marry and make babies" vision. And her brand-new husband Joe is going to side with her, unless he's an idiot. He didn't look like an idiot in Maui, even though he was a slow runner.

Maybe I should've insisted on going with Skittles anyway, and done my best to deflect any attacks against her. That way—

Nate lets out a loud groan. "Oh, come on! How can you win again?" He throws his cards down on the coffee table in disgust.

Yuna gives him a smug smile. "Mad Go Fish skills, man. Mad skills."

"You know that there's no skill involved in Go Fish, right?" I say. "It's all luck."

She gives me a cool look. "Then explain how he hasn't won a single game." She raises a hand, four fingers spread. "Four games in a row."

"Maybe you cheated," Nate says. He's not usually competitive, but four straight losses are probably bugging him.

She goes all Madame Butterfly on him, fluttering her eyelashes innocently. That's a danger sign. Yuna doesn't do that unless she's trying to flirt with you...or kill you.

"How?" she asks. "*You* shuffled and dealt the cards."

"She has a point," Ivy says from the couch she's sharing with Tony. "Unless you gave her the best cards on purpose."

"Why would I do that?" Nate asks.

"I don't know." Ivy shrugs. "Maybe you're in love with her?"

I cough, a laugh caught in my throat. Nate looks at her like she's lost her mind. And I have to agree. Nate loves women, but is never in love with them.

"Are you, Nate darling?" Yuna's eyelashes are fluttering faster.

He scowls. "My heart is impervious. An impregnable castle."

I roll my eyes at his dramatic and superior tone.

Yuna sniffs. "One of these days, some woman's going to bring you to your knees, and you're going to lick dirt off the ground she walks upon."

He shudders. "Gross."

Yuna and Ivy chortle, while Tony merely smiles. I snort a laugh. Nate is fastidious. Even if the ground were covered with flecks of gold, he wouldn't put his mouth anywhere close to it.

"Can we order something to eat? I'm starving," Ivy says, placing a hand over her belly. "Unless Court is cooking?"

Nate blanches. "Definitely not. I want to live."

I pluck a Kleenex from the table next to me, wad it up and throw it at him. "I'm not that bad."

Yuna raises her hand. "No one is risking death tonight." She turns to Ivy. "Since you're pregnant, you should choose."

"That's a good point," I say. "Another one is that pregnant women throw up all the time. Pregnant stomachs that hold on to food are as rare as unicorn horns. She might as well get the maximum pleasure out of eating, especially when she might hurl it back up."

Ivy regards me blandly. "Pizza."

"Sounds perfect," Nate says.

"Agreed," Tony says.

"I want mine loaded with meat and sausage," Yuna says.

I look at her, amazed that she has somehow guessed exactly what I was going to say—again. She maintains that she's Ivy's soul sister, but I swear she's really mine. "You always want what I want."

"It's because I don't have anybody telling me to watch my weight here in the U.S."

"People tell you that in Korea?" Yuna's so skinny that the slightest wind could blow her away.

"It's a long story." She blows out a breath and presses her lips together.

I turn to the two ladies who tag after Yuna everywhere. "How about you?"

"They don't need anything," Yuna says before they can respond.

I look at Yuna's tightly pursed mouth and the scowl forming on her face. They must've upset her somehow. She's generally pretty laid-back and kind. "Sure they do."

"They can ask my mother to feed them if they're hungry."

They must've told her mom something she wanted to keep secret. Yuna's mom can be...forceful, to put it mildly. The entire Pacific Ocean between her and her daughter isn't enough to deter her.

"We will be okay with whatever you're having," one of the ladies says.

"Great," Nate says. "I'm placing an order right now." He starts tapping his phone.

Tony looks at me. "So when are you finally going to introduce us to Ms. Fifty Dollars?"

"I thought she'd be here too," Ivy says.

That reminds me of Skittles' family dinner, which darkens my mood. "She has this thing with her folks. But she said she'd stop by after she's finished."

"Cool. I've been dying to meet Smarties," Nate says.

I run my hands over my face.

"Who's Smarties?" Yuna asks.

Nate gestures at me. "The girl he's dating. He named her after some candy."

I shake my head at his shameless inability to remember. So like Nate. "Skittles, not Smarties. But to all of you, she's Pascal."

Yuna scrunches her face. "That's not fair. I want to give her a name."

I pull back a little. With Yuna, you never know what's going to come next. "Like what?"

"Destiny."

"No. Way too clichéd." Not to mention I had an encounter with a hooker named Destiny in Vegas last year. It seemed like a good idea at the time, since a fortune cookie told me I'd meet my destiny in the far west, plus I was drunk.

But Yuna wouldn't be Yuna if she just accepted my *no*. "It seems so fitting. She *is* your destiny."

I pause. Unlike Yuna, I don't believe in karma or fate or any of that stuff. Shit just *happens*. And it happens when it happens and at the pace it happens. And nothing I do matters. If it did, my family wouldn't have been shattered, Dad wouldn't be asking me to join Blackwood Energy against my wishes, Mom wouldn't be...

I pull myself from the downward spiral of ugly thoughts, not wanting to dwell on the past. "You can call *her*"—I pointed at Ivy —"Destiny."

Yuna shrugs. "Too confusing. There can be only one Destiny."

"Yeah. For Tony."

"I'm pretty happy with just Ivy," Tony says.

Just then, the doorbell rings. Surprised, I turn around. There's no way it's the pizza already. And it's too early for Skittles to be here.

But when I open the door, Skittles walks in. Just the sight of her creates such warmth that pure pleasure washes over me, erasing everything from my mind except light happiness. My bliss vanishes in a nanosecond as I notice she's not glowing. On the contrary: she's looking tense and pensive.

Which, with Skittles, is the equivalent of a normal woman sobbing.

What the hell happened? "You're back early," I say, and give her a soft kiss on the cheek. "Everything okay?" I whisper.

"Yeah," she says. The smile she gives me is about ten percent of its normal wattage.

I want to drag her away and ask her what's wrong, but I feel the intensely curious gaze of my family and friends. I'm not going to get any private time with her until I introduce her to everyone first.

I steer her to the center of the room, then gesture with a flourish.

"Everyone, meet Pascal. Pascal, that's my brother Tony and his wife Ivy. That's Yuna, who is Ivy's best friend and, uh, soul sister."

Skittles blinks. "Soul sister?"

"It's like a soul mate, except it's a sister," Yuna explains cheerfully.

"Oh."

"And that's my best friend, Nate." Over her head, I mouth, *If you embarrass me, you die.*

If Nate sees it, he doesn't react. He just smiles and shakes hands with Skittles. Tony, having spent most of his childhood in Europe, stands, puts his hands on her shoulders and air-kisses her on both cheeks. Nate looks slightly wistful, as though *he* should've thought of that.

"So good to finally meet you," Tony says.

"I've heard so much about you," Nate says. "I hope he didn't mess things up too badly at the wedding. If I'd known, I wouldn't have let him take my jet."

Yeah, yeah, give me shit because I grabbed a twin I didn't know about. Bastard.

"It's okay," she says with a warm smile.

Ivy and Yuna hug her. "I'm so excited to meet you, Pascal," Ivy says. "That's such a unique and cool name."

"And you're gorgeous." Yuna gives Skittles a once-over. "That hair! I wish I had your color."

Skittles blushes, looking utterly cute. "Your hair's gorgeous, too. I always wanted straight hair."

"It's boring." Yuna pouts for a moment, looking down at her long mane balefully. "Court said you were having dinner with your family."

"Change of plans." The smile Skittles gives is weak.

Okay, I've waited long enough. "Let me show her the pizza place's menu, in case she doesn't like what we got."

Before anybody can object, I steer her to the kitchen so we can talk.

"Are you all right?" I ask, keeping my voice low. Tony isn't overly nosy, but the rest? I suppress a shudder.

"Well. Yes and no."

I search her face, hating that I wasn't there to shield her. "Did you have a hard time with your dad?"

"It wasn't that bad," she says. "Everyone *else* was very supportive." Her face is composed, but I catch the small tremor of her chin, the brief breaking of eye contact. "He really meant everything he said on Monday."

"I'm sorry to hear that." *Fucking Steve.* I despise him for being such an asshole, and crushing my feeble hope that he was just off his meds on Monday.

"It's okay. I didn't expect him to change his mind or anything." But the small voice says she's feeling disappointed anyway.

"Hey, Court," Nate yells from the living room. "Stop trying to sell her some fake story you can tell us. We all know what she really thinks about your performance. One lonesome fifty-dollar bill."

What the fuck?

Skittles looks at me questioningly.

How the hell did he find out about the fifty bucks? I look around the room. Tony, my darling brother, seems to be inordinately interested in the ceiling.

"You bastard," I say.

Tony laughs. Ivy shakes her head at him, while Yuna gives Nate a dirty look. "Oh, nice," she says. "Now you're making her embarrassed."

"What she got to be embarrassed about?" Tony asks. "It's really about Court, not her."

Skittles is taking a moment to process. Finally she whispers, "They know about the money?"

"Well, yeah. They also know the spectacle I made in Hawaii."

Holding my breath, I wait. Some women are sensitive about these types of things. But Skittles nods with a self-deprecating smile. "The fifty dollars," she announces to the room, "was all the money I had on me at the time. And it was for the first kiss."

There is a chorus of "oohs" from the room, and Yuna claps lightly. Skittles turns back to me. "Let 'em laugh all they want. That fifty dollars brought you to me."

With a smile, she links her fingers with mine. The same warmth I felt when I first saw her swells like one of those huge, colorful hot-air balloons, filling me until I can barely breathe.

28

COURT

AFTER A PARTICULARLY LATE AND LEISURELY BRUNCH, I watch as Skittles sighs on the other side of the dining table. It's not because she's replete. She's checking her emails and texts, something she's been doing frequently over since her aborted dinner with her family.

Although she puts on a cheery face, I know she's worried about her job situation. She hasn't had a single interview in the more than two weeks since she walked out of SFG. I don't understand why, though. She's brilliant. She asked me to review her résumé last week, and I didn't see anything that jumped out as a red flag.

Unlike her, I'm avoiding my phone as much as I can. Dad's roid-raging pit bulls—I mean lawyers—have been hounding me for days now. Apparently, they really need to talk to me. About what, who the hell knows? But there's no way it can be anything pleasant. They're lawyers for a reason.

As I make my way to the kitchen for another coffee, the concierge calls to let me know a personal courier has arrived for me. I let the guy up, although I'm not sure who would be sending me something. Dad isn't the type to mail anything, except for birthdays and Christmas. Hopefully it's not Mom. She's been quiet since the last hospitalization drama, and I'm hoping things stay that way. I don't have the patience to deal with her issues at the moment. Her manipulative ways are just becoming too much.

She's your mom.

Yeah, no kidding. That hasn't changed, and never will. But somehow that fact only serves to upset me. My gaze slides toward Skittles, now working on her laptop. Look at her. She's working her ass off to be somebody on her own. Even though she's becoming more anxious, and she knows who I am and the kind of influence I can exert on her behalf, she's never even hinted.

The package turns out to be a registered letter. I sign for it and immediately rip it open, walking toward the kitchen to toss the envelope. It's from Percival Langois, one of Dad's lawyers. The letter inside makes my blood boil.

Dear Mr. Harcourt Blackwood,

This is our final attempt to reach out to you. Your father, Tulane Blackwood, is increasingly disappointed with your irresponsible behavior and attitude toward the family legacy. He understands you are currently involved with Pascal Snyder, and that she is seeking employment. Blackwood Energy is more than happy to make an offer and relocate both of you to Tempérane.

I happen to be in Los Angeles this week, and would be delighted to talk with you at any time today or tomorrow, whenever is convenient for you. All you have to do is just respond to my text from earlier this week...

He *happens* to be in Los Angeles. Does he think I'm an idiot? I stop reading, too pissed off to continue. Does Dad really think my refusal to go to Tempérane is about Skittles? Or her employment situation?

I clench my fist. The sound of the envelope crumpling gets Skittles' attention. "What's that? Bad news?"

"Motivation for patricide."

"What?" She lets out a little laugh. "Can't be that bad, can it?"

She doesn't understand how complicated things are. When Dad's hands-off, he can be overly so, even when he knows things are total mess. But when he decides to get hands-on, you might as well try to stop a determined bulldozer.

Personal courier delivery or not, I would normally ignore the letter. But Dad's dragging Skittles into the family issues, and that's unacceptable. Besides, I don't know how far he'll go to get what he wants. My parents don't always understand the concept of limits. So it's time I set some explicit boundaries.

I check my texts and see the one yesterday from Percy, asking me to meet him for dinner today. Bastard. Since I'm feeling less than agreeable, I text back, *Lunch would be better.*

Capital idea, he responds. Palpable relief comes through the bright electric pixels. *What time and where?*

I say twelve thirty and La Mer if he can swing a reservation, laughing to myself all the while. Setting up an orgy between Romulans and Vulcans would be easier than getting a table at La Mer at the last minute.

A few minutes later, he replies, *Done. See you then.*

I stare at the letters. How the hell did he manage that? Not even Nate, who's related to La Mer's owner by marriage, can do that. Then I narrow my eyes. I bet he made a reservation at every top restaurant in the city, just in case. That'd be just like him, because he loathes disappointing his clients. Although if there were any justice, Percy the barracuda would be zapped by lightning every time he set foot into a restaurant fancier than Panda Express.

Skittles' phone beeps. She lunges for it, stares at it for a second, then visibly deflates. "It's Curie. She wants to know if we can have lunch together today." She sighs and collapses onto the couch, her head thrown back.

"You don't want to go?" I thought Curie and she were still tight. Or did I screw things up for them when I threw Curie over my shoulder in Maui?

"I do, but... I'm just being a bad sister. I should be happy to see her, but I just wish it were..." She closes her eyes. "Nothing."

I know exactly what she means. She's been struggling since she left SFG, even though she's trying to hide it. Curie, on the other hand, is doing fine posting fluff on Instagram. I've seen her posts, and she gets paid to mention products and whatnot. Tight or not, it can't be an emotionally comfortable place to be. I give her a hug. "Hey, it's going to be okay. You only need one interview to go well."

"Yeah." She smiles, but it's hollow and forced. "Want to come? She's inviting us both."

It's excruciatingly tempting to cancel on Percy, but I want to make my position on Skittles clear as soon as possible. "I'd love to, but I have a meeting."

"Okay. I'll let her know."

I'd rather be stuck in an elevator with a platoon of flatulent Klingons, but I make myself presentable and drive over to La Mer while Skittles goes to see her sister. Although I've been here before, the place still impresses me with its gorgeous aquarium walls and partitions.

I should bring Skittles here on a date. She'd enjoy it. We should also have a mimosa brunch at Éternité. As a matter of fact, we should hit every nice restaurant in the city just because she'll love it. It'll also be ten million times more pleasant than what's to come.

Percy is already seated, dressed in a gray three-piece suit. Some of the people in Tempérane say his slicked-back black hair and mustache make him look like Clark Gable. I have to agree, especially with his tanned complexion. He grins, showing teeth white enough to blind.

"Court! How are ya?" He's full of Southern bonhomie as he stands to shake my hand.

"Good." *Would be doing great if you hadn't bothered me on my dad's behalf.* "You been waiting long?"

"Nah. Have a seat." He gestures, then sits opposite me.

I notice the half-empty tumbler of bourbon. Percy loves good liquor. Especially when he thinks he's won. Guess it's up to me to show him the celebration is premature.

A server comes over to take our order. Nate told me once never to get the day's special, because it tends to be stuff the chef's trying to get rid of. But that's exactly what I'm going to do, since I'm not really here to eat and don't want to bother with the menu. Percy obviously shares the sentiment, because he requests whatever I'm having without glancing at the menu himself.

"How much is my dad paying you to hound me?" I ask the second our server vanishes.

"The firm's on retainer." Percy smiles. "I'm doing this for your sake, not a billable rate."

"Riiight. How stupid do you think I am?"

"You aren't stupid, son, but here's the problem. You have no direction," Percy says smoothly.

I snort. "I don't need Dad to give me direction."

"Is that a fact?" He takes a slug of the bourbon. "You got yourself a job?"

"Nope. Want to know why?"

"Do tell."

"I don't have to. I don't need to work to put food on the table or make ends meet. Don't need to rush to grab some vanishing opportunity. I can take my time, explore my options—find something that really turns me on and is worth my time and energy." This is going to go straight to my father's ears, thanks to Percy. But I'm not just saying it to annoy them. If money doesn't give you the flexibility to explore your own life, what's the point?

Percy looks at me pityingly. "Like that girl? She turn you on? Worth your time?"

I tense, annoyed he's bringing Skittles up again. "Is this some kind of threat?"

Percy's eyebrows twitch. "Threat?"

"I'm not going in blind like Tony." Cold shivers run through me at the memory of what happened to him—how they hurt Ivy to get to him. "He only got fucked over because he didn't think the family would stoop so low."

"Margot, son. Not your family." His voice cools.

If he believes that, he's an idiot. And Percy is no moron. "Dad was complicit."

"He was no such thing." His tone is suddenly all lawyer.

"He looked the other way."

"And is currently rectifying his mistake."

"A divorce? That's rectifying his mistake? Seriously?"

Percy sighs as though he's tired of dealing with an unreasonable child. "It isn't like you to be getting all worked up over a girl. You didn't care much about Tiffany, although she's a delightful young lady."

His tone says Skittles can't be that good of a lay, and it raises my hackles. "Fuck off."

"Ain't about me fucking off." He flicks invisible lint from his suit. "Your father's very much aware of your current infatuation. He's ready to offer her a job and pay to relocate her if that'll help."

Anger explodes inside me like a fireball, followed by icy fear. I cling to the anger because it's more useful, although the idea that Dad might do something to hurt her, the way Mom did to Ivy, is terrifying. Percy is talking all smooth, doing his Mr. Teflon thing, but there's no way I'm taking anything he says at face value. "You and Dad both stay away from her. She's not a pawn. If he thinks I'm embarrassing now, imagine what it would be like if I really put my mind to it." I give him a nasty smile. "I'll make him wish I was never born."

Surprise flashes in his dark eyes. He knows how messy things are, although he wasn't there when Mom basically said I was just a stand-in for Tony and our dead sister Katherine. He doesn't know Mom would've been more than happy to sacrifice me if it would have meant getting Katherine back.

"Harcourt," Percy begins. "Your parents—" He swallows the rest when our server appears with our entrées.

I toss the napkin on the table and stand. "I've lost my appetite. You can pick up the tab and bill my dad for it."

"He loves you, you know," Percy says.

A bitter smile twists my tightly pressed mouth. When my parents say they love someone, it comes with more fine print than a box of anxiety meds. It's just that other people don't realize that. How easy it is to speak of *love*, especially when it makes you look good. Why, I can do the same. After all, all good sons do, don't they?

I shoot Percy a thin smile. "I love him too. You should let my dad know that as a token of your resounding success."

29

PASCAL

I SPOT CURIE AT OUR FAVORITE PIZZA JOINT. NORMALLY WE would've seen each other at some point since the dinner, but she's been very busy. The price she has to pay for such a long honeymoon.

She looks fabulous, as always. A huge grin, bright eyes. I swear she's glowing like love is radioactive. The diamond ring and plain wedding band glitter on her finger as she waves from the table.

"Wow. This feels so weird," she says when I sit opposite her. "You never have a real lunch break during the week."

"I know. The benefits of unemployment, right?" I force a smile.

She peers at me. "Did you get any callbacks, interviews...?"

I squirm. "Nothing yet, but hopefully soon."

"That's just weird. You have a lot of experience, and you graduated from a fabulous university. I don't understand how you wouldn't have an offer by now. Or at least a few interviews."

"Yeah. Me either." Although Dad said something about how hard it was to get a job. The market isn't *that* bad. I wonder briefly if I'm wrong about Dad. Has he been calling around, blocking my attempts to get a new job?

"Are you applying to places in other cities?"

"No. I'm sticking to L.A. so far. Don't want to move if I can help it." My family's here, my friends are here. And so is Court. I hate the idea of leaving everything and everyone behind. But at the rate things are going, I wonder if I need to expand my horizons.

"You could always come home for Thanksgiving and Christmas," Curie says, as though she understands exactly why I'm hesitating.

"Maybe. But I don't want to think about that right now. It hasn't even been full three weeks yet." I muster up a brave front, doing my best to hide my unease. But it really is odd that I haven't received any responses, even from the contacts I made in college. "So how are things with you and Joe? Got the new place already?"

She sighs. "No, still looking."

"I thought you'd already found one you like."

"We did, but someone else offered a higher price. We couldn't match it." Her mouth quirks down. "I even had a dog in mind to go with the house." Although she adores Nijinsky, she prefers bigger dogs, the kind that thrive with some space. "Then we saw this place yesterday. It looks amazing, better than the one we lost out on. I want it so bad. Look." She taps her phone and hands it over.

I flip through the photos. They show a great home with three bedrooms and a den, plus sizable living and dining rooms. The yard is beautifully fenced with pristine white pickets, and there's a large pool as well. It's exactly the kind of place I'd want if and when I settle down and start a family. "This is fantastic. Did you make an offer?"

Her face goes a little sideways. "Yeah."

"What's the problem? Too many people bidding?"

Curie shakes her head. "It's the owner. This little old Pasadena lady, and she's being weird about it. I feel like she put it on the market just to have people come over, you know?"

"Really? Why would she do that? Isn't it a lot of work to prep a house for showing?" The cleaning alone would put me off unless I wanted to sell for sure.

"Apparently it's a thing among people who are super lonely. My realtor warned me last night when he realized how much I want it." She sighs with frustration.

"But how does he know? Do realtors come with a special radar?"

"The house has been on the market for over six weeks. And you can see what it looks like. I mean, unless the place is crawling with termites or covered in mold, why would it be on the market that long, right?"

I nod.

"So I need to convince her that selling is going to be a good move on her part. A service to humanity, or at least to me."

I laugh at her cheeky grin. But I wonder if the owner will actually sell if she's lonely enough to put her house on the market just to have strangers visit. Then I wonder if that's going to be me years and years from now—no career to keep me busy (from the way my job hunting is going, I might stay unemployed forever) and far from home (because I moved away, hoping to get a job) and lonely and sad and desperate for companionship and...

Ugh. Pascal, get a grip. This isn't about you or your future.

I'm still young. It's only been three weeks—slightly less. I can totally find a job, be surrounded by friends and family and be fine. I know I can.

After we're finished, I decide to go to the mall and see if there's anything pretty that catches my eye so I can buy it to celebrate when I get a new job. It feels weird to not have anything to do and stay home or at Court's all day long. I'm not used to feeling this restless, without any focus or direction. I've been spending a lot of time at Court's, and I'm afraid that at the rate things are going, I'm going to end up like that Tiffany woman—clingy and oblivious. Damn it. Am I going to be exactly what Dad wants me to be?

My phone rings right as I'm about to start the engine, and my heart flutters like tiny, hopeful butterflies are flapping their wings. Maybe it's one of the places I applied to, calling about setting up an interview. I clear my throat and answer.

"Hey, I went by your office today and heard that you quit."

Tom. "Are you calling from a friend's phone?" I ask, annoyed that he got past my block.

"I always have a few extra phones around. You know how it is."

I roll my eyes at his superior "I'm really important" tone. More like people keep blocking his damned number.

"Why didn't you tell me you quit your job?" he says.

"Because you and I are nothing? Because you can't help me find a new one? I have no desire to be a *journalist*."

He doesn't seem to notice my tone. "Well... I heard you quit because of your dad." He *tsks.* "Steve the asshole. Saw that one coming."

Even though my dad's words hurt, I don't appreciate Tom saying crap about him. He may be behind the times in some things, but he's been a great dad in his own way all my life. He took me and Curie to museums and parks, taught us how to fish and swim. I just don't understand how he could go from that to... how he was in the office—manipulative and condescending. Maybe I didn't see the signs because I love him. Or maybe he didn't need to be that way until now because I was young and malleable befo—

"Want to get back at him?" Tom asks.

I'm about to say hell no, then stop. I want to know what Tom means by getting back at my dad. "You know somebody looking for a financial analyst?"

He laughs. "You think like a girl. I don't mean like *get a job.* Think big. Hit him where it really hurts."

"If I thought like you, I'd be an amoeba. And I don't have time for games. Say what you want to say."

"I heard that your dad is laundering money."

I pause, my brain trying to process the words. They're perfectly good words, but strung together like that, they don't make any sense. I let out a laugh, convinced Tom must be high on something. "Call me when you come back down to earth. Actually, don't."

"I'm serious. It's a legit lead."

A legit lead. "Coming from who?"

"I can't reveal my sources. You know that."

I pull the phone away from my ear and stare at it. Who the hell does he think he is? A real reporter? I remember the sensational articles about Court's family. I also remember how he baited Court. A complete asshole.

"Look, I don't know what kind of dirt you're digging through, assuming there even is any dirt to dig, but I'm not helping you."

"Even though your dad blocked you from getting promoted?"

Well, somebody has a mouth the size of Mt. Rushmore. When I find out who, I'll be doing some serious butt kicking, just on principle. "If I was going to get revenge, I'd sue him for discrimination, instead of partnering with scum like you."

"Hey, I get it. You want to protect your daddy," he says. "But does he protect you?"

Something suddenly hits me. "How long have you been working on this lead of yours?"

"A while."

"Did you go through my phone because you thought I was in on this money-laundering scheme too?" Was he dating me in the first place because of it?

"I don't know what you mean." Tom's sounding entirely too offended.

"Bullshit. You know exactly what I mean."

"You should be grateful I'm giving you a chance." He huffs loudly. "Lawsuits can be ugly. This is much neater."

"Yeah, right. You just want to get your trashy piece published."

"Let me help you," he says with the persistence of a snake oil salesman. "Your dad will never know what hit him or where it came from."

"Tom, you're wasting oxygen. Don't contact me again." I hang up.

Now I'm too pissed off to hit the mall. So instead, I go back to Court's place, suddenly needing to see him. He can make me happy—centered.

He's home, tapping away on his laptop on a couch and frowning intensely. Another email from his dad? His relationship with his parents seems so...negative.

He looks up from the screen. "Hey. How'd your lunch go?"

"Fine." I sit next to him and kiss him. Suddenly I don't want to talk about the unpleasant call from my ex and ruin our time together. Tom's like last year's yeast infection—annoying to think about and irrelevant to my present. "What are you doing?"

"Looking for something for Ivy's babies." He lowers his voice. "Yuna already bought, like, two hundred onesies."

"Two *hundred*?" He has to be exaggerating.

"She's had thirty-six shopping bags delivered to Tony's place so far."

"Wow. Isn't a little bit early for a baby shower or whatever?"

"Not according to her."

"Can she afford all that?"

He laughs. "Oh yeah. She's the daughter of the Hae Min Group chairman."

"Really?" I had no clue. The Hae Min Group is one of the largest conglomerates in Korea, its owner family filthy rich and powerful. And she seemed so...normal.

"Her family indulges her," he says.

Is it me or does he sound a little wistful? Do his parents treat him badly? I bite my lower lip. I've been so wrapped up with the confrontation with Dad and my own situation that I haven't given enough attention to what's going on with Court and his life.

He adds, "I feel like I should buy some myself so my nephews and nieces can have something from me." He searches my face. "You look kind of mad."

"Do I?" *And here I thought I was doing a pretty decent job of hiding it.*

"Yeah, because you're usually like a rainbow after a thunderstorm, but right now, you're like the storm itself. What's wrong?"

"Curie asked me about how my job hunt was going. And I told her it wasn't going too great. So..." I sigh.

Court nods. "It is weird that you haven't even had a single interview yet."

His words pierce like arrows, but he isn't pointing it out to purposely make me feel bad. I inhale deeply. "Yeah. You know, my dad was pretty convinced that I wouldn't get a new position.

He said getting a job would be really hard. Now I'm wondering if he's right."

Court shakes his head. "Something will come up. I have faith in you."

Sudden doubts swirl in my mind, spiking my anxiety. "You were right about somebody sabotaging me. And it was my *dad*. What if he called around and asked everyone not to hire me?"

His face sets into a grim façade. "I doubt it, but tell me where you applied."

"Why?" I ask, unsure why his mood has darkened so abruptly.

"To see if I heard anything or know anything about the companies."

I doubt that's the real reason he looks so upset. But I'm so agitated by the lack of employment response that I start to list the places. When I get to OWM, he stops me.

"Okay, it's not your dad," he says, but for some reason seems even grimmer.

"How do you know?"

"Because Gavin Lloyd—the founder and owner of OWM, if you don't know—has a reputation. He does what he wants, and he's not going to refuse to hire you because of what your dad said."

So Dad's right? The job market's just really that tight? The doubts and anxiety twist into a knot large enough to surround my heart. "Do you think I've overestimated myself?"

"No, I don't think so. You're really good at what you do."

His belief in me loosens the knot. But it doesn't totally go away. Maybe...just maybe I should expand my criteria a bit more to include places other than Los Angeles. "Thanks. I'll just send more résumés out and follow up with these companies."

"That would probably be best."

~

COURT

. . .

Although I told Skittles that there's no way Steve told others not to hire her, I decide to check for myself. Besides, he isn't the only one who could mess things up for her. My own father is particularly interested in my personal life, above and beyond what I find acceptable. Part of me wants to believe parents are decent, but I can't afford to be that naïve.

But there's no way I can contact every company she applied to. So I choose Omega Wealth Management. It's the easiest because Gavin Lloyd is close to Nate's family, given that Gavin's mother is dating Nate's great uncle. It won't be difficult for Nate to set up a meeting.

"Great idea," Nate says. "Gavin will quadruple your fortune in ten years. The man's a genius with money."

I nod and smile, since I don't want him to know my exact reason for seeing Gavin. I don't want him to tease me in case I'm wrong, and I don't want Nate to feel awkward or bad about Gavin if it turns out that Gavin did listen to Steve or my dad.

When I walk into OWM, Gavin's assistant smiles at me warmly. She's a curvy redhead with keen eyes and an air of professional competence. Nate told me to be extra nice to her because she apparently runs everything at OWM.

"You must be Harcourt Blackwood," she says.

"Yes, ma'am." I shoot her a warm smile, although I'm certain she knows who I am because of the family scandal. "Just Court to my friends."

"Call me Hilary." She hits a button on her desk. "Gavin, your eleven o'clock is here," she says into a set hooked to an ear. And then, to me: "He'll see you now."

I thank her and step inside.

Gavin's seated at his desk. Dark and lanky, he's an intense man with eyes that seem to pierce you like a pair of laser beams.

"Hello, Court. It's good to finally meet you," he says. We shake hands, and he gestures at a seat opposite him.

I'm surprised at the greeting. He's talking like he he's researched me or something.

"I know who you are," he explains. "Who doesn't? All the stuff with your mother and all."

Right. Of course. It's just...nobody says it to my face like this.

His lips curve. "I hope you aren't upset. My wife says my blunt manner can be off-putting."

"No, it's actually kind of refreshing. I'm glad that you're upfront." Better than people tiptoeing around it, like I'm going to fall apart if they even breathe wrong.

"Good. I don't like to waste time."

Okay. So no need to be diplomatic and look for a good, subtle way to ask what I'm here to ask. "All right, then. There's something I need to know."

"Go ahead."

"Do you know Steve Snyder or my dad?"

"I know them both. Why?"

Damn it. Suddenly I'm nervous, like Pandora about to unlock the fucking box. If I'm disappointed at my dad... Well, he's let me down before. But I don't want Skittles hurt.

Stop overthinking and just ask!

"Did either of them get in touch with you recently?" I say.

"No. We don't really travel in the same circles. Were they supposed to get in touch with me?"

Gavin's face betrays nothing. He must be a damn good poker player. "Here's the thing," I begin. "Pascal Snyder used to work at SFG, but quit recently. She's sent her résumé everywhere, but nobody will hire her. I'm trying to understand why. She's brilliant."

Not even a small twitch. "Did she apply here?"

"She says she did."

He hits a button on his desk. "Hilary, send Pascal Snyder's résumé from HR to my computer, please." He turns to one of his monitors. After a couple of moments, he starts to skim the screen. "You're right. She did apply. We chose not to bother."

Gavin's dismissive tone pisses me off. "Why not?"

"Wouldn't be worth our time. She hasn't been promoted in the last four years."

"So?" I don't mean to, but I sound a little confrontational.

"She was working for her father. How bad do you have to be that not even your own father wants to promote you?"

Shit. I didn't think of it that way. But it makes perfect sense. "Look, her dad is a jerk. He didn't promote her because he thought she should just get married and have babies or something."

"Well, is he wrong?" He shrugs. "Maybe that's all she's good for."

What the hell is up with the medieval attitude from money people? Angry words form in my mouth, but I swallow them. It would be satisfying to yell at Gavin, but it won't solve Skittles' problem. "No, she's very— Look, just do me a favor and give her an interview. And to show you how much faith I have in her, I'll open an account and put a hundred million dollars into it. She can manage it."

He laughs coolly. "Is this your idea of a bribe? That little money isn't worth an interview."

Crap, I forgot. Gavin is richer than a lot of countries. "Just talk to her for, I don't know, ten minutes."

He regards me thoughtfully, then sighs. "Are you doing this to get laid or impress her? There are easier ways." He speaks as though he's trying to help a clueless younger brother.

"I'm already getting laid, and no, I don't even want you to tell her that I was here. I don't want it to look like she got this through some special favor or treatment."

Gavin sneers. "Nobody gets a pity job here. I'm not letting some idiot risk billions, or—worse—my firm's reputation."

"Perfect." I know once he speaks to Skittles, he'll change his mind about her crappy résumé. "So, an interview...?"

He sighs. "I'll give her five minutes."

"Ten. I'm opening an account here, man. A hundred million."

"Still five. Less if I think she's wasting my time. *And* you deposit the hundred mil."

It isn't much, but it's better than nothing. The rest is up to Skittles, and I have faith in her. "All right, all right. But seriously, mark off a little extra time in your calendar. Once you talk to this girl, you'll see that you want her for OWM and thank me for sending her your way."

He gives me a dry look. "We'll see."

30

PASCAL

My apartment smells like cinnamon, sugar and baking apples. I'm making an apple pie for Court, because he's been hinting he wants one. And it's not like I have anything better to do.

I sent out even more résumés, but a vague sense of discouragement clings to me like nicotine on a smoker. I have some savings, but if I don't get a job in the next four weeks, things are going to start getting tight. The last thing I need is an eviction.

You can just borrow money from Curie.

It's an option, but not one I want to use. She's trying to buy a house, and she shouldn't have to support me. I'm a grownup. Maybe I should get a temp job until something more permanent comes my way. I make a mental note to call a few temp agencies.

I check the timer. Half an hour to go. Just about the time Court should be walking in. If everything goes right, the pie will be done about five minutes before he arri—

My cell phone rings. I pick it up but don't recognize the number. *Tom again?* He sure is persistent. I want to blast him for being a dick and take out my frustration with life in general, but I force myself to keep my voice brisk. Just in case.

"Hello?"

"This is Hilary Pryce from Omega Wealth Management calling. Is Pascal Snyder available?" comes a pleasant, professional voice.

Omega Wealth Management? "Yes," I squeak. I stop and clear my throat discreetly. "This is she," I say more normally.

"Ms. Snyder, if you haven't accepted an offer from another firm, we'd like to ask you to come in for an interview."

Holy shit, holy shit! My knees start shaking. I reach out and grab the counter for balance. "Of course. When?"

She lists three dates and times. I take the earliest one. Just in case. There could be hundreds of candidates vying for the same position.

"Thursday at eleven it is, then. Do you need directions to the office?"

"No. I know exactly where it is!" I wince. Was that overeager? Maybe even slightly stalkerish?

"Perfect. When you arrive, please give your name to reception and come to the top floor. Gavin Lloyd will interview you personally."

Oh my God. My heart is pounding, and I can barely speak for a moment. This is a *big* deal. If I can impress him, I won't even need to go for a second-round interview or anything like that. The job will be mine.

"Ms. Snyder? Do you have any questions?" she asks.

"No." I inhale deeply. "Thank you so much. I'll be there Thursday."

"Great. If you need anything, feel free to call me anytime." She gives me her number, and I write it down. My hand is so shaky that the writing is barely legible.

I hang up, then clasp my hands together. Excitement bubbles over, and I can't keep it in anymore. I scream hard and loud. Oh my God. This is my chance. The one I've been looking for.

Although Court's going to get here in less than half an hour, I can't wait. I call him, needing to share this amazing new with him *now*.

"Yes?" he says.

"I got one. I got one!" I shriek.

He laughs softly. "You got a job?"

"No. I have an interview. At Omega Wealth Management with Gavin Lloyd himself!"

"Whoa. That's amazing."

"I know, right? I'm so excited. I don't even know what I'm going to do. What am I going to wear?" I ask as though I've never done this before. My brain feels as sluggish as a spaceship with its warp drive broken.

"You're going to wear your best interview clothes, and you're going to look amazing, and you will totally impress them with how smart and professional you are."

"Yes! That's exactly what I'm going to do. You're totally right." His confident words calm me.

"Meanwhile, *I* will pick up a bottle of Riesling. We gotta celebrate."

"Fantastic." We hang up. But seriously, he doesn't have to bring wine. I could get drunk on water right now.

The oven timer beeps. I take out the apple pie and set it on the counter to cool. Court arrives a little later, carrying the promised bottle of wine.

I dash over and wrap my arms around him. He feels *so* good—like all my hopes and aspirations have come to life in a person. I'm still hopping with excitement. "Oh my God. This is like a dream come true."

"I'm really happy for you." He puts the wine on the couch and runs his thumb over my cheeks. "You're so beautiful when you're happy."

I flush with pleasure. "You're beautiful, too. I really want to thank you for being on my side. And encouraging me and never doubting me."

"How could I not? You're the smartest woman I know. And I know you're going to kill it." He's looking at me, his eyes bright and gorgeous. And suddenly nothing else matters. I pull him down for a kiss. I need some way to express all the bright emotions swirling inside my chest.

Court kisses me back. His large, strong hand cradles my face as though I'm the most precious thing in the world.

His tongue strokes mine, and I purr with pleasure at his taste

—all male, all sweet and dreamy. Mine, he's my man, just surely as I'm his woman.

I put my hands on his shoulders and maneuver him slowly to a living room wall. I push him flush against it and devour his mouth.

His greedy fingers move over my shirt, then slip underneath, skimming the taut, sensitive skin on my belly, leaving trails of heat. My heart hammers, and his races under my palm. I love the way he makes me feel—all hot, reckless and on top of the world. No man's ever made me feel this way before.

How he's making you feel isn't the only thing you love.

The thought slices through my lust like a cold scalpel. I freeze, then pull back.

Court's eyes are dark, his pupils wide. Air saws in and out of him, and heat pulses through me at the need-glazed expression on his face.

Love.

No. It's too soon. We don't know each other well enough to fall in love. Love is what you feel after years and years of being together, like Curie and Joe...or my parents.

"There's no way this is love," I whisper to myself in Klingon.

Court stiffens, his eyes on mine. "What did you say?"

"Nothing," I say, taking a step back. "Want to have some apple pie? I just baked it."

"Yeah...sure. It'll go well with the Riesling." But his expression is dazed, like he understands exactly what was going through my mind and isn't sure about it at all.

31

COURT

IN GENERAL I'M NOT A HUGE FAN OF SHOPPING, AND IT'S doubly bad when I know nothing about what I'm buying. I never knew there were stores dedicated to baby things. Or that there's more than just onesies to baby fashion. Or that they need so much...crap. I pick up some junk wrapped in plastic. A waterproof blanket, really? Then what are diapers for?

I put the blanket back.

The thing is I'm having a hard time focusing because...

Pagh ghotvam'e' muSHa'ghach. Klingon for "this cannot be love."

The words from yesterday fleet in and out of my mind like... waves. Or maybe immortal vampire mosquitoes. Whatever. Skittles didn't mean for me to hear it, so it isn't like I can just ask her to clarify or what made her say it.

So fucking irritating.

Not that Skittles isn't smart for knowing that what we have isn't love. I can't stand it when people throw it in your face like you owe them one because "they love you." Tiffany thinks she loves me, although she's probably gotten over that...sort of. I mean, this is why I like hanging out with Skittles.

So why did it feel like a slap when she said it wasn't love?

I consider for a moment. Not a slap. It was more like...a shock. Yeah. And any guy *would* be shocked. So I shouldn't waste more time thinking about it. It's stupid. It was already stupid of me to pull back from the kiss after she said it, scarf down the pie like my life depended on it and leave her place, with the excuse that she should prep for the interview in peace. I should've just had sex with her instead. Sex solves everything. Well, almost every—

"What are you thinking about?" Yuna asks.

The sudden question makes me jerk my head around. "What?"

"You've been scowling at that onesie like it's the cause of global poverty."

She's staring at me, sipping her mimosa out of a reusable bottle, so people won't know she's started early. Well, it's probably midnight in Korea.

I put down the onesie. "It just looks so small."

She picks it up. "*Babies* are small. And this is a fabulous onesie. See how soft it feels?" She runs her hand over it. "You should get it. It isn't that expensive."

It isn't, until you think about how much it costs per square inch. The whole thing is like a hundred bucks. I can't imagine what a baby will do with a hundred-dollar outfit, but what the hell do I know about stuff like that? "Okay." I turn to a salesclerk near us. "I'll take it."

While the lady rings it up, Yuna gives me a speculative look. "I thought you wanted to do this."

"I do."

"Then why are you so distracted?"

There's no way I can tell her the truth and not go through a Korean Inquisition. And I seriously don't need Yuna starting in on all that *destiny* stuff. "I'm just wondering how Skittles is going to do on her job interview. She has one a couple of days from now."

"Does she? And why are you worried about it? Aren't you going to be her sugar daddy until she finds a job?"

"Of course not. She's too independent for that." Skittles never even hinted.

"Then?"

It's impossible to hide things from someone as nosy and direct as Yuna. Then again, maybe she has some insight. She's a woman, isn't she? "I was just wondering about something a friend said."

Yuna leans closer. "What?"

"He said a girl told him what she feels for him can't be love because..." Shrugging, I clear my throat, heat flushing my neck at the terrible lie. Can't I do better? "He seemed a bit...confused, if you know what I mean."

Yuna raises both eyebrows. "Nate?"

I almost choke. "No, not Nate."

"I didn't think so. He doesn't strike me as the type to worry about stuff like that." Yuna grins easily, like the entire point is silly. "Tell your friend not to worry. People do that all the time."

I gape at her. I'm so stunned that I almost drop the glossy bag the salesclerk hands to me. "They do?"

Yuna nods. "Don't you?"

"Don't I...what?" I say, feeling like I'm losing control of the conversation.

"Say you love them but don't mean it."

"No..." Maybe Yuna doesn't understand what I'm trying to say. Even though her English is amazing, it is her second language.

"I did, once."

"Why?" Couldn't be because she needed anything. Her family is filthy rich.

She looks at me pityingly, like I'm an overly dense bear. "Because I wanted to know what it felt like to say it. And I thought that if I said it out loud, I might feel it."

That makes even less sense than Kant's *Critique of Pure Reason*, which I had the misfortune of reading in college. "Huh?"

"But it just felt so...blah. Like a substandard performance of a Mozart sonata. So I took it back before the guy got any weird ideas."

I don't think that's why Skittles said what she said. Or did she really think I might get weird ideas? And what constitutes a weird idea anyway?

Yuna sighs and pats my shoulder. "Love is like a skincare

product. You gotta try it first, before you know for sure. Sometimes the description sounds great, but when you use it, it doesn't agree with you. Or you use it for like a week, and you start to get allergic reactions or develop hypersensitivity. You know what I'm saying?"

Not even a little. I don't use skincare products, so this analogy is like using calculus to explain geometry.

"But Pascal is your destiny, so it's different with you and her."

"I said it's a friend."

"Ooh, right, a *friend*." Yuna waggles her eyebrows, then pats my arm. "Of course. That's what I meant. That *friend* of yours and Pascal are destined."

"I didn't say Pascal, either."

"Of course. What *could* I be thinking?"

Shit. I should've known she'd figure it out. "Don't tell anybody."

"I won't. I won't breathe a word of your *friend*'s concern." She makes a zipping motion across her mouth, but her lips are wide apart in a grin.

Somehow I doubt she'll keep the promise.

32

PASCAL

"WHY DO YOU SOUND SO LISTLESS? AREN'T YOU READY TO kick ass?" says Curie in her signature cheery voice.

I'm laid out on my couch, staring at the ceiling, phone on speaker mode and lying on my chest. "I *am* ready. It's just..."

"Yeeesss?"

"It's Court. We haven't talked in—"

She screeches. "Did you guys break up?"

"No!" I then tell her what happened in the kitchen. "Normally I would've texted, but he was acting so weird, telling me I need to focus on prepping for the interview and nothing else, before leaving. I actually thought he'd stay for...you know. Sexy time." And why didn't he? He's a guy. He's attracted to me. He knows I'm attracted to him. There was no reason for him to forgo that. It's such an alien reaction.

"Maybe he just really wants you to do well in the interview tomorrow, and you're overthinking it, like you're overthinking how you feel about him."

"But is it really love? It hasn't even been three months."

"Oh, so we're working off Pascal's Timeline, is that it?"

"No, but I wish there were some simple way to check, like a math problem."

She laughs. "I think you love him. And if it isn't love yet, it's getting there. I've never seen you obsess about a guy like this. You usually just sort of keep them around the periphery while you focus on your goals."

Yes. My goals. Court isn't my goal. Impressing Gavin is. "You're right. I can't worry about him on top of the interview. He's probably just distracted and busy right now."

"Exactly. He'll text you soon to wish you luck."

Of course, I tell myself, feeling more optimistic. It isn't like him otherwise. He probably got another letter from his dad's lawyer. How weird is that, a father communicating with his son through a lawyer? But maybe that's what happens when a family has too much money.

"You're going to crush this interview, arise, phoenix-like, from the ashes, and triumph!" Currie says.

I laugh. "It's an interview, not a war."

We chat some more, this time about her house hunting, because I need the distraction, and hang up. Curie is smart about stuff like this. And she's right. Court's going to text me as soon as he can.

A text arrives on my phone. *Hey, it's Yuna. Want to come over for a spa day today?*

For a moment, I stare at the invitation, confused. This must be the Yuna I met at Court's place. It's not like I know another one. But why is she inviting me to a spa day? We don't know each other well enough, and even if we did, I can't really accept, since I need to be careful with money until I get a new job.

And the interview is tomorrow. Just thinking about that makes hope and anxiety rush through—

Another text arrives. *My treat. I need a spa buddy. Can't spa alone.*

I hesitate. It seems crazy for her to offer like that. Spas aren't cheap, and it isn't like we're tight friends. *Are you sure?* I respond.

Very. It isn't that much money. And seriously, nobody can spa alone. It's just not possible according to the Laws of Spa.

I seriously doubt there are any Laws of Spa, but I can't resist her cajoling. Besides, she said it wasn't that expensive, so maybe she just wants somebody to sit and chat with her to do mani and pedi or something simple. And I could use a little makeover before the interview. Some in-spa-ration.

Puns always make me feel better. *Okay.*

Perfect! There's a car waiting for you outside.

A what is waiting where? I shake my head, then decide maybe she mis-texted. *I can drive.*

Yeah, but you won't be able to drive back. Not after we're done.

I frown. What kind of spa treatment makes you unable to drive?

And now that I'm thinking about it, how did she get my number and address? From Court? I'm almost tempted to check with him, but then I stop. I don't want our first text since that awkward evening to be about this. Besides, if Yuna were some kind of weirdo, she wouldn't have been invited to his place, would she?

I grab my purse and step outside my apartment building. And just stare at a blinding white limo with a uniformed chauffeur standing next to it. This can't be the car Yuna meant... Can it?

"Ms. Snyder?" the chauffeur says.

"Yes?" I almost squeak.

He smiles and opens the door for me.

Holy cow. I settle into luxurious leather. The chauffeur says I can have whatever I want from the built-in bar. I thank him, then whip out my phone and text Yuna.

You said CAR, not limo.

A limo is a type of car.

Okay, can't argue with that logic. *I was expecting an Uber. This is seriously beyond amazing.*

All women need to spa in style.

Wow. Thank you.

My pleasure.

I run my hand over the seat. I don't think my face has been this soft since I was five. Oh, man. What have I gotten myself into? Court told me Yuna's the daughter of the Hae Min Group's chairman, but is this what people like her think is "not that much money"?

Is the spa going to be like some misbegotten love child between Versailles and Hollywood? The idea is slightly terrifying. And intimidating.

When I arrive, the place is extremely luxurious—understated elegance and poshness designed to make you feel relaxed and pampered the moment you step inside.

The air is scented with soothing herbs and citrus, and the reception area is wide and airy, with cream-colored stones and tiles. The leather seats are the most beautiful pearly pink I've ever seen. Yuna and Ivy wave from a couch. They're both casually dressed and chatting over what looks like some kind of fruit water.

"I thought you needed a spa buddy," I blurt out, totally confused, but relieved that Ivy's here as a buffer in case Yuna's totally insane.

"I do," Yuna says with a cheeky grin. "How are you, Pascal?"

"I'm good. Hi, Ivy."

Ivy smiles. "Hey."

I sit down gingerly next to Ivy, my butt perched on the edge. I'm still unsure why Yuna needs to have me here, in addition to Ivy. Unless I'm misremembering things, Yuna and Ivy are super-tight besties. "Soul sisters" and all that.

"Okay, so here's the deal. You have to do the prenatal package and send pictures to my mom," Yuna says to Ivy. "She's sent me, like, four thousand texts since last night. Look." She flips her phone over and shows the screen to us.

And Yuna isn't exaggerating. Ivy just laughs.

I stare at the screen. "Good lord. How can *anyone* send that many texts under twenty-four hours?"

"Mom was probably dictating to her team of assistants while getting her feet rubbed." Yuna makes a face. "She really wants Ivy to take care of herself, since these will be her first 'grandchildren.'"

"You're going to get the full treatment, too?" Ivy asks.

"Yes. I need it."

"I could just use a mani and pedi," I say.

"Well, that's a given. I mean, you should do those since you're here, not that your nails need help," Yuna says, her tone rapid and slightly bossy, but in a cute way. "But you should get the works. The massage, detox, everything."

"Um." My head is rapidly adding up how much all those are going to cost. I was expecting mani-pedi, nothing more. It seems crazy for her to spend this kind of money on me, who is virtually a stranger to her.

"Do it. Yuna's paying. Actually, Yuna's mom, probably," Ivy says with a warm smile.

"But..." How do I say that we aren't close enough that I feel comfortable letting her pay for God only knows how much.

"Court said you have a big interview tomorrow," Yuna says. "Massages work better than prayers. I get one every time I have an important event coming up."

I raise an eyebrow. Every time? Really?

"It's true," Ivy says. "When we were studying music at Curtis together, she always got massages before auditions and big concerts."

"Because they deliver results," Yuna says.

It's impossible to say no to Yuna. She's an undercover tornado. Even though she looks all sweet and small, she's a force you just go along with. Besides, you can't begrudge a woman who's determined to give you an amazing time.

And the massages are freakin' incredible. My masseuse finds knots I didn't know I had. By the time she's done, I feel like goo. Utterly relaxed and boneless.

"Wow. That was almost as good as sex," I say as I slip into my robe and then sip a special blend of herbal tea. It isn't sweetened, but surprisingly delicious.

"You can if you go to the right spa." Yuna sighs softly.

Ivy stretches, reminding me of a cat in sunlight. "I feel awesome. Thank you, Yuna. Actually, send my love and thanks to your mom."

"Do it yourself. Photo-bomb her. Like one thousand pictures."

"I didn't take that many. Got a couple, though." Ivy grins a silly grin.

"Next time, I'm hiring a pro photographer." Yuna finishes her tea and gestures for another. "So. Tell me how things are going between you and Court. Sounds like you're getting serious."

Is that what he told her? Maybe he's feeling the same emotions I'm feeling. And the notion makes my cheeks warm and my body tingle for some reason. "He's a great guy."

"He's a fabulous catch. If we had any chemistry, I'd marry him," Yuna says. "Mom would be okay with that, even though he's not quite what she has in mind for me."

"Who does she have in mind for you?" I ask. Does she want Yuna to marry well and all that? Does Yuna need to, given how wealthy her family is anyway?

"Oh, an heir to some huge financial empire. That way, we can cement our merger more strongly. And I'll, of course, deliver the most perfect heir for the both families."

Wow. That's...um...interesting. And really old-fashioned, I guess.

On the other hand, Yuna doesn't seem that upset about it. She just shrugs it off like it's nothing. "Anyway, back to you and Court..." She leans closer. "Do you think you're in love, maybe?"

Thank God I don't have any tea in my mouth. Otherwise, it wouldn't end well. "*Love?*"

"You're blushing."

I fan myself. "It's just hot in here."

She nods. "Of course. Gotcha."

"It's too early," I add quickly, shooting a beseeching look in Ivy's direction, but she is entirely too amused to stop Yuna.

"You only need like a week to know," Yuna says.

"Excuse me?" A week is nothing. A blip.

"You've tried out a lot of different men before, right? It isn't like he's your first."

"Well, uh... No, of course not."

"Right? Men are like fast cars. Unless they repel you for some reason, you ride them for like a week, and then you know if they're going to work out or not."

Oh my God. That's the craziest comparison I've ever heard. Wait until I tell Curie. "What if you need something better and faster later?" I ask, unable to resist.

Yuna doesn't even blink. "That's what divorce and prenups are for."

I shake my head, laughing. She has the funniest ideas, and I like it that she doesn't take everything so seriously. "That's crazy, but I think I love you."

She grins. "See? And we've only known each for, what? A week?"

33

PASCAL

I WAKE UP EARLY, EVEN BEFORE MY ALARM GOES OFF. I'M too wired to sleep more, despite the luxurious massage.

After the spa, Tony picked Ivy up, but Yuna and I stayed behind for a leisurely mimosa dinner. She didn't pressure me about Court or anything. We had some nice girl time, and I really like her. She's a bit cavalier about money—understandable, given her background—but she's also considerate and surprisingly unspoiled. By the time I got home, I was too relaxed and full to do anything but fall straight into bed.

After I shower, I reach for my phone to check the market. Oh crap. I turned it off at the spa at the request of my masseuse and forgot to turn it back on. I missed a couple of calls from Court yesterday, a text from Curie wishing me luck and a text from Court that arrived seconds ago.

Want me to come over and make you breakfast?

I smile at his sweet offer. Maybe I assigned too much meaning to what happened a couple nights ago. He really just wanted to stay away and give me the time and space to focus on prepping for the interview. *Thanks, but you aren't going to make it in time. Traffic sucks.*

I'm right outside your door.

Pleasure surges. I spring-step my way to the bolted door and open it.

Court is standing there in a white T-shirt and denim shorts. A small grin is tugging at the corner of his mouth, and he's holding a paper grocery bag. God. He looks *so* delicious—and hot.

"Hi," I say, slightly breathless, even though the distance between my bedroom and the door isn't far enough to make me exert myself.

"Hey. You look gorgeous and perky this morning."

I step aside, and he comes in.

"I tried calling you, but you didn't pick up," he says.

"Sorry. I totally spaced out. Yuna treated Ivy and me to a girls' day out." I smile. "It was fun."

"Never a dull moment with Yuna," Court says. "If you aren't having fun with her around, you're doing something wrong."

"I bet. The spa was so nice."

He cups my face and brushes a thumb over my cheek. "You look relaxed and happy." He kisses me. "You're gonna kill it today."

"Thanks." I smile, nervous but also determined.

"Anyway, this is my test killer special."

"Test killer special?"

"Yeah. Two eggs, sunny-side up, with a pat of butter, a few strips of bacon and half a grapefruit. It's a simple, balanced break-fast of good protein, fat and vitamin C. No starchy carbs. Every time I eat like this, I do much better on tests. So I figured I'd make it for you."

He's so thoughtful, it makes me warm and glowing inside. It's small thing, but it touches me more than some grand, complicated gesture would. "Thank you."

"My pleasure."

I watch him putter around in my kitchen. It's smaller and less well equipped than the huge, sparkling one in his penthouse. But somehow he seems very at home with an old spatula and a frying pan. I take a moment to enjoy the domestic scene, then start the espresso machine. Curie got it for me on my birthday, and I plan to give myself an extra shot.

"Want one?" I ask him.

He smiles. "Yeah. A latte would be great."

By the time I'm done getting our morning java ready, he places two plates of food on the table. They look yummy, and I realize I can't think of a time I was this pampered and cared for by a guy. The most amazing thing is that I don't even have to hint or ask. He just does it.

"By the way, did you give Yuna my number and ask her to take me to the spa yesterday?" I ask, between bites of bacon.

"No. Why?"

"I was just wondering. It kind of came out of the blue."

"That's just Yuna. She's big on taking care of the people around her. And before you ask, no, I didn't give her your contact info, but she has a way of finding things out. I'm pretty sure the Hae Min Group has a team of top investigators on retainer."

Damn. The possibility never even occurred to me. I lean closer and lower my voice. "You think she has this place bugged too?"

He laughs. "No. She knows what lines not to cross." He watches me polish off my bacon, then hands me a slice of his. "So. You ready to go kick ass?"

"I guess. I mean, I know I can answer whatever Gavin Lloyd throws at me, but I don't know if he's not a jerk like some people say. Some of the articles I read weren't very flattering." At least none of them said he's a sexist from the Dark Ages. That's already a step up from my dad.

"Success attracts haters, and he's very good at what he does. Besides, his assistant's been with him since forever. If he was a dick, she would have left."

"She might need the money, in case that's never occurred to you."

"Ha! She's married to Mark Pryce, the restaurateur. She can quit whenever she wants."

"Really?" I know nothing about her because people don't think assistants deserve the spotlight. But in my experience, they're the ones with real power because their bosses trust them so much. "Tell me about her. Is she difficult? Exacting?"

"As far as I know, Hilary's down to earth. Surprisingly so,

because she had this sensational Cinderella romance and married a billionaire."

"Wonder why I've never heard about her, then." Curie definitely would've said something. She loves high-society gossip.

"Because her husband's family knows how to keep the media out, even though he made a spectacle of himself to woo her. Declared his love on the sides of skyscrapers, and with those smoke planes in air shows. Later he named one of his restaurants for her. Éternité."

"Wow. That's...over-the-top and sweet. How do you know so much? It isn't the kind of gossip I thought you'd follow."

"It isn't. But she married"—he looks up at the ceiling, figuring something out—"Nate's brother's brother-in-law. Damn, that's a mouthful. Anyway, Nate sometimes talks about them."

We finish our breakfast. I start loading the dishwasher, needing a routine task to calm my nerves as the time draws closer to eleven.

"You go ahead and get ready for the interview. I'll do it," Court says.

"You cooked."

"So? I don't mind. Today's your big day."

I smile. "Thanks."

"I know you're going to wow them. I have faith in you."

That brings warmth to my heart. I hate to even think about it before the interview, but I haven't said a word to Dad about the possible opportunity at OWM. Not necessarily because I think he'll wish me ill, but because I'm afraid how I'll react if he tries to be nasty. That makes me a little sad, because I used to feel like I could tell him anything.

I shake myself inwardly. *No negative thinking. I have Court cheering me on.* I can deal with Dad on my own time.

34

Pascal

I rub my hands nervously as I walk into the glitzy lobby of Omega Wealth Management. It's airy and elegant, marble and crystals. Colors are muted and soothing to the eye. Curie would call it money with taste.

I smooth my hands over my best interview outfit: a conservative navy skirt suit and a silk round-neck top in the lightest cream color. My hair's down. I thought about putting it up, but I look better when it's down.

A leggy brunette walks past the security, her glossy mane twisted into a chignon. Now I wonder if I should do the same.

Stop overthinking. The hair won't make any difference.

I know that intellectually. But there are still a billion ants crawling in my stomach.

I really want this job. It isn't just about solving the immediate problem of needing a steady paycheck or staying in the city like I want to. OWM is bigger than SFG. I want to show Dad I'm not just good for being somebody's wife.

I sign in with security, get a visitor's badge and then go to the top floor as instructed. When I step out of the elevator, a sharply dressed receptionist directs me down the hall to Gavin's office.

Breathing slowly to control my nerves, I make my way along the luxurious corridor. Gavin occupies the biggest corner office. A pretty, statuesque redhead is sitting outside. The nameplate on her desk reads Hilary Pryce.

I look her up and down fast. She's younger than I expected. Maybe in her thirties…? Her clothes look expensive, which makes sense, given that she's married to a wealthy businessman. Next to her keyboard stands a gorgeous travel mug that says *A Woman Worth Her Weight in Gold*.

She looks up from her monitor. "Hi," she says, her voice low and warm. It's much huskier in real life.

"Hi. I'm Pascal Snyder. I have an interview."

"Perfect. Gavin's appointment just ended. You can go right in. He's expecting you."

"Oh. Thank you," I say, surprised she doesn't think it necessary to announce me.

I inhale slowly, smoothing my outfit, and recite my positive mantra. *I'm ready for this. I'm just as good as or better than anybody applying here. I deserve a place here.*

Then I walk through the open door.

Gavin Lloyd's office is large and luxurious but also highly functional. Nothing inside is designed for mere pampering, but for optimal ergonomic setup.

The man himself sits behind a huge desk. His hair is black with a hint of brown, his dark eyes piercing. He isn't handsome, per se, but photos don't do him justice. There's a restless energy to him, a slight hint of impatience that the world is moving at a slower speed than he'd like, that doesn't come through in pictures. Or maybe it's just something he's feeling today because of the market's volatility.

He stands and shakes hands with me, his grip firm. "Gavin Lloyd. Nice to meet you, Pascal."

"Same here."

"Take a seat." He gestures at one of the armchairs, then moves to one himself.

Huh. So he isn't going to reclaim the chair at his desk.

"I don't like to waste time, so I'm going to go straight to the questions I want to ask first."

"That's fine." I actually prefer that to a lot of meaningless chatter. I'm too nervous for chitchat, and I expect him to grill me until I feel more abused than a steak charred to bricklike consistency.

And he doesn't disappoint, because he starts off with the recent market movements, then goes straight to more specific questions, thrown at me rapidly and without any pause.

"Which currency would you buy?"

"Thai baht," I say without hesitation.

"Why?"

"Fundamentals look good, and it's been a solid gainer."

"Past performance doesn't guarantee future performance."

"I agree, but there's nothing indicating that it won't continue to perform well. Thailand is making moves to improve its infrastructure, particularly in regards to automobile production. Tourism is also set to in—"

"Who's the most important person at OWM?"

This is too easy. "Other than you?"

"Obviously." A small smile pops on his face.

I smile back. "Your assistant."

"Why her and not one of the VPs who get featured in articles all the time?"

"She's still here, and has a travel mug that says 'A Woman Worth Her Weight in Gold.'"

"Could've been a gift from her husband," he says.

"I doubt that. He would've given her something more romantic and grandiose." Especially based on what Court told me earlier today. "Plus, no husband is going to talk about his wife's weight."

Gavin finally leans back in his seat. "I'm going to be blunt. You aren't an idiot. Actually, you're surprisingly sharp. So why weren't you promoted during your time at SFG?"

Oh geez. I can throw so many different answers, but I'm reluctant to tell him the truth and bad-mouth my dad. He screwed up, whether he knows it or not, but somehow I don't want everyone to know my father is such a medieval relic. "Politics," I say finally.

His expression grows inscrutable. "You're too smart not to know how to play that game."

"Honestly? I didn't know I *had* to play it."

He taps a corner of his mouth a few times, his eyes speculative, like a buyer at a yard sale who's wavering.

Please. Don't let this be the reason you won't hire me!

After what feels like a decade, he says, "We don't do that here. So don't apply what you learned at SFG to OWM."

Ohmigod, YES! "I won't. I promise."

"Good. Then you have an offer. HR will be in touch with you regarding your benefits and first day." Then he names my new salary.

My heart stops, then kicks back, racing faster. "Do you mind if I ask you what position?"

Gavin looks at me funny, like he couldn't believe I'd ask about that of all things. "Senior analyst. Four years of experience is more than enough. You'll find our salary and benefits competitive for this level..."

The rest of what he says vanishes behind a loud buzzing noise in my head. *Holy shit.* Court told me I might get a promotion out of the job switch, but hoping and praying for one and actually getting it are very different. Even though I'm sitting, my knees feel unsteady.

I take a moment to compose myself. Gavin undoubtedly wants me to let him get back to his day's agenda now that we're finished. "Thank you."

"It was my pleasure speaking with you." He stands and shakes my hand.

I walk out, feeling like I'm stepping on clouds. Oh my God. *I did it! I have a new job!*

Doing my best to walk with dignity, I make it to the elevator. I shift my weight front and back, then side by side. Bright energy bubbles inside me. I feel like I could float away like a feather—a very happy feather.

When the elevator doors open to the lobby, I step out, then pirouette, unable to help myself. I swear there's golden light filling me. Can't people tell?

After turning in my visitor tag to security, I pull out my

phone, start texting Court, then stop. He deserves a more personal touch. I'm calling him. I hit the green button.

"Hey," he says.

"Hey, you!" My voice is extra bubbly.

"Guess you got the job?"

"*Yes!* Am I that obvious?"

"The smile gave it away."

Smile? I pull the phone from my ear, wondering if somehow the camera—

Then I notice him on the other side of the lobby, and my heart does a cartwheel and triple flips. He's putting away his phone and waving at me with a bouquet of bright yellow daisies. I dash toward him.

"I can't believe you!" There's so much excitement and pleasure coursing through me that I'm nearly breathless. "What are you *doing* here? I thought you went home after breakfast."

"Well, you know. I figured I'd come by with flowers to congratulate you."

I give him a huge smile, loving the bright sparks in his eyes. I take the flowers and inhale their lovely fragrance, then peer at him through my lashes. "What if I hadn't gotten it?"

A stunned gasp. "In what bizarro alternate universe?"

His exaggerated shock makes me giggle like a teenager. But at the same time, I feel powerfully charged. I could probably single-handedly take down a battalion of Klingon warriors, then destroy a fleet of Romulan ships. And I could do it in ten seconds, with one hand tied behind my back and in high heels and in an impractical bikini girl-warrior outfit. Because, as everyone knows, no female warrior outfit comes with protection for your stomach or legs, just a huge push-up bra made of some shiny metal.

Out of pure impulse and happiness, I kiss him with all the bubbling happiness in my heart, all the pleasure he gives me by just being with me. I can't think of the time I was this impulsive with affection with my exes. I flick my tongue across his mouth for a taste. Court always has that special blend of flavors—sweet, heady and utterly male.

Blood grows hot in my veins, swelling and rushing like rivers after a heavy rain. White heat flares in my belly then spreads all over in waves. The sound of his rough breathing hits me more potently than any seductive whisper. I love how basic and honest his reaction is.

"You drive me crazy," he rasps, his blazing gaze searing my face. "But we need to go somewhere else unless you want everyone at OWM to see you making out in the lobby before your first da—"

"Definitely not." I grasp his hand, linking our fingers tight. "Let's go."

Through the walk to the elevator and the descent to the underground garage, the lust beats strong and hard inside me. I'm already slick between my legs, the air too hot and heavy in my lungs.

"My car's over there."

"Mine's closer," Court says.

I should take my car because that's practical, but I can't bear to be separated from him, not even for the drive between OWM and his penthouse. I let him lead me to his Maserati and drive us to his place like a maniac.

Once we're in the garage of the penthouse, I'm so revved up that even the feel of his naked palm against mine is almost too much.

The engine cuts off. Instead of getting out, we stare at each other for a moment, the air between us crackling. Then, inside the luxurious leathery cocoon, we're on each other.

It's a little awkward to work around the dash, wheel and stick, but they're no match for the forceful urgency of our need. Court devours my mouth, stoking my lust with every lick and suck. I return the favor, wanting to drive him as mad with desire as me. He's utterly magnificent and sexy as hell when he starts to lose himself in lust—in me. He cups my breast through my clothes, and I gasp. It feels good to have him touch me, but I need more.

I get rid of my jacket and top, then push the bra out of the way. He dips his head to flick his tongue across one of my beaded nipples, sending sharp pleasure spearing through me. He pulls it into his mouth, sucking hard. Electric sparks run along my spine, blissful sensations spreading all over and making me tingle to the tips of my toes. I reach out and touch him through his pants. He's hard, and I can feel the pulsing through the fabric.

"Fuck, that feels awesome," he says.

I grip him harder.

"I love it when you do that."

And I love it when I make him feel good.

He lavishes loving attention to my other breast while pushing my skirt up. I hear a small rip as my panties fall away, but I don't care. They're replaceable.

He glides his thumb between my folds, ending on my clit. I cry out, my vision dimming at the hot pleasure.

"You're so damn wet."

"I've been wet since the kiss in the lobby."

He gives me a wicked grin, then licks the slickness from his thumb. "Yum."

"Not fair for only you to get a taste." I tug at his pants.

He obliges, unbuckling, unzipping and pushing them down along with his underwear. His cock's hard, veins thick and pulsing along the shaft. I wrap my hand around it and feel it beat in my fist like a heart. My heart picks up its tempo—harder and faster.

My eyes on his, I run my thumb over the slit and spread the slick precum until his entire cockhead is shiny. His breathing grows shallow and quick. I smile, feeling powerful. Because I want to drive him wild, I slip the thumb into my mouth and suck softly, as though I have his cock in my mouth and this is a prelude to a lusty fellatio.

Court curses under his breath. "You tease. You're going to pay for that."

"Oh yeah?" I raise an eyebrow in a mock dare. The hottest and most delicious anticipation is sizzling over my skin. I've never felt anything like it before.

And I've never even done anything like this before—car sex, and in a *garage*. His penthouse is only an elevator ride away, but it seems like light-years.

His mouth crashes over mine. He kisses me like he wants to own my soul. I kiss him back, wanting his in return. I vaguely sense him move and maneuver. And soon he enters me, his movements sure and steady.

Our gazes lock as he glides in and out of me, pleasure building and building and finally cresting like a powerful wave. I get lost in it, then hold him tight, like he's the most precious thing in the world.

Because he is.

The thought crosses my mind as a second orgasm breaks over me. I clutch him as hard as I can as he joins me in sweet oblivion.

35

COURT

I GROAN WHEN I CAN CATCH MY BREATH AGAIN. THEN I carefully arrange things so we don't crush each other in the Maserati.

Holy fuck. I've never done it in a Maserati before. I quit sex in vehicles as soon as Edgar got his own place with extra bedrooms because comfort trumps almost everything. What is it about Skittles that makes me lose my damn mind?

I turn my head and look at her face, beautifully glowing and flushed with pleasure. Her eyelids are drooping low, and a faint smile curves her swollen lips. The sight wraps around my heart like a hand and squeezes gently. And I know she matters a lot more than I can fathom.

"My God. That was amazing," she says with an overly casual grin. It's like she's sensed what's going through my mind and decided it's too serious for her.

Fine with me. "It was, even though my back is complaining."

She laughs. "My hips feel a little, ah, stretched, too, but we're young. We'll recover."

Then she starts to sit up and right her clothes, pushing her bra down and arranging it so it cups her breasts just so, her top covering her, the bunched skirt smoothed and stretched over her legs. I arch up, pull my pants up and try to make myself as presentable as possible.

"It's a good thing we can bypass the lobby," she says lightly as we exit the car. She runs her hands over her skirt, as though she can magically iron away the creases. "Can you imagine?"

I look her over from head to toe. She looks like a naughty goddess, her hair slightly messy, her lips a little bruised and her clothes mildly wrinkled. And I'm glad nobody's going to see her like this—touchable and sweet...a man's wet dream. It's only for me.

Me.

The sudden possessiveness is startling. I've never felt anything like it with anyone else. But Skittles... She's different. Like a special treasure I want to keep in a safe place only I know about.

"You look freakin' amazing, and the concierge would've been too awe-struck to say hello." I press a soft kiss on her forehead. "But I'm also glad nobody's going to see you like this."

She presses her lips together, but can't hide a small smile. We take the elevator to the top floor, our hands linked. I kiss her fingers, one by one. "We need to celebrate your new job proper-ly," I say.

"Oh, that's right. I forgot to text everyone." But instead of reaching for her phone, she presses closer, her head resting on my arm. "It can probably wait until later, though."

The elevator stops and opens. We step out together, my arm around her shoulders, and stop abruptly.

My mother is in the foyer. I blink a few times, wondering if I'm hallucinating. What the hell is she doing here?

Vaguely I sense Skittles' eyes boring into me. But I can't face her. I don't even know what the hell I'm going to say to Mom, much less Skittles.

Mom's standing still, her chin held regally high. She's gotten thinner. The bodice of her blue dress is slightly loose around the waist and hips. But the bright shine of her golden hair is the same. The weight loss brings out the stark structure of her delicate facial bones.

"Harcourt," she says, her voice like an icicle—beautiful, frail and cold.

"Mom," I say. "How did you get up here?"

"The concierge knows who I am. They didn't want me loitering in the lobby like a nobody."

They should've asked her to go home. I'm going to have a word with them later. "Mom, this isn't the best time—"

"You should introduce me to your girl. This *is* your girlfriend, isn't it?" Mom says dulcetly.

Everything inside me stills for a moment. I don't want to introduce her to anybody, especially not Skittles. But Skittles is watching me, and I know if I refuse, it's going to upset her and make me look like an ass. And her feelings trump my own instinctive urges. "This is Pascal. Pascal, my mother, Margot." I don't say the last name because her days as a Blackwood are numbered.

Mom smiles the gracious smile she gives everyone she deems worth the effort. But her eyes...they stay cool and superior. I can't believe I've never noticed that until now. Is it because I'm older, or because I know what she's really like?

"Hi," Pascal says, giving a small, awkward wave. She probably remembers what she read about Mom.

And the scene hurts because all this could've been avoided if Mom were just more decent.

Condescension flashes in Mom's eyes, but it vanishes almost instantly. Her smile widens, and she reaches out to take Skittles' hand in both of hers. "I'm so happy to meet you. You're the first of Harcourt's serious girlfriends I've met."

My skin crawls. Mom's met my exes in high school, but she's getting around that by emphasizing "serious" as though she's letting Skittles in on a secret—that she's really special. And the thing is, it would've worked...if it were Tiffany standing next to me.

"Oh." Skittles clears her throat, carefully extricating her hand from Mom's grasp. "That's...really nice."

"Like I said, this isn't a good time, Mom. I wish you'd called." *So I could tell you to stay in Tempérane.*

Mom looks at me like I slapped her. "I can't believe I have to make an appointment to see my own son."

Even an appointment wouldn't get her in to see Tony, but I refrain from pointing that out.

"And would it be possible to go inside rather than standing in the foyer?" she asks.

I don't want Mom inside my place or anywhere near Skittles. But what will she think if I toss Mom on her ass? Probably nothing positive. Damn it. It's my fault for assuming that Mom would never come out to L.A. to talk to me. Commercial flights have always been beneath her, and she doesn't have access to the jets Dad keeps anymore, but clearly this is an extreme situation.

"Yeah. We can do it inside, but I can't talk for long. I told Tony I'd see him and Ivy later today," I say pointedly.

My jab fails because she remains coldly placid. Of course; she doesn't think she did anything wrong because Tony supposedly owes her for killing our baby sister. Never mind it was an accident, and he was barely twelve at the time.

We go into the living room. I don't offer her anything. Mom takes one of the armchairs and crosses her legs, while Skittles stands awkwardly, like she's the *persona non grata* in this scenario.

It fucking pisses me off. Mom's the one who doesn't belong here. I take Skittles' hand and squeeze gently. When she squeezes back, the knot in my chest eases. But only a little.

"Percy contacted me," Mom says. "I think it's better if you speak with him and help him to see reason so he can convince your father."

The damn divorce. If I ever see him again, I'm going to ream him for not convincing Mom of the futility of trying to stop the inevitable. "Don't you have a lawyer for that?"

Her gaze flicks to Skittles. "I'd prefer not to discuss family matters in front of..."

Skittles' fingers flinch in my hand, but I tighten my grip. Mom's not going to make Skittles feel like she doesn't belong here.

When Mom realizes Skittles isn't going anywhere, she sighs. "Yes, I have a lawyer. But your father will be more amenable if he's dealing with you."

"You think he's going to not divorce you just because *I* ask?" The whole notion is preposterous. He adored her. I'm just the son who won't color inside the lines well enough to suit him.

"You'll have to work at Blackwood Energy. It won't be a hardship. It's a great company."

"I don't want that for myself." Edgar is already doing it—carrying on the family legacy and providing jobs for all those people. I don't think I would handle the pressure as well. Daily decisions and meetings sound dreadful and utterly dull. Dad already knows I don't have the temperament for an office position anyway, even though he tries. If he could, he'd be harassing Tony to do the same, but he knows Tony's beyond his control. Tony hasn't even taken the trust fund he's entitled to.

If I hadn't taken my inheritance, would Dad be leaving me alone?

"Your father loves you. So do I."

My jaw tightens. "No. Neither of you love me, but that's okay. I'm a big boy now, and I don't need Mommy and Daddy to wipe my nose or bandage a scraped knee." My voice is heavy with sarcasm, but I doubt Mom understands the reason. She and Dad never wiped my nose or bandaged my scraped knees. That was the job of our housekeeper or nanny. "Now, read my lips. *I'm not getting involved in your problem.* You'll just have to accept the consequences of your actions."

"You're going to let your father divorce me? Shame me in front of everyone?" Her voice cracks, just enough to enhance the pathos of her delivery.

Wishing I were anywhere but here, I look away, my neck hot. Why does she have to do this in front of Skittles?

She continues, "Is this how you treat your mother? What does your girlfriend think about it? Women judge their men by how they treat their parents. Surely, you understand that by now. It's how they figure out how you're going to treat them long-term."

"Enough of this bullshit! You don't get to drag Skittles into this."

I start to take a step forward, but Skittles pulls me back. Her face is set in a hard mask. "Mrs. Blackwood, how Court treats you is irrelevant, because I'm not going to behave the way you did. I already know the background to this story. In fact, it's rather widely known."

Mom inhales sharply, her eyes narrowed and smoldering. "You're making a mistake."

Skittles shrugs. "If you say so."

Mom jumps to her feet. "The divorce is going to ruin us!"

I look away, embarrassed and tired of her refusal to accept reality. "Like I said, that's all between you and Dad."

"You don't understand!" Her voice is becoming shrill. This isn't part of her standard routine. She must be desperate.

"Dad loved you enough to let you nearly destroy the family. It's you who killed that love with your actions." I squeeze Skittles' hand, needing the contact to anchor me before I lose my temper enough to do something I shouldn't.

Mom grows pale, then starts shaking. She stares at me coldly, contempt etched in every line of her face. "One day, Harcourt, you'll experience the same thing I am. Don't expect any sympathy from me."

She's the last person I'll turn to for comfort, so she can rest easy.

She stalks away, her stilettos eating the ground. The door slams behind her.

"I'm sorry you had to see that," I say, running my fingers through my hair. It's one thing to be embarrassed about your family's sordid history, but something else to have your woman watch the whole shit show play out with her own eyes.

I need a drink. And a special eraser to wipe out what just happened. I'm so damn mortified that I can't even face Skittles.

"Hey, it wasn't your fault." She puts her arms around me. "She surprised both of us."

I sigh with relief that she isn't disgusted enough to walk out, then hold her tighter because I need her warmth and softness to sooth the acidic burn in my gut. "I'm still going to apologize. This should've been a perfect day for you."

"It *is* a perfect day. I aced my job interview. I had fabulous sex. Your mom's visit... It's just a minor blip. And it showed me you have good judgment."

I pull back to look at Skittles' lovely face. "She's that obviously bad, huh?" I know honesty is important in a relationship, but that doesn't mean I want her to see all my ugly baggage.

"She doesn't deserve you," Skittles says softly. "And your mom isn't you. Don't act like you're somehow responsible for what she did here."

The gentle understanding in her voice is my undoing. And I finally realize why what she thinks about me matters so damn much.

I'm utterly in love with her.

36

PASCAL

COURT IS LOOKING AT ME SO STRANGELY. IS HE STILL worried about how I'm reacting to his mom?

If so, he shouldn't be. I intend to be fully supportive of him, the way he was with me when I was having issues with my dad.

I pull him gently to a couch and push his shoulders until he's seated, then curl up next to him. "Do you want to talk about it?"

"About what? Sex?" he says, his tone light, even though his eyes are still not quite the same bright blue.

"You know what I mean."

"And you know what *I* mean." He puts an arm around my shoulders. "She isn't that important. And she doesn't make a habit of showing up unannounced. It won't happen again. I promise."

The "this is finished" shutters come over his eyes, and I know he won't say another word about it. It bothers me because I swear he needs more support from me. On the other hand, maybe this is his way of coping. Don't I also try not to think about my dad's newly discovered sexist attitude?

Although Court seems okay now, I'm still reeling a little. It isn't because I've never met the mothers of my exes before. None of them were anything remotely like Margot Blackwood.

She's prettier than I thought she would be from the photos. She has amazing bones, and Court definitely got his looks from her, especially his eyes. But unlike him, she has no warmth. I've never met a person so cold. When she held my hands, shivers went up my arms.

I panicked inside, though. I was so worried about making a good impression on her that I freaked out silently about what she'd think, what with me here in my wrinkled clothes and looking like I just had sex.

As the visit went on, it was obvious I didn't have to care that much. Instead of making me relieved, it upset me more. I hate it that I'll never have to worry about how she perceives me. I wish Court had a mom who he could have a tight, loving relationship, not the reptilian Margot. The shuttered and tight expression on his face... God, it hurt like hell to see. He's usually so carefree and laid-back that it never occurred to me he could grow that dark and miserable.

What she said about girls judging their men by how they treat their mom is true. But what I told her is also true. I do trust him. And her cruel parting shot proved me correct. She doesn't have the right to ask anything of him. Not like that.

And I hate it that she ruined our buoyant mood. *Well, you know what? Fuck it.* Court is right. This day should've been awesome. No. It *will* be awesome. I refused to let my dad screw up my self-esteem and goals, and I'm not letting Margot screw things up either.

"You got any champagne? Wanna drink it and have a second round of celebration?" I ask, giving him a come-hither look.

He kisses my forehead. "I have a bottle or two, but I thought you wanted to gloat a bit."

"Gloat?"

Court grins. "If you want, we can hire a plane to skywrite it outside your dad's office. *F U I got a new job!* I'm sure I can find one to do that right now."

I laugh. "You're insane, but the idea does have a certain appeal. In fact, a *lot* of appeal." And my God, it'd be hilarious. I'd give a kidney to see Dad's expression. But... "Let's be realistic. I think texting will work just as well." I start typing on my phone, letting everyone on my contact list know I'm starting a new position at Omega Wealth Management.

It doesn't take long before congrats start popping up on my screen.

Mom: *I'm baking your favorite chocolate cake and cookies this Saturday. Bring Court.*

Rodney: *Congrats! I knew you'd find another great opportunity.*

My other coworkers express similar sentiments. Curie texts, *I knew it! Yay you! We gotta celebrate tonight! I'll grab you after Joe's done with his photo shoot. Dinner & drinks!*

Her enthusiasm makes me grin. I was thinking about a more private celebration with Court, but going out with my sister and her husband is just the thing to erase the funk of the unpleasant visit with his mom. *I'm at Court's. Why don't we meet you at the restaurant?*

Cool. I always wanted to try this new place out. She texts me the name and location of a Mexican restaurant.

I turn to Court. "Is Mexican good for dinner?"

The last remnant of tension vanishes, and his smile finally regains its full brightness. "Sounds perfect."

Great. See you at six thirty, seven?

See you then. And bring your boyfriend.

I put the phone away and look at Court. "That was Curie. She wants to have dinner and drinks. She specifically wants you there."

He gives me a strange look. "She did?"

I nod.

"She isn't going to try to poison me, is she?" He raises an exaggerated eyebrow.

I laugh. The notion is so ludicrous. "You didn't think Dad would, but you're worried she might?"

"Well, I did try to steal her away from her fiancé at her wedding. But only because I didn't know it wasn't you."

I flick a finger across the tip of his nose. "Relax. She won't try to poison you or kill you. Do you want me to give you a signed affidavit?"

"Won't be necessary. I trust you, just like you put trust in me earlier when my mom was here."

The simple, absolute statement puts a lump in my throat. Emotions swell in my chest, and I can't do anything except stare at him. The need I have for him isn't just a physical connection or fun. Maybe at first it was. But now it's deeper and stronger, like we're tied at the soul.

It should be weird I feel that way. I'm too logical for it. But my mind can't think of any other way to describe what we have between us.

"Court..." I whisper. I don't know why, because it isn't like I have anything to say. But I want his name on my lips, to see his gorgeous eyes seeking mine.

My phone rings, shattering the moment. I pick it up, wondering if it's Dad calling to say he was wrong and to congratulate me on my new job.

But no. It's actually OWM's Human Resources department. They want to know when I can start and tell me what I need to bring on my first day.

I close my eyes and tell them I'd love to start next Monday. The weight of Court's gaze bores into my cheek. Part of me is relieved I don't have to examine what I was feeling just moments ago too deeply, but another part of me is disappointed I'm being such a chickenshit.

37

PASCAL

THE RESTAURANT CURIE PICKED IS NEW, AND NEITHER Court nor I have been to it before. Just like her to know all the new places, though. Being a social media addict and an influencer keeps her in the loop.

The music is cheery, Spanish lyrics soaring over rapid guitar chords. The restaurant smells of lime, cilantro, flour tortillas and sizzling meat. Court and I are early, so we go to the bar to order a drink—a margarita for me and a bottle of beer for him.

Over the rim of my glass, I study Court. He changed into a simple shirt and shorts. His broad shoulders and biceps flex and move as he brings the beer to his gorgeous mouth with surprisingly soft lips. I can't decide which I like more—him in his dressier outfit or something this casual and relaxed. He's hot either way. He also looks great naked, too, although that would be illegal in public, even for him.

"What?" he says as though he feels my gaze.

"Nothing. Just thinking you look pretty."

He frowns, although a small dimple appears on his cheek as he tries to suppress a smile and fails. "Pretty is the word for you, not me."

"Really?" Most people—including myself—would usually use a word like "smart" or "nerdy." "Pretty" is for Curie, and I've always thought of us that way, too, even though we're twins.

"Uh-huh. You're gorgeous in that dress."

I flush. I insisted on getting my car from OWM and going to my place to change before coming here. I wanted to freshen up and put on a magenta dress I got last year because it's one of the hottest outfits I own. I didn't want to look like I just wrapped up a job interview, when I know Curie's going to pop up in some cute clothes herself.

She's always perfectly made up and dressed, ready for a selfie or two at any time. I don't usually care about that sort of thing—we aren't in a competition or anything—but I still don't want to appear too shabby and sloppy next to her. So weird that I care so much all of a sudden. I never did until now.

My gaze darts to Court. Is it because I don't want him to think I'm less pretty than Curie? Or wondering how I measure up, looks-wise, to his exes? His opinion is becoming so important—maybe too important—to me.

The door opens, and Curie and Joe walk in together, their arms linked. As I expected, a fresh coat of powder covers her face, and she's in a pretty lavender dress. Joe is in an Avengers shirt and faded jeans, probably having just returned from a photo shoot. He's super busy these days.

"Sorry, we're late," she says, giving me a hug. She always says that when she isn't the first to arrive.

"You're on time. We were early." I hug her, then Joe. Since she wants Court here and I want whatever awkwardness—if any—to be resolved as soon as possible, I say, "So, this is Court. Court, Curie and Joe."

"I know who he is." Joe narrows his eyes and purses his mouth in an exaggerated expression of anger.

"Do I need to start running?" Court says lightly.

Curie elbows Joe in the side. "Oh, stop. You thought it was funny."

Joe's face relaxes into a grin. "Yeah, I did." He pauses. "Afterwards."

"Well then. I'm glad there are no hard feelings," Court says, this time earnestly. And the two men shake hands.

"I was stunned, but really, it was kind of sweet of you to chase her all the way to Hawaii." Curie smiles. "Besides, the only people who make me hold a grudge are ones who hurt Pascal. Fair warning."

"Oh, come on." I love my twin, but she can be overprotective. Besides, I can't ever imagine Court hurting me.

"Well, it's true." Curie makes a fork with her index and middle fingers and does the "my eyes, your eyes" gesture at Court.

He laughs. "No problem. I'll let you put a hidden camera in my place."

I let out a horrified gasp. "Don't give her any ideas."

The hostess comes over and says our table's ready. We move to a booth big enough to seat six. The menu is extensive. Curie skims for a second, then says, "We have to get shots first."

"Exactly. What's a celebration without shots?" I say.

When our tequila shots arrive, Curie raises her drink. "To Pascal and her new job. May she kick financial ass."

"Hear, hear," Court says.

We clink. I knock mine back fast, then bite into a slice of lime as the alcohol heats my sinuses.

"So when are you starting?" Curie asks.

"Next Monday," I say.

"Wow. Quick."

"I had three weeks off."

She nods. Joe and Court decide to get another round, and we knock that back after a toast to Curie and Joe's newly wedded bliss.

The food arrives soon.

"This is a great find," Court says after handing me a tortilla for the fajitas for two that we ordered.

"I know all the good places." Curie grins, waving her fork with a piece of tomato from her taco salad skewered at the end. "If you ever need recommendations, just let me know."

"I don't know how much he's going to call you," I say after a bite, which is delicious. I give her a look through my lashes, dying to see her hilarious reaction. "His brother owns Z, and—"

"What?"

"—I bet he knows all the exclusive digs."

"Really?" Curie asks Court, wide-eyed. She's almost never wide-eyed in person—just in her Instagram feed when she wants to exaggerate.

He shrugs. "Yeah."

"Oh my God. That's *awesome*."

He shrugs. "It isn't bad."

I rub his shoulder. "Especially when you want to have people cut the line."

"You figured that out?" He grins.

"It occurred to me later that maybe you had something to do with it."

"Why didn't you say something?" Curie asks. "You could've come over and invited her to the VIP line."

He shrugs. "Didn't want to impress anybody with my brother's club."

That's so like him. He uses connections he has—like the private jet he borrowed from his rich buddy—but doesn't try to pretend that he's the one with all the things or influence. He always seems to want to be judged for the kind of person he is. And that's sweet and honest. Maybe even slightly vulnerable. And definitely endearing.

As the dinner goes on, Court and Joe start talking about their favorite sports teams. They both love football and basketball, so they go on and on about predictions for draft picks and blah blah blah. It gives Curie and me a chance to huddle away.

Curie gives me a look over a glass of water. "You're crazy about him."

"Is it that obvious?"

"Maybe not to everyone, but I know you. You're in love."

I let out a shaky laugh. "People keep saying that. But it's too early."

"Says who? I knew Joe was it when I first laid eyes on him. Didn't you think that to go to bed with Court the night you met?"

I clear my throat. "That was then, and it's different now. I should give it more consideration if it's going to be a long-term thing."

She laughs incredulously. "What's a long-term relationship except people loving each other so much that they want to stay together as long as they can? I mean, it isn't like you're worried about whether he's rich enough or whatever."

"Of course not!" I bristle like a hedgehog.

"Thought so, because if you were, you wouldn't be my sister. If you love him, you love him. This isn't a math test."

I know it isn't. And that's why it's hard. I can't check my answers, and no matter how sure I am, I could be wrong. I've been wrong before—most recently about Dad. And he was about as much of a sure thing as I thought possible. I assumed he would support me. But he didn't. He still hasn't congratulated me on my new job, and I know he's seen my group text. His silence hurts.

My eyes find their way to Court. The ache in my heart lessens, and I feel whole and happy. Even as my head says it's too early for me to be sure, my heart says that isn't true.

I am in love with Court.

38

PASCAL

I'M SUPER BUSY FOR THE NEXT COUPLE OF DAYS. CURIE SAYS I need new clothes, and I agree. Need something fresh to start off my new job right. So we go shopping Friday and Saturday, and I find a few nice tops, skirts and slacks. And shoes. Curie has a finely calibrated shoe radar, and now I'm a proud owner of two new pairs of the cutest sandals that are also suitable for the office.

Of course, that means I'm neglecting Court a bit. But I don't think it's that bad. He hasn't complained, and even if I'm in love with the man, I don't want to be the kind of girlfriend who has to spend every waking moment with her guy, like a squid with extra-strong tentacles.

Saturday evening, and Court is driving me to my family dinner and another round of celebration, this time with my dad there. He still hasn't said congrats, although I'm certain he's seen my text. I wonder what he's going to say to me in person. It's not like he can ignore me. Maybe he's feeling a little regretful about my quitting. Bet he never thought I'd get a new job with more responsibilities and better pay. *And my very own office, which I didn't have at SFG.* I can't wait to share.

I eye the champagne in my lap. "You sure about this?" I ask Court.

"You deserve nothing less than Dom."

"Isn't this your brother's, though?" I figured out recently that the wine and other pricey alcohol were something Tony left behind.

"He probably forgot it was in the back of the cellar. Ah well." Court shrugs. "Finders drinkers."

I laugh and quit protesting. Most likely Court's right. Or maybe Tony just doesn't care. Either way, I'd like to have a premium bubbly to toast with. I want this to be as special as possible.

We park and walk toward my parents' home together. A pleasantly warm breeze rustles the trees around us. Court's grin is so wide that even my cheeks are hurting.

"What are you so happy about?" I tease. "Is it really that much of a relief that you don't have to be my sugar daddy?"

"Hahaha! I wouldn't mind. But I'm feeling a bit smug because I know Steve's going to be eating a nice, big slice of juicy crow pie."

I smother a laugh. "Well. Yeah. I'm half relieved and half unhappy. I wish it didn't have to come to this." I grow sober. "All he had to do was give me the credit I deserve."

And he still hasn't. Maybe he's been super busy, but part of me is petty and resentful that he's ignoring me.

Court links our fingers. "He wasn't going to do that until you did things his way. And I know something about controlling parents. My dad has been pressuring me forever to be part of Blackwood Energy, even though he knows it isn't what I want. He's used everything at his disposal. Thank God he doesn't have the money angle to use anymore."

And his mother's been pushing him to cater to his father's whims for her benefit. Suddenly I feel bad about complaining. At least my mom's supportive.

He adds, "I think it's gutsy you stood up for yourself against Steve and quit. Not everyone would have done that."

"Thanks."

When I open the door, Nijinsky is the first to greet us with loud, high-pitched barks. Her fine fur quivers every time she yelps. Court scratches behind Nijinsky's ears with a soft smile.

"You're here!" Mom says, coming out with an apron on. "Oh, honey, congratulations! I'm so *happy* for you." She kisses my cheek. "Hello, Court. So good to see you again!"

"Hey, Esther." He grins.

"Come in, come in. Curie and Joe just got here."

We go to the living room and say hi. Then I start toward the kitchen to keep the champagne chilled for later. Curie notes the label and lets out a small shriek. "Is that Dom Perignon?"

I flush with pleasure tinged with a teeny bit of embarrassment at the lavish way Court is trying to celebrate with my family. "Yeah."

"Wow." Curie turns to Court. "Great choice."

"Only the best for my girl." The words slip out easily, and my face heats some more. He winks at me.

"Where's Dad?" I say. He isn't always down here when we arrive, but surely he heard us come in. Part of me wonders if he's planning on staying "busy" and skipping dinner to avoid acknowledging my text.

"In his office," Mom says, then turns to Court. "We're having pot roast again. It's Pascal's favorite," she says, her tone slightly apologetic.

"Awesome! I love your pot roast."

That earns him a motherly smile and twinkle. I go over to Court and hold his hand. "I think Mom loves you," I whisper into his ear. "She never worried about what my exes thought about a Saturday dinner menu."

He kisses the back of my hand. "Only an idiot would complain about a great home-cooked meal. And I love her too. I love it that she's so supportive of you."

Warmth swells inside me, and I wish we could be alone so I could show him how much that means to me.

Dad finally shows up, clumping down the stairs. His steps seem heavier than usual—or is it just my smug imagination?

His University of Chicago shirt hangs loosely around his lanky shoulders. The sight sends a pang through me. He bought it when I got accepted, saying he wanted to show off how smart his girl was. But that didn't last long, did it?

I'm not the only one who notices the shirt, judging by the tight pursing of Mom's mouth or the faint disapproval crossing Curie's eyes before she looks away. Suddenly I'm pissed off. He doesn't get to wear that shirt after having sabotaged me for four years.

"Good. Everyone's here," Dad says casually, like he doesn't notice anything's off. "Pot roast smells incredible, sweetheart."

"Thanks." Mom's smile is a bit forced, tension around her lips.

"Hi, Dad," Curie and I say in unison.

"Hello, girls." Dad's face is impassive, and he isn't looking at anybody in particular. It's almost like he's avoiding making eye contact with anybody. "Welcome, Joe. Court."

I wait for Dad to say something more. Everyone else apparently does too, because they're all quiet. But he doesn't. And that cuts so deeply. It's like he simply refuses to accept good things happening to me because they aren't what *he* wants for me.

"Well, let's eat," Dad says, rubbing his hands together. "The food's ready, right?"

"Yes, and Court brought champagne to toast." Mom's voice is even, but that's not always a good sign. She grows calmer as she gets unhappier or more upset.

She leads us all into the dining room like a queen and her entourage, Joe carrying the pot roast, Curie with a tray of champagne flutes and Mom herself carrying the Dom. Instead of handing the bottle to Dad, she gives it to Court. "You do the honors."

Dad's glare hits Mom and Court. No sympathy from me, though. Mom wouldn't have dissed him if he hadn't done it to me first.

Court smiles. "Sure." He dexterously pops the cork. Curie places the flutes in front of him, and he pours for everyone. There's enough for six with careful portioning. But the petty side me thinks Dad doesn't deserve a sip of the premium champagne.

Everyone stands around the table. Mom looks at Dad expectantly. "Darling?"

This is his chance to redeem himself. And I so want him to say something nice, so I'm not disappointed any further.

We all pick up our flutes. He raises his and says, "To Pascal and her bright future."

Seriously? Would he kill him to say something about my new job?

Court is giving Dad a level, expressionless stare, and I place a hand on his arm. I don't want to get into a huge fight in front of everyone over what Dad said and did. Maybe later I'll confront him and get it out of the way.

The dinner starts once we're seated. Mom serves, although...is she giving Dad the smallest portion of pot roast? She certainly gives Court a plate piled with food.

Thankfully, the rest of the dinner proceeds normally. By that, I mean Court, Mom, Curie, Joe and I chat, while Dad eats silently with an intense focus. Maybe he needs some time to come to grips with the reality that his daughter has a mind and life of her own. But does it take this long?

Mom asks me about the interview, and I tell everyone all about it. I'm proud of how I never faltered throughout it all.

"How nice," Dad says finally. "Although it is surprising that Gavin interviewed you himself. And only the one round, rather than two or three."

I shoot him a sharp look. "Does that really matter?"

"I'm just saying that's generally how interviews go. If I didn't know better, I'd say somebody pulled some strings on your behalf." The smile he gives me is as sharp as a lance, and well aimed.

"Well, I don't know him at all," I say, furious he's trying to diminish my new job. "And I don't know anyone who'd stick his neck out for me like that."

Dad's gaze flicks to Court.

Court raises both hands, palms out. "I had nothing to do with Gavin's decision. If she didn't impress him, he wouldn't have hired her."

Dad lets out a grunt, and heat suffuses my cheeks. I grip my fork so tightly that my fist is shaking. This insult is really just too much. If he couldn't say anything nice, he shouldn't have said anything at all.

Court puts a soothing hand on my arm, his gaze back on Dad. "I know it's hard to admit when you're wrong, but you could at least be happy for your daughter's sake."

Dad puts down his utensils with a snap of his wrists. "Stay out of this, Court. I only want what's best for her."

"And that's what? Embarrassing me in front of everyone?" I say. "I'm not a child anymore, Dad. I know what's best for me, and I can make my own decisions."

"To waste your life doing something you aren't going to enjoy doing anyway? What are you going to do when you want to have children? Do you know that's the biggest reason women in our profession quit? They can't work the hours and still raise kids. It simply isn't possible. Better for you to go into something that won't get in the way of a family."

What the hell? Does he think this is what I need to hear right now?

I put my fork down, too pissed to continue eating. "Really? That's how it is? Well, maybe, just *maybe*, if you were more supportive of the women at SFG, they wouldn't feel like they had to quit their job to have children! Instead of playing into the stereotype, you could create initiatives to make SFG a great place for women. Be a pioneer. But no. Congratulations, Dad, for being part of the problem, not the solution."

"Show some respect, young lady," he says, his eyebrows pinching together ominously. "Especially when you're in my home."

"It's my home too!" I snap. "I shouldn't have to put up with your negativity when something good happens to me just because it isn't what you would've preferred."

He stares like I'm not making any sense. "This isn't about me!"

"It's *all* about you!" I stand. "My God. I can't even have a nice dinner." My voice is brittle, and tears prickle my eyes. I blink them away. I'll be damned if Dad is going to see me cry. I won't give him the satisfaction, no matter how angry and hurt I am.

Court stands. "You know what, Steve? Maybe we should go if you aren't happy to see us." His voice is cold and aloof.

"That's not what I meant. Don't get so worked up—"

"Then what *did* you mean?" Mom says, cutting Dad off before I can. "You made it clear you didn't care about her success. I told you to at least text her, but did you? No, you did not. You couldn't have been a little gracious? Do you have to make it sound like she only got the job because of her connection to Court, rather than on her own merit? I've never been more ashamed."

Curie is glaring at Dad balefully, and Joe looks let down by Dad's attitude.

Dad presses his lips tightly together. "I'm just looking out for my girl. And Court, I'm disappointed in you for fanning the flames rather than trying to calm Pascal down."

Rage coils in my muscles. Cutting words push up, up, up my chest and into my mouth, and I'm sure steam's coming out my ears right now.

Court squeezes my hand. "Well, Steve, this isn't my fire to put out. And why would I bother to fan the flames when you're doing a great job pouring oil all over it?" He turns to me. "You want to stay, or head home?"

Dad's gaze bores into me, willing me to stay put. But I'm done, even though I feel bad about not eating the rest of Mom's cooking, because I know she put a lot of effort into it. "*Home.*"

And I walk out of a family dinner for the first time in my life.

39

COURT

I FOLLOW SKITTLES OUT. THE BALMY AIR DOES ALMOST nothing to calm my fury. I didn't expect Steve to be overjoyed, but for him to be so blatantly hateful...

Fuck.

I want to rage, scream and throw things. But that won't solve anything. It certainly won't change Steve's mind.

We climb into my Maserati. I'm steaming, and so is Skittles. She doesn't need me for any anger fanning. She needs to forget her shitty dad and be happy she got what she wanted.

"You know, we should've asked your mom to pack us some of that pot roast before leaving." I need to break the tension somehow. "Now your dad's gonna get to enjoy it."

She snorts. "Ha. He's probably wearing some right now."

I laugh hard at the image, then link our fingers tighter as I drive down the residential road. "I'm sorry I didn't control my temper better, but he really pissed me off."

"It's okay. I felt the same way. Thanks for standing up for me."

I shrug it away. "Was he this infuriating three weeks ago?"

"Not this bad. Probably because he was smug about me being unemployed." Suddenly, she laughs.

I give her a funny look. Is this what happens when you're at point-of-no-return anger? "What's so funny?"

"Dad. He told me you were a perfect catch because you're young and rich."

"Hey, he isn't wrong. I'm a fantastic catch." Except I don't want those to be the only attributes she associates with me. "Besides, I'm not just young and rich. I'm also pretty nice. Good in bed, too. I bet none of your other boyfriends got paid after a one-night stand."

She giggles. "I thought you were mad I only left fifty bucks."

"That's all you had on you, so you basically paid me your entire fortune at that time."

She leans over and kisses me. "Thank you."

"For what?"

"Being wonderful and supportive."

I smile. I can't remember the last time a girl I was dating thanked me for anything. Now that I think about it, they just assumed they were entitled to everything I have because we were dating. And although Skittles is definitely entitled to everything I have, it's nice to not be taken for granted. "That's the prerogative of a billionaire. Supporting whoever you want."

"Yeah, but it got you on my dad's bad side. Trust me, he won't be thinking you're such a great catch after today."

Oh good. That means I'm not the regressive asshole he wants me to be. "Who cares? It isn't like he and I are going to get married. The only thing that matters is what you think of me."

I feel the weight of her gaze as we stop at a four-way intersection. I glance over, wondering if she'll say something. I know I love her, but does she reciprocate? Don't women usually feel it before men? At least that's what all those headlines on *Cosmo* covers make it sound like.

I let the car start to inch forward.

"Court, I—"

Something flashes in my peripheral vision. I slam on the brakes. "What the fuck!"

My heart racing, I glare at the car in the four-way intersection. It was my turn to go. I was here first!

The driver jumps out and Skittles groans. Tom Brockman, the belly-slithering scumbag. What the hell is he doing here?

I lower my window to give him a piece of my mind. "Hey, dumbass. You were supposed to stop."

"But you did, so it's fine," Tom says. "Look, I need to talk with Pascal."

Skittles coves her eyes.

"Then you should call like a normal human being," I say, still pissed.

"She blocked my number."

I snicker. "Yeah, because she's a normal human being who doesn't want to talk to bottom-sucking barracudas."

Tom ignores me and starts yelling like a lunatic. "Hey, Pascal, you thought about what I told you?"

"No. And why are you here? Are you stalking me?" She starts to reach for the door.

I put a hand on her arm. Getting out to talk is exactly what he wants. Staying inside gives a clear message:

One—he isn't worth the bother of climbing out of the vehicle.

Two—we have no intention of lingering to talk.

Unfortunately, Tom is a bit slow on the uptake. "No, but I know you have dinner with your folks every Saturday. I was waiting to talk to you."

More like an ambush.

He continues, "I'm telling you, you can screw with your dad, and I can make you famous too if you want. You can be the new picture of justice."

New picture of justice? By Tom's definition? I shudder.

"Justice, my ass!" Skittles says. "You mean the new picture of Dysfunctions R Us."

"You know your dad's guilty!"

What did Steve do? "What's he talking about?"

She rolls her eyes. "He thinks Dad's guilty of money laundering."

"Steve? Ha!" That's about as likely as me inventing a Star Trek transporter.

"Exactly. Dad has a lot of faults, but dishonesty isn't one of them. Doesn't matter, though, if the journalist is venal enough. Tom wants me to be his *source*."

Oooh... "And you turned him down, but he can't take no for answer."

"Stop trying to influence my source, Blackwood," Tom says.

"She doesn't want to be your anything, Brockman," I say. "And you know what? You stalking my girlfriend is seriously pissing me off."

His jaw drops. "She isn't your girlfriend."

"Yeah, she is."

"Yeah, I am," Skittles says. She smiles.

Tom glares at me. "Stay away from this, or I'll make you regret it."

"How? Got more trashy shit to say about my family?" I ask extra sweetly, even though I'm seething inside at the memory of what he did say, specifically to embarrass us and make money for himself. "My family tolerated your bullshit long enough. The next time—if there's a next time—will not end well for you."

Hands on his hips, he sticks his puny chest out. "I'm a journalist! I'm protected."

"I know. So I'm not going to punch you. That's beneath me"— I study my fingernails—"and I'll be damned if you get to get my money for pain and suffering and whatever bull crap you throw in my way. But what I can do is sue every publication that buys your articles."

His shoulders slouch a little. "You can't do that!"

"Sure I can. All I need to do is find the people you write about. They might not have the ability to sue you or the paper, but I do. All I got is money and free time."

"But...you can't do that!" Tom says as though by repeating it, he can convince me.

I smirk. "That's the beauty of being a billionaire—doing whatever the fuck I want. And you harassing my girlfriend really makes me want to ruin your career."

Tom turns to Skittles. "Tell him to stop being an ass. He's violating my First Amendment rights."

She shrugs. "I don't think it says thou shalt not be sued."

I snort-laugh.

"You've turned into a complete bitch!"

Maybe I *should* kick his ass. Nobody calls Skittles a bitch.

"No. I just know what I want, and what I want is never seeing your face again," she says, putting a hand on my arm.

"Hear that?" I say. "She doesn't want to see your ugly mug again. If you ever show your face or call her or even breathe too hard in her direction, I'm going to do exactly what I told you."

"You asshole! You think money makes you better than me, but you aren't that cool. You're just a punk with money, but guess what? Money doesn't buy you happiness!"

Skittles covers her face and groans. "What the hell did I ever see in him?" she mutters.

I pat her thigh. "It was before me, so I understand. You didn't have a good, objective measuring stick. Anyway..." I turn to Tom and raise my voice. "Poverty doesn't buy you happiness, either, Tom. So I guess we're even...except that when I'm lying in my bed, on my five-hundred-thread-count Egyptian organic cotton sheets and feeling depressed about all the happiness I can't buy, my girl here will be using hundred-dollar bills to wipe away my tears."

Tom's face turns redder than a baboon's ass. "You'll be sorry!" he cries, shaking his fist like some third-rate actor. For a writer, he sure has crappy comebacks. The sight is even more ludicrous, since his arms are about as thick as carpenter's nails.

Could a sinkhole open up underneath Tom's feet and suck him down into the magma, where he'll be stuck for eternity? Somebody should invent that technology.

He manages to walk safely back to his car, then peels out.

"I actually hope he tries," I say, watching Tom drive away, then starting toward the penthouse. "Then I'll show him I wasn't making an idle threat."

The look she gives is intense and scrutinizing. "You don't make empty threats, do you?"

"Nope. It's bad for the image." I grin, remembering what Tony told me. "Once you start making examples out of a few people, others will to get the hint and toe the line."

Her eyes shine, and she learns over and kisses me, licking my mouth.

I savor the moment, trying not to wreck the Maserati, before she pulls back. "What was that about?"

"You. Being sexy as hell." She runs her tongue along the seam of her mouth. "Tasty, too."

I groan as lust pounds through me. "Fuck. We can't do it in the car again, and especially not in your parents' neighborhood."

"Drive faster," she says, laughing.

40

PASCAL

ALTHOUGH THE DRIVE BACK TO COURT'S PLACE ISN'T TOO terrible—considering the traffic—it feels like an eternity. It's empowering to know I can affect him with just a kiss—a glance and words. Even though he appears generally down to earth and easygoing, he's more sophisticated and complicated than anybody I've ever dated. And the fact that he's shown a few glimpses of vulnerability touches me more than I can say.

I'm hyperaware of his scent, mixed with the subtle leather of the seats, and every flicker of emotion playing across his stunning face. The quick dart of his tongue as he licks his lips, a flash of white teeth, his hand brushing my arm...and the shivers that run through me. The desire that beats in my blood.

He parks recklessly, then jumps out. I dash out and rush to him, wrapping my arms and legs around his shoulders and waist. He cradles my ass and his mouth crushes mine. I kiss him with pent-up lust, devouring him. He molds my lips with his, glides his tongue against mine and nips at me, the sharp sensation sending a hot streak of need all the way to my core.

Oh my God. We might just do this in the garage. *Again.* I don't think I give a damn, though. Somehow when I'm with

Court, I become more reckless, more attuned to my most basic urges.

Court maneuvers us until we're inside an elevator. I feel the hard wall at my back and tighten my hold on him, losing myself in our kiss. I'm already wet, and my nipples rub and ache against my bra. He feels amazing, his hard cock pressing against me, his strong muscles bunching under my touch.

Somehow we're in the foyer, then inside the penthouse. The second the door closes, he pushes me against it, then shoves a hand under my flaring skirt without breaking the kiss. I tug at his pants, undoing the buckles and unzipping and pushing the whole thing down his legs along with his underwear.

I vaguely feel the lace rip, and Court's fingers running along my slick folds.

My entire body is quivering with emptiness. "Now," I demand, my voice low and thready with need.

He thrusts two of his long fingers into my pussy. I clench around them, but they aren't what I want. "No. Your cock."

His face is taut with barely restrained lust, but a grin pops onto it. "I love it when you talk dirty."

"Now, now, n—"

He drives into me, cutting me off with a kiss. I'm so wet that he glides in like a dream, the slick friction positively delicious. I feel like I'm melting, twining myself more tightly around him. The rapid thrusts stoke the heat in my belly until it burns with an incinerating intensity.

"You feel so good," he mumbles against my lips. "I want to do this forever."

"So do I. But after we come."

He laughs. "Greedy."

"Why shouldn't I be? You're mine." The words slip out, but he doesn't seem to notice as bliss twists the chiseled perfection of his face.

I cling to him as he pushes us harder and faster to a blinding climax. When the first orgasm hits me, it's like fireworks are going off in my body. The second one makes me feel like every strand of my hair has been set ablaze.

"Oh fuck, I can't hold back anymore." He grits his teeth.

He pulls out with a groan, and warm wetness hits my belly. I watch him come. His eyes lose all focus as the eyelids flutter downward. He's gorgeous—a masterpiece in rapture.

Then he's wrapping his arms around me like a vise, like he'll never let go. I let him hold me, loving the sensation of having him around me.

"Jesus. You've got me acting like a horny teenager," he says when his breathing settles a bit.

I grin. "The drive got me super hot and bothered, too." And it isn't just my sex drive that ramps up every time I'm around him. My shields drop. It's like I instinctively know I'm safe with him.

He kisses my forehead. "Move in with me."

That jerks me out of the postcoital haze. "Wait. Here?" I point my index finger down. "Like, *here?* Move in here? With you?"

He laughs. "I don't think you said 'here' enough."

Moving in together is the next natural step. I want to scream yes, but are we going too fast? We've known each other for a little over a month now—not counting the one-night stand.

On the other hand, Curie said I'd know when I met the right guy. And my heart says Court is the man.

Screw it.

"Okay," I say.

A huge smile breaks out on his face, as radiant and precious as sunlight after a dark afternoon storm.

"But it's going to take me a while to move everything, what with my job starting Monday. And my lease isn't up until the end of next month."

"That's not a problem. I can hire movers to start as soon as possible, and your place can stay empty until the lease runs out."

I shake my head. "No movers. I hate it when strangers paw though my things." Then I run my index finger along his biceps. "But you can help me move the heavy stuff and flex your manly muscles."

"Should I do it topless?" he asks with an easy grin.

"Goes without saying."

"Deal. We move your stuff together. Both topless."

I laugh. "We won't get any packing done."

"Welcome to the twenty-first century, Skittles. Equality for all." He stares lasciviously at my chest, reaching for my breasts with splayed and wriggling fingers.

Laughing and shrieking, I duck and run. All the while wanting him to catch me and knowing that he'll do just that.

41

PASCAL

AFTER A MORNING SHOWER ON MONDAY, I LET MY EYES roam over my collection of toiletries, sitting on the gorgeous marble double vanity in Court's master bathroom. They look like they fit right in, but at the same time, it does feel slightly surreal. I've never, ever moved in with a guy before. I've lived with a couple, but they moved into my place, not vice versa. I clung to that because I wanted to keep my independence and a home of my own.

But it doesn't make sense for Court give up his place for my apartment. It's so much smaller and not as nice. And where would we put the grand piano?

Since we only had a day, I still have a lot of my stuff at my place. But I brought most of my clothes and all my toiletries because...priorities.

I apply some pink lipstick to finish my makeup and lean back. I thought giving up my space might make me feel anxious, like something's missing in my life. But instead, it feels natural to share his space. I grin. Maybe it's because I'm falling for him. I've never felt this intensely for any of my exes.

But enough sentiment. Today's the first day at my new job, and I want to be on top of things.

I put on a beige scoop-neck top, purple skirt and nude pumps, then go downstairs. Court hands me a spoon. "Greek yogurt and fruit for you, and a bowl of cereal for me."

I take it automatically, then give him a strange look. "How did you know I like Greek yogurt?"

"Because I peeked inside your fridge yesterday. You had ten of them."

Huh. I thought he opened it to grab a beer, which, in my defense, he did. And then guzzled it down.

I devour the yogurt quickly, wanting to get an early start. Court also hands me my coffee in a tumbler. Smiling at his thoughtfulness, I give him a kiss. "You're awfully domestic this morning."

"Just like to be helpful. Have a great day. You're going to kill it."

Laughing, I hurry to the garage and start toward OWM. One more reason to move in: Court's place is closer to the office than mine.

The drive is sweet, despite the crappy L.A. traffic. I already filled out the tax forms and other paperwork for new employees online so I could get started right away. Gavin hiring me is just the beginning. I want to prove myself as soon as possible. Thanks to my dad refusing to give me credit I deserve, I'm at least a year behind on my career track, even with the promotion Gavin gave me. I don't know if I can make up for that, but I have to at least try.

When I walk into the office, the same sharply dressed receptionist with dark hair I saw before greets me. "Hello, Pascal. Welcome to OWM. I'm Sally. Here's your temporary badge."

"Thank you," I say, putting it around my neck. Man, it feels so official—a new job, a new Pascal.

"After ten, the security people will be available to take your photo and make you a permanent one. If you can get it done before five, that will be fine. You'll be reporting to Pete Monroe. His office is over there in that corner." She gestures to my right, then lowers her voice. "He's smart and super cute. But totally taken, darn it."

I grin. It's nice how's she's trying to warn me. "Thanks. But I'm taken, too."

I make my way to Pete's office. It's smaller than Gavin's, but quite nicely decorated. It's ergonomic like Gavin's, but has a softer edge. Maybe he inherited the space from some female executive.

Pete is dark-haired and bright-eyed. He doesn't seem that much older than me, but he's already a level higher. I'm sure Sally's right about him being smart. Gavin didn't build OWM and its sterling reputation by employing fools.

"Hi. I'm Pascal Snyder. I heard you're expecting me?"

He looks up from his laptop. "Hi." He stands and walks around his desk, extending a hand. "Pete Monroe. Nice to meet you." He eyes my purse and the coffee tumbler. "Have you been to your office yet?"

I shake my head with a small smile, slightly embarrassed that it never even occurred to me in my excitement. "I don't even know where it is."

"Tsk. Sally should've shown you." He sighs. "She can be absent-minded at times. Anyway, it's two doors down. We don't do cubicles at OWM."

"I noticed." I haven't seen any, except for the ones for admins and receptionists.

"But since Sally knows you're here, IT's going to bring your laptop in the next ten minutes, and when they do, I want you to work on the documents and projections I sent to your work email this morning, along with some models."

Excitement suffuses me. Hitting the ground running is exactly what I need and want. "Sure."

"As for the welcome lunch, it needs to be next week or something. Hilary will let us know. Gavin wants to come, and that means some schedule juggling."

"Oh." That surprises me. Dad never attended those welcome events at SFG. "Are there a lot of new hires?"

"Nope. Just you and someone else we need to make a decision

on. Gavin doesn't come all the time, but you're his hire, so..." He shrugs with a smile.

The hint of humor in his eyes lessens my anxiety. I thought for a second maybe Pete resented that he wasn't part of the interview process, since he's the one who has to work with me.

"If you need help with your assignment, feel free to ask. We have a vested interest in your success. After all, it's also our success."

I smile warmly, glad to hear that he cares that I do well here. It might just be something he says to every new hire, but it's nicer than my dad's dismissiveness. "Thanks."

I go to the empty office Pete shows me. It's pretty basic—white walls, a few shelves and a desk—but I don't care. I take my seat. The chair is to die for, molding to my back and butt to give me the ultimate comfort and support. I run a hand along the edge of my desk, thrills tingling up my arm. Wow. I feel like I could soar into space right now.

As soon as I put my purse away in a desk drawer, the IT guy Pete mentioned shows up and gives me my laptop, corporate ID and password.

Only four emails pop up on my inbox, which is...surprising. Most companies have hundreds of emails flying back and forth—in a huge list for everyone, then sub-lists segmented by interest, region, industry and whatever subcommittees you're on. I'm actually glad. I disliked wasting so much time sorting through them to find the ones that I actually needed.

Since Pete's assignment is waiting for me, I start on that immediately, determined to do a good job. The first impression is critical. I don't want Gavin or Pete to think I'm a mistake.

Lots of numbers, complex models. Whoever worked on them thought of almost everything. But...

I drum my fingers as the models dump out numbers and projections. I don't really like the recommendations. They all indicate *buy*, but my gut says *sell*. It's the qualitative data that make me uncertain.

Do you really want to challenge the models Pete is giving you on your first day?

Obviously not if they're fine, but...they aren't. I don't want to put my name on a memo with something I don't believe in.

On the other hand, what if Pete's the one who actually made the models? Will his ego be able to handle a challenge? Especially one from a woman?

Ugh. This is so complicated. I hope it isn't some kind of test.

In the end, I decide that all I can do is say what I think. I type up a memo, listing both the model-based recommendations and my own feelings about them. Then I email it to Pete and lean back in my seat, anxiety coiling like a snake in my gut.

It's already a little after one. I got so wrapped up in the work that I didn't realize how much time was passing. I run to a shop a block away from the office and grab a quick sandwich and chips. I'm not really hungry, but if I don't eat, my blood sugar is going to crash.

Back at my desk, I'm finishing the food and wadding up the waxy paper when Pete knocks on my door.

"Hey," he says. "Got a minute?"

Shit. Is he already done reading my memo? Gotta stay cool. He might've not *totally* hated it. "Sure." I toss the paper ball into the wastebasket and take a quick sip of coffee. "What's up?"

"I got your memo." He takes a seat on the other side of my desk and props his ankle on his knee. "You don't agree with the models we've created?"

I watch his face, but it's like trying to read a frying pan. *See? Should've just agreed with the models.*

I clear my throat, pretending a layer of slick sweat isn't coating my palms. "Models are fine, but at the end of the day, they're just tools that require human judgment. My judgment says we should modify the recommendations a little."

Pete arches an eyebrow, then gestures for me to continue.

He's going to fire me. I have to convince him I'm right. "The models didn't account for qualitative data. Which is to be expected, since you can't really capture that sort of factor with numbers."

Without criticizing the beloved models! my brain screams frantically. I go into a rather involved explanation of the qualitative data I discovered, the things I did to try to incorporate them into the calculations, but how they were insufficient.

Throughout it all, Pete looks at me, his face frustratingly impassive, although he's listening intently, his torso angled slightly forward.

"Anyway, does that clear things up?" *Say yes, say yes, say yes.* I don't know what I'll do if he says no in some passive-aggressive way and wants me to go into it more. Some of the VPs at SFG did exactly that with people they disagreed with.

"Yeah. I'm just surprised you wrapped it so quickly and that you actually saw beyond the numbers. When I read your résumé, I thought you were a math geek, and that's what got Gavin interested."

I let myself relax, just a bit. "I like numbers, but the market's made up of emotions, too."

Pete grins. "Precisely. I'm glad we're in agreement. Your conclusion matches mine. Good job, Pascal."

Relief rushes through me, pushing the tension away from my neck and shoulders. "Thank you."

"Seriously, I don't know where Gavin finds his talent, but he sure is quick to snatch it up," he says quietly, a hint of awe in his tone. "We're having a happy hour tomorrow to welcome you to the team, separate from the lunch Gavin's coming to. You okay with that?"

I grin. "Of course."

"Awesome. See you at the meeting."

"Meeting?" I ask blankly.

He laughs. "Check your email for your weekly agenda. It should hit your inbox every Monday morning at nine."

Argh! I haven't checked anything since I grabbed Pete's assignment. "Do I need to prep something?"

"Nope. It's your first day, so just introduce yourself and listen." He stands. "You'll do very well here."

42

COURT

ALTHOUGH I MISS SKITTLES, I TRY NOT TO TEXT OR CALL her. She's busy, and this is her first day. I don't want to get her into trouble by distracting her.

I check my emails. To be honest, I don't know why they're called emails. More like electronic rabbits. I swear every night they fuck and dump ten million more babies in my inbox.

Percy. Ugh. I forward it to my lawyer to deal with. Dad asking me when I'm going to be home. Of course, he didn't write it. That's not how he works. His assistant did, dutifully, just like every quarter. She follows up after exactly seven days if I don't respond. A few emails from charitable foundations, most of which I'm not interested in because I don't know or trust the people in charge. A lot of them are just in it to enrich the founders and administrative teams.

But one from the Pryce Family Foundation catches my attention, and I read it with care. The Pryce Family Foundation is one of a few charities I know that spends most of its money on helping people. It probably doesn't hurt that Elizabeth King, who is in charge, is an heiress who married well, and refuses to draw a salary or charge expenses. She's one of the very few who genuinely wants to change the world for the better.

The email is an invitation to be "sold" at a bachelor auction to raise money for a local pediatric oncology department. Some of the money is for research, but she wants to spend most of it on financial help for the families. The letter contains stories of the struggles the kids' parents face, and how every little bit can help stoke the children's determination and hope to get better. She also has some statistics, but it's the kids that sell me. I won't participate in the auction, since I'm already taken, but there's no way I'm not going to help out financially.

I start typing a response, then stop when the phone rings. My heart leaps.

But it's just Edgar. And I remember that it's about that time for his obligatory call.

"Hey, man," I say.

"Hello, Court. How are you?"

"I'm good." *Huh. What's up with his voice?* "Is Dad there?"

"No. Why?"

"You sound like you've got a larger-than-usual stick up your ass."

"What, I can't ask my younger brother how he's doing?"

I snort. "Not in that weirdly hushed, dignified tone. But since you're asking and Dad isn't around, yeah, I'm doing great. My girlfriend moved in with me."

"Congrats. Is this Ms. Fifty Dollars?"

I swear. Fifty dollars of Skittles. My family and friends may never let it go. "Yes."

"Guess she decided you're worth more than that."

"You know, fifty was all she had on her. She gave me her entire fortune at that moment." It really is a good line.

Edgar laughs. "If that's how you want to explain it."

"You know it's true because she moved in with me, even after meeting Mom."

"Hey now. You came to Tempérane and didn't stop by to see me?" He sounds peeved.

"No, no. She came here."

"*What?* When?"

"Last week. It was fucking weird. It's like she thinks I can stop the divorce. She must've been desperate because I wasn't coming to Tempérane to play my part in her 'hospitalization' dramas."

Edgar curses. "I didn't know she'd do that or I would've warned you. It had to be a last-ditch effort. I guess nobody told you, but the divorce was finalized today."

"Oh." I don't really know what to say or even think. It isn't like I didn't know it was coming. But it sure as hell feels different than I imagined it would.

Before, I thought it was simply a case of just desserts—what Mom deserved for doing her best to ruin Tony and Ivy's lives. She wasn't even sorry about the whole thing. And I was too bitter and pissed off when she said that she never loved me, not really. But now, I'm just sad and disappointed, for her and for all of us. It didn't have to be like this in my family. We could've been happy. Mom could've been gentler and nicer, and we could've been...a real family.

Finally, I exhale shakily. "Did she get anything?" She's always worried about that—getting what she "deserves." Her social standing, her reputation and influence—they all matter to her a great deal.

"The house in New Orleans. And her jewelry, except for the family heirloom pieces. But that's it."

Damn. I doubt Mom's lawyer is a dimwit, because she doesn't like dimwits. "Dad got his money's worth out of Percy."

"Yeah, the man's a fantastic attack dog, if you need one." Edgar pauses for a second. When I don't say anything more about the divorce, he says, "So. You want to work to for Blackwood Energy?"

Aaand there it is. "No. Tell Dad to stop making you ask."

"I did, but he won't take no for an answer. But listen, even if you don't want to work for Dad, you need to think about your future, especially if you're getting into a serious relationship."

I sigh. "What is it you're trying to say? Just spit it out."

"Nothing. Just that it sounds like you and Ms. Fifty Bucks are getting serious, and that means you need to get off your butt and start thinking about what you're going to do with your life. Women don't respect men who sit around and have no direction.

They think men like that are wasting their lives away without accomplishing anything. Which, you know, they kind of are—"

"How the hell would you know?" Edgar, despite being much older than me, hasn't had a single serious relationship. "Besides, I don't need to work to make a living. I'm already rich."

"Oh, I'm sure you can find someone who'll be happy with your money. But she still won't respect *you*."

Acid floods my gut. There's no love without respect. Is that why Skittles said that there's no way whatever she's feeling for me can be love? "Are you saying this to get me to join the company?" I say, hating the anxiety slowly rearing its head.

"No. I accept your decision, even if Dad doesn't. What I'm saying is, you should find a passion—one other than your new girl, I mean." He sighs. "Everyone needs something that fulfills them, independent of their family or the people they love. Otherwise, you know, lives tend to start going off the rails."

I say nothing because I can't refute his point. The acid in my belly lingers long after we hang up.

43

COURT

SKITTLES IS GLOWING SO BRIGHTLY WHEN SHE WALKS IN that it's almost like there's a halo and rainbow over her head. She makes a couple of spins, then wraps her arms around me. "Honey, I'm home!"

I kiss her. "Welcome home, happy girl."

"I *am* happy. The work was *amazing*. My new boss is *great*."

She gushes about this Pete guy while flipping through the takeout menus, stopping on Thai food. "Want to split some prawns in tamarind sauce? I'm starving."

"Sure, but if you're hungry, you should get more than the prawns."

"Don't worry. I'm also going to order green chicken curry and steamed rice."

"Didn't your super-awesome boss feed you?"

"Nope. Too busy working."

I place an order, grab a couple glasses of wine for us and listen to her chat about her new coworkers, her new office and the people she met today. Excitement bubbles within her, as bright and light as champagne fizzing. *I could get drunk off it,* I think, reaching over to take her hand in mine and trace the lines on her palm.

When the food arrives, I sign for it, then bring it to the dining table. She suddenly stops talking, flushing deeply. "I can't believe I've been going on and on about my job." She takes a chair. "Sorry. Tell me about your day."

"Nothing that exciting." I divvy up our food on the disposable plates the Thai restaurant included. Then, very casually, I tell her about Edgar's call—about Mom and Dad only.

Skittles' face softens, and she squeezes my shoulder. "I'm sorry to hear about your parents. I read the articles, but I thought maybe they'd reconcile."

"Yeah, things are a little bit beyond that point now." And saying it out loud lessens the sadness I felt earlier, as though it's one of the steps in accepting the messiness of my family. I give her an extra prawn, since she said she was hungry.

"You can have it," she says.

"You've been burning calories, working that cute little butt off."

"Ha. I was *on* my butt all day."

I steal a piece of chicken from her curry. Chicken for a prawn isn't the best trade, but I'm a magnanimous guy. We eat in silence for a moment. Skittles must be really hungry, because she's scarfing hers down with gusto. Didn't they let her have lunch? Geez. Or maybe she has a great appetite since all her worries about her career are on hold now with the position at OWM.

Then, since the second part of what Edgar said today has been lingering on my mind, I say, "Hey, what do you think I'm good at?"

She licks the curry on her fork. "I dunno. Why?"

"I'm looking for something to do, but I'm not sure what." *Tell me I'm good at everything.* But not like in that annoying pat way people say, "You're good at anything you put your mind to," when they want to throw out a quick feel-good answer so they can stop thinking about your problem.

Most importantly, I want to know what Skittles thinks about *me*. For the first time in forever, I want a girl I'm with not just to like me, but to respect me as well—my talent, my brain, my abilities.

Skittles taps her plastic fork against the edge of her plate. "I think you're good at a lot of things, but the one I like the most is that you're really good at making people happy and comfortable."

I blink a couple of times. "That's it?" I was hoping she'd say something...I don't know...more interesting.

"I'm not saying you can't do other things. I honestly think it's an amazing talent, because not everyone has it, you know? You're really just...*likable*, and you care about people."

Yeah, that's dubious as hell. Like the shit someone would say to appease a useless idiot.

She apparently reads my thoughts, because she starts worrying her lip. "That's what makes you such a great guy," she says. "You remember that time in Maui when I told you my dad was going to poison you and asked for a waiver? It was a joke and all, but you wrote one and didn't even have to think about picking the Make-A-Wish Foundation as the charity would get all your money. I thought it said a lot about you."

"Oh," I say, slightly mollified. "Still, that doesn't seem like much of a skill. 'I'm a likable dude who can make people happy' isn't something you can feature prominently in a résumé or anything. Is it?"

"It's not like you need a job!" Then she pauses and leans closer. "Do you?"

I stiffen, vaguely insulted. "Of course not. I'm not dumb enough to have blown my entire fortune already."

"You know that isn't what I meant. The world needs more happiness, and you have the money and connections to make a difference. And unlike some people, you actually do care." She lets out a short breath. "Not everyone needs a job. Some people should just go out and change the world. I have faith that you'll find a perfect way to do that."

The sincerity in her tone touches the core of my heart. A tide of emotions floods me until I can't find the words to get past it. Finally, I let out a shuddering breath. "It's you who do that for me —make me happy and whole. I wouldn't be the guy who makes people happy without you around."

Shaking her head, she reaches out and holds my hand. "You need to give yourself more credit. If you weren't a good, decent guy deep inside, you would've stayed the not-good guy, no matter who you were with. People don't change just because they're around someone."

That's incredibly sweet and loving of her, and I don't correct her even though she isn't entirely right. She makes me want to be better. She makes me want to change the world for her.

"You don't look convinced," she says. "Let me give you an example that's easier to understand. Let's say I was frigid."

"*Frigid?*" I still have the indentations from her nails last night. And I need to see a doctor to check my ears, because boy does she scream. Not that I mind especially. "No pain, no gain" and all that.

A well-manicured finger goes up to halt my less-than-cooperative thinking process. "It's a hypothetical. Let's just go with it, shall we?"

"Okay. You're more frigid than tits on a yeti. And?"

"What I'm saying is, if I were a naturally frigid person, I'd stay frigid no matter who I was with."

"Whatever. I'd change you."

"No, you wouldn't have unless I were a sensual person deep inside. Contrary to male fantasy, no man has a magic penis that cures all female sexual dysfunctions."

"I never said *all* female sexual dysfunctions," I say, although I did have this particular expectation at one point in my life. "Just *yours*." I point my fork in her direction.

She cocks an eyebrow. "Oh yeah?" Her gaze drops below the tabletop to the V between my legs. "You're the magic man, huh?"

"You thought last night was pretty magical." I smirk. "And not just down there. You said my tongue was magical too."

"Don't recall that. I was distracted, thinking about my new job," she says in a prim, teasing tone.

"Then maybe I should prove it to you again when you aren't distracted about your new job."

Her eyes are bright with humor. And a spark of excitement. "Maybe you should, although I don't know how you can top your claimed super-ultra-magical effort last night."

"Leave that part to me, oh ye skeptic."

44

Court

On Thursday, when Nate calls me to have lunch at Virgo—plus it being his treat—I know something's up.

Virgo is a luxurious new Spanish bistro Mark Pryce—the guy who owns both La Mer and Éternité—opened a few months ago. Virgo is supposedly less exclusive, but everyone who can't get a table at La Mer or Éternité comes, so it's crowded anyway.

"What do you want?" I ask the moment I park my ass opposite Nate at a table.

"Geez, man. I gotta want something to ask you to lunch?" he says.

"Normally no, but you're drinking." Amber color. Must be scotch, his choice of poison when he's happy or upset. "And you look grim."

His mouth forms a curve that could be called a smile if you're stretching the definition the way high-priced lawyers twist the Constitution. "No I don't."

"Yeah, you do. You've got these deep parentheses around your mouth."

Scowling, he checks his reflection in the faceted mirrored

wall behind him. "I'll have you know those are called nasolabial folds."

"You actually know what they're called?"

"How can I forget? Georgette accused me of dumping her for having them. Apparently they're a sign of aging." He rolls his eyes and sighs.

I wince in sympathy. She's a third-tier socialite psycho stalker who set her gold-digging sights on Nate. She decided she wanted to be Mrs. Sterling, no matter what it took. Not that I can blame the social-climbing, materialistic bitch. Nate's family is one of the richest on the planet. Plus she wasn't totally crazy, because she wisely understood that Nate would be easier to approach than his older brother, Justin. Unfortunately for Nate, he didn't realize what was going on and slept with her. Later he figured out she was nuts and tossed her away with the enthusiasm of an Olympic hammer thrower.

When our server comes by, I ask for a mini paella and sparkling lemonade. The drink arrives almost instantly.

"And she's back," Nate says.

"Who?"

"*Georgette.*"

"I thought she was in rehab."

"Not anymore. She says she's clean, and she wants me back."

I almost spew the lemonade. "Didn't you break up, like"—I have to think—"a *year* ago? And wasn't it pretty bad? She tried to brain you with a vase, right?"

"She says she made herself over and is now *clean and worthy of me.*"

My jaw slackens. "Did you see her?"

A couple of jerky nods. "She barged into the medical center yesterday. It was the most awkward shit ever."

"Did she fix her crazy?"

"No, but she did make herself over. I almost didn't recognize her from all the plastic surgery."

Damn. "Bigger tits and ass?" She has a pretty face, but, as I recall, could use some help with her body.

"No. I mean, yeah, that. But her face, too. Her nose and mouth and chin. Jaw line. Enough fillers and Botox to turn her facial muscles into plastic. It's like she cut out the best features of my favorite actresses and glued them onto her face. They look hideous together." Shuddering, Nate knocks back his scotch. "Fuckin' Frankenstalker."

I shudder too. "I know it sucks, but just ignore her. She'll go away."

"She won't. Can you ask Pascal to bid on me at Elizabeth's bachelor auction?"

I stare at him like he's lost his mind. He probably did after having seen Georgette. "Why bother with the auction? Just give Elizabeth money for the cause she's trying to champion with this. Problem solved."

"Can't. I owe her one. She wants a lot of publicity to raise as much as possible, and I already said yes."

"Then swap with her 'assistant.' You know, that Russian dude who looks like an ax murderer." He probably is an ax murderer, not that I'd ever say that to anybody because that man is creepy. I met him once when I went to the Pryce Family Foundation office to see Ivy, and I don't ever want to again, especially in a dark alley.

"Tolyan?" Nate's eyes bug out. "She wants good publicity, not a horror movie."

"Okay, you have a point. How about Yuna? She has the money to bid on you."

"She turned me down. Said if she wins me, her mom's going to send us ten thousand china patterns she's been saving and start planning a wedding." Nate's face scrunches as though he's bit into a slice of lemon. "I like her, but I'm not marrying her, and I certainly don't want the Hae Min Group after me. Barron will murder me."

True enough. His grand-uncle is old-fashioned about certain things. "Don't you know any other women?"

"Lots. But they'd all want to turn it into something more. I could ask my assistant, but she says she doesn't want to because she's worried about what people might think." Nate looks vaguely insulted. "Like it matters what other people think. What she should be worried about is what *I* think of her performance."

This, I can help him with. "Fire her and get a new one who is willing to bid on you."

"Can't." He sighs, deflating a bit. "She's good at her job."

Our food arrives, interrupting his morose self-pity. When our server's gone, Nate says, "You know, I lent you my jet. This is the least you can do. All you have to do is give your candy girl the ticket to the event and tell her to bid on me. I don't care how high it goes; I'll cover everything. Anything to escape the psycho."

I take a bite of my paella. It's done to perfection. Then a solution occurs to me. "Dude! Just eat some bad shellfish and make yourself sick the day of the auction. Problem solved."

"Are you fucking crazy, too? I want to avoid an ex-girlfriend, not die."

Melodrama, thy name is Nate. "Fine. I'll ask, but don't expect Skittles to say yes. She loves me too much to betray me by bidding on you." Truth is, I don't want her bidding on him. Not even to bail him out because...well, damn it, she's mine.

"I'm sure everyone's going to know the score when you guys get married. Poor Nate, dumped like last week's garbage..."

The rest of his sarcastic retort fades behind a loud roaring in my head. *Married? Skittles and me?*

Normally when people mention marriage—and with me in the equation—my immediate reaction is to recoil. Then run, while my skin breaks out in hives. But...Skittles?

She'd look amazing in a wedding gown. More beautiful than Curie, really, even though they're twins, because Skittles just glows. I wonder what kind of flowers should go into her bouquet. Something gorgeous, bright and cheery, just like her.

At some point, when we're both ready, we can have babies. Maybe two, unless she only wants one. One's good, too. Actually, any number's fine with me. Wouldn't it be cool to have a chubby toddler who looks just like Skittles waddle toward me while saying, "Dada," with a baby smile?

Most definitely. And I'll get her an Aston Martin. A stroller, that is, since there won't be any driving for her until she's at least sixteen. And hire a bodyguard who looks scarier than Tolyan to keep the boys away...

"Hey, man. Court. Harcourt Blackwood! Did you hear anything I said?" Nate's voice shatters my pleasant fantasy.

"What?"

"I said, I need to know by tonight."

Impatient, aren't we? I haven't even proposed to Skittles. "Keep this up and you won't be my best man."

He squints at me. "Best man? I don't care about that. I'm talking about the bidding at the auction!"

Oh. Right. "I can ask, but listen, don't get your hopes up."

And later that evening, I tell Skittles very casually about Nate's ridiculous proposal during dinner. I also omit the part about the crazy ex, because Skittles doesn't need that kind of pressure.

Okay, the real reason is that I don't want her saying yes. If she's going to be bidding at the auction, it should be on *me*—not that she'll be able to, since I'm not going to be standing on the block like some side of beef.

But if not Skittles, then who...? Somebody from Craigslist? Probably not. Nate said he didn't want people getting any ideas.

I snap my fingers as the perfect solution occurs. *Tony's* assistant! So what if Wei's male—and heterosexual? Tony often says that Wei's greatest strength is his flexibility. He can do it, and he has zero desire to go anywhere with Nate, not even if it would mean getting his hands on the Sterling fortune.

"Sure, I'll do it," Skittles says.

"Okay, I'll tell Nate you can't..." My head snaps up. "What?"

"He's your friend, and he needs help. I'm willing."

"He doesn't need it that bad."

"Obviously he does if he asked you to ask me. Besides, I've never been to a bachelor auction before. It'll be fun."

"Fun?" When did "fun" change to include getting your heart punched repeatedly? She's supposed to say, "No way am I bidding on Nate, Court. You're the only man for me, even in pretend-world, no matter what."

"You can come along if you want." She giggles. "Besides, it isn't like I'm bidding my own money. I'll be bidding his money on him. Talk about incestuous." Then she rubs the spot between my eyebrows. "Stop frowning. I'm attracted to Nate like...I'm attracted to a catfish."

"A catfish?"

"Ever seen one? They aren't that pretty. I read that Japanese people don't even eat them. Can you imagine being a fish and being rejected by the Japanese? They eat blowfish. Sea urchins."

"Well, yeah. But you're American."

She giggles again. "Want me to demonstrate how I feel about you, Mr. Unhappy Pants?"

"Yes, I think that would be a good, mollifying start."

"Well, then." She puts both her hands on my cheeks and looks deeply into my eyes. "I'll do my best so you don't feel even a smidgeon of jealousy after I'm done." She lowers her lips until they touch mine. And spends the rest of the night proving her case.

45

PASCAL

THE NEXT TWO WEEKS GO BY PEACEFULLY. ACTUALLY, THAT isn't quite right. They go by perfectly. Happily. I love every moment of my job, and adore every moment I spend with Court at home.

Home.

I always thought I wouldn't feel comfortable calling a boyfriend's place "home." After all, it's his, not mine, even if we're sharing the space. Even in college, I never felt like the shared rooms at the dorm were *mine.* Maybe that's the real reason I always insisted on keeping my apartment. But with Court, it feels like home. Every time I walk in, I feel warm and happy. I can let my hair down, relax and just be myself with the man I love.

Perfection.

But at the same time, I wonder if we're on the same page. I can see us heading to the serious territory—the kind that comes with long-term commitment and maybe even a wedding, if we both decide that's what we want. But he's never even hinted he wants to take our relationship to the next level. As a matter of fact, he seems very content with things the way they are. I tap my fingers on my desk and stare at the wall, while my laptop crunches numbers for my projections on the KOSPI.

It isn't that I doubt he likes me. I know he does. But I want more than that. I want him to want to move in the same direction, toward the same goals, I do.

Stop being impatient and greedy, Pascal. One step at a time. You can't force an emotion on him.

Pressuring him would be the best way to repel him. Maybe I'm feeling anxious, because sometimes I could swear we're on the same wavelength when it comes to how we feel about each other.

He values your opinion and thoughts. Shouldn't that be enough for now?

It should be. I mean, he talks about what he's thinking about doing with his life, asks me what I think about some of the charity projects he finds interesting, and we even had a rousing debate about crude oil pricing in the commodities market, one that proved we could disagree without getting nasty about it.

No other man I dated ever took my input into consideration at the level he does. He wouldn't do that if he didn't feel something deep for me, right?

"Hey, Pascal, ready?" Pete says from the open door.

Startled, I check the time on the laptop. *Twelve already?*

It's taken almost three weeks since I started for OWM to hold my welcome lunch. Gavin's a busy man, and his boy wasn't feeling well, then his wife got sick, so he couldn't find any free time. Whatever spare moments he had, he spent at home. His family-man attitude makes him seem more human and likable, changing my perception of him from a cold-hearted, ultra-sharp fund manager to more of a genuine human being.

And it also makes me a tad sad, because it reminds me of how my dad used to be. He took off early from work when I broke my ankle once, just to cheer me up. It's hard to pinpoint when things changed. Or maybe he's always had the medieval outlook toward women, and I just didn't notice because I never wanted to. After all, nobody wants to acknowledge something like that about a person they love.

I gather my purse and leave with Pete and Gavin. Gavin's in

an exceptionally good mood. "Heard from Pete you're doing well," he says. "Damn, I'm good."

"You are?" I say.

"Hey, I hired you, didn't I?"

"Yes, you did." I have to laugh at Gavin's ego. Everyone at his level has it, but somehow his isn't overly obnoxious. It's the general good humor that comes through.

"Pete was skeptical."

Pete gives Gavin a "seriously?" look. "You have to tell her now? Besides, I'm always skeptical when somebody puts a new person on my team without any warning."

"Why?" Doesn't Pete trust Gavin's judgment?

"Because I never know if he's doing it to make me train them or not. He's done that quite a few times before."

Gavin clasps Pete's shoulder. "Only because I know you're good. But I bet you didn't do much training with Pascal."

"Nope." Pete grins.

I smile, thrilled that at OWM, people I report to will actually praise me and value my contribution. I can't think of a time that happened at SFG. That puts a damper on my mood, so I push it aside. *No gloominess. That's all in the past.* I don't have to deal with Dad as a boss, only as a parent. It's been an awkward transition, but I've slowly been working on it. I'm pretty sure it's same for him, too, because since that dinner where Court and I walked out, I haven't seen him.

More people from the office join us until we have twelve. We go to a restaurant Gavin chose—a steakhouse.

"What would you have done if Pascal didn't like red meat?" Pete jokes.

"They have great seafood and chicken. If not, there's always bread," Gavin says, then winks mischievously. "It's apparently gluten-free."

Another coworker from my floor teases Gavin for watching what he eats, and Gavin says he only does it because his wife wants him to stay svelte. I giggle. There's not an ounce of fat on the man.

"Your wife must be very pleased," I say.

"Oh, yeah." He preens.

The lunch starts with a toast to welcome me to OWM. It's relaxed. Nobody says a word about work or the markets. Gavin seems to know about everyone's personal life, asking after their significant others or kids by name. He turns to me. "You have a boyfriend, right?"

"Yup. I'm living with him," I say, not about to hide it like I might've at SFG.

"Great." Gavin's eyes twinkle. "Hope he's good to you."

"Very." I grin. "He's amazing."

"Tell him to keep it up," Pete says jokingly. "Happy homes make productive workers. I've become ten thousand times more productive after I started dating Brooke."

"You mean leave by six every evening like the lazy bum you are?" Gavin says with a mock scowl.

A woman next to me leans over, rolling her eyes at the men. "Don't mind them. They do this all the time. But Gavin doesn't care as long as you deliver results."

I smile. "Thanks. Good to know."

When the server clears our table of the main entrées, I make a quick run to the bathroom before dessert and heading back to the office. As I walk out of the bathroom and make my way to our table, I bump into Cristiano.

"Pascal! What a surprise."

"Hi, Cristiano. Good to see you," I say.

"I thought... Are you joining us late for lunch?"

Us?

He shifts, and I see Dad coming up behind him and freeze. The irony of seeing Dad at the restaurant where Gavin's hosting a lunch to welcome me into OWM is pretty intense.

"Actually, I'm with the people over there." I gesture, slightly uncomfortable. Cristiano has no reason to know I left, but I don't want it to look like Dad couldn't muster up loyalty from his own child. Regardless of our differences, SFG has provided for the family, and its workers are good.

Cristiano's narrow-eyed gaze sweeps them. "Is that Gavin Lloyd?" He sounds stunned. And utterly baffled.

Dad turns slightly red, and the lines around his eyes are tight as he smiles. "Pascal isn't with SFG anymore."

Cristiano stares at me. Guess I look like a traitor to go work for Dad's competitor. But I'll be damned if I feel bad about that.

I straighten my spine. "A better opportunity came up." The kind that doesn't require me to be regressive to suit my dad's antique outlook on how things should be.

"In that case, I'm happy for you," Cristiano says.

"Thank you, sir. So am I."

He nods at me and leaves. Dad gives me a hard stare. "You just had to stick that in there, didn't you?"

"Stick what?" I demand, unhappy that he's angry with me, when I tried to be as diplomatic as possible.

"About the better opportunity."

"What did you want me to say? It's the truth." It isn't my fault he blew it. All he had to do was give me the recognition I deserve.

"You sound so smug, but you shouldn't. Everyone knows you got the job at OWM because of your boyfriend. A hundred million can buy a lifetime of employment." He smirks a little, like he knows a secret nobody else does.

I start to dismiss him, but the number he quoted is too specific. "What are you talking about?"

"Court gave a hundred million dollars to Gavin. Well, he opened an account at OWM for that amount, but it's the same thing. More than enough to pay your salary and benefits for years to come."

"You're being ridiculous." He's only saying this because he's upset and the encounter with Cristiano embarrassed him.

"You weren't going to get an interview anywhere," Dad says. "You weren't promoted in four years, Pascal. People looked at your résumé and probably thought—geez, how crappy is she that not even her own father could stomach moving her up the ladder? You suspected that deep inside, didn't you? And I knew something was up when you got a job with Gavin. Do you know Gavin and Court know each other? Not directly, but through friends. They all hang out in the same circles. So the man you thought was supportive of you was really manipulating you the entire time. And you accused *me* of being dishonest."

I inhale sharply as what he's saying stabs into my heart like a knife. Pain starts, but mentally I put it into an iron box and put it away. I'm not letting Dad ruin the end of my welcome lunch. "You know what? I don't believe you. And I don't even understand why you're doing this when your whole end game is for me to marry Court."

"Because he isn't *going* to marry you. He's just playing around. He wants you to work and be independent"—he curls his lips in a smug line—"so that when he dumps you, he won't feel so bad. He hasn't said anything to you about a future together, has he?"

My mouth feels parched. Dad seems to know every vulnerable point I have and how to squeeze maximum pain from all of them. "I gotta go. My new coworkers are waiting."

Dad says nothing, but as I walk off, I can feel his stare boring into my back. Although I tell myself I shouldn't listen and let him ruin my day, I keep thinking about what he said about Court and his account at OWM. Maybe Dad's just unhappy Court didn't put his money with SFG. Or maybe Dad misunderstood Court opening a new account at OWM. Court could've had it since forever. Rich people have others take care of their money anyway. Or maybe it's as crass and simple as him being pissed off Court isn't doing what Dad wants—marry me, make me quit my job and pamper me like a princess or whatever Dad decides I deserve. Unlike my exes, Court says and does what he wants, and he's gone up against Dad to defend me. Dad has to know Court's been supportive of my choices.

Somehow I manage to get through the afternoon. Thank God. I begin to close all the apps and browser on my laptop to shut it down, then stop. Instead of stewing about what Dad said, I should just check it out. I can access the client list at OWM, after all.

My mouth dry, I pull up the internal database. As I type in Court's name, I start to feel silly. The search result is going to show I'm being paranoid. And I'm going to end up feeling like an idiot for even doing this.

But my fingers move on autopilot, and hit enter.

Harcourt Roderick Blackwood. Client since...

Pain sears my heart as though a needle has lanced it. Then my pulse accelerates, hot blood roaring through me like a swollen river breaking a dam. The date is exactly one day after I got the interview call from Hilary. It's etched into my memory because it brought such hope, relief and anxiety.

Come on, girl. It's probably a coincidence. Didn't he see a lawyer around that time? Maybe the attorney guy arranged this.

But the lawyer works for Court's father, and Court was pissed off about getting a letter from him.

I breathe in and out, forcing myself to go slow, reining in my thoughts. There's got to be a simple explanation for this. He could've joined because he got pissed off after seeing the lawyer and decided to put his money to work so he doesn't have to. Or maybe he got lazy about his finances until the news of my interview reminded him he needed to do something.

Or it could just be a coincidence. Just because one happens after another doesn't mean there's cause and effect. God, that's one of the first things you learn when you're doing analysis.

I shut down my laptop and shove it into my bag. Then, very deliberately, I stand and take a deep breath. *I'm just going to ask Court.* Not accusingly; I'll just bring it up. And whatever explanation he gives—no matter what my head says—I'll accept. Because that's what I owe him for being on my side.

46

PASCAL

THE DRIVE HOME SUCKS. DAMN TRAFFIC. PASCAL'S Twentieth-First Century Law: The more urgency there is, the worse the traffic.

On the other hand, maybe the extra time is good. It gives me a space to calm down, gather my thoughts and come up with a few good ways to approach the topic. I don't want to sound accusing and ruin what Court and I have between us. But how do I bring it up? Just ask point-blank? Maybe mention if he wants to have money there? Gently pry about how he's managing his fortune?

But what if that makes it sound like I'm overly interested in his bank balance? Ugh. That's so not what this is about.

When I finally walk through the door, I'm almost an hour late. Court looks up from his phone. "I was about to text you," he says with a smile, then gives me a kiss. "I was wondering if Gavin was making you work overtime."

"No, he hasn't asked me to do that yet." I clear my throat, relieved he's brought Gavin up first. That way it isn't too weird when I ask him about his relationship with OWM. Right?

Court starts to lead me toward the couch, but I put a hand on his arm to stop him. I don't think I can do this seated. There's too much restlessness inside me. "But if he is doing that, it's to make you more money," I say, watching him so closely that I can almost see individual pores on his face.

"Eh." Shrugging, he rubs the tip of his nose. "He doesn't have to make you work that hard."

Dread unfurls. Why isn't he meeting my eyes? "Why? Did he make you plenty already?" I say, keeping my tone teasing with effort. A huge lid is over the loud words welling in my chest. I promised myself I would trust him—believe him. He could be scratching his nose because it's itchy, not because he's trying to hide how much he's squirming inwardly.

"I don't know. Doubt it, though. It hasn't been that long. Besides, statements and invoices and stuff go to my accountant." He walks toward the couch alone and plops down.

"You don't check?" I ask, holding onto a glimmer of hope. Maybe he doesn't manage his money at all. His accountant does everything, and Court has no clue.

"Of course I check, and he lets me know what's going on, but it isn't necessary for me to micromanage."

My hope shatters like a glass rose. Now I have no choice. "Why did you open an account at Gavin's the day after Hilary called to set up an interview?"

Court's blue eyes flicker. "He's everyone's dream man for that sort of thing."

"But you didn't put your money with him until then."

"It isn't that much. Only a hundred million."

The same amount he said he'd put in at SFG to help me get promoted before I found out about Dad and quit. "Did that have anything to do with my getting a job at Omega Wealth Management?"

Thoughts cross his face like lightning. His tongue darts out to wet his lips, and he scratches a spot on his forehead, near his hairline. "Only partially."

The tremor starts from my chin and lips, then travels to my chest until my heart is aching and my stomach is churning. Even my knees feel weak, and I reach out and grip the back of couch. *You bought me a job there.*

He jumps to his feet. "No! Of course not. Don't be crazy. I'm not that stupid. Look, I met with Gavin, and he said OWM passed on you for something that you didn't do. It's your dad's fault you were stuck at the entry level for so long. Anyway, I convinced him to spare ten minutes. He countered with five because he's a difficult bastard, but he said he wasn't hiring you unless you're good." He stretches both arms toward me in a beseeching gesture. "And you *are* good. You dazzled him, and he had no choice but to give you an offer on the spot. Right? You went in and came out with a shiny new position. A *promoted* position! Do you think he would've done that if he thought you weren't any good?"

What he's saying makes sense in a way. My brain tells me it's very logically laid out. But the feeling of betrayal is still in my heart, and it stabs like a thorn, especially because what I thought I did on my own turned out to be anything but. I would've been nothing without him—a man to make the chance happen for me. Just like Dad had the power to help my career ambition...or not. "I wanted to do it on my own, without any special favors greasing the wheels for me. I thought I was good enough to do it, and it was so important for me to prove to myself, and to my dad in particular, that I'm damn good."

"And you are!"

"No, Court." I shove my fingers into my hair, feeling pissed off and pathetic. "I only got the job because of what you did."

He stares at me like I'm insane. "How the hell can you think that?"

"I ran into my dad today. Do you know how I felt when he told me about what you did?"

"You know he's out to trivialize your career accomplishments. He did that at dinner, remember?"

Of course, but the reminder only makes my heart feel more hollowed. "If what you did is truly innocent, why didn't you say something before?"

"It just didn't seem that important." He spreads his hands in a helpless gesture. "It honestly isn't that much money."

"You paid Gavin twenty million per minute to talk to me!" My voice is loud and sharp with frustration and anger. "You keep talking about how little the money is, like that's enough to undermine the point I'm trying to make and belittle my feelings and aspirations. Maybe my career looks ridiculous to you because I'm making chump change, but it's super important to me. Much more so now that I need to prove that I'm good, especially to myself." And to Dad. It's egotistical and it's stupid, but I feel what I feel, and there's nothing I can do to change that.

Most of all, what I fear is what he said in parting—about Court playing me. That he doesn't see a future with me. That he's been manipulating me. And him being dismissive about the money only makes me more unnerved, like what Dad said is true.

"But you *are* good! Gavin would've hired you even without my account, if only he'd had a chance to talk to you. And I didn't *give* him anything. He has to give everything back when I close the account."

I wasn't even going to answer his justification about how he didn't bribe Gavin, but... "You know, Gavin would've never hired me without your money because he wouldn't have interviewed me. So. You're wrong about that."

"He also wouldn't have hired you if you didn't impress him. And you did that all on your own." Court spreads his hands. "I'm not even sure why you're mad. Are you upset you're working for Gavin or are you mad because I didn't tell you?"

I hug myself. That's a damn good question. "A little bit of both. I just wish I'd known. It's my life, after all."

Court stares at me. "Aw, no, come on. Don't do that." He plucks a Kleenex from the table and moves closer.

Then I realize I'm crying. Damn it. I swipe at the tears with the backs of my hands, embarrassed and furious with myself. "I'm fine. Just something in my eyes." I lie worse than a three-year-old, but I hate crying in front of people. It's so humiliating and ridiculous. "I gotta go."

He jerks to a stop. "Go? Where?"

"I don't know. Somewhere. I need to...have some space and think. What I learned today just sucker-punched me."

I stumble out of the place...and into the waiting elevator. Once I'm in the garage, I run to my car. But in the Acura, seated behind the wheel, I realize I have nowhere to go. My apartment is empty now. And most of my furniture's gone, too—sold on Craigslist.

This is why you don't move in with a guy.

I heave a sigh, then drive toward the small house Curie and Joe share. That's the only place I can go anyway.

I pull up to the house, glowing with bright lights inside. It's pretty and perfect, just like my twin and her life. And she's going to move to an even prettier and more perfect place soon.

My car comes to a stop. I don't even know what I'm going to say. I just need to be around someone who's known me all my life and is going to understand where I'm coming from.

Moving with the slowness and deliberate care of a person who's been seriously injured, I get out of the car, walk toward her door and ring.

The door opens. Curie takes one look at my face, then hugs me hard.

"Sorry to come here like this," I say, sniffing.

"Sweetie, don't even think that," she says, pulling me inside.

The door shuts behind me.

47

COURT

I DON'T CANCEL MY FRIDAY NIGHT PLANS WITH NATE. Well, plans. Nate just called me out of the blue to go clubbing at Z. He said to bring Skittles, but I came alone, telling him she was busy.

That's why she hasn't called or texted since she left eight days ago, I tell myself, even though I texted her until my fingers were sore, and called her until I had to recharge my phone. I even drove to OWM like a lost puppy, but I couldn't make myself go in to confront her. I didn't want people to hear us argue and realize I opened an account there to get her an interview. Not because Gavin and I had any kind of illicit deal, but because I don't want it to affect Skittles' image there. Reputation matters.

But I still stand by my point that I didn't do anything wrong, so what the hell. Okay, so maybe I should've told her about the talk I had with Gavin, but he would've never hired her unless she deserved the job, so it's a wash. Besides, I had other things on my mind. Like her saying how it couldn't be love. So technically it was her fault for distracting me.

Okay, maybe not really her fault, because she didn't know I

can speak Klingon. Or that I have real feelings for her. Feelings that are a mixture of adoration, respect, love and so much more.

But sitting in the VIP lounge isn't the same without Skittles dancing somewhere in the club like before. I almost feel like I can sense her down there, except she isn't there.

"Hey, what else do you think I can add?" Nate's sudden question interrupts my brooding.

"What?"

He sighs, clearly annoyed. "Didn't you listen? Every bachelor needs to submit a date plan for Elizabeth's auction. So I'm saying flying to Las Vegas on my private jet and having a drunken orgy. But I wonder if there's something else I can add to make it sound *really* disgusting."

"Mud wrestling?" I suggest, my voice full of the enthusiasm of a man facing his last meal.

"Not unless the girls are hot. And naked."

"You should say fly commercial economy."

"That's pain and suffering *for me.*" Nate shudders. "Ugh. No."

"Genital piercing. Heard it scares women away." I didn't, but I don't really care that much.

He gapes. "Who the hell told you that?" Then he gives me a closer look. "You okay, man?"

My spine seems to lose all its strength, and I slouch. "Yeah, sure. No."

"What happened?" He stops. "Oh... It's Snickers, isn't it? She dumped you."

"She didn't dump me." She hasn't taken her stuff yet. Girls take all their shit when they're done with you. "Shut up."

"Then why are you here alone, looking so morose and dejected?"

"I'm not alone. As for morose, I'm putting up with you."

Nate snorts. "What did you do to her?"

Whose friend are you? "What makes you think *I* did something?"

"If she did something, you wouldn't be depressed. You'd be pissed off."

Nate knows me too damn well. That doesn't mean it isn't irritating.

"Did you break her heart? Only pay fifty bucks for a dinner or something?"

Pulling back, I roll my eyes. "No." Then I tell him, despite my better judgment because...well, I've already had four scotches.

When I'm done, Nate shakes his head slowly. "For fuck's sake, did you make it crystal clear to her that the money isn't that much?"

I nod.

"Did you also tell her having an account at OWM is actually for *your* benefit, because Gavin's bound to make you even richer?"

Hmm. Did I? "I don't remember."

"Shoulda told her that. I mean, it isn't like Gavin's hurting for clients."

That's true enough. The man's busy and loaded.

"Cheer up, man. A week from now, you're going to look back at this and laugh at yourself for being so down. It isn't worth it. Women are everywhere. As a matter of fact, date somebody in our circle."

"What?" When did Nate become a matchmaker? "Like who?"

"Yuna?"

I make a face. "No. She's like a sister to me." Not to mention she isn't my type. A little too thin. I like mine with soft, round breasts, beautiful aquamarine eyes and long brown hair. Like Skittles.

Fuck.

"You know what? Have about ten rounds, on me," Nate says, patting my back a few times. "You'll feel ten times more clear-headed. And you'll call Elizabeth and tell her you'll be a substitute bachelor at the auction because some shitbag had to pull out last minute because he's apparently too important to help out kids with cancer. You'll date the winner and realize *she* is your destiny. She'll bid more than fifty bucks, and Starburst will become ancient history. Won't even remember her in a month. I guarantee it."

I gaze at Nate long and hard. Maybe it's the alcohol or the lack of sleep...but his suggestion sounds immensely logical.

So I proceed to do exactly that—starting with the rounds of drink.

48

PASCAL

"ARE YOU SURE YOU DON'T WANT TO WORK IT OUT WITH Court?" Curie asks across the dinner table. We're eating late because she and Joe had a meeting with their realtor—the old lady finally decided to sell—and got caught in traffic on the way home. Not that it matters. I don't have much appetite. I only eat because I have to and because I know it's going to worry Curie and Joe more if I don't.

"Doubtful. Sorry I'm here like this." Joe certainly can't want a depressed sister-in-law moping around and ruining the newly wedded bliss phase of his marriage. And I bet Curie doesn't want me borrowing all her clothes, even if we're the same size, or using up all her crazy-expensive face creams.

"No problem, Pascal. You're family," Joe says.

"I just think it's weird. He really seems crazy about you," Curie says.

"What's really weird is that I'm still crazy about him." It doesn't matter what he did or didn't do. My head says he was manipulative and all but lied to me, but my heart goes gooey and achy every time I think of him. I prop my chin in my hand and sigh. "What does that say about me?"

Curie reaches over and squeezes my hand. "You're in love."

"I am. Gah." I stab my salad. "Why *him*? Why did he have to pay my boss?"

"Maybe it really *isn't* that much to him," Joe says. "He's a billionaire. He probably doesn't think about it the way we do."

He has a point. Didn't I see how casual Yuna was about money? Court fits right in with people like her. But I don't. I just can't wrap my mind around using that kind of money to secure an interview. *Argh.*

My phone rings. Is it Court again? He's been calling incessantly, and I considered blocking his number for two seconds before I shoved the phone back in my purse with disgust.

Nope. It's a number I don't recognize. I don't think it's Tom, because he's given up on contacting me after Court's casually delivered threat. Maybe somebody from work...?

"Hello?"

"Hey, you! You...candy bar!" come slurred words against really loud music in the background.

I frown. The voice sounds vaguely familiar, but I can't place it. And it's definitely not anyone from the office. So... "Who is this?"

"Forgot already, huh? I tol' Court women are fickle, Fifty-Buck Hershey Kiss."

It finally clicks. "Nate?"

"Hey, she remembers! Court, she remembers. Court? Court? Aw, shit."

"What's going on?" I ask, worry gnawing at me despite myself. "What did you do to him? How did you get my number?"

"I know shit 'cuz I'm Nate fucking Sterling. We drank. Scotch. Good shit. I only drink good shit, you know. Introduced him to a lot of good shit."

Oh. My. God. *Men are idiots.* "You shouldn't let him get drunk like that!"

"*Me?* You blamin' *me*? It's yer fault."

His accusation pricks at my heart, but I ignore the sting. "I'm not even there!"

I look up and notice Curie and Joe staring at me. I point at the phone and mouth, *Moron,* and move to the living room to deal with the drunken Nate.

Actually, forget that. I need to deal with Court directly. "Nate, put Court on the phone."

"You're dumber than Twizzlers. Can't talk if you're passed out. He's a lightweight pussy. We only had, like...fifteen each? Or fifty." He starts laughing.

That's it. I give up. Nate's waaay too drunk for this. "Call an Uber," I say firmly, while doing my best to hide how pissed off and worried I am. "Do *not* drive."

"I called you Snickers, but Court said you were Starburst. Made him happy or some crap like that 'cuz you shoot rainbows out of your ears."

What?

"But you're just a bitch. A nut bitch! Did you quit?"

"Quit what?" And why am I having a conversation with a guy who's so wasted he's slurring every syllable into sludge?

"The fucking job. If you really think you got it because of his money and yer too proud, you shoulda quit."

I suck in a breath. I haven't quit. But I've been wondering if I should, and his words hit home.

"Did you, Twix? Did you?" Nate demands.

"No," I admit, my voice quiet.

"What? Speak louder. Can't hear you in here."

My cheeks burn even though he isn't here to see me. "I said no."

"That's right. 'Cuz you're, er...phone hippo!"

Phone hippo?

"You're a hippo... Hippo... Christ, hippo-crip! Fuck, my mouth is dry. I need another drink."

"The last thing you need is more alcohol," I say sternly, even though my insides feel like they're going through a blender, and my head is hurting trying to follow this conversation. "Take Court home. And you both need to sleep it off."

"Fuck you, hippo-crip! Fuck you, I drink what I want."

"Nate."

"You can't make me do shit. I'm a free man."

I pinch the bridge of my nose. It'll be easier for me to just go over there or send somebody. Like Yuna. I still have her on my phone. "Where are you?"

"Z. But you can't come. I told the bouncer to kick your ass out if you show. Yer on the blacklist. Never get in. Equal opportunity, Hershey. That's like equal ass-kicking."

A hammer starts beating in my head as I try to parse his drunken raving. I don't care about getting inside Z. As awesome as the club is, it isn't my typical hangout. But the fact that they're at the club makes me relax a little. It's owned by Court's brother. The people there aren't going to let anything happen to their boss's family.

"Bye, Nate."

Hanging up, I close my eyes and draw in a deep breath to center myself. Damn Nate. He isn't wrong about quitting the job. As a matter of fact, I've been thinking about it ever since I left Court's place.

Sighing, I lean against the glass deck door. Curie comes over and puts a gentle hand on my arm. "Are you all right?"

I start to nod, then shake my head. My sister can tell I'm not okay. At all. No point in lying.

She pulls me toward the couch. We sit close, like we used to when we were girls.

"So. Work-related?" she asks.

I shake my head. "Court's best friend. They went out and got wasted. Nate's so gone he kept calling me a hippo-crip."

"A hippo-crip? Is that some new slang?"

We look at each other for a moment. "A big member of an L.A. gang...?" I stop as it finally hits me that Nate's been trying to call me a hypocrite, for God's sake. But the exasperation lasts only a moment. My chest feels like my heart has been scooped out, and I put a hand over it.

Curie peers at me. "What is it?"

"He's right. I am a hypocrite for staying at a job I might not have earned, especially after getting upset with Court about it." Curie's already heard all of it. And since she knows me as well as she knows herself, she wisely refrained from giving too much input, just letting me vent and rant.

"But are you sure? You love OWM."

I bite my lower lip. She's totally right about how I feel about my work, which is why this is so hard. But my gut says I need to do what's right, and what's right is not keeping what I didn't earn. I've never done that, and I'm not going to start now.

Doing the right thing doesn't keep your bank account healthy, my mind whispers.

But not doing the right thing will sicken my soul.

"I don't want a fucking pity job," I say, my voice slightly shaky at the thought. I clench my hands as though that will steady my vocal cords.

Curie nods. "I understand."

Her ready agreement doesn't relieve my anxiety. "I'm being stupid, aren't I? Overthinking everything."

"That's how you are when you're dealing with a big decision. The only one who you just went along with was Court."

She's right about that. I slept with him the night we met because I liked him. A lot. And then... I just couldn't say no to him. Probably because deep inside I wanted to be with him, no matter what excuses I came up with.

"I'm on your side." Curie puts her arm around my shoulders and squeezes. "You always do what's right, whether it's about your job or Court."

"But it feels so scary."

"How come?"

"The one-night stand was easy because I thought it was just one night. But now, I feel more for him." I swallow. "I still love him for all that he is—his smile, his sweet personality and generosity. And I realize now that I reacted much worse than I might have, because seeing Dad's superior smirk just hours before confronting Court put me in this terrible mental space."

Curie nods. "So why don't you unbend a little? He's been trying to reach you, but you've been ignoring him."

"The stakes seem so big." I pick at the skin around my thumb. "And I wonder if Court's attitude is innate, the way Dad's is. Like, because of the way he was brought up, or what he's always been surrounded with. People don't change. Just look at Dad. We just didn't know because he never had the opportunity to show that side of himself. So...if it fails, I'll have nothing except a broken heart."

Curie looks at me long and hard. "So how is that any worse than where you are right now? And what if it works? I know weighing all the risks and probabilities and stuff that makes my head spin is what you do, but sometimes life is about gut feelings. What do they say?"

That's the problem. I don't know. They're like an angry, needy crowd yelling different things as loudly as possible.

"You don't have to answer right now. But you should really look deep inside and figure it out."

And that night, I stare at the dark ceiling and try to listen in the silence. The gut feelings Curie wants me to listen to produce more cacophony than an open market in Delhi, but I start to see the underlying pattern.

Fear.

I'm scared—and humiliated at the prospect of being jobless again...and proving Dad right. I'm terrified I made a huge mistake when I walked out of Court's place—even though I had to before I said something permanently damaging—and that maybe Court exerted more influence on Gavin than he claimed. He is a client, after all, isn't he?

But when my mind starts coming up with what I'm going to say in my letter of resignation, I know what I need to do.

49

PASCAL

GO WITH THE GUT FEELING. JUST LIKE I DID WITH COURT earlier.

That's my new mantra for the day as I get up in the morning and draft my letter of resignation to Gavin. I debate long and hard about mentioning Court, but decide not to because the email could be printed and end up in my record. Gavin probably doesn't want people to know about what Court did. I merely thank Gavin for the opportunity, but I also tell him I don't believe I fit in well at OWM.

My stomach burns because it's such a lie. I love that company. If I could, I'd work at OWM forever. But I send the email.

I sigh, my shoulders drooping. Torn between sadness and regret, I lean back against the headboard in Curie's guest bedroom for a time. I'm officially jobless, starting now. Well, technically I have the two-week notice period, but it's highly unlikely Gavin's going to want me back on the office, knowing I'm not going to be around. It isn't like I have to train a replacement or hand anything off.

I reach for my phone to call Court, but stop because he's probably sleeping off his evening with Nate. I should let him get the rest he needs. Trying to have a relationship talk while being hungover would suck.

To be honest, I don't even know what I'm going to say. I've made so many lists that I can't even keep them straight anymore.

Time to update my résumé and look for a new job—one I'm going to get without *anybody* asking for favors on my behalf.

My phone rings, and I pick it up automatically. "Hello?"

"This is Hilary Pryce, calling for Pascal Snyder." Her voice is warm and professional as usual.

"Oh, hi, Hilary." I clear my throat. "Um. What can I do for you?" Then I check the calendar. I'm not mistaken. It's Saturday. Why is she working on a weekend? I heard from a few coworkers that she doesn't do that anymore. Apparently, it's one of a few conditions for her continuing her employment at OWM.

"Gavin would like you to come to the office as soon as you're able."

Shit. Saturdays mean a day off for most, but not those in finance. "Um. Didn't he get my email?"

"That's why he wants you to come."

Somehow that doesn't sound reassuring. An exit interview can wait until Monday. "Is he upset?" He was pretty smug about his recruiting skills during the welcome lunch, so maybe now he's pissed off.

"Should he be?" she asks in the same warm tone.

Damn it. That's got to be her way of letting me know that she, too, is mad at me. "Okay. I'll be there soon."

I probably owe Gavin an in-person explanation. And honestly, it's probably a better way to end my short stint at OWM. I shower quickly, then dress super fast. For makeup, I opt for mascara and lip gloss. I don't need more than that for the office.

Still, it's ninety minutes later that I reach Gavin's office. Hilary isn't at her desk. Her travel mug is missing too.

Gavin, on the other hand, is in his office, working on his laptop. Even though it's Saturday, he's dressed in a suit. I don't think he owns anything else.

"Hi," I say. "Hilary said you wanted to see me?"

"Yeah, I do. Sit down." He gestures at a chair, taps his

keyboard a few more times and then closes his laptop and turns toward me. "So. What's that notice about? Did you get a better offer elsewhere?"

Oh shit. Is that what he thought? "No. Of course not."

He pulls back in surprise. "You don't have a new job lined up, but you're quitting? Why?"

"If you really want to know..." I inhale deeply and tell him what I discovered about the deal between him and Court.

He listens, then waves me away like everything I just said is about as important as a fruit fly buzzing around. "Pascal. That is the most fucked-up—uh, I mean, the silliest thing I've ever heard. *A hundred million?* Come on. That's"—he casts around for a word—"a joke."

"I'm sorry, but what?" Did he and Court decide to use the exact same excuse?

He leans forward. "Let me clue you in on a couple of things. One, I hate idiots. Okay? *Hate* 'em. Two, I have a few billion bucks in my own account. More than your boyfriend by at least a couple multiples of ten. You understand what I'm saying? So no amount of money can make me put up with some moron who makes me wonder how they tie their shoes in the morning. And three, when there's a hiring mistake through a referral or whatever, I usually correct that in a month and put a black mark on the referee's record. Since I started doing that, which was"—his eyes stay on me, but lose a bit of focus—"I don't know, six years ago? Seven? Anyway, we don't get those anymore."

Well, this is a new side. Gavin's always so nice that it never really occurred to me he could be...like this. "But Court doesn't work for you."

He looks horrified. "Damn right he doesn't. I wouldn't hire him even if he begged me. He doesn't have the right training or temperament for what we do. The only thing he did was ask me to just talk to you for ten minutes, then offered to open an account here with his *hundred million.*" He says it like a Michelin chef talking about a fast food taco. "Like that was going to make a difference to my decision to see you."

Gavin doesn't seem to be faking it. And he has no reason to lie to me. "But you did change your mind about seeing me," I point out.

"Yeah, because he was so convinced that I'd see your brilliance if I just gave you a chance. He sees you and sees perfection. And I said yes because, well... Actually, I'm not sure why I said yes. I guess I just like the guy. But even though I agreed to see you, I had no expectation that you'd be any good."

I swallow. *Court thought I was perfect. He just wanted me to have a chance because nobody else was giving me one.* Oh my God. What have I done?

"But you know what? He was right. You did impress me, which is the only, let me repeat, *only* reason I hired you. And also that's why I then *let* him open an account here. In case you didn't know, I don't allow just anybody to be a client at OWM."

"You don't?"

Gavin shrugs. "Don't have to. Like that guy...Cristiano Cortez. He came to me last week. Said he was interested in moving his business. Apparently he likes you." He flips a hand back and forth. "I'm thinking about it."

Oh my God. That's unbelievable...and incredibly flattering. He's one of the most important clients at SFG. *Does Dad know?* Holy shit.

"But seeing as how you're quitting and everything, I guess he won't be moving after all." Gavin leans back in his chair. "Look. You getting upset with Court is stupid—and quitting the job over it is flat-out idiotic. You understand? Fifty-IQ-type stuff. A guy like him is priceless. I can price anything, but I literally can't put a price on him for you. But I guess we'll see tonight at Elizabeth's bachelor auction."

"What?"

"Court's going to get bid on, and then we'll see what the market will bear for him."

Panic and denial warp through me. "That can't be right!" He never said anything about participating in the auction, and he can't just stick himself in there at the last minute, can he? I mean, aren't the programs already printed out?

"Excuse me, but it's exactly right. I know because my wife's helping Elizabeth put the event together, and she said Court is on as substitute meat—uh, a substitute bachelor."

I jump to my feet. "I have to go stop it."

"Got a ticket for the event?"

No, I don't. Court never got to give me one because... Well, I left.

"Well, then, you might be out of luck. Everything Elizabeth does to raise money is exclusive because she likes to target rich people's pockets. And I wouldn't try to crash it if I were you. Her security is...let's just say, *terrifying*."

Terrifying security or not, I'm not letting some other woman win Court in an auction!

"Look, Pascal, I like you. I like it that you gave notice when you suspected things weren't kosher. I respect that a lot. Most people wouldn't have that much integrity. Anyway, as it happens, *I* have a ticket. They always send me one, and I have no desire to attend because it's boring." He pulls out an envelope from his breast pocket.

"Thank you," I say, reaching for it with huge relief.

He pulls his hand back. "Not yet. You're not going to quit. You're going to work like a dog here because that's what I hired you for. Got that?"

Holy mother of God. He's going to ignore my notice. "Yes," I say, because working like a dog at OWM is exactly what I want to do. Well, with some time off to spend with Court. "Whatever you say."

"Then you'll report to work on Monday as usual." He hands me the ticket. "Now go wild at the auction. They're raising money for kids."

50

COURT

GINGERLY, I CRADLE MY HEAD. IT HURTS SO BAD THAT I'M tempted to chop it off at the neck to stop the pounding.

How much scotch did I drink last night?

My eyes still closed, I roll over to try for a less painful position. My hand brushes a body next to me.

Skittles?

Joy swells as my alcohol-addled brain immediately lights up with her return. I'd be jumping off the bed and dancing if I thought my head wouldn't just explode.

I squint—barely, the light stabbing right through the corneas —and see a large male body less than a foot away. My hungover fog vanishes like a TV being cut off.

"What the fuck!" I scream, my voice hoarse from overindulgence. I wince as my own words stab into my brain like shrapnel. "Who the—?"

"Shut the hell up," he moans, then turns to face me. *Nate.*

I run a hand over my mouth. "What you doing here?"

"Uhng. Guess I passed out last night."

Shit. How bad was it last night if he passed out too? I roll the other way, grab my phone and check the time. Five thirty-six.

And Saturday. The day he's going to be auctioned off like...a gold digger's wet dream.

"You need to go home and get ready. Make yourself pretty for the ladies." Then I groan when his movements make the mattress undulate vertically. Fuck. My stomach is roiling.

"I'm already pretty. And you need to get ready too."

Me? "For what? Lying in bed, dying?"

"You're the substitute bachelor, remember?"

"What?"

"You told Elizabeth."

"I did not." I check my phone. No calls to her.

"Texts."

I check my text history. *Oh, shit.* I told her I would, even though she said I didn't have to. But I insisted. *Always ready to help out for a good cause.*

Great. What was I thinking? Well, the real question is, was I even thinking? Apparently not, because I'm in bed with Nate. At least we're both fully clothed.

I close my eyes and press the heels of hands into my eye sockets. Do I still have to be auctioned off if I pop my eyeballs out?

Probably.

It's for the kids who have cancer, moron. Just do it. Or be the dick who doesn't give a fuck.

But what if Pascal hears about it and gets pissed?

She isn't here, is she? Besides, is she going to be happy with a guy who turns a blind eye to suffering children? She said your ability to make people happy is your greatest asset. Be the man she can be proud of.

Fuck you, brain. You're a dick.

Still, I grit my teeth, stumble to the bathroom and down a handful of aspirin. Two breaths later, I decide that they're taking too damn long to kick in. I need an aspirin IV.

I lift my head and see my reflection, then shudder. I look like a horror movie villain. Bloodshot eyes. Shit, even the skin *around* my eyes is bloodshot. Dark circles the size of moon craters. Hair sticking up like I French-kissed an electrical socket. For all I remember—or don't—I might've done just that.

This is why I don't drink a lot.

But somehow, last night...it just seemed fitting. I taste a bitterness that has nothing to do with old scotch as my gaze lands on the bottles of lotion Skittles left behind. I thought she'd come back for them...and we'd have a chance to talk when she was calmer. But that hasn't happened.

Why the fuck not, Skittles? Why won't you even listen to me?

I close the bathroom door, strip and shower. I need something to make me feel human again, even though I'm feeling deader than a desiccated zombie. A long, hot shower is somewhat refreshing, so now I feel like a brand-new zombie, rather than a hundred-year-old fossil.

After wrapping myself in a robe, I get out. Nate's managed to get himself sitting up on the edge of the bed, his head in his hands. "Do you think I can tell her I'm too sick to be auctioned off?"

"You might dissuade Georgette the psycho from bidding if you throw up on stage."

He perks up a little.

Only Nate would seriously think about tossing his cookies on stage in front of everyone. On the other hand, if I had an ex like Georgette after me...

I let him use the bathroom so he won't embarrass me. I even let him borrow my clothes, because friends don't let friends go out in stale, scotch-smelling outfits. Then we go down to the kitchen to rehydrate. Nate looks like he's headed for the gallows.

"You know, the auction won't be that bad," I say, making some dry toast to help settle our guts. It's supposed to soak up all the extra poison.

He munches on his slice. "How come?"

"You have a backup plan, right? Your assistant is going to bid on you, just to make sure."

"Something like that."

"So you're safe. I'm not. Georgette might decide to bid on me instead."

"No, she won't. You're not her type."

"She has a type?"

"Yeah. Your first name needs to start with an N. Some fortune-teller told her it would guarantee her happiness."

And here I thought I had some crazy exes.

When it's time to head out, I grab an Uber, since Nate and I are in no condition to drive. Nate must be feeling terrible, because he doesn't complain. Not even when it turns out our pickup is a Ford Taurus with a huge rust spot on the trunk.

But the moment I arrive at the Aylster Hotel, where the auction's supposed to take place, I decide I should've told Elizabeth I died and couldn't make it.

Because the hotel contains memories. When Skittles and I were bubbling with the excitement of the first time and high on our fantastic personal chemistry. I still have both when I think of her, but she doesn't. If she did, she would've called by now. And she definitely would know that I'd never do anything to hurt her.

Now my heart hurts more than my head. Maybe I'll die for real and get out of the auction that way.

Nate and I drag each other toward the area where we're supposed to gather. I spot Elizabeth coming toward us with her mouth slightly parted.

Despite the expression of shock, she glows. And is perfectly put together. Like...her skin's perfect, her makeup is perfect and her outfit is perfect. Even her hair is perfectly golden and curled. The only things not photo-ready are her gray eyes, dark with disappointment.

If she'd just yell, that'd be easier, but nope. That's not in her repertoire.

"Who's going to bid on you looking like that?" she says, her voice soft. "Especially you, Court."

"Sorry." I sniff and look down. My left shoe is untied. Isn't that fascinating? "If you're mad, I can just write a check and not terrorize the audience."

She sighs heavily. "My makeup artist hasn't left yet. She's going to fix you up."

I jerk my head, then wince as a shard sticks into a spot behind my eye. "You're going to make me look like a girl?" Is it really too late to get sick? Maybe I can scrape a piece of gum off a sidewalk and chew it. Die of some horrible L.A. street disease.

"You too, Nate," she says.

"*Me?*" He spreads his arms. "Come on."

"We're going to make you look like you weren't out binge-drinking last night. She won't be use mascara and eye shadow, unless you ask." She arches an eyebrow. "You aren't going to, are you?"

"No," I say slowly, still debating the merit of the street gum.

"Then come on. I'm going to make sure I get the right price for both of you."

51

PASCAL

THE HOT RED DRESS I BORROWED FROM CURIE FITS ME LIKE a second skin. She also lends me a strapless push-up bra, saying it goes with a low sweetheart neckline like Klingon and grunting. (She knows me too well.) I add a silver heart pendant for luck and courage.

I step into the luxurious Aylster Hotel and breathe in deep as the memory of my and Court's first time floods my mind. It's a good omen. Right? Maybe the location will remind him of how it was before.

To be honest, I have no idea what I'm doing or how I'm going to win him. Should I put it on my credit card? Do they even take credit cards? And what the hell is my credit limit, anyway? I don't remember, since I never charge more than I can pay off in a month.

But is my money going to be anywhere near enough? A hundred million dollars is nothing to these people. The most I can spend is maybe two thousand.

As I approach the ballroom, I understand what Gavin meant. Security is tight, and the guy who's in charge—or, at least, I think he is in charge from the way he commands others—looks like he eats broken glass every morning to stay mean and sharp. I give him my ticket, and he squints like I shouldn't be the one handing it to him. I swallow, nerves raw. Is he going to kick me out?

"Gavin Lloyd, huh?" he says, his voice gravelly.

My mouth dries. "I'm sorry?" How does he know who the ticket really belongs to? There's no name on it.

"Nothing." He smirks. It transforms him into an even scarier horror show. "Enjoy the evening."

"Thanks," I say weakly, and run inside before he changes his mind.

Although the huge ballroom is full of people, I don't recognize anybody. Everyone seems to know everyone else, though. The buzz of chatter is constant, occasional laughter breaking the hum of words. Nobody seems to care I'm standing awkwardly by myself. No one tries to say hello, either, which is fine by me. I'm too nervous to make small talk, as I realize I'm hopelessly outclassed. Curie has great taste, and the dress is gorgeous, but it's nothing compared to people decked out in dresses you only see on the latest fashion magazines and who have real gemstones sparkling from their ears, throats and hands. No wonder the security guy looked at me funny. My pendant is silver, not platinum. Bet he could tell from a glance.

I pluck a glass of white wine off a passing tray and start to run my hand down the dress until I realize my palms are sweaty. Ugh. This is *not* good. But I'm nervous as hell. Worse than going in for the interview with Gavin. My belly's a full-blown swarm of locusts, gnawing at my courage.

He's going to laugh at you. He's going to pick somebody else. Somebody more like...that woman over there covered in diamonds.

Shut up, I tell my negative self. Who cares if she has more diamonds than Africa? She probably can't do matrix algebra or speak Klingon or be happy watching *Buffy* while sharing a bowl of popcorn. Besides, didn't Nate say I make Court happy because I shoot rainbows or whatever? I don't know exactly what that means, but I'm sure it's positive. Guys don't talk about stuff like that unless they're at least seventy-five percent serious about the girl. Do they?

Soon an MC goes up on the stage, and people start sitting

down. I take a seat in a corner and take a deep breath as the MC talks about the great cause they're trying to fund with the auction. She also speaks of the surprise substitute bachelor, who's not on the program but is bound to make everyone's heart flutter. Harcourt Blackwood is not only the most endearing, but one of the hottest and most eligible bachelors in the country. "Surely, all the ladies can agree on *that*," she says with a titter, "and give him the proper welcome and love he deserves."

Ugh. Acid bathes my belly, and the locusts inside grow more vicious. I put a hand over it, and I swear I can feel the flutter against my palm.

Sweat beads along my hairline. I'm barely paying attention to the MC or the men she brings to the stage. My focus is three hundred percent on the bidding. Holy shit. Most women open with a thousand at least. For some of the more sought-after men, they bid like crazy. I think some of it is ego-driven because they don't want to lose.

I don't even know how much I'm supposed to bid to win Court. He's the most perfect man. But is money enough to show him I'm in love with him?

Probably not after you walked out on him.

Finally he's on the stage. I gaze at his gorgeous face. For a guy who went clubbing and drinking until he passed out the night before, he looks amazingly good. If it weren't for the slightly bloodshot eyes, nobody would suspect anything.

But there's something grim about him. I'd like to think it's because he misses me, but maybe he's just missing a bed and some aspirin. Or maybe he doesn't like the long, breathless introduction the MC is practically crooning into the mic.

Finally, she says, "Now, ladies, show him some love!"

"Five thousand," somebody calls out in front of me. Oh my God. It's the diamond woman. My instinct was right!

"Five thousand one hundred," another says.

"Six," the diamond woman counters.

Damn it. I need to stop this madness before it escalates any further. Nobody's going to get him except me, because I'm the only woman in this room who loves him for all that he is.

"Fifty!" I say.

Gasps go up. Court swivels his head in my direction, his eyes wide. A smile slowly brightens his face like a sunrise.

Relief floods me until I'm feeling shaky and lightheaded. Good thing I'm seated, or I might land on my ass.

"Oh my goodness. *Fifty thousand!*" The MC starts fanning herself.

What the hell? Then I remember everyone else was bidding *in the thousands*. Shit. Is that why he's smiling—because I just committed fifty thousand bucks to the charitable cause?

She continues, "Can anybody—"

"No, I mean fifty dollars," I correct her. "Just fifty. Five-oh."

"Excuse me?" the MC says, taking a step forward. Lines form between her eyebrows, and she stares at me like I'm not speaking her language.

I turn away from her. Court's smile's still there, but his brow is furrowed.

"Fifty bucks. Plus my heart, if that's still what you want."

For one horrible, terrifying, interminable heartbeat, he says nothing. He merely stares.

Did I screw up? Am I too late?

Suddenly, the grin on his lips widens. "Sold!" he says.

I jump to my feet, my fists in the air, exhilaration shooting through me like a rocket. "*Yes!*"

The MC sputters. "I'm sorry, ma'am, but we have six thousand on the floor." She gestures at the diamond lady.

"Her heart is priceless. Nobody can outbid that," Court says, and steps off the stage. "But I'll donate a million bucks to the children you're raising money for."

Oh my God. I'm melting now. He knows exactly what to say and do to make me feel whole again.

The crowd parts as he makes his way toward me. Then he stops three steps in front of me. "You can't take it back, Skittles."

Tears of relief prickle my eyes, and I shake my head. "I won't. Ever."

"Good. I love you too."

My breath catches in my throat. He's telling me he loves me, and I have my man back. So I should be screaming and jumping, but instead my knees shake as tension leaves me in waves. "I love you more, Court."

I don't know which one of us moves first, but his arms are around me, and I have my arms around his neck, and our mouths are fused. In the background, I hear, "But just wait until you see who's coming next!"

52

COURT

"OH MY GOODNESS, I'M SO THRILLED FOR YOU," ESTHER SAYS, clasping her hands. She's so excited that she can hardly sit still on the comfy couch in her living room.

Steve is studying me like a market chart he can't decipher. "So you're going to marry my daughter?" He nods to himself. "Well, can't say I'm surprised. Always comes down to rings and gowns. What does Pascal think about all this?"

"She and I are on the same page," I say, mildly annoyed he's suddenly acting like he cares about her opinion. It's good that she's out shopping with Curie, not knowing this is going on, because she might've said something sarcastic. But I wanted to speak with her parents first, alone, before I pop the question. Call me traditional. "Just so you know, married or not, she's still going to do whatever she wants. That's what I want for her."

Annoyance crosses his face. "What are *you* going to do, then? All alone in your home? It isn't like you're working."

"Steve!" Esther says.

I raise my hand. "It's okay. Your husband has every right to ask that before giving me his blessing." I turn to Steve. "Look, it doesn't matter what you say because I'm not going to be her shackles. I want to be her wings so she can soar."

His expression turns even more mulish. All he has to do is pout to complete the look. "Is that so?"

"As for your question, Pascal says that my talent is making people happy. So that's what I'll be focusing on. I'm already looking into championing some causes in conjunction with the Pryce Family Foundation and Blackwood Energy's charities department." That's about the extent of the involvement I want with Dad's company. He's happy—for now—because he thinks I'm giving in.

"You could do something more important," Steve says pettily.

"What's more important than doing what I'm good at, something that makes people happy?"

"Darling, stop being stubborn and give him your blessing. I'm certainly giving mine. They're perfect for each other."

Thank you, Esther. You're going to be my favorite in-law.

Steve purses his mouth. "Fine. You *better* make her happy, or I'm going to personally kick your ass."

Normally a lanky man in his sixties threatening me with physical violence would make me laugh. But this is a father's sentiment, and I respect that. "Of course."

I scratch Nijinsky's belly before heading out. Esther invites me to stay for tea, but I have a lot of things on my plate today.

My phone rings just as I climb behind the wheel. *Nate.* "Hey, man. How's the date?" He's finally taking his assistant, who won him at the auction, out to Vegas. During the auction he actually said his ideal date would be a drunken orgy, although I don't think he and she had one, drunken or otherwise.

"It's...good. Great. Nothing goes wrong in Vegas."

Probably not, especially when you're as rich as Nate and it doesn't matter how much you lose.

"Hey, listen," he says, "is a wedding ceremony valid without proper witnesses?"

Huh? Where the hell did this come from? "I don't know. Don't you have lawyers on retainer for that sort of questions?"

"I'm not asking them. Google didn't help, but I thought you might know."

Everything inside me stills. "Uh... Nate? Are you okay?"

"Yeah, I told you that already. Hey, can you ask your lawyer?"

"I don't have a lawyer. Percy's Dad's lawyer."

"All right. Never mind." He hangs up.

I stare at the phone. What was that about? Then I say, "I'm doing fine, too, thanks for asking," and start the car.

I have her parents' blessing. I have the ring. And I have the place (not Z, even though Tony said I could use it if I wanted). It's going to be freakin' perfect.

53

PASCAL

WHEN I ARRIVE AT Z WITH CURIE AFTER A DAY OF shopping, we don't go to the regular line. We go straight to the VIP line, and the huge, bearish bouncer who let us in last time smiles.

"Hey, Pascal."

"Hi, Zack." I smile back.

Curie winks. "Hello, handsome."

"Handsome? What does your husband think about that?" the bouncer says. "I mean, it's true, of course, but..."

"Nothing, because he knows he's the handsomest in my eyes."

I giggle at her deadpan delivery, but I also know it's true. Joe and Curie are super tight, just like me and Court. Although I was worried that things might be awkward or somehow different than they were before, our relationship couldn't be better. Curie told me it's because every trial that doesn't kill us makes us stronger. Not that I plan to repeat the experiment ever again.

Zack lifts the rope, and we go inside, weaving through the pounding music and the crowd. The gang's already on the upper level—Tony, Ivy, Yuna, Edgar, Joe and, most importantly, Court.

He looks breathtakingly gorgeous, his eyes smiling at me. I

slide next to him on the long, round seat and kiss him. "Missed you."

"You too."

"You were only apart for a few hours," Edgar says.

"You don't get it because you don't have anybody you love," Court replies.

"You mean, I'm a rational, normal human being."

Court arches an eyebrow. "Let's put it to a vote."

"Don't be so mean to us," Yuna says in a cheery voice. "I love being single and not missing anybody."

She and Edgar high-five each other. The two women who always tag along after Yuna look pained. Huh. Maybe they're tasked to keep her away from men she has no plans to marry. Or maybe they're worried she might take Edgar out for a week-long test ride.

I turn to Ivy. "How are you feeling?"

"Pretty good." She puts a hand on her still relatively flat belly. "It's fun to be out and about." She gives Tony a teasing look. "He's been keeping me home, worried I'm 'overdoing it.'"

"If he could, he'd carry her everywhere," Yuna adds.

Are Tony's cheeks turning red? It's sort of cute because he seems very...intense and focused normally. "If I don't take care of my wife, who will?" he says. *Awww.*

"I agree one hundred percent," Joe says, putting an arm around Curie and pulling her closer.

Tony nods. Mr. Vindicated. "Exactly."

Court takes my hand. "Wanna go dance?"

"Yup."

"Me too!" Yuna stands, then tugs at Edgar. "Come on."

"Me?"

"I can't dance alone."

His face scrunches. He's definitely going to say no. *Poor Yuna...*

But he rises to his feet with a long, heaving sigh. "All right, fine. Let's go."

"He's really accommodating," I say to Court.

"He lost a game of Go Fish to Yuna before coming here. They

bet that the loser would have to do whatever the winner wanted tonight...within reason."

We reach the dance floor. I sway for a bit to the pounding beat, then let my body do what it wants to the rhythm. Court is close to me, his large, hard frame moving with the music and me.

Just a small brush against my arm...then my chest...then he's standing behind me, his hands on my hips. Blood runs hotter and faster in my veins, lust throbbing through me.

One song becomes two. Then three. His breath fans my ear. I shiver, every square inch of my skin prickling and responding to his nearness.

And I'm already wet.

I link my hands behind his neck, pulling our bodies even closer. My eyes on his, I kiss him, just a small, quick flick of my tongue. The need inside me kicks up a notch.

"Let's get out of here," he says.

"Yeah?" I smile.

"Need someplace more private, don't you agree?"

His erection presses against my belly, and my knees are growing weaker. "Yes."

He links his fingers with mine, then tugs. I follow him, laughing breathlessly like a teenager about to do something unspeakably naughty.

As we go past Yuna and Edgar, who are still dancing, Yuna gives me a huge wink. My cheeks flame, but I don't care *that* much. It isn't like she doesn't know we're an item.

Court leads me past familiar city blocks until we reach the Aylster Hotel. I grin hugely. "Again?"

"Of course. It's our lucky place."

"Totally." Where we had our first time. And where we reaffirmed our love for each other at the auction.

He doesn't stop by the front desk, though. He whisks me straight to the waiting elevator. He hits the close button repeatedly until the double doors close with nobody but us inside.

"You already have a room?" I ask.

"Mm-hmm. The same suite we had last time."

Damn. That's perfect. "Confident, aren't you?"

The grin that never fails to make my heart swell with love pops onto his face. "I thought I might get lucky tonight."

"Only tonight?" I arch an eyebrow. "I think you got lucky last night, and the night before, and..."

Laughing, he cradles my face between his large, warm palms and kisses me hard. I open up, feel his tongue glide against mine and taste a hint of tequila and him. Yum.

White heat unfurls, making my nipples bead and my clit ache. I rub myself shamelessly against him.

The elevator stops, and the doors open. We rush out into the hall. This time, Court finds the right suite on the first try.

As soon as we're inside, he pushes me against the wall. His mouth crashes over mine, and I devour him with all the unrestrained hunger growing within me.

This is our get-lucky place. And *we* are definitely getting lucky tonight.

54

PASCAL

I ROLL OVER, FEELING THE SOFT, LUXURIOUS COTTON SHEETS against my skin. I lost count of the number of times we screwed, but I'm slightly sore—in all the right places. Maybe we can do it again. It's only... I open one eye to check the time on the bedside clock. Ten. On Sunday. Definitely more sex. Then a shower. Then eat. Or maybe a shower, then more sex, *then* eat...

I shift toward Court, then stop when I see his side of his bed is empty. I still and listen for any sound from the bathroom. Nope, nothing. I touch the pillow. It's cool against my hand.

Huh. Where did he go?

I start to sit up, then stop when I see something on the indent of the pillow. A fifty-dollar bill...folded into a heart.

I pick it up with a smile. How adorable.

"Pretty good, huh?" Court says, coming in from the living room. He's already freshly showered, a towel wrapped around his tight waist.

I eye-fuck him. Because a body that lean, strong and gorgeous deserves it.

"Oh. So you're too busy admiring this"—he sweeps his hand over his six-pack—"to give some love to my origami heart?"

I tilt my chin up primly. "Not my fault. You're the one flashing me." Then, since I don't want to make him feel like I'm ignoring his effort, I run my index finger along the edge of the heart. "Did you fold this yourself?"

"Yup." He grins, taking his spot on the bed. He shoves the pillow behind him and leans against it. "I thought it symbolized our love for each other. Fifty bucks and your heart."

I flush, absurdly touched by his sentimentality. "We don't need a physical token. I'll show you my love every day."

"And I'll show you mine...but maybe you can keep this safe for me." He puts a hand over my heart.

"Okay." I hold the fifty-dollar heart with more care, then realize something's off. I can feel something round and hard inside.

"Open it," he whispers.

My pulse racing, I open it, taking care not to rip the note. Inside is a platinum ring with a huge diamond in the center, set between sapphires on either side. I place a trembling hand over my lips. "Oh my God. Court."

He gazes at me with love shining in his beautiful gaze. "Pascal Snyder, you're the center of my universe, the keeper of my heart. I love you. Will you marry me?"

Tears prickle my eyes, and my pulse pounds like it's ready to gallop away. I start to say yes until I realize something. He didn't ask me in English. He asked me in...Klingon?

Oh. My. God. *He speaks Klingon?! Shit.* My mouth parts. He understood what I was saying all this time? What the hell *did* I say? Anything bad? Panic gums up the gears in my head, and I can't think. Finally I say, "tlhIngan Hol Dajatlh'a'?" *You speak Klingon?*

"Actually," he says, "I speak English *and* Klingon. I'm a man of many talents."

"But you speak Klingon! All this time!"

He nods. "Since I was about twelve."

Squeezing my eyes shut, I groan.

"Don't worry, you didn't say anything *that* bad. Besides, I think it's awesome you speak it. We can communicate in secret whenever we want."

Well, yes, if you want to look at the positive side...

"Hey. You haven't answered my question." He looks at me with blue eyes bright with love. "Will you marry me?"

I kiss him. "HIja'. A thousand times HIja'. But it's going to be a long engagement. I'm going to plan a ceremony we'll never forget."

"Whatever you want," he says.

But I already have what I want—Court Blackwood, speaker of Klingon, center of my universe and keeper of my heart.

THANKS FOR READING *STEALING THE BRIDE*! I HOPE YOU enjoyed it.

Would you like to know when my next book is available and receive sneak peeks and bonus epilogues featuring some of your favorite couples? Join my VIP List at http://www.nadialee.net/vip.

TITLES BY NADIA LEE

The Sins Trilogy

Sins

Secrets

Mercy

The Billionaire's Claim Duet

Obsession

Redemption

Sweet Darlings Inc.

That Man Next Door

That Sexy Stranger

That Wild Player

Billionaires' Brides of Convenience

A Hollywood Deal

A Hollywood Bride

An Improper Deal

An Improper Bride

An Improper Ever After

An Unlikely Deal

An Unlikely Bride

A Final Deal

~

The Pryce Family

The Billionaire's Counterfeit Girlfriend

The Billionaire's Inconvenient Obsession

The Billionaire's Secret Wife

The Billionaire's Forgotten Fiancée

The Billionaire's Forbidden Desire

The Billionaire's Holiday Bride

~

Seduced by the Billionaire

Taken by Her Unforgiving Billionaire Boss

Pursued by Her Billionaire Hook-Up

Pregnant with Her Billionaire Ex's Baby

Romanced by Her Illicit Millionaire Crush

Wanted by Her Scandalous Billionaire

Loving Her Best Friend's Billionaire Brother

ABOUT NADIA LEE

New York Times and *USA Today* bestselling author Nadia Lee writes sexy contemporary romance. Born with a love for excellent food, travel and adventure, she has lived in four different countries, kissed stingrays, been bitten by a shark, ridden an elephant and petted tigers.

Currently, she shares a condo overlooking a small river and sakura trees in Japan with her husband and son. When she's not writing, she can be found reading books by her favorite authors or planning another trip.

To learn more about Nadia and her projects, please visit http://www.nadialee.net. To receive updates about upcoming works, sneak peeks and bonus epilogues featuring some of your favorite couples from Nadia, please visit http://www.nadialee.net/vip to join her VIP List.

Made in the USA
Monee, IL
21 May 2023

34233409R00198